Noir Fire

A Gritty Speculative Fiction Anthology

edited by

Valeria Vitale

&

Djibril al-Ayad

Futurefire.net Publishing

ISBN-print: 978-0-9957265-2-9
ISBN-electronic: 978-0-9957265-3-6

Contact:
editor@futurefire.net
http://futurefire.net/

Contents

Acknowledgements

The editors would like to thank: M. Bennardo, Zoë Blade, Curtis C. Chen, M.L. Clark, Mame Bougouma Diene, Fábio Fernandes, R.S.A. Garcia, Gwen C. Katz, Damien Krsteski and Benjanun Sriduangkaew for early discussion of speculative and progressive noir; Brian Olszewski and Regina de Búrca for proofreading the final anthology.

Introduction

Valeria Vitale & Djibril al-Ayad

This anthology was born from the love of a genre, perhaps more cinematic than literary, and a passion for mixing themes and palettes on the page. But it was also inspired by a deep frustration at the shortcomings of some classic examples of that genre, and the conviction that many of the amazing and diverse authors working in speculative fiction today are doing better, more inclusive, progressive work.

Noir is famously difficult to define. Compared to other genres, it seems to be more about atmosphere and aesthetic than a set of rules. This may be why in noir, clichés are not something to avoid, but a beloved ingredient that readers expect to find. The Italian writer Gesualdo Bufalino once said that detective stories are very popular because they are reassuring, maybe even cathartic: the culprit is discovered, questions are answered, justice is served and the establishment restored. Everything finds its resolution. With noir, in contrast, things remain un(re)solved, criminals often get away, a sense of loss and futility assails the protagonist—who is usually worse off at the end of the story than they were at the beginning.

What then explains the longevity of these stories? And more, how will the genre evolve and change via contamination with other genres and literary traditions, while remaining recognisable? What are the elements that must be present for a story to be noir? What can be removed or substituted or played with?

In this gritty speculative fiction anthology, we have assembled a splendid table of contents that brings us all the atmosphere of noir, without conceding to reductive or offensive stereotypes. All the heartache that we want to feel while reading noir, without losing sight of empathy and solidarity. We are very pleased with the range of settings, from the neon lights of cyberpunk contamination to the earthy colours of ancient cities of stone and mud.

And of course Futurefire.net Publishing specialises in progressive speculative fiction, under-represented viewpoints, and social-political consciousness. When we put out the call for submissions, we were hoping for stories that would play with and even subvert the noir clichés that we all love to hate. Reader, we were not disappointed. From the light-touch parody to stories that looked nothing like noir on the surface and yet delivered all those feelings of loss and betrayal mixed with the fondest of love and the desire to lose everything for that single cause, or person, that we believe are the true mark of excellent noir tales.

We wanted stories that were refreshing takes on noir, and we are proud to say that the authors in this anthology delivered exactly that. Not only have our stories packed noir up and sent it to more, and more diverse settings than rainy American and French cities; and not only have our authors brought noir tinges to ghost stories, fantasy, myth, fairy tales, outer planets and virtual realities. They have also used noir tools to chisel new, more progressive (and more interesting) tales. We have banned sorry-ass white, misogynist male detectives. We got rid of the appropriation of non-western cultures to evoke exoticism or distrust.

So beware of any damsel in distress that you may meet in these pages. You'd be a fool if you thought she was waiting for a protector. And never underestimate those silent, background characters. Some of them may try to kill you.

Why do readers want these stories with no resolution and filled with pain? In spite of all the tough talk, a lot of noir anti-heroes have human decency, and endeavour to keep it alive. Beyond what they say, their actions suggest that they do believe in friendship, loyalty, solidarity. Sometimes in love. At others even in justice. If they have seen enough during their lives not to expect the good guys to win, they still struggle to be better than the crooks, the traitors, the polluters, the abusers, the corrupted and the corruptors. They will fail, but you'd better believe they'll try again. Like Pandora who, after releasing all the darkest shit in the world, still sees Hope at the bottom of her box. That is, I think, what we love in noir, that Hope survives against all odds, sometimes even against the protagonist's best intentions. But it's there. Hope that maybe not today, and maybe not tomorrow, but one day, one day we will do something worth it, we will make this right. We just have to put some ice on our black eye, and steel ourselves to try again.

If on flicking through these pages you have the impression that you've picked up the wrong anthology (what do an old grandfather visiting family, a deranged seer lost in a labyrinth, a troubled youth with his zombie lover, have to do with noir?) we ask you to trust us. Suspend your disbelief, your distrust and your expectations, and bear with us. We promise you, these stories are filled with noir and will not let you down. You'll notice the grandfather has a checkered past sometimes lurking visibly close to the surface. You will discover the mix of tenderness and desperation between the two boys who seem to animate a Hopper painting (well, if Hopper had painted the undead).

And you may find that a dishevelled woman, abandoned to die underground in a dark place full of ghosts can be an incredibly intense and poetic femme fatale.

For although the protagonists of this volume may include gods and demons and monsters, as well as A.I.s and robots and cyberpunks, and are sometimes surrounded by ghosts and visions and memories; although the criminal gangs have monstrous heavies or hive minds or terrifying technologies and dystopian aspirations—they are still the trappings of noir. Updated, subverted, questioned, improved or reimagined, garnished with science-fictional, fantastic, horrific, weird, surreal or unreal elements, they go places noir itself may never have dared to go. Dare you go with them?

Challenge your expectations, and enjoy all the shades of our authors' unique noir palette.

The Fox and the Snake

Timothy Yeo

On Sundays, the shrine entrance choked up with humans hailing from different countries. Their skin colour didn't matter to me, so long as their yen shone purple. I put on my mask—red and white patterned plastic with two ears sprouting at the top—and morphed my face into a gormless young girl's. Standing below the orange gates next to the fox statues, I held up my basket stacked with worthless knots of paper. When the tourists came streaming in, I would be ready to present them with valuable charms forged by the monks of Mt Takao, a thousand yen apiece.

My phone rang. I saw the caller ID and lowered my basket. How did she get my number? After I had bled her and her mother dry for all they were worth, she should know better than to get entangled with me again.

"Hello?" I answered, retreating behind a statue.

"I have a job for you, Kevin."

Rachel sounded deeper, more level. It must have been four years by now.

"Who's Kevin? I think you have the wrong number."

"I don't care what name you have now."

Some tourists were staring at this weirdo standing off the path. My mask twisted into a lunatic's scowl, and they quickly walked away. "Look, miss, I'm hanging up now."

"I want you to deceive a god."

That perked my ears up. Like Tokyo, Rachel's home was a developed city that traded in coin instead of altars, and to my knowledge I had been the only true divinity to grace the island.

"What are you talking about?" I asked.

"Let's meet at Changi Airport. The toast café on the third floor."

Where we had our second date. "What time?"

"Seven pm."

"Not sure if there's still flights."

"See you there," she said and hung up.

There was absolutely no reason for me to entertain her. Although— it did sting that another deity had apparently moved into my territory. I threw away the basket and found a deserted spot behind the food stalls. With no one to see me, I sat down, took off my mask, and began to trace new patterns.

I was impressed. Now the bangs had cleared from her face, the baggy clothes were gone, and a top and slacks combination completed the working professional look. She didn't recognise me because I had the mask on, so to her I seemed like another clueless Chinese tourist wandering in from the Arrivals. I had wanted to see what she looked like when she thought she wasn't being watched. I thought she would be awkward, glancing around nervously. But an unfamiliar steel gaze was stamped on her face.

I crept up behind her and removed my mask. She looked at me. I studied her hard for any signs of surprise.

"Let's go inside," she said without a trace of emotion.

I followed her in. "Not going to ask me how my flight went?"

We sat down. "Do you know anyone named Bai She?" she asked.

"I'm hungry. Wanna grab a bite?"

"Not at all."

"I'll order for both of us." Before she could protest, I hailed the waitress for two servings of honey toast. Our usual combination: avocado for me, strawberry jam for her. From the corner of my eye I continued searching her for any cracks in the armour.

"Stop being childish," she said. "We didn't meet here to joke. I need you to deceive Bai She."

"Who?"

"A naga spirit."

I had dealt with a few vicious naga in the golden days. Although these snake entities usually resided higher up the map in East Asia. "A naga incident here is a rare occurrence."

"It's staying at Sherry's house."

Calling her mother by given name now? Rachel really had cleaned herself up.

"How's she doing?"

"Still worshipping anyone who smiles at her."

"Worshipping the naga?"

"Bai She's doing what you did. Sinking her teeth in while disguising it as a smile."

"Don't be so cynical."

"I mean literally. She's feeding on Sherry every night. Like a vampire."

This wasn't unheard of. Snakes were ravenous creatures. Sometimes naga kept pets, walking food sources to be snacked on every now and then.

"Why not just leave the house?"

"Sherry won't leave her. You know how she is. She's thinks Bai She's her long-lost daughter."

"What, her real one not good enough?"

There. A slight tense in her knuckles, her chest inhaling in one sharp breath. I made a show of looking away. The waiter came and placed our two orders on the table, along with the sharing plates. Rachel reached for the spoon, but I beat her to it.

"Here you go," I said, cutting out a piece for her. Triangle shaped, dashed with a stroke of strawberry, just how she liked it. She accepted it stiffly and took a bite.

"What makes you think I can help?" I said.

"You're a conman, aren't you?"

"More accurately, a mischievous fox spirit."

"So do your conning. Deceive the naga. Make her think Sherry's got a rare disease, or something."

"You know I'm more elegant than that."

"There's three conditions. You update me every day. Don't break Sherry's heart. And you never contact me or Sherry again once the job's done."

"You haven't even mentioned what you're paying me."

"The knowledge that you've righted your wrongs to your former lover."

Obviously a twisted joke, but neither of us laughed. She looked down and cut me a piece. Square shaped, avocado on each corner, just how I liked it.

"I already have redeemed myself," I said.

"Yeah, sure."

"Back then, you would never talk back to me like that. Now look at you."

"I've learnt how to deal with lying bastards."

"Exactly. I've already taught you enough—"

She hurled her entire meal at my face. The plate spun out of her hands halfway, smashing into the pillar behind me. A shard shot out and grazed my neck, dripping warm blood down my skin. The waiter dashed over to help.

I put on my mask. "Everything's okay," I told the waiter. "Her hand slipped."

The waiter left and I turned to look at her.

"I'm sorry for that," she said. "Let's continue."

"It's okay," I said. I wanted to take off the mask, but if I did everyone around would see the blood.

The payment was everything left in her family's savings account, which in my currency totalled to six hundred thousand yen. I could make that amount easily any week of the year. There was no need to stay in this foreign country and entertain an unprofessional client who scarred me with cutlery. Although—I had already forked out a large fee flying here on such short notice. Might as well make this trip yield a net gain.

"Bai She needs a babysitter," Rachel had said over dessert. "Since she gets angsty cooped up alone in the house."

"What? How young is she?"

"Looks and acts ten years old. She'd love a kindly old man like you."

My real face was spotted, wrinkled, and sporting stubble. The older you looked, the less you were trusted. Therefore, the babysitter's visage would be that of a young college student, still barely two steps out of the nest. I hung an ad on the lamppost with my newly improved face beaming in the foreground. Within that day Sherry called me over.

She was even more of a mess than I remembered. Her makeup spilled all over herself, barely hiding her smile lines. She had periodic shivers that only calmed when her hand wrapped around a pack of cigarettes. She moved and talked slowly, like an Alzheimer's patient twice her age. The naga had only accelerated her degradation. After a routine where she forgot her house keys and had to dig through her bag several times, she finally led me towards Bai She's room.

A thin white snake greeted me at the entrance, coiling up my shoe. I regarded its open fangs, wondering whether its reach was far enough to strike my skin.

"Hope you don't mind," Sherry said. "Bai She loves her pets."

I counted at least four snakes lounging around: two more hanging off the desk, one perched atop its master's shoulder. Bai She was smaller than I had pictured. She wore a summer white dress and sported two very squishable round cheeks. Upon seeing me her entire being lit up and she threw herself forward, wrapping herself around me in a tight hug.

"Mr. Lye!" She shrieked out my false name in pure joy. Then she disengaged and bounced over to her 'mother'. From just a few seconds of observing their interaction, I could tell how deeply the naga's fangs went. Bai She would be any hungry mother's dream. She begged Sherry not to go to work today, nodded furiously when told to be a good girl, and screamed in laughter when her cheeks were inevitably pinched. It was a performance so grand, even I had the urge to tug on my own mask.

Sherry went to work, leaving us alone with a stack of board games. Now it was only me, Bai She, and her four snakes. We played the two-player version of President using a deck of cards, and although I tried to play badly, she really did have the mind of a ten-year-old. After forgetting the formula for a full house, her lovely features screwed up and she began sniffling. Quickly I discarded my ace of spades down my sleeve and made her win. Like clockwork she was all perky again, kicking away the cards in her celebratory dance. Eventually she got restless and zipped out of the room, singing a nursery rhyme about the forest. I fought my way through all the junk in the house to chase after her, catching her legs when she was halfway out the second-floor window, screeching laughter ringing in my ears.

Sherry came back soon after and showered me with thanks. I had passed her two-hour test. She now wanted me to come over every single day of the week.

I said goodbye to the two of them and left—making sure I peeled the snake off my shirt first. But as soon as I turned the corner, I jogged back round to the back of the house. Sherry's room was on the second floor. I scaled the wall to reach the balcony, hid behind the wall, and waited.

After about an hour I heard thumps. Sounds of a body slamming against the floor, travelling right up to where Sherry's bed must be. I peeked through the curtains and saw Sherry, eyes glazed and lips trembling, nearly half off the bed. Bai She's body coiled around hers in a vice. I saw the naga's fangs cleanly, biting into its victim's neck.

A hiss. I looked down to see a snake nudging my foot. I gently brushed it aside and climbed down.

"See?" Rachel said. "I wasn't lying."

For dinnertime, we were having steak at a restaurant I remembered well. Our fifth and sixth dates, to be exact.

"You left out the part where she keeps four snakes."

"Is it a problem?"

"Naga aren't normally so powerful to have familiars."

"I don't know what that means."

"Means that this naga's dangerous. You could double my fee and it still wouldn't cover hazard pay."

Rachel went quiet. She cut out a cube of meat from her steak and placed it gingerly on my plate.

"The money's all I have," she said. "Check my bank statement."

10

I placed her offering in my mouth. It was delicious—every single meal I had eaten since landing in this country hadn't disappointed. "From what I saw, Sherry doesn't have much time left."

"So can you do it?"

"Well, she's a monster, but she's also far too young."

"And that's your speciality, isn't it?"

I bit back a smart retort, considerately remembering Rachel's earlier outburst. Instead, I tossed her a triangle-shaped piece of steak and declared I would take this job.

And it was going to be a relatively easy one, which I suppose justified its cheap price. When Bai She had fed, her movements were that of a child with no restraint, splashing blood onto her dress. This was no calculative predator who chose their victims carefully. Bai She had latched onto Sherry for the same reason Sherry had latched onto her—on a whim. Such connections were child's play to break. I could simply rub the thread between my fingers, applying pressure until it snapped.

Having a developing mind, Bai She craved intellectual stimulation, something her 'mother' could never provide her. During these babysitter sessions I introduced to her a variety of children's games. Blackjack, Solitaire, Crazy Eights. When she graduated from playing cards, we moved on to the board games. I made all the appropriate moves—praising her when she got something right, encouraging her when she was on the verge of tears. Soon her snakes crowded at the door whenever I arrived.

With phase one complete, I started slipping in extra hints. That Sherry was too stingy to buy the more expensive game sets. That it was lucky I was here because Sherry never wanted to play games with her. On the side, I lifted small trinkets from Sherry's bag. Her lipstick, mirror, things I knew she valued and hated losing. A few whispers here and there, and Sherry found these items turning up in Bai She's room, next to the snakes. On the next bloodsucking session I eavesdropped in, Sherry wasn't the passive victim anymore. She was sitting up, repeating the same questions over and over. Bai She responded, her mouth half-full, that she didn't know what Sherry was talking about. There was no anger in their conversation, not yet. That would come later.

I gave my report to Rachel in the park while she enjoyed a cone of ice cream. As I updated her on my progress, she stopped licking, and threw her treat into the dustbin.

"Put on your mask," she said.

My mask was unsheathed, over my head—Rachel was the only person in the city who I allowed to see my real face. "What's wrong?" I asked.

"You're disgusting to look at."

"That's an ungrateful thing to say."

She didn't back down this time. "Could you stop getting so close?"

I pulled down the mask to imitate a famous male movie star. She shifted to the other side of the bench, looking away.

"This needs to be done," I said. "You hired me for this."

"Sure, because you know what's best."

At least I had freed her from her mother. That woman lived in her own world, bumbling through life with her heart swinging from her sleeve, poisoning her daughter with her sickly love. After I had emptied her safe, my one wish for her family was that leaving wounds would teach them how to properly heal.

But the daughter hadn't learnt completely after all. She brooded on the bench, still struggling to contain her emotions. While waiting, I took a glance around the park. I recognised the rose shrubs, the morning-glories, that alcove surrounded by a pair of sunflowers. When we had first kissed, it had been on the path leading down to the Lily Pond, where silent pink bulbs bloomed and skaters darted across the still water. There she had whispered in my ear things she had never told anyone else, like her deepest darkest fears, or the password to her bank account.

"Want to take a walk?" I asked. She needed to cool off. "They revamped the Lily Pond, I heard."

She remembered as well as I did. "You've got some nerve."

"Rachel." Once again, it pained me I couldn't deliver this with my real mouth. "Back then, we were in different roles. I was desperate for scraps. You were young and naive. Now the roles are different. You're my client, and I'm doing a job. That's all there is. That's the way people work. This time, you have to trust me."

We ended up taking that walk. I hung a respectful distance behind her, but I couldn't help but notice that when I inched closer, she didn't protest.

A week into the job, I finished removing all of Sherry's failsafes: her cigarettes, her pills, her lemon scented mints. Even her 'daughter' was taken away from her. Bai She had a new present, a ball of yarn to practice Cat's Cradle with. After every babysitting session, I would assign her a different problem, so that she spent her nights on the string and not on her victim—a victim who was now no longer willing.

The nights of feasting grew shorter. Neither party was enjoying it anymore. Outside their bedroom, I could hear Sherry asking where the hell Bai She hid her bottles, even pushing the girl's teeth off her prematurely. To a young mind like Bai She, this once docile mother turning feral must have come as a shock.

When the world around you stops making sense, you latch on to the handhold that feels the most familiar. By week two I was certain I had mired my little snake girl into complete confusion.

When I next opened Bai She's door, I was nearly knocked over. The snake that normally greeted me was now twice its previous size. Another snake slammed into my leg, trapping me in the corner. The last two flanked Bai She on either side. She had the string in her hands, frayed from constant practice. Yesterday's pattern had been a difficult one, too. This girl learned fast.

She lifted her head and flashed a bright smile. "Mr. Lye!"

The snake released me. Catching my breath, I made a show of admiring her Cat's Cradle handiwork, remarking (somewhat truthfully, this time) that she was nothing short of a genius.

I decided on Love Letter today, because she was so skilled with games now, she could graduate to the kind with social deduction. I dealt the cards and we took turns trying to guess which members of the king's court were in our hands. I bluffed that I had the Guard, but eventually revealed my King, who had the power to knock her out of the round. As she waited for me to reshuffle, I noticed her smile dissolving into a frown. At our feet, the snakes skittled round restlessly, their red pupils tracking my every movement.

"I saw your mother earlier," I mentioned innocently. "She seemed angry at something."

That was the signal for Bai She to let it all out. "I don't understand her!" she exploded. Four different snake jaws opened to hiss. "She says I'm a bad girl, but I didn't even do anything!"

"She said that? But you've been very polite to me."

"Right?! It doesn't make sense."

"Maybe," I suggested, "she's saying something that's not true."

"What?!" her eyes widened. "Why?!"

"That's how people work. Sometimes, people lie."

"Not her," her cheeks puffed, on the verge of bursting from this sudden revelation. "She's the best mother in the world."

The chair behind me cracked. A snake wrapped around it, muscles bulging, splintering wood near my lap. She didn't seem to notice. I decided to leave it at that for now. The seed I had implanted was stirring wildly in her mind. I could already see her taking the lesson to heart, as her eyes turned dark and her mouth curled down, and as she shot out a finger to reveal my card as the treacherous Spy.

The movie theatre, date number twenty. It was easy to spot Rachel among the younglings. Her head was a few meters taller, her sharp blazer putting all college jackets to shame.

"Nice snakeskin." I nudged her branded bag. "Trying to impress someone?"

"I came from work."

When I updated her, she frowned. "She broke a chair?"

"Destroyed it, yeah."

"You said she was dangerous?"

"Children throw the most violent tantrums. If she finds out I'm lying, she'll tear me limb from limb."

"Oh, shit."

"Don't worry. I can take care of myself."

"Couldn't care less. I'm talking about my mother. They way you've put it, you've turned her into a villain. What if Bai She—"

"Don't worry about that."

I explained to her the full plan. She squirmed on her feet, trying to hide how impressed she was. A couple drifted past us, chatting about how the latest caped crusader punched the bad guy into space. I ran my eye over the movie schedule: there was another showing starting in ten minutes.

In the darkened theatre, she continued giving me orders. "Just in case, I want you to get Sherry out of the house."

"If you're really that worried, just move back in."

"We aren't on speaking terms. I know a few friends she has in Japan. I'll arrange a trip."

"You can do that?"

In the darkness, she didn't notice me slip off my mask.

"I'll just say Sherry's dying of cancer. The sort they are, they'll happily drag her on an extended bucket list vacation."

"Proud of you," I said. It felt great saying it, without the mask to muffle my voice. And now I could study every shadowy contour of her face, without her stopping to interrogate me.

"Sure. I'll leave it to you to convince her."

The opening credits started, and the audience hushed. After seventy minutes, the heart-pounding climax arrived where the monster had the hero in its grasp. It was a very well-crafted scene, calculated to put the audience on the edge of their seats. Rachel gripped her right armrest, the one closer to me, such that her fingers were inches from my own.

When the world falls out from under you, you latch on to what feels the most familiar.

Bai She grew really good at bluffing. Of course, I bluffed that her bluffing bluffed me, but nevertheless there were a few rounds where she genuinely surprised me. On those occasions, where her Guard card was revealed to be the magnanimous Princess, she unleashed a joyful laugh as her snakes whacked the cards out of my hand.

Her familiars were used to me by now. At any given time at least two would be slithering under my shirt, rubbing their fangs against my pulsing veins. Bai She and Sherry never met at night anymore. I was Bai She's new target now. The next step had to begin quickly.

First came the favour to my client. Rachel's extra orders were unnecessary and only created further risk. Although—I supposed if Sherry was out of the picture, it would make my job easier. When the call from Japan came, she dithered predictably, but I was on hand to convince her that during her absence, Bai She would come to love her again.

Bai She handled the departure well. With Sherry gone, the entire house became her territory. Snakes chewed up the tablecloth or sunbathed over the sink. When I went to loot Sherry's room, I walked into a cloud of cotton. Where Sherry's bed had been now lay a pile of broken wood and stuffing.

On the start of the third week, nestled amongst a bodyguard now thick as her elbow, Bai She threw me an angelic smile. "I got you, Mr. Lye! Gooot you!"

Her voice was lost over the constant hissing in my ears. "Good one," I replied, gathering up the cards again.

"If my mom plays, I'd thrash the shit out of her, right? Right?"

"No question," I declared. "You're a genius."

A prick on my neck. As gently as I could, I pried the snake off and laid it on the floor.

"Mr. Lye," the snake demon said. "Would you like to stay over tomorrow night?"

Finally. I had reached the point where I had Bai She's complete trust. The plan now approached its final phase. For this, I would pile the thread with one final burst of weight. I would take her out, treat her like an adult. The arcade, a delicious meal, maybe even a little wine. Make sure our last day together was something she'd never forget. Then, when approaching the climax, where she was already lying on her bed in eager anticipation, I would pop off to the store for some drinks first.

She would never see me again. Later, when emerging confused from her room, she would find our board games ripped to shreds. The entire house ransacked, silverware from the cabinet gone. Her snakes having vanished, assumedly to be sold in the black market (in actuality I would break their necks and throw their corpses into the river). She would also realise her distrust of Sherry was misplaced, but the thread had long since snapped. Bai She would never be able to form another connection again. She could suck on prey all she wanted from then on, but the blood would come out dry.

She would learn an important lesson that day. And be all the better for it.

The karaoke booth was tiny. We squeezed together on a single ottoman until our thighs were touching. There was a musky smell here, the scent of untended plaster. Coloured lights flashed around us at puzzling intervals, and a song from twelve years ago belted out of the box television. Two cans of cheap beer sat on our laps.

I delivered my report. This perfect outcome was imminent. Bai She would stop being a naïve child, and Sherry would lose her poisonous crutch. Would Rachel prefer to make payment by wire or cash?

Her shoulders relaxed. Using the alcohol as an excuse, she even let out a satisfied sigh. "Give me your account number," she said.

She waited for me to negotiate. Suddenly demand an extra cut, or wrangle for more jobs. I said nothing and buried my mask in beer.

"Why did you help me?" she asked.

"What kind of a question is that?"

"The money's cheap change to you. I know that."

"Then why did you offer me in the first place?"

"Because you were my only hope. And I'm still amazed you agreed."

"Alright. I'll be honest. It's because you're such an easy mark I couldn't resist coming back."

"Seriously!?" She flashed me a smile for the first time—a blatantly artificial one. "You really thought I would fall in love with you again?"

I threw my hands up. "Guess that didn't work. Damn it."

The lights dimmed as the singer launched into a crooning ballad. I got up and yelled for the receptionist to bring us a second round.

"So," Rachel said, tracing her finger idly on the seat. "This is our last meeting, then."

"What a sad occasion."

"Since it is, let me thank you formally as an adult."

"Oh?"

"You did a good job." She stood up. "I guess your soul can rest easy now, having redeemed yourself."

"No more sleepless nights for me."

She nodded to me and walked towards the door.

"Wait," I said.

"Yeah?"

"Not going to sing?"

She paused with her hand on the doorknob.

I was only half paying attention to the game. I couldn't help thinking how I was going to miss this country. The weather was needlessly hot, and no one spoke Japanese, but three weeks here and it felt like a return to home.

"Mr. Lye," Bai She said. Her innocent eyes peeked out from her cards. "Why do people lie?"

"Bai She, I've told you before. People are people."

I would come back soon, I decided. Probably in December, during Rachel's leave, where we would take a cruise around the island and take turns stealing each other's food.

"But isn't it better for people to understand each other?"

I looked up at Bai She, genuinely proud of how far she had come, how much she questioned.

"Listen well, Bai She. You should never want to be understood. Use your words carefully. Hide your wishes with a mask. If someone guesses who you really are, then you've lost the game."

All four snakes circled round me, thirsty for blood. I knew she wouldn't make a move yet. She was entirely dependent on my command.

"Mr. Lye," Bai She asked, "is that why you lied to me?"

I did a perfect job. I was confident of that. Laying down the foundation for weeks, ensuring no mistakes slipped through the cracks. That was why, as the snakes tore off my mask and burrowed into my cheeks, I realised the fault didn't lie with me.

"Goooot you." Tears were streaming down Bai She's face, and she was smiling. "You liar."

I tried to reform the mask, to construct a plea for my life, but angry fangs darted out to split the plastic into pieces. I collapsed, choking on my own skin and blood.

"That woman," Bai She said. "Who was she? She showed me proof, though. She's not a liar."

But she was. A soulless, ungrateful, beautiful liar. When had Rachel decided to betray me? Back in the karaoke room, where she learned the plan was already complete and it didn't matter whether I was alive or dead by the end of it? Or had she already visualized my mangled corpse at the lily pond? When her hand rested on mine in the theatre? When she thanked me with those earnest eyes? When was it?

The scar on my neck, on our very first meeting in the airport. It hadn't healed, because Rachel hadn't forgotten.

It was growing cold. The demon brought her foot down, again and again. I started to give in. There was no point getting angry any longer. My little girl had grown up to be a fine young woman. The only regret was that I would never get another chance to play the game with her again.

The Stars, Their Faces Uplifted in Song

M.L. Clark

Transfer orders reached me in active storage—awake but shelved, attentive only to the smaller sounds of silence: the hum of ventilation shafts, the occasional click of distant footsteps, the minute grind of locks on other doors.

Call them my meditative years—four and a half, give or take, since the last serious incident on Loris Prime. Just don't ask why I logged into storage after putting that sorry case to bed. Fatigue doesn't hit an AI the same way it might a Natural Intelligence, and for all the cynicism in my personal profile, the notion of growing too jaded or spooked for detective work, as an NI often does, won't pass muster either. The best I can offer is that time passes differently for AIs: every sluggish, human second its own eternity, and yet, what are four-plus years to someone with whole centuries in their wake?

Unfolding and unplugging myself to answer the official call, I made note of all the points along and under my 'steel frame operating at suboptimal efficiency: plastics thick with particulate; liquid wiring that had just begun to crystallize; phase-shifting nanoprocessors in need of realignment. Minor fixes, all, but important reminders of my own mortality—gradual though it would be, unless I hastened things along.

My associate had been sent straight from Network HQ—meaning straight from basic training—to join me on the journey out. He was young as recruits went, but then, they all seemed childlike to me, from the freshest to the most seasoned NI in the outfit. This wasn't just my age talking, either: Everyone I'd been programmed to care about had died generations past, and I suspected that, for whatever reason, self-actuation had lessened my ability to build a similar rapport with others since.

Hearing tell of this suspicion, a previous associate once suggested that maybe we weren't so different after all—humans, that is, and AIs. At the time, 58 and widowed, he maintained that his heart had been permanently wearied by its losses, and though he saw youthful optimism all about him, he knew he'd never again join in. I accepted this as his view for as long as he held it, and then, when he was 62, likewise accepted word that he'd found a man who taught him to laugh and cry anew. Granted, though, this was forty-odd years ago, and they're both making their way back to stardust now, so he wasn't entirely wrong: I'd be joining him and all other NIs, eventually, on that protracted road.

In the meantime, the kid before me was of the nervous, jumpy sort, and as ill-fitting in his Network jumpsuit as he seemed in the hush of the storage lockers. When he spoke he cleared his throat first, as if in competition with the silence for my attention.

"If you need a moment to get—ah—dressed?"

If I'd still had a synth-skin I might have smiled. I'd worn one such outfit or another for centuries: the first the body of a Companion with ample female attributes, the next a broad-shouldered male number, and the rest all variations therein. But the naked chassis had its benefits, too; it "breathed," as an NI might say of their birthday suit.

Instead I declined his offer by making directly for the shuttle, as the Network surely knew I would. My associate jogged to keep up while rattling off details of our case: Twenty-three dead monks in a mountain-dwelling community on a hunk of rock so old, so remote, and so apparently bereft of commercial value that at first I thought it no wonder the Network didn't want to waste "real" agents on the case.

"Witnesses?"

"Just one—the only surviving monk."

"And what does he say happened?"

"He doesn't."

"Scared into silence, huh?"

"No, just—too busy to talk."

The kid almost bumped into me when I stopped short at the loading dock for a passing luggage car. The ticker for our own transport flashed its final boarding call.

"Too busy for a murder investigation?"

His cheeks and ears reddened as we took our respective seats. "Well—ah—that's the tricky part, Detective Bennett—sir. See, the monk won't stop singing long enough for anyone to get a word in edgewise. And the locals say he can't. Their people—they believe the universe was sung into being, and the monks' job is to keep it going. For as long as anyone remembers, the monks have been holding the universe together in song—in shifts, of course, but without pause. So now the locals are terrified because if he stops... well, he won't stop, sir. Not with that much on the line."

"Well, that's a damned nuisance. What's your name, kid?"

"Yes, sir. Hersh, sir."

Out the nearest viewscreen, Hersh and I watched Loris Prime fall away.

I skimmed all pertinent files from Hersh's sig-card during the last minute of the flight. The hunk of rock we'd landed on had three official names: its Network designation, its everyday name, and its sacred name. Only three would be unusual, if not for the planet's culturally homogenous population: just under a quarter million calling Cog "home."

Cog was a planet of relentless mountain ranges, many containing caverns large enough to port three shuttles through, side by side, with room to spare on either end. But if Cog had ever held lucrative mineral and metal reserves (and some signs pointed to interplanetary mining operations thousands of years back), they stood depleted now. What remained was a multifaceted people, their skins a patchwork of colors, shapes, and sizes, with agrarian traditions haphazardly merged from what might have been as many as twelve original sources, and a persisting caste system not unusual for colonies their age and size.

The way Hersh had told it, today's Cograns were nobodies in the Network, but from the report that wasn't quite true: their use simply lay elsewhere, in communication relays and intelligence-gathering, two services which—at the shit end of a particularly cold and inhospitable solar system—these people could perform with greater ease and discretion than most. So maybe there was more to my reassignment than first appeared.

Either way, the Cogran who met our transport was taller than the average native, and from the accessories on his outerwear, more affluent, too. Sev Franz, he called himself—Sev being a designation not unlike "Father" or "Reverend" in other parts of the galaxy, but with the added implication of "mediator" or "peace-maker." There was no official police force on Cog, where most communities numbered in the low thousands, but each had an upper-caste council that met to discuss various infractions therein. Sev Franz introduced himself as one of seven such councilors from the community of Pagora, which encompassed the mountain cavern where the world's monks—a population already in sharp decline in recent years—lived and worked and held the universe together in song.

"Striking place," I said, as he directed us to the primary crime scene. "Cog's what, now—thirteen, fourteen billion years old?"

Sev Franz shot me a puzzled look, but if he'd hoped to read anything off my naked 'steel frame, its impassive ocular sockets and rigid, empty jaw, he could only be disappointed. "No, of course not. Closer to—well, five billion, I suppose. But surely you know that."

"And your people? Do they know that, too? My files suggest strong literacy rates, no major panic about modern medicine and the like. And yet, the universe is billions of years older than your world, and your people are terrified that it will *end* if the singing stops?"

Sev Franz's mouth parted. "Ah," he said, winking. "Yes, I see now. I suppose it all sounds incomprehensible to someone like you—a *robot*, yes?"

"AI will do. Just 'robot' would be the equivalent of calling you a mammal, or vertebrate, understand?"

"Absolutely. But the point remains, no?"

"No, I don't find it incomprehensible."

"Because you already find humans irrational in everything we do?" Sev Franz glanced in amusement at Hersh, but the kid was trying his best to appear professional, only the flushed tips of his ears conveying his own uncertainty.

"Well, you are, but no." I affected a sigh to set the NIs at ease. "No, I was originally programmed to worship, myself. One person, mind you, but to me she was a god."

"I'm not so sure that's the same…" Sev Franz started, before a look of discomfort passed over his face. "Then again, who am I to say it isn't?" His next smile was all business—big and toothy as he clapped his hands and gestured to a narrow cavern entrance, no more than an unadorned crack along the mountainside. Only from the wear along its edges (the rock worn smooth by many palms over many generations) could one begin to guess the meaning of this place. We entered the recesses of the mountain one by one.

Our narrow walking path opened into an antechamber many meters in, after which various markings of civilization—mosaics, friezes, metalworks, and free-standing sculptures, all given the impression of movement by torchlight—flooded our field of view.

"Shouldn't this place be cordoned off?" said Hersh. "For genetic testing?"

Sev Franz looked ready to tousle the kid's hair. "Already done, son. Took you two a while just to get here, remember?"

Our timing was relative, of course. Network logs showed that three days had passed on Cog since the incident, with the lone surviving monk hooked to a saline drip as he sang the song of the world alone in the temple's inner sanctum. For me and Hersh, though, it had been just under a day from Hersh's briefing to our joint arrival. Plenty still refused to travel in the Spiders—giant mechanical structures, vaguely arachnoid in form, at the outskirts of every known solar system, opening their arms to approaching vessels and transporting each to its desired coordinates—but even those who shuddered at such machines still benefited from their use. Hell, the Network itself, as a web of resources spanning the known galaxy, had only become possible after decoding and adapting to such alien technologies.

"And beyond this passage?" I nodded to a corridor wreathed in images of monks—some reading, others buried with saintly glosses, still others in transcendent acts of prayer. "The temple?"

"After you." Sev Franz gestured and I obliged. Hersh alone stumbled as we reached a balcony from which the whole mountain seemed to give way—its interior rising hundreds of meters to a ceiling entirely painted over, but also descending hundreds of meters more into pitch-black void. Once I'd adjusted my visual settings, I could make out five other balconies around the circular perimeter, while at the chamber's center, along a pillar that ran the whole height and depth of the cavern, lay a second sphere—a room from which the brightest lights emanated through intricate gaps in the stone. The whole temple was filled with song: deep, raw, and simple—at times no more than a guttural *ahhh* that proceeded from this second sphere and reverberated throughout.

Though I assumed our lone monk lay within that room at the center of the pillar, I could not so easily surmise how he'd entered the inner sanctum in the first place. I turned to Hersh to speculate, but his gaze was fixed on the trick of the shadows that made the temple floor seem infinite. His forehead beaded with sweat.

"Afraid of heights?"

"A little."

Sev Franz came between us, peering over the ledge. "Our oldest stories speak of monks climbing down the sides of these walls, crossing the base of the cave, and scaling the pillar for their turn at song. See? You can even make out the footholds on either side—a bit run down now, but passable with the right equipment."

"Needlessly elaborate, wouldn't you say?"

"Oh no, Detective. It all accords quite well with our beliefs—man crawling out from the depths and into the light." And he went on, with a lilt in his voice:

Little children, least of the universe,
Turning their voices heavenward—
The planets, the stars, their faces
Uplifted in song—
Who will keep this symphony in motion
When all the little children are gone?

I allowed Sev Franz a generous silence before asking, "How do we cross now?"

"Oh, it's simple enough. Here—" And he wrapped both hands around a heavy, rounded stone by the passageway, dragging the knob from one side of the balcony ledge to the other. In so doing, the underside of our platform unfolded into a springy mesh bridge spanning half the cavern. "We've just had all these retracted to give our dear brother peace in this difficult hour. He has a hard enough task without being troubled by Pagora's townsfolk, however well-intentioned their journeys out."

Or their interest in finishing the job. I tested the tensile strength of our narrow walkway and its railings before leading the party on.

"But what if he wanted to leave the center chamber?" said Hersh. "Could he even operate the bridges from inside?"

Sev Franz's baffled look was all the answer either of us required.

On the way to Cog, I'd wondered why Pagora's sitting council hadn't conducted even the simplest yes/no interrogation with the lone surviving monk, irrespective of his need for constant song. To see Brother Yuco in the heart of the temple, though—sinewy with age, slumped in grief and exhaustion, a blanket wrapped about him, IVs in his arms, and his head shaking a relentless *no no no* while eleven crime scene markers held vigil all about—I understood at once the futility of such an exchange. The monk, however, was not alone; by his side knelt a woman, also old by human standards, to whom had clearly fallen the task of keeping Brother Yuco awake and full of universal voice.

"Marin Bris," said Sev Franz, touching her shoulder when she turned and scowled at the sight of me. "This is Detective Bennett and his junior associate, from the Network. They're here to help."

"What in blazes we need a robot for," she said. "And one with more skull than face—Stars preserve us, people're going to think Death's come to mark the End of Things."

"It'd be fitting, though, wouldn't it, given the circumstances?" I said. "However competent your ministrations, we both know Brother Yuco can't keep this up forever."

"You shut yourself with that talk this instant." Marin Bris glared at me, then Sev Franz. "You've told him we're training the next lot even now, haven't you? They'll be here in time—he's only got to hold out a little longer, don't you, old man? Oh, come now, don't start that again—"

Hersh twitched and made to speak when the old woman ran her palms over Brother Yuco's tear-stained cheeks, but I caught the kid's wrist, and with a confused glance my way, he held his tongue instead. Together we watched Marin Bris kiss the salt from the monk's eyes as he shook his head and intoned another verse from the Cograns' ancient song.

"Come along, then," said Sev Franz. "I assume you'll want to see where the other twelve were murdered? We know they died first, in their beds, done away with by the same incineration tool we found at the bottom of the temple, and which the murderer ultimately overheated to the point of destroying all genetic evidence. Granted, the real puzzle is how the other eleven were killed *here*, in plain view of one another, and from so many angles, but we have all those stills on file already. I imagine you've already reviewed the lot."

I nodded at this last, but lingered just the same at the edge of the inner sanctum. "Although I'm not so certain that's the puzzle here."

"Oh?" Sev Franz halted halfway across the mesh bridge, blocking my associate's passage. Hersh clung desperately to one railing and shut his eyes against the depths below.

"Just think of it." I surveyed the intricate carvings along the pillar and throughout the walls of the outer cavern, its acoustics perfectly suited to the monks' millennia-old task. "You believe your song upholds the universe. You train for years and gather in shifts to meditate, to pray, and to sing. You shut your eyes, clear your mind, and hear only the force of that collective music—until it starts to go out, one precious thread after another. What do you do at first except sing louder, assuming—as is only reasonable at the time—a much milder explanation for all the other voices dropping off?

"So by the time you realize just how much silence has crept in, even if you *do* open your eyes and see the killer, and all your brothers' corpses around them, how do you orchestrate response without giving up the song? Let's say there are half a dozen monks remaining— *maybe*, at best—when the severity of the situation finally reaches them. That's still half a dozen men trained only in slow, communal action, and now suddenly required, with frantic glances alone, to decide who'll make the first move—and how, against such a silent but deadly weapon—while the rest try to keep the universe alive. Those just aren't good odds for survival, Sev Franz. Not among your kind."

Our Cogran mediator did not reply at once, and when he did there was something distinctly angry about his soft-spoken "I see," as if to say—*You must think us all fools*. But Marin Bris did not hesitate, or equivocate, in her own howl from the heart of the temple.

"OUT!" came her personal song of the universe, as she clutched a now profusely weeping Brother Yuco. "OUT OUT OUT OUT!"

Hersh had his own disapproving look by the time we reached the living quarters, and gone was the eager "Yes, sir" when I asked him to inspect each monk's cell. I asked Sev Franz if he'd give us a moment alone, to which the mediator readily agreed, claiming that other Pagoran business called to him anyway. I turned to my associate.

"They teach passive-aggression in basic training now?"

Hersh's cheeks grew a livid pink. "You always that horrible around people in mourning?"

"Marin Bris, you mean, or Brother Yuco?"

"Both. Either. The hell does it matter." Hersh cast about the room in that nervous, twitchy way of his. "You read the files, didn't you? You know they're both Ang—lowest of the low on this colony. So twist the knife in the wound, why don't you? Picking on two scared old people who could never've advanced in the first place except through the Order, and even then don't get much say about all that's gone on."

"Not quite. Only the men ever advance." Hersh's nostrils flared with what I took to be exasperation as I went on. "Fascinating, isn't it? Cograns believe the song of the universe must begin with the lowest of the low, swelling until it reaches the stars themselves. In practice, that gives a few Ang men social mobility in exchange for sterility, and so ironically creates a *new* lowest class of Cogran: the Ang woman, for whom no such deal is on offer. Some follow Ang men into the mountains, sacrificing their own fertility in turn, but their lives here are not easy. *Heaven's whores* would be my translation of the Cogran term."

"There are women like Marin Bris on my world, too," said Hersh, his arms now minutely trembling. "Shunned as class traitors for leaving oppressive homes, then exploited for the rest of their lives by the people they gave up everything to serve."

"And you're Ang yourself, I take it—or the equivalent on your world." I waited for his reply, but Hersh only studied his hands. "It shows, you know. You've got the look of someone who doesn't think he fits in, who's just waiting to be found out. Who thinks he needs to defend his right to the very air he's breathing, the room he's taking up."

Another pause on my part; another silence on Hersh's.

"No wonder they paired you with me. Kid as jumpy as you, on assignment with a regular NI? That'd just be asking for trouble—for both of you. No way the Network risks your sorry ass *and* some human vet's just to see if you'll cut it in the field."

At last Hersh's head snapped up, his face and neck fully flush with anger. "I passed my entrance exams like anybody else. Top third of my class, too. Nerves of steel in a shuttle cockpit, or behind the controls of any other vehicle you can name. I joined the Network to serve the galaxy and improve the reputation of my people, and so help me, Detective Bennett—*sir*—I'm going to do that, whether you like it or not."

I laughed: a rare, spontaneous gesture that made me wonder if I'd overlooked other repairs. If I still had synth-skin I would have affected wiping the corners of my eyes, too.

"Settle down, Hersh. Who the hell cares what I like or don't like? I'm just the asshole AI running your first assignment. I mean, good for you, having dreams and shit. But see how easy you make it? Getting pissed because some unresolved angst hits an angle of the case the wrong way? That's the kind of emotional baggage that leads NIs to violence, so get used to me pushing it: I'm running a homicide investigation here. I can't always back down or play nice if I want to learn about the people involved."

"Yeah? So what'd you learn from upsetting the old lady like that?"

I affected surprise as best I could without a human face. "Plenty. Why, didn't you?"

Hersh clearly couldn't tell if I was joking or not, so with a severe frown he returned to his inspection of the monks' cells, silent at first but eventually getting into the rhythm of his labors, and at times even calling out the amused likes of: "Got some letters in here!" "Man, Brother Timu was a slob!" and "Brothers Wye and Kildew were sleeping together!"

I kept my replies short and mostly neutral, with the occasional bit of encouragement whenever warranted, and by the time we left the mountain, Hersh seemed almost a different field agent—not completely over the worst of his restless mannerisms, granted, but more comfortable, at least, in his persisting annoyance with me.

Only twilight greeted us when we left the mountain, with even wildlife apparently in short supply on this fragile, gutted world. We soon learned that Sev Franz had indeed been called away by important business—the arrival of temple novitiates from far-off villages—but we hadn't been forgotten; once we passed into town, we were escorted to a large enough hut that Hersh could sleep well apart from me. While I charged from my portable energy drive, he picked at a local delicacy of rice and beans.

"Thoughts on the good Sev Franz?"

Hersh paused in that way most socially-aware NIs do before responding, trying to convey serious consideration where most AIs, when left to their own devices, would simply churn out every relevant response.

"For someone who believes the world might end at any moment," said the kid at last, "he's pretty calm. But uptight in other ways. Especially about anything theoretical."

"Not surprising, given his job description. He's their front-of-house: the man who tends to their day-to-day spiritual needs *and* their political ones. And now he serves as Cogran's representative to the stars, too, which would be quite a tall order for anyone."

Hersh opened his sig-card, a projection screen hovering over his dinner. "It's all pretty new for them, isn't it—Network ties, trade benefits, the chance of leaving this rock? I mean, 'Cog'—it even sounds worthless in the galactic tongue. Someone should tell them how it translates on other worlds. Maybe get them to put in for a name-change."

"You might be surprised how many would take pride in the name's translation, if they knew it. We're talking about a culture that boasts of low beginnings, remember."

"Not all of them, though. Not people like Sev Franz." Hersh's facial features were so expressive I could almost hear the gears in his head turning. He pointed at me with a spoon. "Sev Franz talks a good talk about his faith relying on the lowest of the low, but he seems pretty happy to be in another caste himself. One with plenty of mobility, and wealth, and best of all, the assumption that the universe just *wanted* things this way. That he'd earned all his luxuries and the confidence that comes with them just by being born."

"Not bad," I said—and meant it; the kid had potential—"but what's it to us?"

Hersh shook his head. "Honestly, I don't think he cares if we solve the case or not. He's already fixing the parts that matter to him, turning the whole temple back into a well-oiled machine, so if we can't figure this shit out, it's no skin off his back. Hell, he might even come out of this looking *more* useful to his people if we leave empty-handed."

"No reason for him to knock off twenty-three monks, then, that you can see?"

"Nope." Hersh wiped his mouth and sat up. "And you—sir?"

I didn't reply, and Hersh went back to his meal, speaking again only after pushing his plate aside. By then, in the time it took Hersh to say "What I *don't* understand—", I had over a dozen rejoinders queued, like *...could fill the whole mountain temple. ...would stretch between one Spider and the next. ...thankfully won't bring about the ruination of any important civilizations.*

We weren't ready for that kind of banter, though, so I played it straight and let him finish: "—is why we're here at all. I mean, yeah, it's sad that almost all the monks on this world got wiped out, and upsetting that these people think the universe might end because of it, but what's the Network's angle? Because we both know they have one."

I affected an unnecessary pause of my own. The kid was perceptive, but not yet able to extrapolate beyond his own experiences. "Of course they do," I said. "But it's obvious, isn't it? It doesn't matter if the world actually ends or not—the trouble is that someone might have killed those monks *thinking* the world would end if their song did. *That's* the kind of terrorist mentality that alerted the Network to this case. *That's* why they sent us: on the off-chance we're dealing with someone who might have access to the whole Network through the Spiders, and a death wish for the universe to boot."

"But if Brother Yuco stops singing and the world doesn't end—"

"Then our perp will either be humbled by how wrong they were, and maybe even give him or herself up, or else they'll retaliate in even more extreme ways—ways that might *actually* bring the universe to its knees. It's just too big a risk to be ignored."

"If our perp wanted to end the song, though, why leave Brother Yuco alive? Man, I wish they had surveillance cameras on this dump. I get that the temple's a sacred place, but still—we could've wrapped this all up remotely with just a camera or two."

I nodded and stood to retire. "Different cultures, different practices. It's a good question, though. We'll know more when we talk to the family."

But Hersh only frowned at me. "You don't already know who did it, do you?"

Without a synth-skin, I didn't even bother feigning a smile.

"Night, kid. See you at dawn."

We made it to moonfall before being roused by a disturbance in the scrub-bushes just beyond our hut. Hersh had his hand on his holster when I opened the door and sighted three figures hunched and quarreling in the dark.

"That's enough," I said. "Present yourselves." I was ready to give chase if they ran, but instead the one in the middle stood up sharply, then shoved the smallest into the light spilling from our hut.

"Take her when you go," he said. "Please. She's ruined if she stays here."

The third figure, a woman perhaps in her late twenties, was crying and shaking her head. The child before us looked half her age at best, and when Hersh saw the bruises all along the child's arms, he swore in a language I didn't recognize.

"Who's done this to your daughter?"

The man seemed startled by the obvious connection, then impatient. "It's nothing compared to what will happen if she stays. She's in love with one of the boys they've taken—she's a fool. She'll follow them all to the temple just like that old crone did, and bring shame upon my family. It wasn't supposed to be this way."

"You did this to her, then?" Hersh's hand was back on the holster. I was half-inclined to stay silent and see what he'd do, but the Ang man's last words intrigued me.

"Tell us," I said. "How was it supposed to be?"

He hesitated, and seemed poised to speak until the child's mother pulled at his arm.

"We can't," she said to him. "Too many have died already for this foolishness. There will never be an end to things."

"There'll be an end to your beating your daughter, that's for certain," said Hersh. He advanced with weapon half-upraised, gesturing at the child to get behind him. I admit to almost crushing his wrist until he let the service piece drop, the child still frozen between her parents and us. Hersh shot a furious glance my way as he cried out and nursed the injury.

"Is that it, then?" I said. "Do you really think bringing about the end is the answer? Better to destroy everything than live another day as you do?"

The woman spat in the dirt between us. "You want to talk destruction? You ask that old hag, Marin Bris, what right she had smuggling tools and the like into the temple. There's nothing sacred to her kind once they go up. You don't understand what those whores are capable of—the wrath that comes of a lifetime's selfish indulgence. She was old, see? Too old. They were fixing to be rid of her, so why not repay 'em with murder?"

"Village gossip," Hersh spat back. "That woman won't leave Brother Yuco's side."

"Then we're on borrowed time," said the man, his expression ashen. He took hold of the child by an elbow and tugged her into the shadows. "It's no use now, trying to run—Come, Isla. We must pray."

Hersh started after them, but I held his shoulder too firmly. "The hell's the matter with you," he said, and kicked a 'steel leg instead. "We can't just let them get away."

"I'm not," I said. "But you still need your sleep."

Hersh gave no sign of comprehension at first, but when I began to walk away his brows shot up. NIs might take a little longer, but they more or less get there in the end.

"Hey," he said, crouching in the dirt. "Here." He tossed his firearm my way. I crossed the barrel over an ocular socket in salute, then gestured again for him to go bed. This time, to even my surprise, he obeyed.

I didn't pursue the wretched family, though explaining this neglect to such a young and emotional NI would not be possible. In the morning I'd tell Hersh I'd spoken with the father and put the fear of the Network into his superstitious head, and Hersh would accept this both because he'd never known me to lie and because he wanted to believe that things would turn out better for the child. Never mind that a culture is rarely changed overnight, this girl's problems ran wider than her immediate, frantic family, and the Network has a strict policy against removing natives from their worlds. Some hopes, I knew, were clung to not because they made sense, but out of sheer despair at the alternatives.

What did strike me, though, was the woman's backtracking—how she'd launched into a tirade against Marin Bris as if to deflect from initial words she hadn't meant to say. The idea of a death cult was not out of the question on a world as stark as this one, with the Sev Franzes of society contentedly running lower castes into the ground, but if there were natives willing to destroy the universe in order to make their suffering end, surely they already had their next target lined up: the young boys training to take Brother Yuco's place.

I took the main Pagoran road—now ill-lit in the dead of night—to the compound where the children had been gathered. Sure enough, sentries were stationed at all corners. I raised a hand to one by the entrance and he glanced nervously at me. I highly doubted the glint of my 'steel frame in near-darkness was for him a reassuring sight.

"Any disturbances tonight?"

"Just you," he said, jutting his chin. "We've strict orders to turn everyone away."

"I'm here on behalf the Network, running a—"

"Yeah, we know," said the man, his voice growing heated. He swept his rifle through the air between us. "Just—leave this place alone. Sev Franz's orders."

I nodded to the light coming from the compound windows: no song; only changes in the shadows. "Sev Franz is here now? *Working* with the little boys?"

The man's expression hardened at the inflected word. It was almost tediously easy to rile an NI this way.

"Sev Franz is a great man," said the sentry. "And he's only ever had this planet's best interests at heart. There's nothing he wouldn't do to protect our people—even from themselves, if it ever came to it."

"Do you think it might have, three days ago?"

It took the sentry a few seconds to grasp my meaning, after which he looked at me in disgust. "*If* Sev Franz needed to kill twenty-three monks, putting our *entire universe* in peril in the process, you can bet there was a damned good reason for it. *If*. Now get away, will you? Before I call the others."

I bowed and clicked my 'steel heels together, the farce of the gesture entirely lost on this little NI. For the next few hours I observed the compound at a distance, monitoring its perimeter more acutely than the sentries ever could, but no covert Ang force—or any force—appeared. The only real movement was in the predawn hush, when a slight chill settled in the air and a figure slipped from the front doors into the street. From his gait and the way the sentry greeted him, there was no mistaking Sev Franz, in all his eminent apparel.

When he'd passed fully out of sight, I stole back to the guest hut and woke Hersh with a good shake to the arm. He groaned, passing a hand over his eyes. "Time already?"

"If it's not already too late."

That got his attention, groggy as the poor NI remained.

Dawn met us halfway along Pagora's main road, somewhere between the upper-caste residences and the downriver slums where the city-Ang resided. From then on we were greeted by dozens of hardened bodies and startled faces—more so than even the strangeness of my chassis could explain.

"They look terrified," said Hersh, whose yawning had just abated. "You think that shit of a father passed the message on, that we're not to be messed with?"

I didn't reply, but sure enough, the Ang hid their gazes even from my young associate, and only by inference, from darting eye movements when we asked, could we extract any information about where Brother Yuco's sister lived.

Yuco Mera was an old woman herself, but already deep into the day's labors of washing and folding while tiny Ang children settled about her, peering at her work or playing in the dirt. She had the calmest expression of any of the adults we'd seen all morning, though her long-whiskered brows carried a weariness perhaps indicative of grief.

"Sister Yuco," I said—and that caused her to crook her mouth and grunt *ha*.

"Mera," she said, scrubbing hard in the basin before her. Out the corner of my eye I saw that the children had taken a shine to Hersh, and he to them. I let them be.

"Mera." I crouched to eye level. "We're from the Network, come to investigate the murders up in the mountain. Your brother—"

"Good as dead." Mera flung a sopping wet blanket onto another pile. "And everything with him."

"You mean the universe? It's been around a lot longer than your planet, Mera, let alone your Cogran monks."

Mera cast a tired look my way. "Ever think maybe it's all in reverse, spaceman?"

"You mean, the universe created retroactively? Its entire past arising the moment the first monk on Cog broke into song?" She nodded so gravely then that, for the first time since my arrival, I truly longed for synth-skin, and the gentleness of the smile I could have managed in reply. "Cograns are tremendous storytellers, Mera. I'll give you that."

Mera grunted, flinging another garment on the stack for drying. As she did, Hersh and I both caught sight of a faded tattoo on her inner arm—a blue circle with a line spanning its radius and extending beyond the circumference.

"What's that?" he said, and from the heat in his voice I could tell his past was getting in the way again. "They don't mark you here, do they?"

Mera covered her arm and looked away. "No child," she said. "Some in the city think it's all a great line, the universe—from the lowest to the highest—but we Ang know otherwise. The universe is a circle of unity, and needs all of us to survive."

"Your brother believes that, too?" I said. Mera nodded. "And Marin Bris?"

Mera snorted and returned to her scrubbing. "Only circle she knows is the one she's been making for decades between temple beds."

Hersh visibly blanched—young NIs and their horror over the thought of old and rutting flesh. I had all I needed, though, so I bowed to Mera and stood.

"But that's not what I meant," she added softly, and when she looked up this time she seemed as nervous as all the other Ang we'd seen. "About everything ending with him."

"I know," I said. "And for that I'm truly sorry."

Maybe it was surprise that allowed her to accept my hand then. Maybe not. Either way, Companion though I'd once, long ago been, with just the 'steel chassis a little squeeze was the only comfort this old AI unit could provide. It was high time we were moving on.

Hersh had to sprint to keep up as I made for the temple. Though he quizzed me with glances all the while, I would say nothing until we'd entered the mountain, crossed the mesh bridge, and found ourselves observing the Order's newest monks as they prepared to take over from Brother Yuco, who was more groaning than singing from his place on the floor. Marin Bris still knelt beside him, stroking what threads of hair remained and tucking his blanket in, while two medics stood ready to carry him out at Sev Franz's word.

"Marvelous timing," he said, gesturing at the nervous young boys in their robes, fresh from crash courses in—at the very least—the Cograns' ancient song and ceremonies. "You bear witness to history in the making. Cog has sadly declined in its practice of taking tribute, which is why our monastic numbers were so perilously low to start— but no more. These boys have all been volunteered by their families, who've been amply rewarded in turn. With these faces we will begin anew, building a better, stronger Order—and oh, you will see our results the galaxy over! How the very stars will burn brighter in the coming years!"

As if to signal their agreement, the boys at that very moment picked up Brother Yuco's fading refrain, and the whole cavern reverberated with a song far deeper and richer than any (I must admit) I'd ever heard before. Hersh himself looked ready to give way before the majesty of the performance, and there were tears in all the other NIs' eyes. I allowed them their moment of rapture before tapping Sev Franz on the shoulder.

"I would speak to you, Sev Franz, in the antechamber. With Brother Yuco."

"Of course," he said, and gestured to the medics, who took his cue and hefted the old monk out, Marin Bris clinging to one flagging hand.

Even in the antechamber, though, surrounded by various artifacts of the ancient Cogran peoples, the tremendous song of the young monks presided. To be heard at all, I spoke slower than usual, and ensured each word was especially firm. Sev Franz insisted that the medics be sent out before I went on, but I in turn insisted that Marin Bris stay. After a moment's hesitation, he nodded, and I surveyed my little audience.

"It's all over, Brother Yuco," I said. "But you know that already."

The dying monk blinked at me, silent at last, but still profusely weeping.

"You can't mean to accuse *him* of all this," said Marin Bris, leaping between us with clenched fists despite her years. I sympathized, but continued speaking directly to the monk.

"You couldn't kill yourself, too, because you weren't trying to end the universe—only the caste system here on Cog. You had to make things just fragile enough in the Order to force your fellow Cograns to take stock of their fragilty, and hopefully compel them to distribute the load more equally. To make singing the universe *everyone's* job, and so lift the Ang from an oppression the whole practice right now reinforces."

Marin Bris and Hersh both cast startled glances at Brother Yuco, then me, then him again. "You couldn't have," said Marin Bris. "All your friends. Your brothers."

"He didn't," I said. "That's clear enough from the stills—the inconsistent trajectories of each incinerating shot. They were probably all in on it: the whole Order taking their lives in hope of a better tomorrow, and leaving behind only the oldest, the frailest—"

"—the lowest—" Hersh muttered.

"—to shoulder the load until the rest of Cog came to its senses." I turned again to Brother Yuco, who made what I could only assume was the first grief-sound he'd been able to utter on his own behalf since the whole ordeal began.

"Dear Brother Yuco," I went on. "In all my years, in all my travels, I wish I could say that such transcendent acts are always enough to change the world, but the efficiency of the upper castes here is its own, fearsome thing. You won't triumph in this moment—but you and your fallen comrades join a long line of people across the galaxy who at least have tried."

Now it was Marin Bris's turn to moan, and fall to her knees, and bury her face over Brother Yuco's chest while the worn-out old monk—who had all on his own, without pause or reprieve, sung the universe for days now—took his last, ragged breaths.

"This doesn't surprise you in the slightest, does it?" I turned to see Hersh confronting Sev Franz, who in turn blandly smiled at me.

"It's as you said, Hersh," I said. "Different expectations for different castes." I nodded to our Cogran mediator. "We'll be filing our report within the day, of course."

Sev Franz shrugged. "Write whatever you want, but just remember that the Network's word doesn't count for much among my people. If your report is made public, though—if this is the view of Cog you release to the system at large, when we're on the verge of so many new alliances—I will personally ensure that every Cogran knows Brother Yuco went mad and killed his fellow monks. In one fell swoop he'll go from savior of the universe to deranged nihilist, and his family will live in infamy for the rest of their days."

Marin Bris threw a cutting word the mediator's way, but Sev Franz seemed unfazed, even bored. "Do what you need to *in private*, though, and Cog will forget the unsolved murders in a moon or two, but I guarantee that the legend of Saint Yuco will live on. My people will give thanks and sing praise-songs to his family tree for centuries."

"Or at least until Cog gives up this nonsense of singing the universe altogether." I knew this, at least, would annoy him.

Even then, he was quick to obscure his irritation by humming. "You know, Detective Bennett, you keeping mocking my people's beliefs, but I wonder if you ever reflect on your own. The universe we've always known is one we've always been told needs song to exist—and lo and behold, there has always been song. Meanwhile, the Spider that brought you here—do you *need* to know how it works to accept that it does? Or whatever turned you from advanced program to sentient being—do you know *precisely* where the distinction lies? Are we really so different, you and I?"

His smile told me what he wanted then: the NI mediocrity of *I learned something from you, now learn something from me.* In this game, I'd parrot his earlier words—say, "I'm not so sure that's the same..." and affect some AI equivalent of discomfort before adding, "Then again, who am I to say it isn't?" After, we'd grimly shake hands, equals at the end of a bitter case, and I'd take Hersh with me to the nearest Spider, Marin Bris would wither away, and Sev Franz would go about his business with a renewed lightness in his step.

But I didn't ape a word of it. Maybe couldn't. Instead I put Hersh on the next transport, off to his second assignment with what every rookie loves best: an outlandish tale of working for a hard-ass to grease the wheels with new associates. All the better for him, too, that *this* hard-ass was made of both piss and 'steel: the vast narrative terrain he'd have at his disposal! I almost smiled a naked-chassis smile to see the young shit go.

Strangely, though, it would be whole minutes after my own transport out before I realized what I *should* have said to Brother Yuco, Marin Bris, and Sev Franz in the temple's antechamber: that time spent within the Network brought its own, uncontrollable revolutions. That travelers from distant worlds, brimful with distant ideas, would one day topple the caste system where even the most valiant acts of Cogran resistance had failed. That my report, though classified for now, would eventually be released, and Brother Yuco's true heroism reclaimed then by his people. That one day I would return to bear witness to all of this, and more, and tread upon Sev Franz's long-obscured or infamous dust.

Or so I hoped—though the very delay in this realization gave me pause, and inclined me towards a service station before putting in for my next assignment. But I suppose even an AI must take great care with repairs if it wants to live long enough to hear the universe sung in just the right moral key. Too much time in stasis, and everything decays.

◉

A Prayer to St Jude

M. Bennardo

As Madame Cassie turns off the neon all-seeing eyeball in the window of her shop, she spots that man standing on the other side of the alleyway. She's seen him before, but not here. The first time, it was in Atlantic City in her original shop when he sat across the table from her, with two police detectives standing behind him. That was three full years ago, but ever since she's seen him again in each and every new place that she's moved to, one by one, up and down the shore.

Tonight, he's leaning against the doorway of a shuttered up t-shirt store. It's the shoulder season and the storefront she rents here is off-boardwalk in an alley, so there aren't any other people in view. Instead, there are about twenty gulls picking at dropped popcorn between Madame Cassie and that man, but the birds don't seem to mind the man. Nobody ever seems to mind him. Nobody except Madame Cassie, that is.

He's a big man with a completely shaved head. He's facing across the alley in the direction of Madame Cassie's shop, but he isn't exactly looking at her. That's because he's wearing dark glasses, with two big white eyes painted on the perfectly black lenses. The eyes are painted like cartoons eyes: big leaf-shaped whites, light brown irises, with perfectly centered jet black pupils applied by a Sharpie pen, and a set of curly eyelashes ringing the top and bottom lids.

They are Madame Cassie's eyes and they are Madame Cassie's glasses. Or at least they are an identical match to the pair that she keeps in a case on her table. The first time she ever saw that man, she asked him to wear those glasses. But Madame Cassie doesn't know how he came to have a pair just like hers, or why he is wearing them now, or why he is standing outside her shop. Whatever the reason, it can't be anything good.

Swiftly, Madame Cassie drops the blinds and shuts out the light in the shop. Tomorrow, she will think about how soon she can leave and whether after three long years there is still anyplace else left for her to go on her fading map of the Jersey Shore.

Next morning, Madame Cassie turns on the neon eyeball at nine o'clock as usual, but she keeps the blinds shut. That way, it won't matter whether that man shows up, because she won't have to look at him and won't know if or when he appears.

Just a few minutes after turning the sign on, a woman Madame Cassie has never seen before knocks tentatively on the door as she pushes it open and calls into the shop, "Hello? Are you open?" But the woman doesn't wait for an answer, and walks in still talking. "I'm sorry for coming in without an appointment, but I've got a terrible problem and the girls at the hair salon said that you could help."

Madame Cassie is used to these kind of entrances, so even though her mind is still thinking about that lurking man across the alley, she smiles and nods, motioning to the empty chair across from her. "That's all right. You're missing something? I can tell. But don't worry: we'll find it for you. Just sit down there and we'll talk it through."

The shop is dim with the blinds closed, but Madame Cassie doesn't miss a thing as she sizes up the woman. Not too young, not too rich. All the while the woman is saying something about her mother's ruby bracelet, which she wore for the first time in five years and now like a fool can't find anywhere.

Instantly, Madame Cassie knows that the mother is dead and that the bracelet is valuable in more ways than one. Madame Cassie can practically smell the sick feeling on the woman, just like you can smell a terminal illness on a patient in the hospital. A strong feeling like that is not necessarily good for her work: thick desperation is a hard thing for Madame Cassie to see through, but she has done it countless times before.

"They said it would be twenty dollars." The woman takes out a single twenty dollar bill and holds it out in a shaking hand.

"Don't pay it to me," says Madame Cassie, rebuffing the money gently. "Pay it to St Jude. He's the one who's going to help us."

At that, Madame Cassie takes out a St Jude candle from the box under the table and places it in front of her. It's not the whole candle, just the painted glass holder with the actual candle scraped out. The woman slips the twenty dollar bill inside, curling it neatly so it stands up straight with half an inch of the bill sticking up above the rim.

Madame Cassie nods and moves the candleholder to the middle of the table. Then she says: "Here, put these on."

She is holding out those dark glasses with the cartoon eyes painted on them, a perfect match for the pair that man had been wearing the day before. The woman looks at them doubtfully, but Madame Cassie is used to these objections. She knows that the glasses look goofy, but they are an indispensable part of her work.

"These glasses are the only way I can see through your eyes," says Madame Cassie. "As long as you wear them, they give me the power to peer into your life and look around, and maybe to see something that you have missed. If you want me to look for your mother's irreplaceable bracelet, then you'll have to put them on."

Then Madame Cassie offers the glasses again, and this time the woman takes them. After she sets them on her nose, she looks around the shop. "I can't see anything. It's all dark now."

"It doesn't matter," coos Madame Cassie, patting the woman on the hand. "I'll see for you now." Then she tells the client to focus and take ten deep breaths and clear her mind as much as possible. Then she says: "All right now. Take me back to the last time you know you know you had that ruby bracelet."

Then the woman says: "Well, I know I had it last Monday. I put it on special, as a lucky charm, to go to the doctor. I remember it caught on my jacket pocket when I was taking out my keys to lock my apartment door, but I made sure it didn't fall off. After that, I'm not so sure. But I know I went to work, then to the doctor during my break, then because it was such a nice day I took a walk along the boardwalk on the way home—"

Madame Cassie holds up her hands. "No, not like that. You can't go so fast. Take me back to the first thing and start over. That jacket pocket where the bracelet got caught. And this time you have to tell me about the jacket. You have to tell me about the pocket."

The woman's brow crinkles and she makes a motion as if to take the glasses off. But Madame Cassie says: "No! Please leave them on." So far, the fog of desperation is only getting thicker. All Madame Cassie can see is a swirling yellow cloud of sick feelings, and she is starting to doubt that she will be able to break through. She has to calm the woman.

"What I mean is that you have to tell me what it feels like when you put your hand inside that pocket. Think about it and describe it to me. Is it warm and fuzzy like a pocket lined in down, or is it cool and slick like a pocket in a windbreaker? Does your hand sink all the way in like it won't ever come out again, or does it only fit partway like the pocket is fighting to keep your hand out?"

Slowly, haltingly, the client answers the string of questions. Soon enough, she starts adding extra details that Madame Cassie doesn't even ask for, and Madame Cassie smiles and leans back in her chair, nodding encouragingly. The sick yellow fog is still swirling and boiling around, but occasionally a pulse of something clear and solid comes through: the dyed purple wool of the jacket, the flash of fine gold links, the blaze of a big beautiful ruby.

"Good, good. Now tell me about the walk to work. Do you look through the peephole before you open your apartment door? Does it open onto a hallway inside the building, or on a walkway outside? When you lock the door, is it just one lock or two locks? Do you take an elevator down, or the stairs... ?"

And for half an hour, this mundane interview continues. Madame Cassie never lets the woman move on to the next moment of her day until she is satisfied that what she sees in her mind exactly matches the description that the woman is giving. It takes a long time and makes for a very dull conversation, but Madame Cassie doesn't know any other method. Probably she has heard more descriptions of jacket pockets, junk drawers, couch cushions, car seats, handbags, and filing cabinets than anybody else in the state of New Jersey. But for a twenty dollar fee, she and St Jude always have time to listen to one more of the same.

And Madame Cassie never asks stupid questions like: "Did you try turning all your pockets inside out?" Or: "Are you sure you emptied everything out of the drawer?" Or: "Do you think it might have fallen behind the couch somehow?"

The fact that this woman has come to Madame Cassie and put twenty dollars in the St Jude candleholder means that she has already thought of all those things herself. She isn't here for such obvious and trite advice. She is here for Madame Cassie to see something that she could never have seen on her own.

And as the woman answers the questions, Madame Cassie sees more and more details. She sees the small grey trapezoid of outside window, just visible from the woman's desk at work when she cranes her neck. She sees one leg crossed over the other, and the foot on the end bouncing in preoccupation in the waiting room of the doctor's office. She sees the weathered wooden fences lining the dunes on the way back home, miles of thin beaten slats held together by twisted rusted wire, striving mightily against the elements to keep the sand from overwhelming the boardwalk.

And at last, after thirty minutes of questions and answers, Madame Cassie sees the missing ruby bracelet and knows exactly where it is.

But Madame Cassie doesn't say so. Instead, she takes the St Jude candleholder with the twenty dollars still inside and sets it on a shelf behind her where several other identical candleholders already stand. Then she hands the woman a card with the prayer to St Jude written on it. "Why don't you go home and look one more time? If you say this prayer every morning for the next nine days, I'm certain that you'll find the bracelet before the tenth day. But if you still can't find it, then you can come again after ten days and take back your twenty dollars if you want."

When the woman takes off the dark glasses, there is disappointment in her eyes. Obviously, this is not what she expected. No doubt she had been hoping that Madame Cassie would give her a location where she could go to lay hands on the bracelet right away. But Madame Cassie doesn't work that way, not with any of her clients. She has taken this woman all the way up to the threshold, but now she will have to walk through it by herself. That is the best that Madame Cassie can do.

A few minutes after the woman leaves, a man comes in. There is nothing tentative about his entrance: he bangs open the door of the shop and sweeps inside, making a beeline for the open chair at Madame Cassie's little table.

"I'm glad I found you," he says. "I've lost the goddamn keys to my storage unit again."

"Hello again, Mr Catallus," says Madame Cassie. "Always so nice to see your face." She is already putting a St Jude candleholder on the table, and the man is pouring a cascade of quarters into it from a plastic Ziplock bag.

"It's all there, eighty quarters. I double-counted this morning, in case I found you here. I thought it was you, from what the ad said in the newspaper. But why did you move again? And why did you change your name? First Ocean City, then Sea Isle City, and now Wildwood. You have to start leaving forwarding addresses!"

Madame Cassie only shrugs. "Oh, that's me. Always moving. I just get the itch and I have to go."

She hands him the dark glasses and he immediately puts them on. Then he leans all the way back in his chair, his arms crossed on his chest, his head thrown back until his nose and the unblinking cartoon eyes all point at the ceiling, and he starts talking without any prompting by Madame Cassie about the keys and where he last saw them and what he did step by step on that day.

When he's done, Madame Cassie says: "I can see them pretty well already, Mr Catallus. You're getting very good at this. Why don't you go home and look one more time?"

Mr Catallus laughs and claps his hands together, just once. "That's what I wanted to hear. If you say I should look, then I know I'll find them. It won't take any nine days either! I have a buyer who wants to pick up an armoire I have in that storage locker tomorrow. Five hundred dollars, cash!"

"All the same, we'll keep St Jude over here in case you need to come back."

"I'll come back all right. You know I'm always losing those goddamn keys." Then Mr Catallus folds up the dark glasses and sets them down on the table, picking up a prayer card as he does so. Madame Cassie wonders how many of those cards he has at home already. A dozen? Two dozen? But she understands the importance of routine. With a thing like this, if you can get it to work once then you don't change anything the next time if you can help it.

Madame Cassie almost smiles, but by then Mr Catallus is opening the door to leave. And suddenly the image of that large bald man leaning against the shutters of the t-shirt store flashes through Madame Cassie's mind. It's as clear as anything she has seen in the past hour: as clear as the ruby bracelet and the keys of the storage locker. Is it a memory or a premonition? Or just an overactive imagination?

Madame Cassie turns her face away and frowns hard, averting her eyes so she cannot see out the door as Mr Catallus leaves. Memory, vision, whatever. She will not be seeing it today, not until she figures out where she can go next.

The rest of the day's clients are less interesting. Madame Cassie doesn't only do lost and found, after all. She also reads tarot cards and palms and horoscopes, and that's what all her other clients want for the rest of the day. Madame Cassie knows she doesn't have any special talent for those things, so she just follows the usual formula and says what she has learned to say.

Her real gift is with lost and found. In all the years she has been doing it, only a few people have ever come back for a refund. That's how Madame Cassie knows that it really works. Sometimes she thinks she should charge a lot more, and focus only on that, give up the rote tarot readings and so on. But who knows if changing the fee might make it stop working? And besides, she doesn't want people to think she is too good at it. She doesn't want anybody to get the idea that she's infallible.

But reading tarot cards and palms and horoscopes is easy. With tarot cards, you just deal them out from the deck and tell a story about what you see. You don't have to coax visions out of yellow clouds of boiling bad feelings, seeing and then politely ignoring all kinds of things that the clients don't really want to reveal to you.

On a tarot card, everything you need is already right there, printed in plain view. Take the Fool, for instance, stepping off a cliff and into danger with one foot on solid ground and the other foot about to plunge into the precipice. Something is distracting him, maybe the flower in his hand or maybe the mountain scenery in the distance. His dog is nipping at his heels, maybe blindly following its master to destruction or maybe trying to warn him away from the edge. The story is a little different every time, but it always comes out of what's already on the card and you never have to see anything you don't expect to see.

"But you don't really see, do you, Madame Cassie?" That's what people ask her all the time. Ignorant people who think there is no such thing as second sight. "If you could really see," they say, "you'd just tell your clients where to look. There wouldn't need to be any nonsense about praying for nine mornings and all that. It's just that people come to you and talk things through, and then they get their own ideas. So when they go home, they can see what they couldn't see before."

Madame Cassie doesn't respond to words like that, but they do trouble her. After all, she made the dark glasses with the cartoon eyes herself when she first started out, just as a gimmick to help her stand out from all the other fortunetellers on the Boardwalk in Atlantic City. She hadn't meant them to be magical, not really. They just turned out that way.

The same thing happened with the St Jude candleholders. Madame Cassie knows as well as anybody that St Jude is the patron of lost causes, and that St Anthony is the patron of lost items. But she had found an unopened box of twenty-four St Jude candles at a junk store for only fifteen dollars. Even if it was the wrong saint, she figured that they would make another good gimmick. But as soon as she started using the candleholders and the glasses, she started to see. To really, really see.

So when people say she doesn't actually have any second sight, Madame Cassie knows it's not just her that they are insulting. There's a higher power involved, even if it doesn't make any sense that St Jude or any other saint would want to have anything to do with her, an unimportant old woman who was never a very good Catholic in the first place.

Once, not long after she saw that bald man for the first time, she packed up the painted glasses and all the candleholders in a box with the idea that she would throw them away. She had been scared by that man and didn't want to mess with any higher powers anymore.

But the knowledge of that higher power was also what stopped her. For how could she ever walk away from something so all-seeing? How could she dare to cut ties with something so clearly supernatural, so beyond human understanding? Madame Cassie didn't know what kind of deal she had made to attract this power, or what forfeit might be claimed of her if she ever broke the deal, or what kind of angel or demon would come to claim it. So she decided not to change anything. Always, that was the safest thing. Just keep going the same way and never change. And if things get too bad, then just move on to a new town and take a new name and hope that the bad won't find her again.

At the very end of the day, Madame Cassie can't resist taking a peep outside the window. The sun is setting and the sky is darkening, glowing unearthly blue over the t-shirt store across the alleyway. Her neon sign burns red in the window. And between the two glows, there's that bald man wearing the dark glasses leaning against the door, just like Madame Cassie had guessed.

Madame Cassie curses herself for being so weak as to look, and she curses him too, for the day he came into her life. It's always the same: once the bald man starts coming, he never stops until she packs up and moves to a new place.

Through the glow of the red all-seeing neon eyeball, Madame Cassie suddenly sees herself as she was three years ago, back in Atlantic City, back in her original shop. She misses that shop, with its cozy collection of knickknacks assembled over thirty years, and her little claw-footed table and her worn leather chair. She misses her old self too. She had been more energetic then, less grey, with a twinkle in her eye.

But then, still in her mind's eye, she sees that bald man come in. He comes in following two police detectives, and Madame Cassie feels her forehead crease into a frown and her stomach start to pinch itself in pain. This is what comes of people calling Madame Cassie a miracle worker, of people believing she has a hotline to a higher power. Because once people believe that, then they don't just come looking for harmless things like ruby bracelets and storage locker keys anymore. They come looking for real things instead.

So Madame Cassie sets her face in her most unfriendly expression. She always thinks of her grandmother's English bulldog when she puts on that face, trying to look as stubborn and stupid and mean as she can. "What does he want?" she asks brusquely, nodding her head at him. "You know this doesn't work. Not for things like this."

"Come on, Madame Cassie," says one of the detectives. "We wouldn't come here if it wasn't serious. And what's wrong with it anyway? It's good advertising for you."

She squints at the bald man, but she isn't really looking at him. Suddenly, she realizes she is play-acting this grouchy crone just as much as she play-acts the wise and soothing aunt with her other clients.

A little shiver runs up her spine and for a second she wonders why she can't do it for real. Why can't she turn him away without putting on a face and assuming a character? She really doesn't want to talk to this man, after all. She really doesn't want to hear about whomever he has lost. So why does she feel like she's just pretending?

"Who is it? His wife? How long has the foolish woman been gone?"

Madame Cassie still isn't looking at the bald man. She's looking at the police detectives instead. She's hoping if she ignores the bald man and he gets offended, then he'll just leave.

But then the bald man answers. "She's been gone two weeks," he says. "I haven't seen Miranda in two weeks."

And everything drops out of Madame Cassie, leaving her barren and hollow. And she remembers that this is why she play-acts all the time. Because if she was doing it for real, then this is where she would drop to the floor. This is where the big deep darkness inside her would swoop up and eat her whole. And it still does. It still happens. But at least it doesn't show on her face.

"Two weeks," says Madame Cassie. "You boys really are desperate now."

And then she is sitting down at the table and taking out one of the St Jude candleholders. She hands the bald man her dark glasses with the eyes painted on them. Because it's too late already. It's too late to explain that it just doesn't work if the client doesn't know the place where the thing has gone missing. That Madame Cassie can only see through the client's eyes, and that it doesn't work if the missing thing has been stolen away and hidden in a place that the client has never seen.

"This is the last time," is what Madame Cassie says instead. She stares down the two police detectives, who are slouched against the wall of her shop, their hands in their pockets as they watch her with the bald man. "I never want to see you two back here again."

She gives the bald man a St Jude prayer card and tells him to put it into the candleholder. The candleholder can't be empty, but she doesn't dare charge him any money for something she knows will never work. And thank God that it won't, she thinks to herself. Thank God I don't have to worry about that! At least, thank God, I'll never have to see whatever terrible things there are to see.

Then Madame Cassie blinks her eyes and she is back in herself again, back in her new shop, and she is alone. Outside, there is the darkening sky and the t-shirt store and the bald man leaning against the shutter. But that's outside, through the glass of the window and beyond the flickering red light of her neon sign.

Madame Cassie's mouth tightens into a grimace. Then she shuts off the all-seeing neon eye and lets the blind fall across the guilty window.

Madame Cassie knows that not every lost thing can actually be found in this world, and also that not every lost thing that can be found is good for the person who is looking to find. Sometimes things are better left unfound, and that's why Madame Cassie never tells her clients exactly where to lay their hands on anything. It's why all she ever does is take them to the threshold, leaving it to them to walk through the door themselves. That last step is theirs alone to take. Whatever might happen afterward, that last step is not her fault.

Madame Cassie also knows that the bald man never did find what he was looking for, and also that he never really was looking for it in the first place. Madame Cassie knows that he hadn't lost anything that day that he came to see her. Madame Cassie knows that he was the one who had been trying to hide it.

Madame Cassie takes a fading map of the Jersey Shore out of her purse and moves it into the light of a lamp. She unfolds it and her finger moves up and down the coastline, reading the names of tourist towns dotting the big blue empty side. Too many of them have already been crossed off in red ink. Those are the places she's already been to, and the places she's already left behind.

Then Madame Cassie wonders: Does she really have it in her to do it again? To pack up her things in the old cardboard boxes that are splitting open after so many moves? To load up her van in the early morning hours and leave this town and her rent deposit behind? To rattle off down the quiet dark highway, living and working in the cramped squalor of her van until she can scrape together enough for first and last month's rent on a new place?

Madame Cassie has lost almost everything she has ever owned in the past three years, moving from place to place. But she never lost the candleholder that holds the St Jude prayer card that the bald man put inside. Each time she finds a new shop in a new town, she unpacks it and sets it out. When she leaves, she takes it down and packs it away again. She has just never figured out anything else to do with it.

But now she picks it up. She holds it in her hand, rolling it around until St Jude is looking up at her. How is that prayer supposed to go? Though she has recited the words a thousand times with clients, Madame Cassie has never really prayed it in earnest and only a few phrases come to her now.

St Jude, the friend of Jesus.

Pray for me, who am so miserable.
Come to mine assistance in this great need.
That I may receive the consolation and succor of Heaven
In all my necessities
And all my tribulations
And all my sufferings.

But what had St Jude ever done for her? What help had he ever been? If he had done anything, it was to put the burden of second sight upon her, and that was what was crushing her now.

Suddenly Madame Cassie is up on her feet and opening the door of her shop. Suddenly she is out in the alley and barreling across it. The bald man in the dark glasses is still there but he doesn't even look at her.

The seagulls squawk and scatter before Madame Cassie's approach, but the bald man just stands there, still wearing those dark glasses with the painted eyeballs. In all the years he has been appearing to her, Madame Cassie has never before approached him like this, and she half expects him to vanish in a puff of smoke. But instead he just stands there, looking exactly the same as he always does.

"What do you want?" screams Madame Cassie, louder and angrier than she knew she could. She knows she isn't play-acting now. She is a single raw nerve, worn to its end. "What do you want from me?"

But the bald man doesn't do anything. He doesn't flinch and he doesn't answer her. If he were one of her tarot cards, she could just look up in the book what he's supposed to mean. But instead, all she can do is keep asking. Keep trying to get him to respond to her, to tell her what he wants so she can give it to him and finally be free again.

In a fury, Madame Cassie raises her hand and throws down the St Jude candleholder that holds his prayer card. It makes a dull pop on the concrete of the alley, but it doesn't break apart because the sticker wrapper with St Jude's image keeps all the pieces together. Through it, Madame Cassie can see the candleholder is webbed with cracks, broken into shards. But still it clings together. She stamps down with her foot, trying to grind the fragments apart.

"Don't you hear me?" she hisses. "Tell me what you want!"

As far as Madame Cassie is concerned, she already gave that man the only thing he could possibly want, the first time she saw him. Because that time, she really had seen. The day he had come into her shop with the police detectives, the boiling yellow mists had separated and she had seen everything.

Madame Cassie had seen exactly where the bald man's wife was hidden. She had been able to see because the bald man knew the place.

And Madame Cassie had known exactly what that meant. The wife wasn't actually lost. She had been put away, and the bald man had been the one to do it.

And Madame Cassie had just sat there, still talking to the bald man, still acting her part, not even skipping a beat. Inside, she had been heaving with horror and fear, but outside she had looked just the same as always. Then at the end, Madame Cassie had just said the same thing as always, too scared and sad to say anything else: "Take this prayer card and go home. Say the prayer every morning for the next nine days, and if she's there to find then I know St Jude will lead you to her."

And now Madame Cassie is face-to-face with him again at last. From inches away, she looks up into the leaf-shaped whites of the painted-on eyes. She looks up into the light brown irises. She looks up at the sickening curls of the eyelashes. Madame Cassie looks up into the deep black points of the permanent marker pupils.

Then she reaches up and she starts to scratch. Boiling with dread, she scratches at the paint with her nails. It flakes away, falling in a snow around her hand. She knows now that the bald man isn't appearing because he wants something from her. She already gave him everything he wanted, the first time she saw him. She already put everything back into his hands: letting him make the decision whether to pray or not, whether to look or not, whether to find his missing wife or to let her lie where he had put her.

No, that man doesn't keep appearing because he wants anything. He keeps appearing because Madame Cassie must want something from herself. And whatever that might be, it had to be under that paint. So Madame Cassie scratches and scratches and scratches, and doesn't stop until the paint is all gone.

But under the paint, the glasses are still dark. Madame Cassie still can't see what they are hiding. All she can see is herself: two images of her pleading face and staring eyes, one in each lens, her expression wild and despairing, and her hands reaching down toward herself in duplicate reflection as she takes the bald man by the shoulders and tries to shake him loose.

"Just tell me what you want!" Madame Cassie says, tears in her voice this time. Because she knows that she isn't asking him anymore, and she knows that he won't be the one to answer.

"Just tell me what to do!" Madame Cassie says again. But she knows already what the bald man is: that he is a door, and the she is herself at last standing at the threshold, and has been for three full years now.

"Just tell me! Just tell!"

But the bald man doesn't say a word. He doesn't move either. He just looks down at her, through his impenetrable dark glasses, and Madame Cassie looks up into her own reflected self.

"Just tell…!"

But she doesn't need the answer in so many words. She knows what it must be already. It's the same answer that anybody would give to anybody else at the threshold of a door:

That now that she is here, she must take the last step herself.

Terminal City

Zoë Blade

It's three in the morning when I find Spark's body. I've come into the store early to perform some extra work while my boss is asleep. I know there's something wrong when the door isn't locked and the fan's on. I smell it before I see it, a putrid smell I can't put into words. I walk behind the counter, and that's when I see him, on his back, staring up at the ceiling, a pool of congealed blood surrounding his body, soaking into the dusty wooden planks that serve as the floor. He must have been like that for a good few hours, because the rats are already there, licking at the sticky red puddle. If you're not actively working in K block, the entropy envelops you, devours you. Food, as in meat, as in anyone not strong enough to fend them off, is eaten by the rats. Between the planks, I can just about make out the cable and light store below ours, a dark red puddle staining their counter. Mr. Wu won't be happy tomorrow morning.

The cops say it was a robbery gone wrong. The till's empty, but it doesn't add up. Not that they see it that way. As far as they're concerned, everything adds up just fine, all neat and tidy like columns in a spreadsheet, and they move on to their next case, save for a single cop guarding Spark's door for a few hours. All they're good for is targets. While I answer their mundane questions—Did I see anyone looking suspicious? Did I know anyone who might have a grudge against Spark?—my transponder's wirelessly interfacing with theirs, silently cloning their badges, copying their private keys to my personal stash. It's a dangerous move, sure, but worth it for the access it grants me.

I'm not saying I know better than them. Maybe I just care about Spark a whole lot more than they do. It just doesn't sit right with me. There are plenty of stores in the area, most more profitable than ours. Bright, loud arcades, full of electromechanical gambling machines that must have a good few hundred coins in each of them. Off-licenses. Hell, even the dentist next door probably has more in his cash register than we did.

So I decide to do a little research of my own. My boss, David, calls it denial. Trying to get my dead co-worker back. But it's not like that. We were friends, sure. That's why he talked to me. Why he told me he was onto something. And those crazy eyes of his, back when they had been alive and animated, had told me he believed what he was saying. He was building something. Something he believed was important.

David, being the sentimental type, gives me the day off—without pay, natch—and I pay Spark's place a little visit.

Although we both work—worked—topside, where the rain's thick and during the day you can occasionally even glimpse sunlight, we don't—didn't—make anywhere near enough money to live there. Spark's apartment is deep in the bowels of K block, like mine, beneath all the stores you feel reasonably safe in without a weapon. Where the constant onslaught of rain is replaced by drips running down walls made of decaying wood, rusting iron, and concrete. Where the only light is provided by fluoros hanging limply from the thick braids of cables that people use to syphon electricity off of one another, swaying as people walk hurriedly along the planks of wood that serve as the floor above.

Back when it was built, K block was all concrete, high ceilings. But such luxury soon gave way to economy. Nothing so wasteful could last very long in a microcosm of pure supply and demand, and space was so very much in demand. The first squatters retrofitted iron skeletons like climbing frames on every floor, filling them with wooden planks. Now the whole thing's layered like a rotting cake. Twice as many floors, each half the height. Then they went out onto the roof, and they built up.

The bowels live up to their name. Maintenance pipes scattered throughout seep raw sewage into thoughtfully placed buckets or, worse, puddles with the optional plank of wood providing a handy gangway. There's so much steam coming out of the tiny factories and kitchens that in some parts, you can't see further ahead than two or three people. You have to rely on your memory to guide you. It would be enough to make you faint, but you wouldn't find a clean surface to faint on.

It doesn't really have an outside so much as endless corridors, and if you want to get home, you have to hope the stores between these corridors and your apartment are all open, although of course they always are, workers pairing up to alternate twelve hour shifts. If you're lucky, you can afford to fortify your ceiling with tarpaulin, somewhere between your neighbor's floor above you and your light. Spark was into tech enough to concentrate the little money he had into buying whatever he needed to keep his workbench going, so at least it'll be reasonably dry there.

There's a cop guarding Spark's door, trying his best not to show how uncomfortable he is in his uniform. The door to Spark's place isn't in a corridor so much as the back of a noodle bar, just a meter or so away from the open fire of the kitchen stove, but the graying, weathered looking chef dutifully ignores us as he fries his product. My stomach grumbles, awakened by the aroma of fresh food, but I can't eat right now.

I get into character, putting on my well-practiced look of routine boredom. The cop's transponder makes a friendly electronic chirp, signifying that someone with the correct privileges is in proximity. As far as it's concerned, I'm Lieutenant Emily Long. It flashes up her badge number on its miniature Nixie tubes. I hope he doesn't look down at it. He presumably works with the real Emily Long. It's a hell of a risk, trying to pass for a cop without a uniform. I stay calm, focus on my breathing, and walk up to the door as if I have every right to be there. But already his eyes are on me, looking me up and down, studying my giveaway K block native clothes. He looks down at his transponder, at his co-worker's badge number.

"Listen," he says, reading the number, "I don't know who you are, lady—" but by the time he looks back up, I'm already gone.

From behind, I reach around his neck with my arm, trying not to let his flailing arms unnerve me, squeezing just enough to make him pass out for a few minutes. It's over quickly. "And you never will."

The chef focuses intently on his craft as I slip into Spark's apartment, leaving the cop in a heap on the floor, too heavy to drag inside.

Spark's apartment stinks more than most I've visited. I tug on the piece of string hanging from the bare bulb in the center of the ceiling, and the place lights up. The few dishes he owned are all piled up in the washing up bowl, waiting to be taken to the nearest public tap and scrubbed clean. I half expect a rat to crawl out of the pile of circuit boards and cables lining the floor. Even by K block standards, Spark didn't really seem to believe in furniture. Not a second chair or coffee table at any rate. He wasn't the social type. Didn't entertain houseguests much. He was a worker, like me. Driven by this sick compulsion to always make things, to always take things apart, to fix them, to make them more efficient, or simply to understand how they work, until you fall asleep at your workbench at sunrise. Sunrise. You'd be hard pressed to remember what that was after a few days down here.

His place isn't really an apartment, it's a workshop which happens to have a microwave, kettle and washing up bowl. A lone shelf holds a cassette deck, but no actual tapes. There's a dustless gap where presumably tapes were until recently. Odd, I never had him pegged for much of a music fan.

A wooden ladder leads up to the top bunk of what must have once been a bunk bed, although now it's little more than a few planks of wood with a mattress, pillow and faded cotton duvet on it, looming over what would have been the bottom bunk, the centerpiece of the tiny room, his workbench. A door the other side of the room unfolds to reveal a toilet. On those rare occasions when he took a shower, he must have ventured out into the city proper. It's the kind of place your mother—not to mention your amygdala—warns you to stay away from.

Most of the workbench is buried under a mess of wires, and the whole thing is stained by dozens of blobs of congealed solder, scarred by a thousand tiny scratches. It tells a story, a story of single-minded obsession. It's clearly the place where he carried out his passion in life. KT seventy-twos, your standard issue catties, lay strewn about the place in various stages of disembowelment. For tech, this place looks like a rogue doctor's makeshift emergency room and morgue all rolled into one, only without the sterility.

But I'm not interested in what's on the operating table, so much as in what *isn't* there. There's a gap. A clearly defined area of no clutter, where there should be... something. Just as nature abhors a vacuum, so did Spark's own personal chaos. At any given time, *something* would have been the center of focus, but right now, the desk lamps, the magnifying glasses, the clips, everything that snakes out from the frame at the back of the workbench points to an empty space. Something was on his workbench until recently. Where is it? *What* is it?

I head back out into the noodle bar, carefully walking around the cop's gently breathing body. I try to nod respectfully to the chef, but he refuses to make eye contact with me. In K block, you live to be his age by minding your own business.

Next stop's my place. I have some money and water in my backpack, plus a hacked transponder, ratty receiver, some spare batteries and my keys, but not much else. I need to eat. I need to sleep. I make my way through the labyrinthine narrow hallways that pass for the streets of K block, letting years of memories guide me while I concentrate on more pressing matters, until suddenly I'm at my front door.

Immediately, I can tell something's wrong. My transponder's vibrating. I glance at its tiny screen. My silent alarm's been tripped. Every inch of my body suddenly screams at me to get out. I try to hide it, to just carry on walking past as if I never intended to go in there. Suddenly breaking into a jog would be too obvious. I walk past, as casually as I can, hoping no one's worked out exactly where I was when I looked at my pocket and is putting the pieces together to work out it wasn't a coincidence. But it's too late.

Just as I'm about to turn a corner, there's a loud burst right by my head. I turn around to find the chipboard sheet that serves as a wall has a new hole in it, right where my ear was. I'm suddenly aware of a sting of pain. I put my finger up to my earlobe and then look at it, at the small streak of blood. There's screaming the other side of the wall, where presumably someone wasn't as lucky as I was, while the people this side who can see the shooter have enough sense to dive out of the way, more or less silently, giving this shadowy figure a clearer shot at me.

I give up any pretense, and I run. I never see who's behind me. I don't turn back to look. I just keep going forwards, guided by years of experience, avoiding all the dead ends and flooded rooms as I dive left into a belt maker's place, straight past a teenaged boy, maybe Brazilian, clanging away at a counterfeit big brand buckle so intently that he barely seems to notice me, then right into a noodle factory, past huge sacks of wheat, a bunch of rats and two elderly Chinese women shouting at me in their native tongue, up a ladder onto the wooden floor above, along more stores, down another ladder, and along the solid concrete ground floor again, running towards the bright light at the end, until I finally manage to burst free into the real world, running and squinting in the golden sunrise, the cool breeze on my skin at last. If I've just been reborn, maybe it's time to become someone else.

After a few more blocks, I slow to a gentle jog, then finally just a brisk walk. I reach into my backpack and pull out my sunglasses, presumably a cheap imitation of some famous brand I haven't heard of. My assailant's probably long gone, deep in the bowels of K block, like anyone who wasn't born there. No one can outrun a native, no matter how fast they are, because it isn't about speed. It's about direction.

It's time to prepare for my next move. I already stick out more than I'd like in the city proper, not having the money needed to look the part. I make my way to the public showers, and spend a small fortune there, washing the congealed blood off my ear and neck, along with the odor of a dozen different eateries and factories. I even buy those little sachets of shampoo, conditioner and hair gel, re-spiking my short, black hair. Looking in the mirror, I'm finally satisfied that I won't be thrown out of anywhere, even if I could do with a change of clothes.

Sophia's place is the nicest out of the three of us. She works for a Kao Telecom authorized repair store on J block. The difference between her job and ours, between her apartment and ours, between her life and ours is night and day. Literally. Her place has such extravagant features as windows that overlook the apartment block across the street, even letting in a bit of sunlight; a much larger room, one you could actually call a studio apartment while keeping a straight face; her very own private shower; and elevators, so I'm not out of breath when she tentatively opens her door, pulling its chain taut.

"Rain!" she exclaims, her face lighting up. "Hey, listen, can we do this later? I'm just about to head off to work. How's this evening for you?"

"Spark's dead," I say matter-of-factly. I feel a pang of pain in my head, but manage to hold the tears back.

Sophia drops the smile, her eyes widening ever so slightly, searching my face for a sign I'm playing some sort of trick on her. "For real?"

I nod solemnly.

"You'd better come in." She closes the door, flicks off its chain and swings it wide open, stepping off to the side as I make my way past her and into that beautiful apartment of hers, bathed in natural sunlight. It smells faintly of potpourri, or perhaps incense, propagated by a small, quiet, battery-operated fan on the coffee table, blowing a gentle breeze around the room.

As much as I try to avoid it, my eyes always wander towards the artwork on the walls. Hand painted by Sophia herself, depicting beautiful women of all shapes and sizes in various types of erotic confinement. All strictly consensual, she always goes to great pains to assure me, making me wonder just how fictitious the encounters depicted actually are. Pain's something she probably knows a lot about, connoisseur-like. The paintings are good, from the vibrant colors that make them seem glossy and hyperreal and the perspectives that seem to reinforce the viewer's dominance over the subjects, through to the symmetry of the pieces, and other signs of thoughtful balance. She says she sells them for a high three figures each, sometimes even more. Nice side business.

She certainly looks as well off as she is. Her taste is refined. Even dressing for technical back office work like I do, she's wearing a fine wool sweater and designer jeans, not cheap knock-offs like everyone on K block. Golden colored bracelets adorn her wrists, making a pleasant jangling sound whenever she gestures with her hands, and subtle make-up emphasizes the beautiful contours of her eyes. Her curly, black hair falls gracefully down to her shoulders. When she hugs me, I can smell perfume, much fancier than the simple deodorant at the public showers.

I want to say something comforting to cheer her up, but I can't think of anything.

She makes us both a coffee, fresh from her own machine and as dark as her soft skin. I tell her everything. Well, almost everything. Finding Spark's body. Searching his apartment. My plan.

Standing on the rooftop above my target's apartment, waiting for Sophia's signal, I can see the whole decaying city. Phone cables tether the buildings together like mooring lines, as if without them they might simply drift away. I let my gaze follow one of these cables from a neighboring building all the way to this one, raindrops dripping down from it onto the concrete floor beneath my feet. It's peaceful up here. Just the groaning of the turbines, the clatter of the air conditioning, the rain on old concrete and metal.

In my line of work, repairing KT equipment, if you're the curious type, you learn a lot of tricks. You learn how to make a logger board you splice between the catty—the cathode ray tube terminal—and the modem. This board intercepts and stores all the keystrokes going out and all the display characters coming in. Of course, with only a few K to play with, you can't store them locally. You have to ship them out to another account on the net. We have a lot of customers. On the days you're bored, you rack up a lot of usernames and passwords. A lot of accounts. A lot of secrets. And a lot of places to stash them.

You start trading them with acquaintances—"friends" wouldn't really be the right term, people like Spark and Sophia and me don't really have friends. It can become an obsession, like collecting schematics for boards you're not supposed to know about, let alone access, or phone numbers for people who aren't supposed to exist, and certainly aren't supposed to be on the grid. Spies. Assassins. Ghosts in the machine. In my circles, we collect all of these.

The three of us know—knew—more about KT's networks than KT themselves do, so whatever Spark was up to, they were probably the first people to object to it. Even if it wasn't them who killed him, they're likely spying on us all, so I can always see if they have any useful information. I already have the accounts of various people at KT. The only problem is that KT actually cares about its employees. Each person has certain designated places they like to log in from, and anywhere else is flagged up as suspicious. The target's apartment is generally your best bet. Luxurious, forty meter squared apartments like Sophia's, personal to just you and your optional spouse. It gets better. If you're a city proper hacker like Sophia, you can afford your own KT seventy-two terminal, black market, serial number etched off. And if you're a K block hacker like me, you know how to splice a line. Plug yourself right into the junction box, crocodile clips over his apartment number's regular jack. You set up an umbrella on a tripod, you plug your catty into the juice the box has along with the spliced line. Now, as far as the grid's concerned, you're in his apartment. You have to wait for him to leave, so you know he's not going to be logged in at the same time, from home or anywhere else, then, *then* you can log in as your target. It's time consuming. It's risky as hell being up there looking like some demented, high tech gargoyle squatting under the wind turbines. But it works.

My ratty receiver hooked into the back of the catty, tuned in to a disused frequency, I patiently watch the steady pulse of the bright phosphorous green cursor. Finally, a sliver of text appears, nudging the blinking cursor out of its way. Just a jumble of characters. A glitch in the system, as far as anyone else is concerned, if they happen to hear it. Just noise. But it's my signal. It means Sophia's seen the target, one Mr. Eugene Langford, leave his office building for lunch. I flick the switch on the back of the catty, switching it from the receiver back to the spliced line, and I'm greeted by the login prompt for Eugene's apartment. I enter his details, my fingers flying along the keyboard with professional precision. Sure, it's a risk, but some things are worth it. Some things, you just *have* to know.

And now, for the first time, I have everything. Access to the whole of KT. Something I'd never dared to see before. Hoards upon hoards of data, of raw information. Salaries. Bills. Patents. And *real* secrets. Information about potential rival companies. Things they aren't supposed to know about. Things they *wouldn't* know about if they weren't spying on their customers, and a monopoly to boot. Other people's inventions. Spark's invention.

Once I see Spark's files, I make my move. The idea is to copy them across to someone else's account, then from there to the next person's, hopping across to five different people. People I've never heard of. People I've never hacked before. People I can't be traced to.

I switch the terminal back to the receiver, the ghosts of countless alphanumerics fading into the abyss, replaced with Sophia's message comprised of only a handful of random looking characters. Nothing else accompanying it yet. Good. I switch it back to the spliced line, and the text reappears. My fingers moving deftly over the board, I log into the first stranger's account and make a hidden dot-directory to stash the files in, then switch back to Eugene's account and perform a remote copy. One down, four more to go.

I switch, and for a split second I freeze. Staring me in the face is Sophia's second signal, signifying that Eugene's just walked back into the building. Shit. I make a mental note not to panic. I close my eyes, take a deep breath, and open them again. I work quickly but methodically, careful not to make any spelling mistakes. I delete all my activity from Eugene's shell history log, then log off. It can't have taken me longer than twenty seconds after I first noticed the signal, and it can't have been more than a minute since I last checked for it. So a minute and a half from getting the signal to logging out, tops. That's cutting it uncomfortably close. I hope he took the stairs.

Then I'm back on the street, bulky machine under my arm, and no one's any the wiser. I perform the other four hops from a public terminal where I feel slightly safer, but only once I'm back in Sophia's apartment, the rain and police sirens a mere background noise, can I do something remotely approaching relaxing.

I've always felt that Sophia's apartment is the perfect place for relaxing. There's something comforting about someone who's so open about her sexuality.

"It worked then?" Sophia looks down at my boots, and the trail of wet footprints behind me. Whoops.

I look around for somewhere to put down the heavy machine.

"Anywhere's fine," she suggests.

I put the catty down on an empty chair. "Yeah, it worked. I got out a minute and a half after your second signal, max." I look Sophia in the eyes. "I saw things there, things they shouldn't have had. Spark's things."

Sophia's expression softens. "You look exhausted."

"It's been a rough day." I still can't bring myself to tell her about the shooting. I don't want her to worry about me unnecessarily.

"No kidding." Sophia gestures towards her bed, at the other end of the room. "You want to lie down for a bit, take a little nap?"

"Can't. I have to work out what to do next."

"Well you can't do that if you're tired. Trust me, you'll be able to think better once you're rested. *Then* you can strategize."

"It does look kinda tempting... are you sure you don't mind?"

"I insist."

I take off my army boots and curl up on Sophia's bed. That soft, cozy, luxurious bed. "Thanks. Maybe I'll just have a little nap, just for five minutes."

When I wake up, there's a thin blanket over me. I open my eyes, glancing out the window at a ninety degree angle. It's twilight, and the rain's stopped. Inside, the soft wall lights are on, and the place is starting to look almost like home, only more spacious and opulent.

I blink a few times, eyes adjusting, and tentatively sit up on the bed. "Why didn't you wake me?"

Sophia's the other side of the room, behind a canvas, brush in one hand and palette in the other. Her black, curly hair's tied back in a cute high-up ponytail. She talks to me, her voice softer than usual, but keeps her eyes focused on the canvas. "Sorry hon, you just looked so peaceful and calm like that. I didn't have the heart to wake you up. You've been through a lot today, you earned some rest."

I awkwardly amble towards her, unsure what to say. What comes out of my mouth is: "Thanks."

She smiles at me briefly, finally looking away from the canvas. Her eyes are slightly puffy, her cheeks still drying. She misses Spark, just as I do, and she's better at expressing it than I am. She searches my face for answers. She looks like she wants to know what to do next to fix this, but it can't be fixed. Spark's dead, and nothing will bring him back. The best we can do is ensure that whatever he was doing will live on. "So, what now?"

"Now?" I glance back at the bed, and next to it, the rack of jackets and dresses above the piles of neatly folded tops and jeans, at some of the rack's more exotic outfits. They aren't exactly proudly on display like the artwork, but they're still something she simply refuses to be ashamed about. I smile, for the first time since I found Spark that morning, as the next part of my plan solidifies in my mind. "Now I go shopping."

A short trip to the outer rim of K block later, where it's cheap enough for me to afford but not overtly illegal enough for the store owners to get hassled by the cops, my purse is lighter but I have a new outfit and matching boots, not at all to my taste but something I can use to blend in, where I plan on going. It's sticky on the inside and has a bullet hole in the back, lovingly patched with matching black PVC. Shops on K block, you don't ask questions.

I'm back at Sophia's apartment by nighttime. "Hi honey, I'm home."

"I should make you a key," suggests Sophia, her hair down again. She leads me inside once more, closing the door behind me.

I put my plain white plastic shopping bag down on the impeccably varnished wooden floor—stores on K block don't exactly go out of their way to advertise themselves—and make my way to the canvas. Now that she's finished, I can't help but sneak a peek at what she was painting. When I see it, it catches me a little off guard. It's just like her other artwork, and just as with the others, I can't imagine who the freckled redhead depicted in this one might be. Maybe she really does make all these muses up out of thin air.

"You look disappointed." Sophia pouts, mocking me. "Thought it would be you?"

"I know you better than to think you'd take advantage of a sleeping friend."

Sophia grins playfully. "You're awake now."

"So there's a chance yet." I grin right back. "Is it OK if I change?"

Sophia raises an eyebrow. "Sure, go ahead." Now it's her turn to act nonchalant. She sits down on her couch and flicks through a glossy fashion magazine.

I take off my backpack and my regular clothes, little more than a sports bra, combat trousers and army boots, all plain black. They're revealing in their own way, showing off my midriff, but not particularly sexy, merely functional in K block's climate of constant heat, rain and sweat. Then I take out my new outfit and try it on. I'm sweating before I've even finished zipping it up.

Sophia glances up from her magazine. "Want a hand?"

"No, I got it." It takes me a good few seconds of waving my hands behind my back, but eventually I manage to finish zipping up the outfit at the back of my neck. The boots are next, going almost all the way up to my knees, and they have impossibly high heels. I have to sit on the floor for a good five minutes while lacing them up. I stand, shaking. Balance myself. Pace back and forth a few times, slowly at first, figuring out how not to stumble.

"You come into my apartment unannounced, several times in one day, you get me to call in sick so I can tell you when some guy's having his lunch break, and now you're performing a little strip tease and dressing up game in front of me. What do you think this is, my reward? I mean, I know you must be feeling pretty shocked and all, but is there anything you'd like to tell me?"

"Not yet." I walk up to Sophia's fan. The trickle of cool air is nice, but nowhere near as strong as I need right now.

"Alrighty then." Sophia goes back to her magazine.

"May I?" I crank Sophia's fan up to full tilt, its drone now drowning out the sirens outside.

"You might even get it to do something, you got some new batteries." Sophia doesn't even glance up from her magazine this time.

I swap out the fan's batteries with the ones in my backpack, freshly charged ones I'd bought from Stu, a neighbor of mine with a cluster of solar cells perched on a little spot he rents on a K-block roof, where the top layer of iron and wood is sprouting up like so many trees.

I put the fan back on the coffee table, then get the bottle of water from my backpack and carefully pour a dribble of it into my hand. I rub the water into my face, make my way back over to the table, and bend over, hands on boots, my wet face taking the full brunt of the cool air. I close my eyes. The sensation of a cool breeze flying right into my wet skin is sheer bliss.

When I open my eyes again, Sophia's standing over me, looking down at me. "Can I keep them?"

"Sure," I say, looking back up at her, "you give me one of your paintings."

She smiles. "I didn't think they were to your taste."

"They're not," I admit. "Not really. But fencing one of those, I could get us a few years' worth of electricity."

"You know," says Sophia as she walks over to the kitchen part of the room and takes a bottled drink from the fridge, "it's not really called fencing if it's legal."

"Ever the intellect." I straighten back up and spread my arms, posing for her. "How do I look?"

Sophia takes a long swig from her cool drink, then looks me up and down. Her lips are wet. "Inspiring. But… "

I raise an eyebrow. "But..?"

"The look's incomplete." She walks over to her bed and sits down, picking up some dark eyeshadow and a brush from the bedside table. "May I?"

I think about this for a second. Growing up on K block, I hardly ever indulged in such luxuries as make-up. It felt almost odd to wear it, and letting someone else apply it would have felt stranger still. But this is my friend, and I trust her. I walk over to her and sit down on the bed beside her. "Sure, if you think it'll help."

Sophia smiles, and unscrews the small round container of eyeshadow.

What seems like maybe twenty minutes of foundation, eyeshadow, eyeliner and lipstick later, she adds one last artistic flourish, then just sits there scrutinizing me for a few seconds, looking for flaws and apparently not finding any. Finally, she relaxes, her look turning into one of appreciation, admiration of her own work. "There, perfect. Go ahead, have a look." She gestures towards the full length mirror beside the bed.

I look at my reflection with fascination. The catsuit shows off my curves in a way I'd never feel comfortable doing, but with Sophia's impeccable make-up artistry, I really look the part. The reflection's mine, same brown eyes, same epicanthic folds, same short, spiky black hair, but she actually looks like someone else, some twisted sister of mine. Not a character I'm playing, but a whole other person with her own inimitable sense of style. She grins with me. "It's perfect, thank you!"

"You're not going to go out dressed like that, are you? You'll get mobbed."

I hadn't even thought of that. "What do you suggest?"

Sophia riffles through her rack of jackets and outfits, then pulls off an old trenchcoat and hands it to me. It's a little big, but still serviceable. You can hardly tell what I'm wearing underneath, at least. I transform yet again into someone else, someone less sexual and more simply... stylish. I smile, and my reflection smiles back at me, beaming with confidence. I take a swig of warm water from my bottle, half in disbelief at the more attractive woman in the mirror copying my every move and making it look better, purposeful. Suddenly I see a strange mark on my bottle, then relax a little when I realize it's just lipstick. I make a mental note to refill it from a public tap on my way home, then remember that Sophia has running water in her kitchen. Such luxury. It's the little things.

"Hey, can I use some of your water?" I ask.

"Go ahead." Sophia gestures towards her gleaming metal sink, complete with both hot and cold taps.

I walk over to the sink, and empty out the warm water from my bottle. Then I fill it back up again, with fresh, clear, *cold* water, until it's overflowing like a beautiful statue that serves as the centerpiece of an ornate fountain. I take another swig from it, of deliciously cold water, then fill it up again.

Sophia watches me, apparently amused at how something so simple can be so important to me.

I smile back. She wouldn't last a week in K block. It would eat her alive. I nod at one of her paintings. "You ever been to Cravache?"

"Not my style." Sophia's curiosity sounds piqued.

"Really?" I grin, unable to hide my dubiousness.

"There's more to a sexuality than your partner's sex, or what you do with them. For my sexual encounters, like my artwork, everything has to be just right. The lighting. The outfits. The devices. The predicaments. There's a certain class to what I do, and frankly, that place is just too trashy. No offense."

"What do you mean, no offense? I don't go there either!"

Sophia frowns. "So why are we talking about it?"

"Because right now, I really need to go somewhere that's *not me*. Somewhere that doesn't fit my profile. You wanna come with me?"

"That doesn't even *begin* to make sense."

"You coming or not?"

Queueing outside the cloakroom, our hands freshly stamped, double doors protect us from the onslaught of noise deafening the crowd on the dancefloor. That is, aside from the brief moments when those doors swing open to let someone through, swallowing them whole, and ear splitting screeches threaten to give me a headache. The rest of the time, we're protected from all but a dull murmur of throbbing basslines. Still dangerously loud, but more like physical movement, a vibration in my stomach, than noise. The place smells of stale sweat.

I hand Sophia my coat—her coat, technically—and she passes it along to the woman behind the counter, who's sporting black and purple ponytails and decked out in an impressive latex corset of her own, but looks utterly bored. Sophia then takes off her own jacket, revealing her outfit: a low-cut latex minidress that shows off her cleavage, putting my cheap PVC catsuit to shame. Heads turn. Sophia smiles, radiating a cool, nonchalant confidence. I'd consider feeling jealous if I wasn't trying to blend in. Her boots are like mine, only they look almost new, they taper off to dangerous looking stiletto heels, and she knows how to walk in them. Together, we certainly look the part, our outfits so shiny you can almost count the lights on the ceiling just by looking at their stretched, warped reflections on our bodies. She must live for clubs like these, where she can have any woman she wants. If I look like I fit in here, I can't imagine the upscale equivalent where Sophia fits in, a whole subculture of impeccably dressed playthings eager to do her bidding.

The doors swing open again, and I ignore the sudden onslaught of noise to peek past them, scanning the room, looking for those glowing screens, and wow do I find them. I can't even work out why such a place even *has* a seventy-two, but there they are, a whole row of tables with them, up against the far wall. A moment later and they're gone again, obscured by the doors.

"Let's go over—" Before I can finish the sentence, I feel a tight grip around my neck. I turn around to see Sophia grinning at me, her arms stretched out, her hands fiddling around behind my neck. I must have a puzzled look on my face, as she grins at me, an evil, condescending grin, and pulls her hands away again, holding a key.

I tentatively feel around my neck. Sure enough, she's fastened a collar around it, with a metal D-shaped ring at the front and a padlock at the back. Even the woman behind the counter looks amused.

"Very funny," I say. "Are you going to give me the key?"

"Sure." Sophia is positively beaming. It seems to be all she can do not to laugh. The next thing I know, she's reaching into her handbag and pulling out a dog leash, snapping the end onto my collar's metal ring. Her voice has changed, and not just to speak up over the muffled music, if you can call it that. I've only heard her talk like this once before, when I paid her a visit while she had company. It feels weird suddenly having this tone of voice directed at me this time. "Once we leave, and not a second earlier."

I sigh. This isn't exactly how I'd planned it, but I figure I can't really fault her for blending in. It's the perfect cover. "Fine. Let's go over to a terminal at the far—"

"Shh," soothes Sophia, stroking my hair. She's enjoying this more than I'm strictly comfortable with. Wanting her to notice me is one thing, but this is taking it a bit far. I make a mental note to get her back one day, assuming I make it that long. At any rate, I can't entertain a revenge fantasy right now. I have to keep my mind focused on the task ahead.

But Sophia has already gone. I feel a curious tugging sensation on my neck, pulling me sideways. I suddenly realize what's happening, turning around in time to see the chain stretching taut all the way to her hand. She's leading me—literally—through the double doors, across the dancefloor, to the far wall. The cacophony of noise, smells and sights envelops me. The dancefloor reeks of fresh sweat, latex, and even precum. People dance and lead each other astray in roughly equal measures. I try to play along, glancing at some of the other patrons and emulating the submissive ones. I keep my head down, trying not to focus on Sophia's swinging hips as she takes me on a long tour of the place—too long—parading me around the dancefloor like a beloved pet she's showing off to her peers.

As masters and mistresses lead their slaves off the dancefloor and into the bathroom to perform sordid services for them, Sophia leads me off the dancefloor to an empty table, where she corners me in, and I finally got a chance to see what was worth killing a man over. Spark's files. Schematics and machine code. Timestamped just *after* his death.

"So that's what this is about?" shouts Sophia, still affecting her dominant's voice, looking over my shoulder at the terminal's display.

"May I speak?" My own voice has only the merest hint of sarcasm. Mentally, I'm still in the world of raw data, not experiencing my immediate surroundings enough to work out whether I'm even joking or not.

"You may," decides Sophia.

"I know they did it. I can't prove it, but I know they got his files after his death, and the only way they would do that is if they were the ones who killed him."

"So that's why we're here? To prove it?"

"No," I said reflexively. "I just told you, I *can't* prove it." With a slight sigh, I mentally detach myself from the terminal and reattach myself to reality, the questionable smells, the intermittently blinding lights, the piercing music, my aching neck, and my friend.

"But that is why we're here, these files?"

"Yes. What, did you think I was trying to seduce you in a moment of vulnerability?"

"Honey, I *still* think you're trying to seduce me."

"So, what, you're happy to just go along with that and take advantage of me?"

Now Sophia looks downright offended. Angry. She yanks on the leash, pulling it uncomfortably taut, forcing my face closer to hers. "Maybe I'm keeping an eye on you to make sure you won't do anything you'll later regret. You're not the only one who's emotionally vulnerable right now, you know. I lost a good friend too. And on top of that, in the last fourteen hours, I've sheltered you, I've engaged in industrial espionage with you, and I've even indulged your little fantasy or whatever the hell this is, even though it hurts to be teased like this, knowing nothing will ever come of it, and I *didn't* want to round the day off by having you running back to my apartment again, this time with tears streaming down those pretty little cheeks of yours while you tell me all about how you went to a place like this without someone who cared about you watching over you, and how someone here took advantage of you. So yes, I'm playing with you, but no, I don't take our friendship lightly, at least not as lightly as you seem to. If I must look after you like a pet, I'm going to keep you leashed like one, and not let you out of my sight. OK?"

I swallow hard, looking up at her impassioned eyes, and nod solemnly. When I next speak, it's barely more than a squeak. "Sorry."

"Apology accepted." She nods at the terminal. "Now do what you do."

I nod compliantly, and Sophia gives the metal chain some slack. I face the terminal again, and begin to focus once more.

Compared to getting the files, copying them from one compromised account to another is easy. Personal accounts have lax security. No one cares if someone logs in twice at once. I copy the files from one of the accounts to another, log in as that person, and copy them from there to another, and so on, from Steve to Jane to Sarah to Michael to Paul. Eventually, I settle on Evelyn Chung, and from there e-mail them to a printing service. I copy Chung's private key to someone else, and repeat the five-hop ritual.

"How much do you want to be a part of this?" I ask Sophia.

"Do you have to ask?"

"It's risky. I'd like to store someone's private key on your account."

"Whose?"

"No one in particular. Just a random person on my list of compromised accounts."

"Why not store it on your account?"

"That's what I was going to do, and physically grab it from work. But I can't, it's not safe." I sigh, deflating slightly. It's time to come clean and tell Sophia the whole truth. "I've already been shot at today."

For the second time today, Sophia searches my face for any kind of indication that I'm joking. When she doesn't see one, she closes her eyes and takes in a deep breath, coinciding with a momentary lapse of the music's caustic, heavy rhythm, a calm little moment of bass, chatter, and the occasional distant slapping and cheering. She lets the breath of air out again, slowly, finally opening her eyes once more. "Well, that explains the ear."

I lean in slightly, loosening the chain a bit. "You knew about that?"

Sophia frowns again, although not as severely this time. She gestures wildly with her hands, almost accidentally snapping my neck off in the process. "Who do you think put the blanket over you? You have any other watchful guardians I should know about?"

I look down at the chain, taut again, unable to meet her gaze. She's right to be angry at me. I didn't realize how much she had to be angry about until now. "I'm sorry. They traced him to me, but you're clean. You're my safehaven."

Sophia stares down at me, and this time I can't escape her gaze. She looks right through my body and into my soul. I must have looked pitiful in that moment. Finally, she gives me her decree. "I'm in. Store her key on my account."

"Thank you." I'm not sure if I look appropriately apologetic or merely grovelling. I face the terminal again, Sophia giving the leash a bit more slack, and I copy Evelyn Chung's private key one last time.

"You want to explain your plan now?" asks Sophia.

"Sure." I log out of the terminal.

"You done?"

I nod. "I figure KT killed Spark, and tried to kill me, because of these files. I don't know what they are yet, but clearly they're important. Can't read them here, though. The schematics are vector files. Can't view them on a catty. I have to print them out to know what they are. The rest are machine code, M sixty-four by the looks of it. I've just run them through a disassembler but it'll take me a good few weeks to reverse engineer this much undocumented source code. I'd rather do that in private, with a pen and paper, so I'm gonna print those too. There's a printer's not too far from here, over on the other side of J block, so I'm sending the job there. Given how today's turned out so far, however, I'm not just going to waltz in there using my real name. So I figure we go back to your place, change back into our regular clothes, I use your interface to rig up my transponder with Evelyn Chung's private key, then I head off to the print store posing as her and collect the printouts."

Sophia stands up, looming far above me, and tugs on the leash. "Isn't that dangerous? Can't they trace what you're doing and just wait for you at the store?"

"Theoretically, yes." I take the cue and shuffle along to the edge of the seat, then stand up, only wobbling slightly. "But they don't know about Chung. And they don't seem to know about you yet."

"Yet?" Sophia turns around and walks back onto the dancefloor, with me in tow.

I stumble after her. "It's just a matter of time until they mine our social network, regardless of whether I store anything on your account or not. I'm not going to lie to you. They're probably going to come after you regardless of what I do. But if we do this first, it should give us just enough of an edge to outmaneuver them."

Sophia leads me straight through the middle of the dancefloor, pushing the doors on the other side wide open. "So... some assassin's probably going to turn up at my door, but don't worry about it, we should have a printout by then?"

I follow her lead as best I can, trying not to fall over in the combination of impossibly high heels and being led by my neck. Once we're past the doors, at least I can think properly once more. "In essence, yes. Look, I'm sorry about this, but I'm not bringing it on you any more than Spark brought it on me. Just by knowing each other, we're already involved regardless of what we do."

Sophia unclips the leash and throws a key at me. It bounces off my clumsy hands and onto the suspiciously sticky floor. She gives two tickets to the woman behind the counter. "So how's this printout going to make everything better?"

I pick up the key without thinking, getting a few appreciative stares from passers-by before I realize I should have bent my knees more. "I don't know yet. Leverage, maybe. I'll figure that out later. Right now, we just need to get it and see what it is, because until we do that, we don't have anything. Even someone of your status, a citizen of the city proper, they can still just get rid of us all and make it look like a series of unconnected robberies and muggings." Finally, I manage to unlock the padlock and give it back to Sophia, along with the collar. I rub my sore neck. "Still with me?"

Sophia puts on her jacket, then throws her old trenchcoat at me. "It doesn't look like I have much of a choice, does it?"

In the dimly lit hallway outside Sophia's apartment, my ears are still ringing. I can barely hear what she's saying.

"OK, now I'm going to teach you how to use a welcome mat," she teases as she gets her keyring out of her handbag, finds the right key, and unlocks the door.

It swings wide open to reveal a man in a suit, older than us, maybe in his late thirties, looking like a ghost white salaryman, pointing a silver colored pistol right at Sophia's face, standing right there next to us. The man glances at us both and smirks. He probably wasn't expecting to get both of us at once. We made it easy for him.

Before I can think what to do, Sophia has kicked him in the crotch with the full force of a stiletto heel and is grabbing my wrist, pulling me back down the corridor, down the stairs, away from the echoes of the concrete walls exploding with bullets and into the relative safety of the bustling crowd outside. It's all I can do not to stumble in my block heels. I suddenly have a newfound respect for femmes.

"I think," says Sophia as she pulls me through the crowd, "that we just ran out of time. New plan?"

"One second." I struggle to think of something. The crowd's a blur, and I just ignore the sea of faces, letting them wash over me as Sophia leads me as far away from her apartment block as she can, as unpredictably as she can. "You're right, we're out of time."

"So what's your plan?" Sophia sounds serious and urgent.

Running out of options, I suggest the impossible. "We've got nothing to lose. I say we be ourselves for a little while."

Sophia leads me into a deserted back alleyway, steam rising from vents in the ground, then out the other side, to another crowded street, parallel to the first. "Elaborate."

We keep running. Miraculously, I don't fall over. "We still go to a printer's, but without a private terminal, I can't copy someone's private key to my transponder. Even if we somehow found a public terminal with the right interface, it wouldn't work. It takes time. It's suspicious. So we don't. We go to a printer's as ourselves. I set up a new print job, in my real name or your real name, and we walk in and pick it up."

Sophia talks in short bursts, between breaths. "*That's* your plan? To just waltz right into a printer's using our real names? Forgive me, but I thought that's exactly what you told us *not* to do, back in Cravache."

Struggling to keep up, I barely manage to say a whole sentence in between panting. "If we move quickly enough, we might be able to make it in time."

Sophia slows down to a brisk walk, catching her breath. She looks back at me. "*Might?*"

Once I catch up with her, I follow suit, grateful to finally have a chance to get my breath back. "Hear me out. We find the four or five closest printers, we queue up the job in all of them, then we go to just one of them and pick up the printouts. He'll have to guess which one we're at, so we'll have a good chance of not running into him."

"Unless they have more than one person after us," points out Sophia, her face lit up by the neon lights, alternating between the primary and secondary colors of a twenty-four hour café's animated sign. "Did you get a good look at your tail last time? Was it the same guy?"

I let out a grunt of frustration. "I hadn't thought of that."

Sophia sighs. "Any other options?"

"None come to mind."

Sophia opens the café door, her voice resigned. "Come on. Just remember to keep your coat on."

An old guy sitting at the table next to ours scowls at us until he leaves a few minutes later, but no one says anything. We have a cup of coffee and a sandwich each—the first thing I've eaten all day, I suddenly realize—and I set up five print jobs, two as Sophia, two as myself, and one as Spark. All the while, Sophia is drumming her fingers, nervous like. It distracts me, but I don't say anything. The way

I figure it, she's more than entitled to feel nervous. Then we pay our bill and head off to the closest print store, one of the two I used my own name for.

The print store turns out to be a regular convenience store that happens to have a cheap laser printer on the counter. My heart's beating hard in my chest as Sophia and I walk up to the counter.

"I believe you have a printout waiting for me," I tell the guy behind the counter.

"Name?" he asks.

"Rain."

He smiles in a way that seems slightly creepy. "Pretty name."

"Thanks." At least he's not complaining about how short my hair is. Maybe that's the magic of Sophia's make-up skills. Maybe I blend in with polite society a little more now. I glance down briefly at the trenchcoat, making sure it's buttoned up. It is.

"Pre-paid, all accounted for." The old man hands me a thick stack of papers. "Happy reading."

"Thanks." I open the door, Sophia the other side, and that's when he walks in. The salaryman. Mr. Ghost white. He spots her first. I see him grab his gun, as if watching it in slow motion. I look around for something, *anything* I can use. I grab a glass wine bottle off the shelf and swing it into his hand. I picture the glass smashing everywhere, the floor suddenly washed with liquid red, wine with a little blood mixed in, but the bottle doesn't break. It must have hit him pretty hard though, as he screams in pain. The guy behind the counter starts shouting at us, but words don't register.

I get ready to swing it again, but there's no need. Sophia kicks him with her heel again, this time in his stomach, and he doubles over. I shove the bottle back onto the shelf, and we run out of there, back into the street. The shouting is replaced by human traffic, and we're back to running through the crowd again, only this time I'm carrying the printouts at last.

Sophia takes the lead. "Follow me."

"Where are we going?" I gasp.

"Somewhere close. Somewhere we can blend in. Somewhere we haven't been shot at yet." She holds up her hand. First I think it's so I can keep track of where she is, but then I realize she's showing me the ink stamped on the back of it. Cravache.

"You have to be kidding me."

"It's just around the corner from here, and you seemed so keen to go the last time. Didn't you have fun?"

The pounding so-called music actually gives me a headache this time, but at least no one's staring at us here—aside from the occasional look of approval—and at least Sophia doesn't leash me this time. Finally, I can go over the schematics, colored spotlights and the occasional strobe lights providing a suitable ambience, giving them the splendor they deserve, something that black ink on white paper alone just doesn't do justice to.

They're beautiful, both in purpose and in elegance. A computer small enough to fit in your home. Instead of renting a seventy-two and buying cycles on a frame, you can solder together one of these babies and have a whole computer to yourself, right there in your room. A CPU, a text chip, a modem chip, all things that video terminals have, but in addition, a ludicrous amount of memory. Dozens of K. Enough to fit in whole programs. A modified modem that lets you frequency-shift key your data right onto your own personal stash of audio cassette tapes. Then it's no longer a dumb terminal. It's a tiny computer in its own right, capable of running whatever software you want, and no one can spy on you. It's privacy. It's beautiful.

My first thought's to build it, natch, but that wouldn't be enough. KT had already killed Spark, and taken a pop at Sophia and me. I mean, we're good, but we're not *that* good. We can't outmaneuver them forever. Maybe they hadn't caught up with us yet, but they would eventually. Information spreads pretty quickly on the net, no matter what kind. With enough dedication, everything can be traced.

That's when I hatch the final stage of my plan. This invention was by Spark, but it's not his. It's not mine or Sophia's, either. It's everyone's. That's who I have to give it to. Everyone.

I log in as the illustrious five once more, one at a time. From each of their accounts, I can e-mail one point seven million people, using a glitch in the ubiquitous mail server that I learned to exploit a while back. There are eight million, seven hundred thousand people in this city with their own private—whatever *that* means—account on the KT frame net. In the morning, they'll all wake up. Maybe a few dozen thousand know how to solder. Each of them will be able to make their own private, personal computer, and each of them can make them for their friends, too.

I set up the first batch of e-mails, my finger hovering over the enter key, and that's when I feel it, something hard pressed against the side of my waist. I turn around, refamiliarizing myself with my surroundings. Sophia has gone, not that I really blame her. In her place is the salaryman, that stupid grin back on his face.

"No one around to kick me this time," he says. He's so close, I can smell the mint on his breath. I look down at his bloodied hand, wrapped around the grip of his pistol, the barrel pressing against my waist.

I nod at his hand. "You should get that looked at."

He sneers. "Move your hands away from the keyboard. Slowly. Now."

I look him in the eyes. "I suppose if I press this key, and e-mail all these people, your client or employer or whoever will just go in and delete them all anyway."

He nods.

"You know what?"

He looks ever so slightly unnerved, but too cocky to really feel threatened. "What?"

"I don't care." I look past my assailant to the crowd behind him. The slaves. The masters and mistresses. One particular woman with curly hair, who I'm increasingly proud to call my friend. The salaryman turns around to see who I'm looking at, but it's too late. Sophia punches him in the cheek at the exact same time I try to prise the gun from his hand, pointing the barrel up at the ceiling, away from me. He fires it, destroying a light in the process, small shards of glass flying towards the crowd. There's a burning smell. Screams. Running. The place empties out, and I take the gun safely off the man as Sophia pats him down, making sure he hasn't got any other tricks up his sleeve.

She looks down at me, a warm smile greeting me. "Doesn't he know you're spoken for?"

The few people left in the room have no shortage of restraints, and are polite enough to help us out. With our would-be dispatcher safely apprehended, I finish sending the e-mails, all of them.

I look down at the salaryman, disheveled, cuffed and bleeding. "A word of advice: try datsusara."

"I think we'd better leave," suggests Sophia. I nod, and she offers me a hand, pulling me out of the seat.

"Your place?" I ask.

"Depends. Can I paint you?"

I look up at her, grinning. "Maybe."

Sure, this man will be back on the streets soon enough. Maybe he'll come after us again, maybe even with some co-workers. At least now I can follow the first rule of a gunfight: bring a gun.

KT will see what we've done before morning, I'm sure. Try to stop it. Over eight million e-mails from just five accounts has to get noticed somewhere. Maybe they'll delete almost all of them. *Almost all.* Nothing stays hidden in these streets. And now, with a little luck, KT might not be a monopoly forever. Maybe people can finally start to make their own machines, their own languages, their own protocols. A chaotic, haphazard, organic mess, just like home. And maybe that would be a beautiful thing.

Nightingale's Lament

Laura Gregory

The bird was leaning against my desk when I returned to my office. Gripping my pistol, I came around the corner, but this wasn't a threat. It was a client: hip cocked against the scarred oak, cigarette trailing smoke, scarlet lips and high cheekbones. A mosaic of feathers etched across their scalp and down their arms. A sheath of red silk enveloped them, sharp collarbones and gaunt chest on display. I holstered the gun. "It's not office hours."

They flicked ash from their cigarette. "I work late nights."

I opened a drawer and dropped a pile of photographs inside. My latest solved case. The mayor's wife having an affair with her chauffeur, who was also in bed with the mayor's competition. You'd think the elite would be more discreet, but they got high on power, forgot about people watching from the gutters. I could always use another case, but working with the eldritch patrons of the city came at a cost. Too many poor humans like me ended up dead. First, I needed to know why they were here. I switched on the desk lamp and they folded themselves into the chair opposite, elbows pulled in tight, but legs reaching for miles under the desk.

"My lover, Ardito Cirillo, was killed. I need you to find out who did it." Their voice was hushed but lyrical, like water tumbling over rocks.

"Police investigate murders. Why don't you start there?"

"They ruled it a suicide. But I think my boss paid them off. He's my prime suspect."

I crossed my arms. "And who is that?"

"Don DiGiovanni. The Mad Wolf."

Mafia. Biggest boss in town, then. I tripled my fee. "And why would he want your lover dead?"

They shifted in their seat. "He was ambitious, you know? Always had a side hustle going on. He was one of the Don's men but maybe he stepped outside his place."

I pushed the ashtray across the desk and watched the light dance up the golden fletching on their arm as they tamped out the cigarette. I could have gone for my own but I'd quit last year. Doctor's orders. Half a century was too old to be playing with fire.

"What can you tell me about that night?"

"Nothing."

"This is going to be one hell of a difficult case then."

They sighed and something in my chest ached fiercely. "I don't remember. I get these lapses in memory. Amnesia, like waves in a storm… I was at the lounge the next night, wondering where he was, he always came to see me sing. Everyone was looking for him, but they would, you know? Put on an act, even if they'd killed him. I've seen it before. I went home at dawn, my house is by the bay, edge of a cliff, and he was there at the bottom. Been shoved off. He hated heights, he never would have fallen on his own."

"Where do you work?"

"The Bacchus Lounge. I'm a singer. They call me The Nightingale. Gale for short."

"And what are you?"

They held up their hand, looking at the feathers imprinted on their skin and shaking their head softly. "I don't remember."

I locked the drawer with the photographs and opened another, taking out my blood pressure pills. I popped one, knowing I was too old, knowing this bird would be the death of me. But I pulled out my notepad to start writing down the facts. "I'll take the case."

I didn't go to The Bacchus Lounge until I'd done my groundwork. My buddy in the force pulled up the report, it did read as a clean suicide. A bit of crumbled rock at the cliff edge with no signs of a struggle. Even the trajectory measured for someone who had leapt, as opposed to being pushed or slipping down. Of course, all those details could be falsified, but what was the cover up?

I had them run The Nightingale too. They'd come into the country six months ago, sponsored by Don DiGiovanni for his nightclub act. Their classification was eldritch—other. No help there.

Sussing out Ardito's business contacts, I discovered he had investments in a nightclub that wasn't owned by the Don. That could get him in hot water. But no major debts. Only minor crimes on file. He seemed like he was trying to get clean, go legit. Maybe he'd just wanted out and it earned him a death sentence.

I filled my pistol with silver bullets before heading to the club. Mad Wolf wasn't a metaphor, blood-in and blood-out involved the lycanthrope strain in this gang. I asked if Ardito was initiated but Gale denied it, too low on the ladder to be part of the pack. Forensic reports confirmed it: blood results were pathetically human. Drug and alcohol free. High cholesterol. I sympathised.

The Bacchus Lounge was in an old train station. The roof centered on a circular dome laced with ironwork. A massive birdcage hung down from the apex, draped in moonlight from above. Tables spread out below, patrons drinking and waiting for the entertainment. A stage was set up with piano and string quartet, absent of performers. I stood in the shadows until the bartender noticed me. Ronny was a vampire contact I'd used in the past. He slipped away from the customers and gestured me backstage, his fangs just peeking out, white flashes in his smooth, dark face. I slipped him a hundred dollar bill and it disappeared in a sleight-of-hand gesture.

"This one's new, still impressionable. I've convinced him you're a friend of Ardito. He'll talk but don't linger long. Don't want Mad Wolf on my scent. I might bite but I can't fight off a pack of wolves, alright?"

My target was standing at attention in the hall, gaze vacant as I walked in front of him. Ronny did good work. I reached to shake his hand and it was like we'd been buddies for life. He told me all about Ardito shaking down debtors and his murders of rival gang members; he wasn't a saint. This could be a retaliatory strike, but a fall from a cliff wasn't much of a message. Not their style. They'd gunned down an informer on the busiest street at daybreak last week. I didn't suspect them of being stealthy.

I may just be human, but all prey knows when a predator is going to pounce. I looked back and there he was, the Mad Wolf himself. I was caught, no way around it, but I didn't have to throw Ronny to the wolves. I released Tony's hand and the hypnosis left him. He scampered for shelter and I strode towards the Don.

"I'm looking into the death of Ardito. His family hired me." I didn't want to put any heat on Gale.

Don DiGiovanni was around my age. His voice was loud but flat. "I know what you and Tony were talking about. I read lips." So he was deaf; I'd never heard rumour of it. "Ardito had potential. I warned him but..."

A door opened and Gale emerged from their dressing room, this time wearing black silk. It revealed a fine layer of down had emerged to cover their chest. All the feathers along their arms had sprouted barbs that sparkled in sharp metallic glints.

Mad Wolf watched Gale approach. "Lycanthropes aren't the only creatures controlled by the moon. When I found them, washed ashore on the Sicilian coast, I thought it a gift from the Gods. A golden goose. See how packed it is out there? Every night, they draw a crowd. But now, maybe it's a curse." He sighed and jerked his head. Dismissing me.

I caught up with Gale at the door. Their nails, beneath a lacquer of red paint, were long and curved. They glanced down at me and their irises had turned pure black. "I'm starting to remember," they whispered. "There were others before Ardito. He wasn't the first to disappear."

Suddenly Mad Wolf grabbed Gale's arm, fingertips digging into flesh. "Get onstage, eh? *In bocca al lupo.*"

Gale watched the Don go, their glare piercing his back and their voice a hiss. "*Crepi il lupo.*"

I should have left. Last time the mob warned me off, I'd been pissing blood for days. But the birdcage was on the ground. Gale sashayed through the spotlight and I couldn't cross without interrupting the show. A pianist started playing as the cage was lifted up. Pale light from the waxing moon fell on Gale and the entire room exhaled their collective breath in a sigh.

When Gale started to sing I suddenly understood why they were suspended above the crowd. It wasn't just some tawdry burlesque twist. It was for security. As piercing notes of love, loss, yearning and heartache escaped into the air, I wanted to reach them, embrace them, with an urgency I wasn't sure was intended to protect or punish. And I wasn't alone. The entire room had come to their feet, some even standing on their chairs, anything to be closer to the song. In his private booth, only Mad Wolf remained seated. He tipped his glass at me and I took that as my final notice. I burst out of the exit with the notes of The Nightingale still infiltrating my ears.

All the clues dried up. I interrogated everyone Ardito had come in contact with his final week. None of my sources could confirm a rival gang hit. No one in Mad Wolf's pack had a grudge. I grilled his mother so hard on if he had suicidal thoughts, I made her cry. She denied it, her suspicions, like Gale's, on foul play. I had no answers but I had to end my case. It had been haunting me. The Nightingale had been haunting me. I didn't dare return to The Bacchus Lounge, so I sent a message through Ronny, who slipped a note in their dressing room.

I waited past midnight. I didn't trust myself to be enclosed in the office with them. Instead, I stood at the towering window in the landing, the gothic proportions of the building still feeling too small. The moon was full and lit the entire hall. I heard the front door slam below and then delicate steps up the flights of stairs. There was an odd noise, like fabric dragging on the floor. It was the tips of their golden feathers, having fully formed into heavy, lustrous wings. Their hands had fused into black talons. Their face was still human and their eyes were full of sorrow.

"Don't talk." I held my hand up, aware of the power of their voice. My other hand clutched my pistol in the holster, if only for cold comfort, because I knew the silver bullets would have no effect. This was no lycanthrope before me. "I can find no proof Ardito was murdered. All evidence points he went willingly."

Tears seeped out of Gale's eyes. With no fingertips to catch them, they merely let them fall. I wanted to wipe them away, but I planted my feet on the hardwood.

"I remember..." Gale's sigh was a melody. They flexed their wings, shimmering in the darkness. "I've lost so many others I loved."

I felt my will breaking, reaching towards them. "Please, be quiet."

Gale shook their head, sobbing, a wail emerging from their mouth. It was music. It was ecstasy. It was a siren song. I rushed to them but they were running, wings unfolding, until they smashed through the window and out into the moonlight.

My feet raced to follow, leaping off the stone ledge to chase the siren as they soared into the sky.

But I had no wings.

And I solved it too late.

We Are All Wasteland on the Inside

Benjanun Sriduangkaew

She is dying, the old spymaster, when I visit her house. Spread all over the room: lethargic on the bed, a hand (thick, callused) pinned to the ceiling, a leg (long, shapely) dangling from a bookshelf. The rate of her decay has been rapid, toxins mating and making nations in her body, fighting wars and creating cultures and making history that expresses in the bioluminescence blotting her skin. It looks editorial, opal tones and swallowed sea-storms, and would have made her the star of a body-mod exhibit. Jellyfish chic, arising salt-thick and hungry from the deep.

But still she breathes, and when she sees me, she says, "Help yourself."

The bar is fully stocked, red bottles and faceted cups. Clean stirrers, cleaner glassware. She has a housekeeper, some fresh-faced (as they eternally are) upsorn-sriha newly out of the forest: the sandals left at the door are telltale, delicate gold and shaped for hooves. For my drink I pick smoky wine and red petals that dissolve in the alcohol, giving up spice and salt and sour. I skip the coconut syrup that's supposed to go with the cocktail. Sweet things are not my province.

I settle on a chaise longue. It's distracting, her collapse, the slow agony of a body pushing free of each other as though they are similarly polarized magnets. Phantom limbs have sprung from the sockets of her arm and leg. They curl about her, boneless, barely real in their pallor. Her torso is intact otherwise, the head still firmly joined to the rest. A pre-murder scene, avant-garde and carefully posed on sheets and headboard for maximum statement. She must be on anesthetics, medulla oblongata sloshing in drugs, but her eyes are steady, her voice smooth and uninterrupted by intoxication.

"I'm your assigned legal executor." A sip: as hard-hitting as I expected. She has good taste and the means to satisfy it, though I can't imagine she has enjoyed anything lately. "We'll need your authorization to unseal your will, Khun Jutamat."

Her mouth pinches. A smile aborted late-term. "I don't have one."

That's news to me. I know she has close family and two ex-wives. "Your property will revert to the state."

"I'll be dead and money won't matter to me. I didn't ask for you specifically on account of your law degree. You worked with police."

"Yes, ma'am." I have worked in many things: theater, accounting, a stint in forensics and vice. Mine is a timeline in disarray, but so are most people's. Much of life has become debris and dead skin after Himmapan, the convergence event.

Jutamat's poltergeist arm stretches unsteadily, the movements more like limp rubber than bone and muscle. Undulating, repulsive. "It's a good range of skills. Much more important than one's bank balance or where that balance goes after one expires. You and I, we'll solve my murder together before I go."

In Jutamat's garden there is a tree, old, its canopies dripping star-shaped leaves. Gold, green, tipped in stark white. It is heavy with a crop of makkalee fruits on the cusp of maturity and independence from the bough. I have never seen one of these trees; they don't grow just anywhere and resist attempts at cultivation. Only at the liminal edges do they flourish, where Himmapan hovers and seeps into city, black loam making sludge of asphalt, green radiance splattering traffic signs and sidewalks. Where birds fly too close to that border they disappear, the dirt-crusted pigeons and smoke-stained crows.

Accordingly there are no birds here or butterflies, no ants or amphibians. All is clean. Not a blade of grass is too long; no weeds or infestation of fungi touch the earth, no mark of worm or insect hunger on petals. Frangipani, lotuses—either Jutamat favors those, or no other flower would grow. Symbols of passing on and peace, respectively. Appropriate perhaps.

Myth tells that makkalee fruits are alluring and sweetly scented. Reality is less glamorous. They smell faintly vegetal rather than like palm sugar, jasmines, or some heavenly blossom. On the ground one of them lies fallen and premature, ivory skin bruised from impact and seeping blue sap. I turn it in my palm, tracing the contours of full breasts and small waist, flared hips and thick thighs. The face is rough, a work in progress, but there is already a nose and mouth defined, eye sockets deepening. The ones on the bough are shaped similarly. All makkalee fruits from the same tree look alike, replicated over and over in some internal mold, the way dolls emerge from a factory.

"Have you ever met one of them full grown?"

I put the fruit down. Jutamat's wheelchair labors, for all that her body can't weigh that much anymore. Shreds of her ghost leg get stuck in the mechanism, between joints. "Can't say I have, ma'am."

"Poor conversationalists. They only think of the soil and the air, rain and sun. Not much else; I can't imagine what hermits in legends see. But then, mythical hermits tend to be ugly and desperate." She wheels forward. It continues to be a struggle, looking at her directly. The eye protests. Optic nerves flinch. The mind attempts to reconstitute what is there and fails. "Rumor has it that eating makkalee will cure any ill. Incorrect, of course. My housekeeper planted this, by the way, to keep her company—not many Himmapan natives live in the neighborhood. Would you like a bite? Think of it like molded chocolate or marzipan."

"I will pass, thank you." I don't consider myself squeamish. But still they look humanlike and, given time to ripen, they will talk like humans too. Pastiche personhood. "I don't think I am the person you want for this." A simple arrangement of paperwork, what will go where, a list of beneficiaries and then a cut for the tax collectors. That is what it should have been.

"I'll be the judge of that. You were police, more or less."

"Less rather than more." With effort I focus on the banal details: her thinning hair, the indented scar on her chin. "What makes you think there's a crime to figure out, a perpetrator to bring to justice?"

"Justice has nothing to do with it, Khun Oraphin. I seek satisfaction and, from your records with forensics, you seem to have a nose for the strange. When you were very young, you were lost in Himmapan for a day, I understand."

A day to my parents; a month to me. It wasn't a bad month—Himmapan is kind to children, and I was twelve going on thirteen, sufficiently young and sufficiently pure—but I returned changed, one of the first to have made the crossing before true convergence. No one believed me, at first, until the parents of another child went on air. Talk shows, taken seriously by nobody, and then a handful of lost children grew to a dozen, a score. We became a generation. Himmapan, the domain of many things, but foremost among them the eagle and the serpent. When I open my hand I half-expect to be clutching a feather the color of clear night, the color of polished cobalt. This is a hallucination that's seated itself deep inside me, parasitic, cancerous.

"I suppose I was, ma'am." I never say anything else. Not the details. Not anything.

"Stop calling me that. You aren't my servant." Her flesh leg twitches; she is trying to cross it, but the other one is insubstantial and does not obey. I wonder if the amputated leg, alone in that room, flexes and pulls with effort. "I was one of the people poring over your case file, back then. It all looked like a threat to national security at the time."

Sixteen years ago. "What'd you like me to do, Khun Jutamat?"

"Help me figure this out," she says. "My fortune isn't going anywhere. It's not inconsiderable—you would know. It would serve a dead woman poorly, but you're alive and prone to stay that way for decades yet. Sort this out and I'll sign it all to you."

Her assets are significant, no denying that. My thoughts dart—avarice is so magnetic—to the possibilities, the fantasies, the horizons out of reach. Money is not all, especially in the changed world, but it is still much. Humanity does not function without a currency. We've knotted ourselves too tight to go back to barter and an exchange of labor, to discard the coins and the notes and the checks. Even those of the forest are becoming like us in that way. "Your family isn't going to be happy with me."

She issues a low chuckle, a sound of paper rustling on wood. "What does it matter, whether they are happy? Come, I'm not dying any slower. The sooner we get started, the better."

To trace any curse, the most obvious and essential first step is to examine the site of its effect, in this case Jutamat's body parts. There will be a piece of buffalo hide, a fragment of tooth or finger-bone, as vector for malice. I imagine the housekeeper on her dainty deer hooves dusting the celadon and polishing the teak floor, precise steps as she cleans around these lost limbs. Not everyone can afford upsorn-sriha staff, hard workers as well as supreme ornaments. All the rage in any establishment of class and currency, any household of taste and opulence. For myself I can't stand those quiet, hooved girls, but I am no tastemaker.

With gloves on—best practice must be followed—I pull down the detached limbs. The hand is first and hardest, speared in place by a reptilian tongue of glistening iron. It bleeds when I bring it down, though Jutamat evinces no reaction save mild amusement. The leg—it is a whole leg, complete, from thigh to tiptoes. Fetching it is simple; handling it less so. The weight of the limb is hot and heavy, confrontational in its gross mortality, the bones and muscles and wrinkled skin at the knees. I seize it around the ankle at first, then reverse my grip when I realize that the position would put the thigh much too close to my face. Maneuvering it awkwardly to a sofa I put it down and try not to think on the intimacy of this. The detachment happened right at the point where it joined the groin, clean.

The leg smells faintly of shower cream, not the cheap type: this is essential oils, bergamot and frankincense, an underlying note of subtle fruits. The poison must have preserved the parts entirely, suspended them in the moment of amputation. "What were you doing when this happened?"

"I'd just come out of a bath. That was the first one." Her voice falters, only just, then resumes smooth: lifetime-practiced control sanding off the edge of trauma. "How does it end?"

"Your head." Not that I have seen it in action but there are reports and studies. Few ailments of supernatural sources have not been catalogued, compared, cross-referenced into mundanity. We forge the changed earth through empiricism and remorseless analysis. The poets and dreamers thought they would be ascendant, but after all it's people like me and Jutamat who thrive. Pragmatists who know how to move through the world, and know how to move it in turn by levers and hand-wheels. "It's mostly painless. As far as I know, ma'am."

Jutamat makes a noise through her teeth, strained and thin and high: distilled panic. "Two to five months, though they say it escalates toward the final stage."

"Do you have enemies?"

"In my profession, at my age, who does not? Unless one is devoted to nothing but pushing pens and shuffling papers. Any number of people, domestic and foreign, would want me gone." She sips from a glass of anchan tea so cold it radiates, mentholated and lambent. "After sixty I'd have thought they would leave me alone to die naturally. I guess not. Should've smoked and drunk more."

The past doesn't relent and deeds like hers don't fade, not that she needs reminding. When I open her detached hand it feels exhibitionist—perhaps voyeuristic?—to be caressing, touching, playing with an older stranger's appendage. Her palm is empty: I'd expected a sliver, a thorn, the swell of a small tooth hiding under skin. The obvious carrier of a curse. If only, for once, existence would oblige by being simple. "Have you been having dreams?" Sleep paralysis, a ghostly face greenly lit. The paranormal is predictable in its symptoms, easier than viruses and cancer to diagnose, more straightforward by far than the caprices of human flesh.

"No dreams. No, that's not quite true. One dream. A khrut. Young. Female. Four arms. She's sitting on a chair. Blue like her feathers." Her expression pinches: this is not a woman used to sharing her dreams. "She's singing, I suppose, but there is no sound. Like you are receiving faulty signal, visual without auditory."

I look at the leg, perfunctory, pushing at the skin and peering behind the knee. "I will need to consult."

"Who, a shaman?"

"No." The leg falls from my hand and rests, limp, on the table. It will leave smudges on the glass and the housekeeper will have to wipe that away. She will have to put the limbs somewhere, too, arrange them in neat order. Maybe a mannequin, custom-made to Jutamat's build. "I will get back to you as soon as possible."

Throughout all this, she has not asked how to stop the toxin of unmaking. Some curses are like the common flu. Others are cousin to genetic defects, unliftable, incurable. It sits there inside, cystic slag hardening to fossil, a seismic fault-line in the soul. The only answer is passage into the next life.

Reincarnation is the true panacea.

There's nothing magical about Krungthep. The writers and artists were wrong, and what once resided within their fantasias and imagination are now everyday—everywhere. Metaphor and allegory no longer serve, having turned literal overnight. Even the statues and stencils in Suvarnaphum have come alive, adopted as vessels for the creatures they once depicted as fictional. What is the point of words on pages, or nielloware etchings or delicate carved ivory, when the genuine articles are full of voice and viscera?

It's strange: others who have wandered into Himmapan as children, the ones I know, none of them turned to art when they grew up. Not painting or sculpting, not the piano or the jakhe, neither verse nor prose. Those from the forest make better images and music than we do in any case. Maybe we are *meant* for brute industry and surgical calculation while they are built for the rest, including philosophy.

Every time need summons me to Suvarnaphum, I bring vast quantities of food. They trend red, a menu selected for the carnivore's palate. The giants can eat fruits and vegetables like anyone else, but they enjoy those no more than a child, and unlike a child they don't need to worry about cavities, caloric intake, diabetic futures. Himmapan beings can eat as much as they like, gobbling up carcinogens and cholesterol with no cost or effect.

The giants make their home where first-class passengers used to check into Thai Airways, under a pavilion of banana leaves that never brown. Few travelers venture near for fear of the giants' appetite, and not without reason. There have been disappearances, though never remains. There have been questions, though never investigations. I do know for a fact that the giants are tremendous eaters and that they leave no bones.

All three are home today, reclining on cushions made from hammered bronze and holding plates made from black nacre. Empty. Around them, the walls gleam with tableaus of holiness. Prince Siddhartha stepping on the lotuses of his birth; Prince Siddhartha forsaking his palace to seek the ascetic's path; Prince Siddhartha triumphing over demonic temptation.

As one the giants look at me, or at least turn their attention. Each of them has four faces apiece with eyes to match, their gazes reading existence in compound. Their faces are theatrical masks, red and blue and green, bristling tusks like machetes. Wood and acrylic transmuted to sinew and iron. I've asked them why they don't wear their own flesh and get answers in verse that leave me no more enlightened. They have an abiding love of Sanskrit, which I never bothered learning (does anyone, who was once spirited away?); that is the province of a government liaison (I avoid that entire division—too many fetishists).

"Child," one of them says, "you did not come empty-handed; we can smell."

This is a ritual—they don't talk without a bribe. The styrofoam boxes I brought are damp with blood and grease: cartilage flavored hot and sour, dripping meat just barely rare, plastic jars of namprik and dry chili. Pork, beef, the animal is nearly moot. As long as it is flesh that once belonged to a walking creature, flesh that once housed cardiac muscles the size of a fist. I don't think much of vegetarianism, but if anything could turn me herbivorous it would be them, not religion or even health problems.

Once they have filled their plates, the blue one says, "You look in want of a tale."

The green one chuckles, a sound like a landslide about to begin. "We tell stories not to excite or intrigue, but to harden their truth."

(*Don't you have names?* I asked. *The crunch of femur and the slide of tongue on new guts*, they said. I didn't ask again. You could call them Morrakot, Tuptim, and Pailin, but those are such soft names next to their predator might.)

"I don't. I need to know—" My breath trembles, cuts short, a juddering knock against my teeth. "I need to know if Panthajinda is alive."

They look at one another. Enough eyes to spare, still, to look at me too. "You left a wound in Himmapan, child." This from the red one, though they all have the same voice, asphalt and seismic calculus. "It seeks to restore itself, in khrut-shape or not."

I was a child, I could say; I did not know what I was doing. But the actual meat of it, the reality, is what it is and will not bend to my excuses. "Let me talk to her." What remains of her.

The green giant opens their mouth, and keeps opening. Past the unhinging of jaw it opens, a gaping hole lined with bright tongues and red teeth. I have seen it before, and don't look away, but it's not a sight

I wish on anyone. The tongues and teeth roar and blur into a vermillion haze. Himmapan colors bleed into that with difficulty. Sometimes I don't think the giants are from the forest at all; it is a place of green and gold and opal radiance while the giants are red on red inside, a hungry insatiable mass.

The image stabilizes and there is Panthajinda, enthroned, eyes shut. When I left her and Himmapan, we were both children, but her echo—spirit remnant, dregs at cup's end—has aged, tall and strong, her four arms immaculate. Two for the wings, two for human things. Droplets of water in her black-sun hair, on her gilded throat. She looks asleep; of course she looks asleep, a goddess at rest.

How do you begin to apologize, even if it wasn't your fault. How do you start to grieve, when you are as good as the murderer. The giants don't judge or condemn, but they don't have to.

We don't talk; what communication occurs is at a preverbal level, the sensation of elevating pulse and heart knotting into stone, the memory of dying. Wisdom passes from her to me in impressionistic blots, truths on mortality and samsara that turn like barbed wheels. The dead don't have secrets to keep. They tell you everything, everything. All you need to do is ask, all you need to have is the stomach to bear.

I promised myself I wouldn't cry; it leaves me small and brittle, robbed of dignity. I break this promise, every time.

On the train ride home I watch a girl, seventeen maybe, compulsively blotting her face. Sheet after sheet; she is too sweaty and the air conditioning too sluggish. At the far end of the carriage, two kinnaree murmur in quiet conversation, fair salaries and weather, the merits of birdseed and imported fruits. Their foreheads and noses produce no excess sebum. Their eyelashes are voluminous without the requirement of mascara, their lips pink without the assistance of lipstick, their skin lustrous and poreless without the help of foundation. Enough of them and the cosmetics industry will go extinct entirely. Himmapan women make farang supermodels look pickled and haggard, farang celebrities overpainted and swollen with botox.

Back at my apartment, I take out the lockbox that has accompanied me from move to move down the years, home to dormitory to apartment. It's small and mundane, a dial lock to guard it and not much else. Few pieces of jewelry are attached to my name and all of them reside here, but the diva of the show is this: two bangles beaten thread-thin, clinched together by a star sapphire. The one gift from Panthajinda that she intended to be the first of many. Funny really; it was given to a child, but somehow it's stretched as my wrist grew, the gold so soft and so warm. I rarely wear it. For two days I don't leave my apartment, pulling blackout curtains over the windows, double-bolting my door, switching off my phone. An anechoic chamber, liberated from human interaction.

On the third day, I return to Khun Jutamat's house, the bangles gleaming on my wrist. I'm dehydrated, famished, and my head is full of feathers.

She isn't home, but one of her staff lets me in on her instruction. Wait in the garden, they say; she'll be back shortly from the hospital. Perhaps some miracle cure has been found, last-minute. Most likely not.

Her garden overlooks the Chaopraya, which isn't what it used to be, that mucky sewage-blighted self. After Himmapan and Krungthep collided the river has been running clear, its skin lacerated nacreous white, smelling of cleanness and paya-nak and—toward the sea— mermaids. To filth the waters is to court incredible misfortune, swifter and harsher than falling apart slowly. So much converges, so much moves inexorably. What Himmapan brought is not magic but consequence. What happens to us, inside, is a wasteland.

The upsorn-sriha housekeeper steps, dainty, onto the verandah. The tray she carries holds a perspiring glass. Her eyes are downcast, demure. You always forget the damage an upsorn-sriha can do, they all have this look of harmless grace, their delicate feet made for running. Away, you think, because of the folktales. Kinnaree, upsorn-sriha, makkalee fruits, all the girlish things of the forest who exist to be captured, painted, admired.

I take the glass, gazing into it, the milky tea. Its flat, bright orange the same color a child might shade in a sun. I think of drinking it in one big gulp, emptying the glass just like that and grinding the ice to dust in my mouth. "Is this painful?"

"Pardon, ma'am?" Even her voice is ordinary. Her face too, plain and homely as though she's been particularly cursed among a species made for breathtaking beauty.

"Whatever you added to the tea. Will it put me to sleep without pain, or do you mean for me to suffer like Khun Jutamat did? Or worse."

Her gaze meets mine, direct, before fixing on the bangle. The star sapphire that is so like the color of Panthajinda's wings. "She was meant to be a queen among khrut."

"I remember you now." A handmaiden, or childhood companion. Panthajinda didn't give her much attention during the time I was in Himmapan; I was novel while the upsorn-sriha was not. She used to hover just out of sight, dutiful and a little sad, I thought. "You must've been there when she died."

"She wouldn't have been there near the river, had you not slipped. So close to the territory of her enemies. They were at war; still are."

It's not as though I need reminding. The war between nak and khrut, that forever enmity between those of the water and the sky. Serpent against eagle. As a child I didn't understand it; as a child I thought only of Himmapan as a vast playground, freer than any Krungthep street. "I couldn't have known." That the nak would drag her in and drown her; that her wings—strong on land, impossibly mighty in flight—would be deadweight in water, no use at all. "She was a child."

"She would have grown to rule and command. They destroyed her as they would any weapon. I will avenge her, but their logic wasn't unsound."

The nak spared me, once my purpose as bait was past. Because I was a human child, they said, and to take a mortal life was a sin. Not so with another of Himmapan kind. With others of the forest, any tactic was permissible, any death a justification unto itself. "Would this even bring her back?" Killing Jutamat, killing me.

She stares at me, unblinking. Do deer need to blink, I wonder. "It's not the flesh—Khun Jutamat, like you, is mortal—but the essence, the karmic heft. Some are bound for better destinies than others. You should pay for what you did, but your place on the wheel is far beneath what I require. Khun Jutamat is gold. You are dross."

How strange that the spymaster is, evidently, possessed of greater virtue than most. Than me, though that's no surprise. "What is still there..." My breath comes out thin. "It's not her anymore."

The first hint of anger: "What do you know about my liege."

Nothing, nothing at all. An image, a memory. The dead bears no resemblance, a distant cousin to their living selves. Less. "How many more do you need?" Counting cargo, reducing it to simple arithmetic.

"If I find a single shining soul, rich and pure, it will suffice to give her a new body. I will need nothing more."

"Isn't this prohibited for you." Human lives: Jutamat's and whoever else's, before and after. How many in total, I could ask, balancing a checkbook. Murders against one resurrection, crimes against one act of reparation.

Her hands twitch; her shoulders coil, tense. "I may be exiled. But I will see her back."

Isn't that what love is like, after all. What I feel for—about—Panthajinda is tangled in an ideal. I slide the bangles off my wrist, hold them out to the upsorn-sriha whose name I have not asked (and would she tell me? No). "Take it. More yours than mine."

She might move to slap it out of my hands, out of pride. Instead she takes those thin gold threads and puts them onto her wrist. Slimmer than mine, and already the bangles appear to fit as though they'd been made just for her. She doesn't offer, *But she would have wanted you to keep them.* No quarter.

When she's gone, I drink the tea. Not too sweet, not too much condensed milk. It's just right and it's just tea, unburdened by the acrimonious acid of poison or curse.

When she was still alive, I asked Panthajinda what Himmapan would have been like untouched by human imagination; how the wars would have played out, how each race would have evolved, deific and alien. *Meeting you is the best thing that ever happened to me, Oraphin,* she said. *I can't wait to see your Krungthep, all your skyscrapers, all your lights. We could go to school together.* After she died, I asked her again, and it was then I learned that the dead do not use words, do not speak. Instead she showed me an image, a dark line stretching forever, drinking all light: an event horizon, full of ruin, the endpoint of Himmapan crossing over. There is no room for dreamers.

On the way out I take a final look at Jutamat's lost, forlorn limbs, stacked together in the living room. Two legs, one arm. Soon she will be simply a human torso, and then not even that. Maybe that is the future. An epidemic of disassembly and all of us lying exposed, apart, awaiting the end.

I will be there too. By then Panthajinda will have come back, picking a path through the vision she foresaw. She will glide on her taloned feet, the upsorn-sriha at her side, and stop by my body. For one last time, I will see her again.

I Will Make You Remember Me

H. Pueyo

Cacau arrived late in the afternoon, when Sebastián Minami was about to close the office he rented every month. The two had exchanged some emails during the past week, and he only knew a few things about her: she was a Brazilian immigrant in desperate need of a private eye, and didn't want to discuss her case until she met him in person. Not that it mattered. He was about to take a well-deserved break from work, there was no need to know any further information. She could—and should—find somebody else to help her.

"Do you know Mr. Minami?"

Sebastián looked left and right, pretending to find an imaginary secretary in his disorganized cubicle before adjusting his round rimmed glasses.

"That would be me."

"Oh," she murmured, still touching the frosted glass of the door with her fingers. "I'm sorry, I didn't mean to—"

"It doesn't matter. You wouldn't be the first to ask." Sebastián began to tidy his desk. He regretted not using Callari, his father's surname, to avoid this kind of situation, since every time he used his mother's name he heard all types of uncomfortable comments, and they all began with *I never would have guessed...* "I'm sorry to say I have bad news for you, miss... Romero, right? I know why you're here, but I'm about to go on vacation, and can't help with your case."

"You don't know why I'm here."

Correct—he didn't. What he did know was that his head was about to explode with an ache that began from behind his left eye, and all he could do to ease the pain was knead the sensitive area with one hand while the other searched for the blister pack in the pocket of his tweed sport coat.

"Try me, then."

"I need someone to investigate my past," said Cacau, firmer than before. "I don't remember anything."

Sebastián swallowed a pink pill without water.

"I'm afraid repressed memories are out of my jurisdiction, miss," he said, closing his laptop to put it inside his satchel. "Why don't you decode? There's a clinic in this building, if you're interested. Fourth floor, room 43."

"For the same reason you haven't done it." Cacau pointed at the blue box hidden behind a pile of books that said *Dolofrix Forte, codeine phosphate and paracetamol.* "I don't want any lunatic who studied three months of neuroengineering messing with my head. Why do you need those pills?"

"Fair enough," said Sebastián, walking toward the door. He was much taller than her, and had to bend to maintain eye contact. "You have one dinner to convince me to accept your case. But you'll pay."

There was a restaurant he enjoyed at the corner of the street of his office, cheap and calm, with the same old waiters and the same old clients, in a familiar porteño fashion. Sebastián liked their food and the comfort of his routine, but he avoided taking women there for two reasons: the patronage was mostly masculine, and it was not an adequate scenario for a date. But this was a business meeting, and she was the one trying to impress him, not the contrary.

Cacau glanced at the men with the corner of her narrow black eyes—the cook, the waiters, the other clients talking to each other and laughing out loud. Finally, she decided for a table near the window, away from everybody else.

"I'm listening," said Sebastián. The waiter brought their drinks and a basket of bread. "Lucky for you it's not an extramarital case."

"It started when I moved from Porto Alegre two years ago." Cacau played with the bottle of grapefruit soda bubbling in front of her, thin white scars visible in the pale yellow skin of her fingers and wrist. "The problem lies in the fact that I don't remember the first six months of my time here. Whenever I try, my mind goes blank."

"Do you remember why you decided to come to Buenos Aires?"

"I don't remember *anything*, Mr. Minami."

"College, maybe?"

"I didn't even finish high school."

"How old are you?"

"Twenty-three," answered Cacau.

He was surprised to see she was not as young as he had imagined, but it was still too young to find her attractive. *Ten less than me.*

"Work?"

"I work at home."

"Which field?"

"Art."

"Family?"

She pressed her lips together. "My parents arc dead."

Sebastián narrowed his hazel eyes behind the glasses. The waiter appeared with two milanesas: a regular steak for him and a vegetarian one for her, both with salad, lemon, and French fries. He had to admit to himself that her problem fascinated him; he guessed the gap in her memory was caused by a traumatic event, but he didn't know if that alone could erase six months of a person's life.

"I might be interested, Ms. Romero, but…"

"Wait," Cacau interrupted him, glaring at the table of blue-collar workers eating and making jokes on the other side of the restaurant. "Are they taking pictures?"

"Pictures?"

Sebastián turned around. The men were eating pizza and taking pictures of their meeting, but there was nothing extraordinary about it: only laughter, conversation and a good amount of beer.

"I think so."

"I have to go," mumbled Cacau, getting to her feet. She threw several pesos in front of him, and ran toward the entrance door.

"Miss…" Sebastián tried to say, but his eyes were focused on the table. It was too much money, and she had eaten only half of her food. He hurried to pay the bill, and ran outside to find her.

Cacau was sitting on the pavement, a ghost under the soft light of the lampposts. Her dark eyes were lost on the cars that came and went and on the swift pace of passersby, but seemed unable to compute what she saw, making her look like a statue instead of a person.

Sebastián took a pack of cigarettes from his coat and placed one between his lips before sitting by her side.

"Do you smoke?"

Cacau didn't answer. Her hands were holding the lower part of her red t-shirt, twisting, twisting. The smoke of his cigarette danced with the wind, reminding Sebastián that it was too cold to be outside at this time of the year.

"What was that about?" Sebastián tossed the change into her lap, and it fell between her arms onto the washed-out jeans of her overalls.

"I don't like pictures," said Cacau, her voice devoid of any feeling. She turned to him, looking at his shoes. "Detective?"

"Sebastián."

"Would you mind taking me home?"

A strange request, but Sebastián didn't question it. He called a cab and repeated the address murmured by her, and they were left in front of a nice old building in Caballito. Thinking that would be all, he began to walk toward the nearest subway station, but Cacau grabbed his sleeve and pointed at the door with her chin.

"Wanna come in?"

The rest happened too quickly. Cacau guided him to the elevator and kissed him, Sebastián pulled aside the straps of her overalls and lifted her shirt, pressing her body against the mirror of the elevator. She smiled, unbuckling his pants, not at all like the flinching girl he found in the street.

"This is considerably unethical, Ms. Romero," said Sebastián, lifting her by the thighs. It wasn't the first time he had done something like this, and he was afraid it wouldn't be the last.

"Maybe I like unethical," replied Cacau. "Do you?"

Sun crept through the windows of the living room, forcing Sebastián to open his eyes. Pink melted into strokes of orange and white, telling him it was early morning and reminding him of where he was. He had slept in Cacau's bed until the middle of the night, but a particularly strong headache woke him up, and he spent forty minutes walking through the living room until he was able to take a nap on the couch.

Her apartment was bright and colorful, with shelves full of books, knitted pillows, plastic blue and green glasses scattered on a round wooden table, and several illustrations hanging on the walls. The paintings were all of women: naked, delicate, dismembered, their ethereal expressions embellished by viscera, bloodless and soft, peaceful corpses unaware of their own fatalities.

"You almost gave me a heart attack," said a small voice behind his back. Her pixie black hair was disheveled, and Cacau wore only his shirt and a pair of black panties. "I forgot we fucked last night."

"I didn't mean to scare you."

"I don't usually allow guys I sleep with stay in my house, that's why." Cacau made a sign for him to follow her to a narrow kitchen. She poured a glass of orange juice for him, and drank the rest from the bottle. "Sorry for yesterday, by the way. I don't know what happened to me."

"It was definitely an unusual start to an investigation." Sebastián smiled and rubbed his eyes. The soreness had traveled to his shoulders, causing waves of pain that went from his neck to his lower back. "We can start whenever you want."

"Want facturas before we start?" Cacau offered a brown paper bag full of buttery pastries: milk buns, cream puffs, little cannons filled with dulce de leche, and a couple of crescent-shaped medialunas.

Sebastián chose one dripping with sugar and took a bite.

"Are you running away from the subject, Miss?"

"If you saw me naked, you can call me Cacau. What do you need?"

"First, I'd like to see what you have here. Bills, tickets, journals, anything that helps me reconstruct your life from two years ago."

"Sure, but I'm a bit of a hoarder." Cacau walked to her bedroom and Sebastián followed, taking with him the juice and the facturas. "Things can be hard to find."

Her bedroom was just like the rest of the house, with adorned walls and gleeful sheets, Christmas lights hanging over the headboard, tons of notebooks, and art supplies. There were unpacked boxes inside the wardrobe, clothes of all kinds, stuffed animals hidden in a drawer, plastic dolls, and countless objects that seemed to have no point besides random collection.

"Those are the things I brought from Brazil." Cacau pointed at three cardboard boxes. "I never opened them because it's just paper and I didn't know where to put it."

Sebastián tied his brown hair in a low ponytail, and both of them sat cross-legged on the floor.

"When did you realize that your memories were missing?

"A couple of months ago, taking a bath." Cacau licked her fingers after eating another pastry. "I was washing my hair and lost consciousness for a couple of minutes. When I woke up, I started to think about it until I realized I couldn't remember what I did during the first months here."

"You passed out in the shower?" Sebastián raised his arched eyebrows.

"It's nothing serious. I wasn't hurt."

"Go on."

"This paper says I rented this apartment half a year after the trip." Cacau stretched her small body to open another drawer, and gave him the papers: contracts, rent, passport, even the bus ticket of her trip. "The problem is that I don't know what I did or where I stayed before that."

Sebastián skimmed the papers, and stopped when he found a three by four picture of Cacau with a shaved head before turning his attention to the notebooks, the only photograph he would find in her entire house. The other boxes had nothing particularly personal, consisting mostly of sketchbooks with the same disturbing images he saw in the living room, and some notebooks that had never been unpacked.

"Are you sure you never decoded?" asked Sebastián. Cacau looked into his eyes for an instant before focusing on a dot on the floor. "Passing out is a common side effect, especially in illegal clinics. It's also common for ex-addicts: you might feel a strong revulsion, or even pass out if in contact with the source of addiction."

"I think I would know if I had." Cacau frowned. "Doesn't everyone?"

102

"There's also the money factor. You don't seem like you would be able to afford it." Sebastián grabbed another cream puff. "Not memory removal, at least."

"You know a lot about decoding. Why?"

"I almost did it once."

"For the cluster headaches?"

"How did you know?"

"Gut instinct. Besides, I had those for years. Spent a great deal of my teens in hospitals." Cacau smiled, proud of her deduction. "Your eye drops, your voice changes, and you're constantly covering your eye with your hand," she added, pretending to remove her own eyeball. "I did that too."

"You'd be a good investigator, but you're not entirely right," answered Sebastián. "Ever heard of the Ezeiza killer?"

Her pitch-black eyes sparkled when he said the name.

"The one who raped and killed six women? The bodies were found near the airport. I followed the case," said Cacau, too excited for someone who had just "followed" the story. "He got caught after kidnapping a cop."

"Me."

"*You?*"

"Not the killer, of course." Sebastián grinned. "The cop."

"You're a cop?"

"Not anymore, as you can see. No. I was fired after that."

Cacau crawled to his side, looking at Sebastián intently.

"Because you were kidnapped? That's unfair."

"Of course not," Sebastián replied, and his temples began to throb. "I was fired because I was addicted to morphine and refused to decode, not because of that incident."

"Oh."

"I tell you this because you're not very orthodox yourself." Sebastián shook a piece of paper with another violent illustration. "Obsessing over serial killers and all."

"Your headaches started after that?"

"Why, did yours start after something?"

"I don't know," said Cacau. "I don't remember when they started."

"Well, I do. It's somewhat pathetic, in retrospective." Sebastián closed his eyes, still feeling drowsy. Sometimes, even when he was happy and productive, there was an imaginary hand burying itself into his left eye, trying to pull whatever was inside him out, just like Cacau had described. Then, it was gone, as fast as it had begun. "The doctor said the stress likely caused the cluster headaches and the fibromyalgia, and that both could *at least* have been mitigated by decoding."

He tried to sound as casual as possible, but his throat dried up and the pain got worse. *I don't care, he told himself like a mantra. I don't care anymore, I can talk about it.* But, unlike Cacau, he did remember the source of his stress, and his face, his eyes, his sweat, the ceiling of the shipping container, the six hours inside of it, and every bit of his body that hurt, and kept hurting without any reason after so long.

"Why didn't you decode, then? Money?"

"No, my department was willing to cover everything. It was a scandal, you see." His long fingers touched the leather cover of a notebook. "The downside was that they would have the right to access all my memories regarding the case, which I found distasteful."

"But…"

"Miss Cacau," he interrupted her, tired of talking about himself, and lifted three rolls of untouched wrapping papers. "You're not a bit of a hoarder. You are one."

Cacau opened her mouth to reply, but a piece of paper fell on his lap, from the inside of one of the rolls. Sebastián held it in front of his face: the note had been folded many times and had signs of the years, but the writing was still legible, and it clearly belonged to her. There, written many times as if Cacau was trying to remember something important, were seven usernames: mariadagraca01, mariadagraca02, mariadagraca03…

"Who is Maria da Graça?"

"I need a favor, Javi," Sebastián started, holding his last cigarette while looking at the screen of his phone. The man on the other side of the line grunted.

"Again? That's all you ask nowadays: favors, favors, favors! What am I, your business associate?"

"As you know, I don't have many friends," he chuckled, trying to find his lighter. "Come on. Write it down."

"Tell me."

"I need any information you might find about a Brazilian immigrant called Cacau Romero da Silva."

"Who?" His old workmate was the only person he still talked to besides his clients, and it wasn't uncommon for him to help Sebastián with private investigations.

"My new client."

"Is Cacau a male or a female name?"

"It means 'cocoa' in Portuguese," replied Sebastián. "Not sure about the gender."

"It's a girl, right? You only ask me to help when you fuck the client, you promiscuous slut."

"It's important, I swear."

"Yeah, sure." Javier sighed, sounding disproportionately tired. "Is that all?"

"Another thing," Sebastián said, smoke covering his own face. "I also need any information you can find on someone called Maria da Graça."

Sebastián and Cacau were lying on the floor of her living room, staring at the ceiling. Both of them were shirtless, and the private eye was trying to find any relevant clue about her on his phone.

"Are you sure you don't know any Maria?"

"I already told you." Cacau rolled eyes, stretching. Rows of scars covered her arms, hands, thighs, and some were scattered between her legs. "That's a really common name. It could be anyone. Why are you obsessed with it?"

"Gut instinct. I feel like that paper is important. Maybe she was an enemy?" He suggested, his left palm covering his eyebrow and epicanthic fold. "An ex? A friend who posted a picture you didn't like on social media? You still didn't tell me why you hate pictures."

"I just don't like them." Cacau rolled over his chest, taking the phone from his hand. "Can't we do that later?"

"I thought you wanted to discover what happened to your memories as soon as possible." Sebastián tried to ignore her breasts touching his stomach, and pulled the phone back.

"I'm thinking about giving up," she said out of nowhere, her hand toying with the zipper of his pants. "Maybe I'm wrong and my memory just sucks."

"Are you dismissing me?"

"If you're fucking me just because I'm paying you, then yes, of course I am." Cacau laid on her back again. "If you want to keep doing it, no."

"Cacau," Sebastián tried to argue. "I'm confident I can…"

"You know what? I invented it." Cacau offered an almost perfect replica of a smile. "Sorry. I guess I was bored."

She was lying. Sebastián could see it in her round face, in her low voice, in her blank eyes. She was not only lying—it pained her to do so.

"I don't believe it."

"I lie, Sebastián," Cacau insisted, shaking him by the arm as if he was denying the obvious. "That's what I do. Everybody knows."

"Who's everybody?"

Her lower lip began to tremble. Perhaps they were, indeed, in the realm of repressed memories, because he felt like he was touching something, a feeling so raw and intimate she was unable to completely hide within herself. Cacau covered her chest with her hands, despite the fact that he was not looking or even thinking of touching her.

"You don't understand." Cacau looked even more fragile, twisting her body to hide herself from him. "I'm going to pay you for the time you lost in this nonsense, but this investigation is over. I'm not someone like you, who went through something serious; my memory is just horrible, I shouldn't have bothered you with this..."

"I want to continue more than ever."

"There's nothing, there's really nothing, nothing, nothing!" Cacau shook her head repeatedly, getting more aggressive as she continued. The fingers that covered her light skin turned into claws, grasping meat and forming red lines in her breasts to rip them apart. "I'm sorry I made you believe in me—I'm stupid, stupid, stupid, I always fuck up like this! I invent problems to complain about them, it's nothing, Sebastián, it's nothing!"

It was nothing, he remembered himself saying after leaving the container. *It was nothing. You're overreacting for nothing.*

"You gave me enough proof to believe that's not true."

Cacau stopped talking, glaring at one of the shelves with wide eyes. Then, she began to laugh.

"Which proof? Gut instinct's no proof, that's the problem! You don't even have a proof I even forgot a thing!"

"You're the proof!" It was his time to shake her, holding her shoulders. "There is a reason you forgot, but the proof is written all over your body, in your reactions, your scars, the ones you did and the ones you clearly didn't. I knew in the moment you ran from that restaurant that...!"

"Stop, stop, stop! Stop allowing me to be a spoiled brat, stop touching me, stop, stop...!" Cacau squirmed out of his arms, running toward the kitchen, but Sebastián caught her again.

"Cacau, listen to me." Sebastián held her by the head, forcing her to look at his face. When he did, he realized there was something under her hair, a volume that should not exist.

Cacau had no chance to answer. The second he touched the protuberance in her scalp, her eyes went white, and she passed out.

His phone vibrated, and Sebastián stared at the screen. The only reason he accepted it was because it had Javi's face attached under the contact name, and he needed more than ever to believe there was a clue to be followed in Cacau's case.

"You found something?"

"Good night to you too, asshole," answered Javier.

Sebastián crossed legs, sitting at the side of Cacau's bed while she slept.

"Yes or no?"

"I'm emailing you the info I got on the Romero girl, but it's not much. Just basic data, and some tracks on what she did here. Nothing illegal."

"Did she decode?"

"Eh?" Javier sounded confused. Sebastián took a deep breath before continuing:

"Neurodecoding. Did she?"

"Not that I know."

"Okay. What about Maria da Graça?"

"This is where things get tricky," Javier said. "It's a very common name in Brazil, apparently. There's a celebrity with the same name, and a district in Rio de Janeiro."

"I'm aware."

"*But* I know some guys from the Brazilian border, and I'm trying to contact them. So stay tuned, and check your inbox."

"Thank you." Sebastián ended the call and looked at her again.

After Cacau lost consciousness, he dressed her, took her to bed, and checked the back of her head. There, below the thick strands, were three rough scars with wire ports, typical of clandestine decoding.

"Hey," Cacau murmured, yawning. She had brown circles underneath her eyes and her lips were dry.

"You passed out."

"I know."

"Cacau…"

"Decoding scars," she interrupted him, predicting his next words. "She has them."

"What?"

"*Me*. I have them."

"Yes," Sebastián agreed, stroking her hair. Cacau placed her hand over his, trying to find the ports as well.

"That's why I pass out. It's the security system."

"Well, you wanted a concrete proof—now you have it."

It was the sixth clinic he entered and left without any progress. With it went his hopes of not driving or taking the subway, as one of the clinics was located inside his building, and the others were near his house. His entire body hurt now, from the neck and back to the wrists and knees. Sebastián chewed on a pill, allowing its bitter taste to contaminate his gum.

"Have you seen this woman?" Again and again he asked, showing a picture of Cacau with a shaved head, ready to complete the procedure. Only in the eighth clinic did he have a positive response, this time from the secretary.

"I saw that one, I did," said the woman with a lazy voice. "In college."

Sebastián frowned. "Can you please tell me more?"

"Strange girl. A bit of an accent." She took the picture from his hand, and traced Cacau's face with a fingertip. "Maria something, I think."

"Maria?" Sebastián echoed, trying to keep a straight face. The list of names returned to his head. "Yes, Maria. Did you study together?"

"Oh no, I was just the librarian," the secretary continued. "She studied that neuro stuff. Always after the decoding books. Day after day. Asked me an awful lot of questions when she found out I worked here part time. Then she quit and I never saw her again."

"Can you help me with something?"

It took her a small fee to accept, but with it he was able to access the library database with the woman's card, and found not only the fake personal data of Cacau (Maria da Graça da Silva, 24 years old, Neural Engineering), but all the books she rented (*The Brain as Software, The Brain as Hardware, Decoding: A Step Towards Transhumanism...*).

Sebastián shoved the books inside his bag, and took them to her apartment. *Here's the lunatic who studied three months of neuroengineering*, he wanted to say. Instead, he began to talk as soon as he crossed the door:

"I found Maria da Graça." Sebastián showed one of the covers. "It's you."

"What?"

"This is the name you used during the months you don't remember, probably to decode yourself," Sebastián continued, talking with the characteristic local accent that made everyone sound like they were singing. "I'm still not sure what the usernames mean, but I think now we can safely assume you erased your own memory. The question is: why?"

"Sebastián." Cacau was still standing in front of the door, holding one of the books against her chest. "I'm not a scientist."

"My guess is that you were studying this for a while. Remember what you told me when we met? You don't want someone messing with your head. So you did it yourself."

"Is that even safe?"

"You tell me."

"I have no idea what you're talking about."

"This is it, Cacau!" His usual calm voice turned frantic. "This is the answer you were searching for! You erased your own memories, but to retrieve them…"

Cacau leaned against the wall, like her body could no longer hold her weight.

"I have to decode again."

Sebastián's expression softened when he saw her face, so sad, so lost, and he smiled.

"I can be there with you, if you want me to."

Cacau closed her eyes, sitting on a dental chair to wait for the procedure. The room was tiny and clean, at least compared to the filthy corridor they had to go through to reach the clinic, with cables snaking through the floor like black snakes. Sebastián sat by her side on a stool, watching as the doctor connected two thick wires to the back of her head. Once, he had almost been in her place, but now he didn't know what to expect.

"I'm ready." Cacau took a deep breath, and he touched her shoulder, flattening the striped shirt she was wearing.

"It'll be quick, since she has the ports already," said the doctor, eyes focused on the screen. "Since her head's prepared, there's no need for surgery. Which is good for you, it makes it cheaper."

"Is that all?" Sebastián asked, concerned. The screen didn't show any image, unlike what he imagined, and just looked like an antique computer with black screen and green numbers, files and letters. "Her mind?"

The doctor chuckled.

"In a way, yeah. Are you sure about the date of the deleted files?"

"Memories," corrected Sebastián. "But yes."

"There's nothing here." The doctor typed quickly on a keyboard that covered a large portion of the desk. "She really went all the way. Let me try something else."

Sebastián watched in silence, and a long list of names popped in the screen:

mariadagraca01.dec
mariadagraca02.dec
mariadagraca03.dec
mariadagraca04.dec
mariadagraca05.dec
mariadagraca06.dec
mariadagraca07.dec

"There!" He pointed at the names, his heart racing. "Those are the files we're searching for."

"I'll restore them, then."

Cacau squeezed Sebastián's hand, small fingers wrapped around his. The first file began to load on the screen, and her body convulsed, chest and limbs quivering like she was receiving an electric shock.

"NO!" yelled Cacau. Her cheeks lost color, and cold sweat formed in her forehead. "No, no, stop this, please, no, no, *no!*"

She tried to reach the wires behind her head, but both men jumped to stop her.

"Don't let her!" the doctor warned, trying to stop her with one hand. "If she plugs off now, she might have permanent brain damage, and I don't want to get arrested."

Sebastián crouched to hug Cacau with his thin arms. "Cacau," he whispered, face against her face. "You need to calm down."

"If he doesn't stop right now, I *will* pull the wires."

"You chose to do this, remember?"

"I know what the name means. Maria—" She touched her own head, fingers curled around short strands of black hair. "I know I said I wanted this… And I do, I still do, but not like this, not here, not all at the same time…"

Sebastián looked at the doctor. "I don't think she can handle it."

"The file might be corrupted if I stop now. I can't take responsibility."

But Cacau was lost in thought, far from himself and the clinic, far from Buenos Aires, in a private place no one could reach her. Sebastián nodded, and the other man canceled the restoration process, unplugging the wires from her head after turning off the computer. They stayed silent on the subway train, and only talked again in the elevator of her building:

"I don't want to do this ever again." Her hand touched the lower part of his shirt, trembling. "It's not the right way."

"Want to talk about it?"

"No." Cacau pulled him closer, rubbing her face against his chest and using one of her free hands to open the button of his pants. "I don't want to talk anymore."

Someone knocked on the door. Sebastián would rather stay in bed, but he forced his sore limbs to move and checked the spyhole. The person on the other side of the door was not the one he wished to see, but Javier, whistling distractedly and looking at the wall. He unlocked the door, wearing the same clothes as the day before and smelling like cigarettes and beer.

"What do you want?"

"I should quit being your friend," complained Javier, slapping his face with two stapled files. "You're talking like I'm not doing you a favor."

"Sorry. I'm not feeling great."

He really wasn't. Cacau stopped contacting after the last time they had sex, and didn't answer any of his subsequent messages. Usually, he wouldn't have cared—he spent years telling himself that he would choose casual sex over commitment any day, but ending what they had, whatever it was, left a bitter taste in his mouth.

"This might make you happier," said Javier, but he stopped to make a strange expression. "Or not. It's not the most exciting read."

"What are you talking about?"

"Maria da Graça, of course!" Javier sat on a chair, and offered a cigarette. "I found her."

"Found her?" Javier blinked several times, as if he wasn't speaking proper Spanish. "What do you mean?"

"Listen. I'm not working for her anymore. She dumped me."

"Maria?"

"No, Cacau," grunted Sebastián, trying to find another blister pack in the pockets of his coat. "They're the same person."

"Oh, so you already know," commented Javier. "You're probably feeling like shit. I mean, I told you so! It's not a good idea to get involved with clients."

"I am, in fact, feeling like shit, thank you for noticing."

"Then don't read it." Javier hid the files, covering the front page with his own jacket. "It's depressing. And graphic. Thank god I don't work with this kind of case. I'd kill myself."

Sebastián squinted eyes, and stole the files from his hands. Javi tried to get them back, but Sebastián was taller and willing to behave like a child.

"Seriously, dude. Not the right time."

"Thank you for your help!" Sebastián used his best telemarketing voice, and guided him to the entrance. "Off you go."

After locking the door, he sat on the sofa with the papers in hand. He needed to do something: to see, read, to give her the answers she sought and might already have. Part of him—many parts, *all* of him—was desperate to understand Cacau, and a hint of fear and excitement brewed in his chest when he opened the file.

Unfortunately, no determination in the world prepared him for the nausea he felt after reading the first line. The report described a large police operation eleven years ago, focused on dismantling a child pornography ring in the south of Brazil. They had tracked and arrested seven adults involved in the production and distribution of thousands of videos and pictures of children aged 1 to 11 for two decades.

Sebastián felt his body sinking into the sofa, centimeter by centimeter, strand of hair by strand of hair. "Some of the children interviewed have reported..." said one part. "... 3 to 9 in the COPINE scale," continued the other. *This is not the proof I wanted to give her*, he thought, and the hole in his chest grew larger. One of the oldest children, whose real name was C.R.S., was referred to as "Maria da Graça" in the distributed material, and had been left to the care of her maternal grandmother after her father was arrested...

Sebastián swallowed two pills, and took a large breath. *I need to talk to her.*

"Cacau," he typed. "I have some documents that might concern you."

●

Sebastián stared at the ceiling, lying on the small couch of his office. The pain was not as bad as before, but he had to take breaks during the day to keep working. His new client, Mrs. Mendoza, wanted to know if her husband was cheating on her, just like many other married individuals who knocked on his door. Although he was used to handling this kind of job, he had to change positions, now that his treatment consisted in taking appropriate medication, exercising, and resting instead of abusing opioids, as he would have preferred to.

"We could eat something first," said Cacau, sitting on his chair and drawing on a notebook. Her hair was still short, but it was longer than before, secured by clips of many colors. "Something sweet."

"You're addicted to sugar, Ms. Romero," answered Sebastián with a subtle smile. "But yes. We could."

Cacau smiled, focused on the doodle of a faceless maimed woman. At times, he found himself surprised by their current arrangement. One year had passed since the night he gave her the police reports without any expectation of hearing back from her, and a few weeks of uncertainty followed. She read the files alone, and only contacted him again half a month later, asking him to meet her in her apartment.

It's strange, Cacau told him then, and Sebastián felt back to the moment where he first stepped home after the hours he spent inside the container. *It doesn't feel like it happened to me.*

"I'm dying to know if the guy's cheating on her or not." Cacau closed the notebook and helped him back to his feet, massaging his arms with arnica cream. "I mean, what an asshole."

"I think he is," answered Sebastián. "Most of them are."

I want to remember, she had said before, and he insisted she would, someday. *I want to feel like my memories don't belong to somebody else.*

"Gut instinct?"

"Gut instinct."

Sebastián smiled and kissed the top of her head.

"Let's go, then. I'm starving."

avenging the sorrow

Lam Ning

My elderly neighbor greets me on the morning of the first autumn storm with a large cardboard box full of stray kittens that she has just clubbed to death. She holds a stained wooden baton at her side, looking out with dismay at the falling rain.

I speak up first. "Good morning, Mrs. Chey."

"The trash," she complains. "All full. Where I can throw this?"

"Call animal services," I suggest. The rain is loud on my umbrella.

She groans with impatience and tries to close the front of her bathrobe with one hand. She is in flip flops, grey hair tucked under a woolen cap.

"You go that way?" she asks, gesturing at another dumpster across the street. "You take this?"

For a while, I've worked as the local handyman. So it's not an unusual request, and I don't want her to just leave that pile of death by my front door.

"Alright."

"Okay! Thank you!"

Her children raise pigeons in their backyard, so I suppose her actions are understandable.

I take the box from her and start across the street.

A wreath is tied to the telephone pole by the dumpster, its flowers drenched from the rain. A stack of bouquets rests underneath it. Someone has left an open umbrella to protect the roadside memorial.

When a girl dies on the streets of Aki Sao, her family will cover the sidewalk with roses, carnations, and mums, until the pavement overflows with petals of yellow and white, red and pink. Her friends will build her a throne, draped in vibrantly colored cloth and lace. The walls of nearby buildings will be marked with graffiti crowns and angel wings. The neighborhood will whisper her name for years, until the echoes fade.

When a son of Aki falls to the streets, they light candles and leave beer bottles where he breathed his last. They bring flowers to his mother. Strangers won't cry for him, but they will respect the space where he once laid, even just for a little while.

It is now the end of summer, after the fall of the last regime, and the streets are flooded with both flowers and candles. Soft petals take flight every time a bicyclist passes by, and they fall among the plastic bottle caps and cigarette butts that always litter the sidewalks.

It is the nature of the changing of the guard that the blood of the youth is spilled. In this world, we cannibalize the newest generation with every end and every beginning of a dynastic cycle. It is a cull that has long since filled the oldest of our cemeteries and keeps our crematoriums burning, day and night.

This circle cannot be broken. Revolutionary leaders, crime lords, and petty tyrants—all rise and fall like public housing units when the market is high. We burn enough incense for the smoke and joss to enter our waking dreams. There is no family that does not have an escape plan. We are all swimmers, and we all know how to find the mainland by dark.

They don't want us there either. But we're just trying to live. If you've never rushed a barbed wire fence at a border crossing, clawing through a haze of tear gas, you could never understand what drove us to it. There's no use in explaining it to those who have the privilege of a homeland.

For us, there is no hope in expecting help from outsiders, from the global community, from sympathetic foreigners or public figures. We no longer have faith in anything other than ourselves, and even then, the trust between our own tends to run thin.

This season, there is a new ruling party in government. And no one cares.

I reach the dumpster and lift the box to toss it in.

But as soon as I do that, something inside the box starts crying.

Of course. Of course. I should have known. Death is never clean.

General Andar is an old friend. On days when she is doing field work, I find her husband at the clinic, which they run out of their garage. The front room of the house is used as a client receiving area. Their family lives in the back, evident on most days by their small grandchildren running throughout the place.

The floor is made up of hard wood tiles, with large rugs that are nailed down. It is always swept clean, and even the children know to keep their toys on the tables and shelves so that their grandfather can move his wheelchair around without any trouble.

Back in the home country, he had been a veterinarian. But that ended the moment he arrived at these shores, the refugee of a war no one remembers. He drove a taxi for many years, back when the transportation service was run entirely by syndicates. He retired from that with a bullet in his knee. After his children graduated from school, he regained his veterinary license so he could practice again.

When I step in through the front door, closing the umbrella while balancing the box on one arm, he is behind the reception desk, head turned toward the front window. Across the street, a mechanical crane sits in the parking lot of a two-story warehouse. It seems that air conditioning units are in the process of being installed on the roof. The crane is probably meant to do the heavy lifting. But work has come to a stop, likely due to the weather, and the units now wait covered in tarps on the back of a flatbed truck. There are no workers in sight, and the heavy hook of the crane dangles from its cable, motionless under the rain.

Doctor Andar is just as still in his chair, his eyes never straying from the massive piece of equipment.

He had four sons, once. Two were killed, one each, by the two different factions fighting for control of the home country. A third died in a drone strike by a foreign ally. The fourth is an adopted child, and the only son to survive.

He also has daughters. Fortunately, they are well.

"Good morning."

My voice pulls him back, somehow, and he turns to me. The look in his eyes is impossible to describe. He's traveled the distance of half the world and at least two decades with just a simple glance.

"My friend…" He rolls his chair around the desk. "What have you brought me?"

"Well, it's—"

I am interrupted by the tiniest of cries, coming through the box.

"Ah, I see. A cat. And very young."

"There are many," I explain, "but only one is still living."

"A massacre."

"It wasn't me this time."

"Yes, I hope not. Come. We go back."

The furniture and cabinets in the office are old and outdated, like the rest of the building. But some of the medical instruments are new, and the exam table is adjustable in height. Dr. Andar can stand for short periods of time, but often he will work from the height of his chair.

I set the box down on the table.

He pulls a lever to lower the table. Then he opens the box.

It is a mess of small mangled bodies, dark matted fur, and crushed skulls. Urine, blood, and other fluids have all soaked into the cardboard. And buried in with all that, something moves and cries out. Again and again.

The doctor reaches into the box with gloved hands and pulls out a black kitten. It kicks vigorously with three legs, while the fourth hangs limp.

Dr. Andar nods as if pleased. "Welcome to the world, little one."

Poverty has a distinct odor to it. Like old kitchen pipes and unwashed bodies. There are many parts to it: rusted cars on cinder blocks, naked toddlers playing in a yard cluttered with discarded plastic, used adult diapers collected by the front door. And, often, flies in clouds around the mountains of trash bags.

I work for a local landlord. Mainly, I handle minor repairs in the buildings that he owns.

None of his properties are in good condition. He blames this on the low-lives that rent from him. They call him a slum lord in return. I mind my own business.

Today I'm replacing a bathroom stop valve in a unit rented by two families, which they have kept in better shape than most. It's a quick job. I'm almost done when there is a hard thumping on the front door. Then, men's voices.

The yelling can be ignored at first. But it's followed by the sound of the front door crashing open, furniture overturning, something breaking. More shouting.

If someone is trying to start a fight, I don't need to be here. There is a back entrance I can leave through if necessary.

But when I step out into the small hallway, the disorder has suddenly ceased.

At the kitchen table, sits the abuela of the house. She is blind in one eye and only has blurred vision in the other, according to her grandson. A scarf covers her head, in place of hair that has been falling out in clumps over the last few weeks. I only know because I'm called here often for one thing or another.

She tilts in the direction of the front entrance and in a raspy voice worn down by the years, calls out for her grandson. His name is Alejandro, and he is standing by the table, a thin kid of about twenty, though, when he speaks, he betrays a mind far younger than that.

Now he answers her with a stammer. "Um…"

From the open doorway, three men crowd their way inside. A shoe rack by the entrance has been overturned, scattering children's sneakers and old sandals across the floor. A glass vase once full of pennies lies broken, shattered to pieces.

My boss has enforcers, debt collectors, eviction specialists. Most in his position do.

The three of them see me and stop. I recognize them. Their eyes have that shine of off-brand biosystem augmentation. It's been the trend these days for young people to turn themselves into comic-book yakuza, complete with special effects and acrobatics. I'm too old school for that, but I can't really blame them. It's the rule of the eternal arms race. Once someone builds a bigger sword, everyone else is going to start building their own. The research says that it takes years off of your life. Granted, if you're taking part in the neverending gun opera out here, chances are you won't live long enough to worry about it.

Occasionally, my path crosses over with that of the enforcement branch of my employer's organization, though I do my best to avoid it.

It isn't my place to interrupt what's about to happen. This looks like a collections call.

But their eyes are actually fixed on a target that's behind me.

I turn just as I hear the sounds of a beaded curtain being swept to the side.

He's wearing white today, and he glides by me with the ease of a swan.

"Hello!"

His voice is gentle, upbeat, birdlike. He's wearing a surgical mask. He barely glances at the mess in the front room and instead meets the eyes of the three collectors.

Their leader lets out an audible sigh, a mixture of frustration and pure exasperation. "Why are *you* here?"

"Good to see you, Kim!" His eyes squint every time he smiles. It's obvious even through the mask. "I'm working. Can I help you?"

"Where's Javier?"

"He started a new job today. I don't know when he'll be back. But he did say to give this to you."

A white envelope appears in his hands, stuffed full, secured by rubber bands. This he offers to Sokhem, who eyes it with suspicion but eventually takes it.

For a moment, an awkward silence takes over.

Then: "Would you like some cake?"

It's a question asked with such genuine intent that the rest of us flinch in unison.

And that's when I notice that there is a store bought cake on the table, still in its pink bakery box. The lid is folded open to reveal bright colorful frosting. Something suitable for a child's birthday.

Sokhem fumbles out a reply. "Uh, no thanks."

"Oh. Are you sure? What about your friends?"

"Nah, we're good. Gotta get going. See you later, Kiku."

The three of them leave.

Alejandro, Javier's little brother, looks confused, but he kneels down and begins to pick up the mess that's been left on the floor.

Kiku, my boss's son, goes to help him.

Abuela reaches across the table to turn on the small portable radio. A daytime talk show comes on, flooding the room with noise and laughter.

I finish the work in the bathroom. Then I go outside to turn the water back on. After I test that the faucets are working, I pack up my tools into the carrying case.

Back in the kitchen, abuela is chewing pumpkin seeds with the radio volume up high. The lid of the bakery box is now closed over the birthday cake. It seems that the grandson had just wanted to take some pictures of it. He is staring at the screen of a little pocket camera when I come through, deep in a conversation with Kiku about bearded dragons, all the while never making eye contact.

The shoes are back on the rack. The floor is swept clean of broken glass, the pennies gathered up into a small jar and placed on a shelf, as if nothing happened.

I only nod at them and make to leave without a word.

But Kiku meets my eyes. He then lays a hand on Alejandro's arm. "I like lizards too. I hope you get to have one as a pet someday."

"Yeah, me too…"

"You should save the cake and have it with the rest of the family when they get back."

"Oh. Sure."

"I have to go now. I'll see you next week, okay?"

"Okay."

"Happy birthday, Alejandro."

"Thanks."

"Bye, Mrs. Gutierrez!"

The old lady grunts in response and waves a dismissive hand in the general direction of his voice.

I'm already out the door. But Kiku catches up to me.

"Can we go together?"

"Sure."

"Thank you."

The rain is still coming down. It's an el nino year. I hold the umbrella over both of us, which is not difficult. He stands only about as tall as my shoulder.

"Kiku" is his street name, so to speak. His given name means light and hope.

When we say that someone is like a flower, we are usually speaking of women. There is something vulgar to the effect when you say it about a young man.

My boss's son, his youngest, is like a flower. He seems to take much more after his mother in looks than his father. He has her same pale delicate features and slender build. My arm could probably encircle completely around his waist. His movements are marked by a kind of softness that's both endearing and unsettling. And yet, as rough as the neighborhood is, he has almost no enemies here, which is rare.

His only real enemies may be his own father and half siblings.

My boss barely acknowledges the existence of his youngest child. And by law, he doesn't have to. Kiku's mother was a mistress, not a wife. But he may have taken care of both of them just to appease her. She is known to be a dangerous woman.

The clouds open up a bit as we make our way down the street. But even as the sunlight breaks through, the rain won't let up.

"How have you been?" He's wearing soft black gloves, and he laces his fingers together as he walks. He has a noticeable limp that he does his best to hide.

"I'm fine. You?"

"Yes, me too."

"That's good."

"I haven't seen you since…" He pauses and looks up at the sky. "It was spring, wasn't it?"

"I guess so."

"I was thinking about you. You never keep in contact. So I can only hope for the best."

"Nothing personal. I was just busy."

"Oh. I know that you always are working. I am too."

"Where do you work?"

"I am still doing home care for the elderly."

"Okay."

"But tomorrow I have an appointment with a photographer."

"A what?"

"Photographer."

"For…"

"A modeling job."

"What?"

He actually laughs a bit at that. Something about my face must have set him off. "Why are you so surprised? Are you saying I'm ugly or something?"

"No. But that just seems... I don't know. Are you going by yourself?"

"Yes."

"You should bring a friend with you."

"Okay. Do you want to come?"

"I have jobs lined up tomorrow."

"Oh. I think I'll be fine."

"It can't possibly pay enough to be worth the trouble."

"You sound so serious."

"How else should I sound?"

"I just wanted some pictures for my portfolio. I'm auditioning for a play next week."

"Oh. I see."

"I saw an ad for a small theater group. They're planning a Shakespeare event."

"Are you trying out for Prince Hamlet?"

"No, I'm trying out for Ophelia."

"Oh."

"You're making a scary face right now."

"Am I?"

"I'm taking the train tomorrow. I'll be back around five. Evening time. If you want to meet up with me, I can tell you more about it then."

We've reached the gate to his apartment building. I've backed myself into a corner with the conversation. There isn't an easy way out of it.

But before I can give an answer, he tells me, "Wait here."

He lets himself in through the gate and rushes up the steps, disappearing through the door of his unit.

When he comes back out, he has a small box with a lid over it. It's the type that people use to store keepsakes.

He hands it to me with both hands, sliding it sideways through the bars of the gate.

"When you were cleaning out your mother's things," he said, "I saw you put this in the trash. I don't think you really looked at what was inside."

I take it from him and tuck it under an arm.

"I'll see you tomorrow, right?" he says. "Five p.m. East-nine station."

"Sorry, I'm busy."

"Oh, it's fine. Some other time then."

"Hey…"

He stops mid-turn. The rain is already soaking into his black hair.

"Don't get so involved in your father's business. Especially with, you know, tenants and clients, things like that. It's best to just leave that alone."

He nods his head vigorously. "Don't worry about me. My father and I, we never fight over these matters."

He waves at me from the other side of the bars and runs back inside.

The Wei Fang and Keiko story begins at a tattoo shop.

Boss was young, and the country was new. Keiko was a former private-school delinquent who had learned how to ink in a drug dealer's basement. Skin art and graffiti are sacred around here. Keiko's skills, even in the beginning, were always noteworthy. At her height, she was a legend.

Wei Fang sought her out for some minor work. A poppy for his right shoulder. It was purely decorative. A lot of us wear the poppy. It's the cash crop of low-lives, the currency of our night markets—our honorary national flower.

But when Keiko's reputation grew, the boss went back for something more serious.

She completed two sleeves for him, and a back tattoo. By the time she started the work on his back, they were already involved. He wanted a traditional symbol of protection, like the stone animal statues that usually guard the homes of the elite. He asked for one lion, a male; she gave him two, a male and a female. A mated pair. To watch over him.

What we wear on our skin can have several meanings. Often personal, sometimes a joke. But for those of us who walk the knife's edge and linger a bit too long in shadows along the water front—those of us who are awake at hours when others sleep, who hold the secret grievances of the powerless and unfortunate—it is necessary to seek out the protection of a higher power. Even those of us who know that we don't deserve it, because we ourselves contribute to the pain and misery of societal dysfunction. We who are outnumbered and outgunned in every war—what we wear on our skin is an incantation, a blessing, a defensive spell. For many, it's the last layer of armor we have. Those of us destined to fight the world—its laws, its broken systems—and lose, we carry what form of asylum we can.

The rumors say that Keiko, our back-alley priestess—patron saint of anarchists—had this type of power, and the ability to bless those of her choosing. But she'd made a mistake in wasting that power on a man who was both conceited and married.

She became the permanent resident of a convalescent home after an overdose. One night, years ago, she took a hit of a street synthetic and flat-lined. She was brought back, but she did not come back whole.

In the practicing community, it is not unheard of. Sometimes, the drugs help you reach the world beyond this one. Many do it to talk to their dead ancestors. It's a journey that may take you away from your body for a time. Sometimes, you come back. Sometimes, you don't.

She lost the ability to speak that night. Keiko survived in a half-comatose state, neither present nor absent, but something in between.

Wei Fang hired me to perform an exorcism at his estate around that time. He had a fear in him then. It was like the fear of retribution. I did what I was hired to do.

Now there are moments, when I'm out on the street, or near the Arowana, the tattoo shop she used to run, or near any of the other places she used to frequent, when I do start to sense a dark presence. It is, at times, menacing, and other times, sweet. It is a thing that is capable of harboring both love and malice. I only ever nod respectfully at the invisible beast and keep moving, away from its jaws.

I can feel its intentions, its will, and its hunger. And I want no part of it.

I have no plans for the night. I gave up both cigarettes and alcohol years ago. So, after dinner, it's just me, the evening news, and Madam Mui on vinyl.

It's almost time for bed when I decide to open Kiku's box.

Inside, there are letters. Handwritten on paper. Each in its own envelope, postage stamped and marked.

In her final years, my mother had mentally regressed to her younger self. The letters are from her. She was writing to someone whom she thought was a female classmate. They went to school together, decades ago, but lived in different villages. The stories she wrote were a combination of things that could have happened in her childhood. They are surprisingly lucid and vivid in detail.

And for every letter she wrote, there is one that she received in response. Written in colorful ink, usually bright purple or pink. Always saying encouraging things. Telling her to study hard. Inviting her to make plans for the future. Sharing the occasional intimate secret. These are the words of a young considerate friend.

The return address on these letters is Kiku's. The address my mother was sending to is also his.

She used to always call him by a different feminine name every time she saw him. She decided at some point that he was that one old friend of hers who wore her hair in a bob and could sing in contralto, like a famous singer of the time. Whenever I stopped by her apartment, which was every day in the evenings after work, she would address me as "uncle."

Kiku would never correct her. He would only say, "Oh, another one of your father's friends?"

"Yes. You've met him too, Li-li. He's a pilot like my dad."

"Oh! Can he take us flying?"

"Not in a military plane. It's not allowed."

"Oh, that's too bad."

"Were you ever a dancer?"

"What?"

"Were you ever a dancer?"

"No. I mean, yes. I used to be one. But I was never very good at it."

"I think you should try it again. You look like one. I was a dancer too... a long time ago. I used to dance for the queen."

"Then you had way more talent that I did."

"Is the sun setting?"

"Yes, I think it is."

"It looks nice."

In her last hours, at her bedside, Kiku became a much adored younger sister, one who had died from pneumonia years ago. I was my father then.

I don't think about it often. But judging by the content of the letters, it seems that Kiku knew more about my own mother than I did.

At the very bottom of the box is a plain manila card. Addressed to me. A prison postcard.

It's been years, but I still remember exactly what it says.

I return everything to its original place and close the lid. I make space for the box on the top shelf in my closet. One day, I'll go out to the water and build a bonfire and burn it and cast the ashes into the ocean.

Tonight, I go to bed early.

When I sleep, I dream about my father and the koi pond we had in the old family house. In my dream, I help him feed pellets to the fish, the metallic shine of their scales flickering in and out of sight as they swim through the dark waters. He tells me that I should call my brother, the accountant, who lives on the mainland with his wife and their two kids and a family dog in a nice house in a safe upscale neighborhood.

"Okay, Dad," I say. "I will."

And I mean it.

But while I am down in the throes of REM sleep, a barrage of shots pop off from the street just outside and below my window. Semi auto, small arms fire. I count nine shots before I fully wake up.

In the middle drawer of the dresser by my bed is where I keep one of my guns. I also keep a small lamp on top of the dresser. Its weak light stays on all night, dim enough so that I can sleep, but just barely bright enough so that I can open my eyes in the middle of the night and see what's around me.

I reach over and take out the gun without sitting up. I keep it at my side, finger out of the trigger, and wait.

The other light, the red security bulb, is off, and the amber indicator on the panel shows that the alarm is armed but silent. Meaning, nothing triggered any of the sensors near my windows or doors.

Outside, there is frantic yelling and crying.

A mother, wailing for her son.

Somewhere in the distance, sirens scream.

I return the gun to the drawer and go back to sleep.

The smoke shop on the corner sells a type of candy that was popular where I grew up. Since I quit cigarettes, it's the only reason I have to go back there.

This morning, flowers and candles are clustered together near the front door.

Charlie—business owner, Oak Town original, and the last of the true O.G.s—usually mans the counter. That's where I find him, rolling up his anxiety meds with calloused brown fingers so he can smoke them later. The hair under his spotless navy blue baseball cap is grey, curly, and white.

My candies are waiting by the register.

"This can't go on," he tells me, and lights up. "They got two more. A guy and his girl. High school kids. Got shot off a motorcycle right outside. She was on his back. Looks like she never let go. Just held on 'til they both bled out. And that's how they went. Like Romeo and Juliet, huh?"

I hand him my cash over the glass display case. "Romeo and Juliet was a suicide."

"Well, then, I guess all we got here is just some straight killin'. Bonnie and Clyde. Except they didn't do nothing to deserve it."

"Did anyone come and ask to see your cameras?"

"What, you mean the cops? They the ones doin' all that shootin' last night."

"Ah, I see."

"They was aimin' for somebody else. The poor kids just got in the way. Don't matter anyways. Cops just gon' blame the clowns that got away. Call it another public service killin'."

Charlie's been around. He remembers the old drug wars. He's seen generations lost. He's seen opposition movements run their course, seen their heroes and villains come and go with the ebb and flow and fury that both topples regimes and also builds and sustains them. He knows where we're heading because he's already been there.

My son and his grandson both did time at the same correctional facility. But for two very different reasons.

Some days, through our mutual cynicism, we talk revolution.

But today—

"How's business?" I ask.

"I've had better weeks. All those flowers outside. Puts folks in a mood."

"Maybe it's a good sign."

"A what?"

"It means that people still care."

"Man, I tell you. I wouldn't mind never seeing so many goddamn flowers ever again. Just make the bullshit stop."

"I hear you." As part of the weekly ritual, I usually bring him coffee from the donut and dim sum place next door. Today, I add an order of shu mai to it.

"She gave me extra," I say before he can protest. "I can't eat it all."

"Well, in that case…"

Behind the counter, a body shifts under a blanket. There's a worn down couch back there, against the wall. Stretched out across it, Charlie's grandson turns from us and pulls the blanket over his head, until only the stray ends of a few short dreadlocks are visible.

The old man's grandkid is not a career criminal or a sociopath. He just got sent to corrections when he should have gone to psych. Happens more often than it should, I suppose. He never hurt anyone other than himself. He just needed meds.

But the market price went up on that, last I heard.

At least his grandfather has access to homeopathic remedies. A while back, I even gave him the business card of a reputable acupuncturist I knew. So far, the kid's been maintaining.

Charlie picks up the bag of food and sets it on the corner table next to the couch.

I take my candies. "I'll see you later, sir."

He waits until I'm almost at the door before he speaks up again.

"Your son was in here a couple weeks ago." Charlie's voice is quiet but unwavering. "He didn't ask for nothing, and I didn't say nothing to him."

Outside, the wind picks up leaves and flower petals. I watch them spin and tumble until they scatter.

"Just thought you should know," he finishes.

I look back over my shoulder. "Thanks."

"No problem."

Then I push open the door and step out. The sun is bright but the air is cold. Autumn, as they say, is a time of change.

An was born during the famine years. He cried often.

I spent most of that time out on deployment.

The war ended badly for us. We arrived to the sanctuary city as illegals, and we were treated as such.

By then we had already lost our elders and the weakest of our young, those too fragile to survive the endless walking through minefields and the cold nights drifting through open ocean. We carried them as far as we could. Do you understand? We carried them as far as we could.

In this interim holding cell for the leftovers of someone else's foreign policy misdemeanors, we were all outcasts, and An seemed to make few friends.

There were nights when my son would wake up screaming at phantoms only he could see. And he'd come running to me, too scared to sleep, too scared of sleep, crying that if he fell asleep he'd never wake up. And so I'd stay up with him, hold him at my side, let him curl up against me with a blanket over him, until he eventually got too tired and drifted off, and I'd stay awake to count his breaths, to make sure he still breathed, and I'd keep watch until morning when he woke up again.

We convinced ourselves that he only needed time to adjust. Much in the same way we had convinced ourselves that our cultures would survive in the new world, that our family bonds were strong enough to withstand the pressures of assimilation and the global market and the trauma of the wars we don't talk about with outsiders, a hidden history that never made it to the evening news broadcasts, that never earned more than a footnote in the core curriculum of public education.

I should have known better, in retrospect.

In truth, no wars are cold.

I remember Mai, standing with me at the docks—its nighttime waters quiet, her suitcase at her side. She looked up into my eyes and asked if we were failures as parents, right before she boarded a ferry for the mainland and never came back. I had no answer for her then, nor have I found one in the many years since.

The East-nine station is near my old precinct. I wonder if anyone I know is still there.

A part of me wants to pay a visit. But there is a candlelight vigil gathered near the train station this evening, and I'm not a fan of large crowds anymore. So I keep it moving.

It is late by the time I reach my block.

He's standing there, under the streetlight, a few steps from my duplex. Again, he's wearing white, though the pants, like his gloves, are solid black.

His head is bowed. And as I watch, he kneels in the street, reaches down, and scoops something up into his arms. When he gets up, he stumbles a bit to get his footing, as if the weight of what he's carrying is too much for him.

Then he turns around and sees me.

He looks tired. In his arms, he's holding the body of a large black cat, its fur damp and dirty. There is a small pool of what must be blood on the ground. It leaves stains on Kiku's sleeves as he cradles the dead animal against his chest.

After a moment of heavy silence, he tells me, "I was just passing through. I decided to stop by and see if you were home. I found him, lying here by himself. I noticed a few days ago that one of the other cats—the black one with the white feet—she had kittens. They're all dark, like this one. I think they're his. Ever since they were born, he behaves differently. He is more protective of this area. This area belongs to him. And he wants to defend it. His ears are all torn up because of his fighting with other cats. See this? He has a bit of grey fur still in his mouth. He must have grabbed onto something with his teeth, and he never let go of it, even though it killed him. He did it for those babies. He did it to protect them. I'm going to go bury him now."

Kiku walks past me.

I ask him, "Where?" Concrete surrounds us, not much dirt anywhere.

He stops. "Do you want to come? I'll show you, if you want."

I follow without even meaning to.

We go under an overpass and down a set of crumbling steps into the parking lot of an old warehouse. The chain linked fence is barely standing. The building has been vandalised and empty for some time.

There is access from a side entrance. To my surprise, the darkness is offset by an overhead window, which lets in the light from the street.

A motion sensor triggers other lights along the hallway floor.

By the time we reach the main room, I've figured out where he's brought me.

This is Keiko's old shop.

Because I used to help my father raise koi, I know the sound of softly stirring water. There is a canal that runs behind the building, and the levels rise during storm years.

When my eyes adjust to the dark, I realize that the entirety of the base room has been flooded.

We are on the second story of the building. Below us, the first floor is submerged in black water. And it isn't calm water. There is turbulence under the surface.

A small light flickers to life when Kiku takes another set of stairs down toward the pond. At the last step, he bows and kneels. He reaches to his neck and unties the scarf he's wearing. He uses this to gently cover the dead cat in a burial shroud.

He presses his palms together, fingers to the sky, eyes closed. A prayer pose. Then he carries the animal's body and lays it over the water. And lets go.

Of course the body sinks beneath the water and disappears.

But I feel the change in the air almost immediately. My face is cold, blood drained. I grip the steel railing of the staircase. Below me, the waters begin to thrash.

My eyes pick up a shape. Silver scales emerge from the pond's surface. Something larger than a normal fish, something serpentine in its movements. A fin takes form, then disappears. A dark eye and a mouth, maybe, glides by.

Without warning, water splashes violently, the thing launches itself up into the air, and I catch the full figure of it, its complete mass, in the half-light. Metallic silver, dragon-like, its long body sails in an arc over the pool before diving down back into the depths, sending a wave of water crashing against the surrounding walls.

After a while, the surface is calm again.

Kiku has not moved from his place. He finishes a near silent incantation, hands together, before raising his head. He looks back over at me.

I descend the last few steps between us.

He slumps forward, and I reach out to grab him before he falls into the water. I guide him to sit down on the bottom step. Then I take a seat next to him. And ask nothing about the ritual. It would be offensive to do so. There is a code among practitioners, even those of different sects and different cultures.

Kiku is breathing heavy. He sweeps wet bangs out of his eyes and nods at something in the darkness.

I follow his gaze to a wooden structure nailed to the opposite wall. It looks like a box, with double gold-hinged doors that open from the front. Its corners curl up, like the gates of a temple. It is accessible by a second floor walkway.

A shrine, I realize.

"My mother kept it empty," Kiku explains. "This is so that those who come in here can choose for themselves what is inside. They can find something in their heart and place that thing, whatever it is, inside. And they may bow to that, rather than an idol. Because, out here, in this country, everyone is so different, we can't know what deity they worship, if any. So as not to be inconsiderate, she left it empty."

His words echo through the chamber walls. "The side entrance is always open. Sometimes people come and leave offerings. Some even spend the night if they have nowhere else to sleep. But no one stays longer than that. Often, I find that people will come here to cry, or to scream, or confess their sins and ask for forgiveness. I don't always know what they're looking for, or from whom. I just listen. If there is a secret or a wish that you need to say out loud, but dare not to, you may come here. Speak it here. This place will take it from you. And it will bear some of the weight for you."

His voice has fallen to a whisper. He is exhausted. Without asking permission, he lays his head on my shoulder.

The shirt he's wearing is fashioned after a traditional garment. The sleeves are long and wide, like wings. The enclosures are embroidered and complicated. No one really wears such things anymore except for performances or ceremonies.

But I realize, after some scrutiny, that the buttons on his shirt are misaligned. He's fastened them out of order. The one near his neck hangs by a loose thread, leaving his collar area exposed.

The more I stare at his clothing, the more asymmetry I find. It looks wrong. Threads have been torn apart.

I want to know his reason for coming by my apartment earlier. Did he need me for something?

I won't ask it here. I won't ask it now.

"Do you have a wife?" he says.

That throws me off a little. "Used to. Not anymore."

"Do you still speak to her?"

"Occasionally." Mai calls me exactly twice a year, mainly just to make sure I'm not dead. We have an understanding between us.

She was my family's choice for me, not mine. But we learned to live as a couple. We have some feelings for each other. One can't call it romantic love, but we do care for each other, even in separation.

Kiku asks me, "Would you go to her if she needed you? Would you help her if she were in trouble?"

"Yes."

He smiles. "You seem like the type that would."

"I try."

I have a feeling he just needs to hear someone say it.

Suddenly I have the urge to put my arm around him.

But actions have consequences. And I am not in a position to take those kinds of risks.

You don't really know me, Kiku. So don't make assumptions about my character.

I ain't lying though.

It's been some time, but Wei Fang once put out a hit on his youngest son.

I turned down that job.

It's bad luck, and even worse manners, to drown a bird that is both helpless and means no harm to others.

In the end, Wei Fang hired someone else. And so Kiku was beaten unconscious with a metal pipe as he walked home from school one day. He survived, but he's walked with a limp ever since.

Kiku had been accepted into a university to study dance and traditional theater. On stage, he was well known for playing female roles. He was pretty good at it. Not that I would know anything about that. Strange as it may seem, my father had taught me to be kind.

But men like Wei Fang cannot tolerate embarrassment of any kind. A family shame must be erased. A source of humiliation should be pulled out by the root.

But he'd made a mistake in sending an amateur to do professional work.

Kiku dropped out of school to heal from his injuries. He never went back.

The money that was supposed to go to his tuition went back to his father.

As far as I know, Wei Fang never made another try.

If he comes to me again, my answer will be the same.

At this point, he should know better.

I won't move against Keiko. I have my reasons.

There was a day in spring, years ago, when a little girl disappeared from the backyard of her home. A canal ran behind the house, so there were immediate concerns that she could have drowned.

That girl was Bopha, my brother's young daughter.

We searched for her throughout the day and well into the night. I didn't want to give voice to the suspicions in my heart.

An had come home that afternoon with wet clothes and no explanation for it.

Bopha's body was found days later, having floated to the surface of the water.

An showed no emotion throughout the ordeal.

My son, by then, had grown into a stranger. Because of the nature of my work, I could not see him as often as I would have liked. My options for employment were limited. In securing safe passage for my family years ago, I had incurred a heavy debt, one that I had to repay. I did what I had to do. But it all came with a price.

My brother and his wife blamed themselves for their daughter's death. They were both exhausted from long hours working on the graveyard shift. They slept during the day and hadn't noticed her missing. In their grief, they surmised that she must have snuck through the fence and fallen into the water.

But Mai held conference with me one night. In whispers of her mother tongue, a language our son no longer spoke nor understood, she told me about the dead animals she'd found over the years at the edge of the canal, near the house. Mostly rats or squirrels, sometimes pigeons, or even cats. The cats disturbed her because they had been bound with shoelaces. It was obvious that they had been killed. The reports she'd made to animal services went unanswered.

I suppose that a mother would know her child best. More than a father who was often absent.

I wanted to believe in our son. But I also trusted Mai's instinct.

My brother broke down the day we scattered Bopha's ashes in the sea.

I watched my son closely that day. An looked like he was trying to cry but couldn't. I remember putting a hand on his shoulder. He stood stiffly and said little.

Six months later, another child disappeared. She was older than Bopha and just a little bit younger than An.

Her body never turned up, not in its entirety. But her right foot did, still encased in a small pink shoe, washed up on the banks of the canal.

Her mother recognized the shoe immediately. A footprint was also found to still be recoverable.

She was called Rose, and she was Keiko's first-born, Kiku's twin. Undoubtedly they had the same father. But Wei Fang only ever acknowledged one. For illegitimate children, he would only ever acknowledge a boy.

Back then, I was still with the department, but the case wasn't assigned to me. I'll never forget how quickly my colleagues gave up on Rose. They let it go because there were higher priority issues back then. The whole thing went cold.

Keiko, however, did not let it lie.

And so, one night, she overdosed as part of a sacred ritual.

And in my house, that same night, An woke up screaming.

Whatever Keiko did, whatever she summoned, it was powerful, and it must have hit its mark. Those of us who come from similar practices received our fair warning in the silence that fell throughout the city, a strange spiritual quiet that seemed to keep every scavenging animal off the street after sunset. A shadow rose up from the urban undergrowth, spread its wings, and took flight, swelling into existence like a tsunami or some other force of nature.

Around 0300 the power went out.

I woke up while the rest of the house slept on as if they'd been sedated.

And something that may have been Keiko, or something called forth by her, made landfall—tore its way through the streets—howling, roaming—in search of prey.

In his room, An had become catatonic. He would not speak or move. For days, he'd been trying to conceal the wound on his hand, an injury that took the shape of a very humanlike bite mark.

I covered him with a blanket and left, sealing the door behind me. I marked it with a protective sign, re-enforced by my own blood.

I crept into the kitchen, alone, and lit a candle. And I waited.

Eventually the beast came to my front door. It had taken the form of a dog. But it could not easily breach the barriers I had placed around the house. So it growled and paced and clawed at the walls of the spirit shield.

Between Keiko's power and mine, there is a difference in magnitude. How much, I did not want to find out. I am a mediocre practitioner at best. Knowing your limits is an undervalued character trait.

Fighting her was not my intention.

So I opened the front door and stepped outside. I went out into the street to confront what was waiting for me.

The demon dog hunched over with its head down low, menacing but ever so patient. It was visible by moonlight in the darkened street, a monster the size of a house—half-shadow, half-flesh, a collar of bone, its body branded by his mistress's defensive lettering.

I did not have enough blood in me to stop it if it chose to attack. My only option was to kneel.

And so I did.

My brother had blamed himself for his daughter's death, and so I would also take on the responsibility of what my son had become.

A life for a life seemed only fair. I figured I had lived long enough. There's already a grave in the homeland we lost that bears my old name.

Keiko's spirit dog was the judge, jury, and executioner. And it took only a moment to make up its mind.

When I was young, I had once played Russian roulette with my father's revolver. What it takes to pull the trigger is impossible to quantify. In the last second before the hammer strikes, the totality of your existence plays out in your mind. Memories from the past become as intense as your present reality, brought to life by the realness of the situation playing out before you. And whether they are good or bad, these things that make up your life, it no longer matters. Your time is your time.

It is then that everything leaves you, and you will be taken over by the most real sense of peace you will ever know.

And so—

Click.

The beast lunged at my throat.

Behind me, the door slammed open. And a single gunshot rang out.

The dog staggered and stopped. A wound formed on its body. Its blood dribbled down one leg and pooled into the street.

The scent of gun powder was in the air.

I looked behind me.

Mai stood in the doorway, arm raised in front of her, my 9mm in her hand.

The dog seemed to take her in with almost human eyes. Then, as if coming to a decision, it rose up onto its rear legs and leaped into the sky. It became something else, sprouted large black wings, adopted a new shape, and disappeared into the dark.

I got up. Went to Mai. Put a hand on her shoulder.

She lowered her arm and leaned into my chest. I wrapped my arms around her.

"I couldn't let you do it," was all she said.

I am on call almost every night. Some weeks are slow. Others are busy.

The phone rings a little after midnight. I am dreaming about my father's koi again. Whenever I dream like that, it is always a sign.

Wei Fang may be awake at any hour. He sounds fully alert when I answer.

"I have a small matter," he says. "But it must be dealt with immediately."

He gives me an address. It's to a vacant lot that he's recently purchased. A large box has been dumped there, and he wants it removed to a public dump site. Now. Because construction workers are showing up early in the morning to begin building, and he can't afford any delays.

I don't ask for specifics. I have a utility vehicle, and the drive isn't far.

Late night rain washes over my windshield. I always keep an umbrella in the car, even during drought years.

The lot is situated behind a car dealership, next to two apartment buildings still under construction. It is a desolate location. People often use the space as a dumping ground.

The box is on the side of the road, next to a chain link fence. Something about it puts me off. I pull up next to it and approach it slowly.

It is a wooden crate. Not too large that it won't fit in the back of the van. When I shine my flashlight on it, I notice that the top lid has been hastily nailed in place. The nails are in contorted positions.

The wood is sharp and new, though rain-drenched and scratched up on the surface. It is a little unusual for a person to use brand new material just to throw something away.

I lay a hand on top of it.

Something is strange about this.

A layer of wet dirt covers the lid. I sweep it away with my fingers.

Beneath the mud, there is a mark, drawn in blood. A seal.

I drop the umbrella. With a pocket knife, I cut my outer forearm and let the blood run over my hand. Then I press it to the lettering. The barrier is weak. It breaks easily under my hand, taking the wooden surface with it. I toss the broken pieces aside.

And then—

My face is suddenly cold.

I remember.

"Would you go to her if she needed you?"

Yes.

I would.

But is it too late now to do the same for you?

Is this heart still beating?

It is.

Then.

Why—

Why name yourself after a flower of mourning?

Is it because—

No. Nevermind.

We go together, now, you and I. One last time. Through these streets.

I won't scatter your ashes to the sea.

Though one day, you may do so for me.

The General herself opens the clinic door. She's dressed as if she were up late working. And it only takes one look for her to fully assess the situation.

She lets me in, bolts the door, sets the alarm, and leads me to the back. Along the way, she knocks on a door in the hallway, opens it, and says something softly in her language. Another voice from within answers her. Then she closes the door and motions that I follow her into the treatment room.

She hits the switch, flooding the room with fluorescent light.

The steel exam table is open and waiting. She covers it with a towel and several layers of sheets.

I lay Kiku down on top of it.

"What happened?"

"I don't know."

Dr. Andar appears at the door, pushed in his chair by his teenage daughter, Leila, as he finishes buttoning a knitted shirt.

"What did you bring me this time?"

I empty my wallet onto the table.

"That doesn't answer the question, my friend."

"He's breathing," the General says, as she attaches him to an ancient monitor that's probably meant for animals.

"Ah. Let's bring out the oxygen."

"Saturation is low. BP and heart rate are running high."

Leila slips around me to pull things from the cabinets, her movements well rehearsed.

"Did you find him in water?" the General asks.

"No."

"His clothes are wet."

"I know. It's raining."

"He looks like he was submerged."

At some point, Kiku opens his eyes, coughs out water, and tries to fend off the hands that are on him.

He only stops when I press my palm to his forehead.

He tries to say something but doesn't have the voice. The left corner of his mouth has been sliced open.

They are removing his clothes. Leila brings a blanket.

His body is covered in wounds. The cuts are superficial, not deep enough to kill. These types of injuries are intended to cause pain.

There is also a ring of red abused skin around his throat.

He submits to the treatment with only a few tiny nods in response to the questions he is asked. His eyes tear up when the General goes into him with the stitches. He reaches for my hand and doesn't let go.

When she is finished, she bandages the worst of his wounds and assures him that he's done well. He tries to thank her, but his voice cracks and breaks. He looks like he's about to cry again.

There is talk of a scan for head trauma, though his vitals look good now. They have to make preparations, and I agree to stay up with him in the meantime.

They leave us alone for a little while.

He struggles to sit up. I have to help him. There are no pillows. He leans into me instead.

I don't like physical contact. This is fine, though.

Some time passes before he says anything. He whispers, as if his mouth is in pain.

He talks about his father.

"I knew he would never love me. But I didn't know how much he could hate me."

Then he covers his face with bare hands and cries.

He must have known all this time that his father was the one who had hired a hit on him years ago.

The General returns with folded clothes. "These used to belong to my son. They should fit you." Then she gives me a look. "Are you helping or being a nuisance?"

"I swear it's not my fault this time."

"You say that every time."

Leila comes in. She is carrying the kitten, the same one I had brought in a week before.

"I thought you might want to see him," she says. I'm not sure if she's talking to me or her patient.

It doesn't matter because Kiku is already reaching out towards her. She gently deposits the small animal into his hands.

His voice is a coarse sound, as if he's spent the last few hours screaming.

"What's wrong with his leg?" he asks her.

"It was broken," she says. "But it's healing on its own. The orthopedic surgeon said there's no need for surgery."

He smiles a bit, but only one side of his mouth moves. The other cheek is stitched shut and taped over. "You'll be okay," he whispers and holds the kitten close to his chest.

"You can have your old job back if you want," she tells me.

"It's a young person's game, Amal."

The General nods. "Sure. But your time's not up yet."

Rain pelts the roof. We stand together under the overhang near the back entrance. She tucks her hands into her coat pockets. She's watching the parking lot and the dark quiet street beyond.

I tell her, "I'm fine doing what I'm doing."

"Being an accessory to attempted homicide?"

I inhale long and deep and let it out.

"Do you like your job?" she asks.

"I just do what I'm told."

"Did your boss tell you to come here tonight?"

I don't need to say it.

She is, of course, right on all counts.

"Do you need a vet tech?" I ask.

"Are you interested?"

"I meant for the kid."

"Ah. Well, he does seem good with animals." She shakes her head. "I don't know where you find 'em, Sam. But I feel bad that he got caught up with you, of all people."

"I know."

"Take care of that one. And he'll take care of you."

"Don't get it twisted. We're at least two decades apart."

Her laughter rolls like smooth thunder over the sound of rain.

In the morning, Wei Fang calls with a job for me. He's sending me to clean out one of his properties. The address is Kiku's apartment.

He asks if last night's assignment is complete. I tell him that it is. I'm not lying. The box did make its way to the public dump site, like he wanted.

It is early, and I didn't get much sleep. I check the bedroom before I leave. Kiku is wrapped up asleep in a blanket. I watch him long enough to see that he's still breathing. Then I leave without waking him.

I arrive to his apartment to find a junk hauler's vehicle already parked in front.

Inside, I find the usual three, Sokhem and associates, breaking apart furniture and throwing things into trash bags.

They rip apart cabinets and take hammers to the tables and chairs. It's easier this way. Like dismembering a body.

Then they start tearing into the shrine. And that is a problem for me. A holy object has to be properly decommissioned. Otherwise, the ground beneath it becomes cursed.

I turn my back, raise the fingers of one hand upright, in front of my chest, and offer a quick prayer.

Evil often spawns from tragedy.

In the bedroom, I find a small box of what could only be mementos, including a small piece of jade in a red cloth envelope. There is also a zipped up money pouch. These things I tuck under my coat.

It is understood that everything is fair game whenever Wei Fang has one of his properties cleaned out. The occupants never return.

Sokhem and his friends come into the room after me to continue pillaging. There is a jewelry box with gold and silver pieces inside. I leave that to them.

They know me. And they know that I never take things. I only do the job that's asked of me, nothing more.

The mood today is unusual. No one is speaking. Even as they pocket valuables, no one smiles or laughs.

It doesn't take us very long to clear out the place. Most of Kiku's life seems to fit into a modest collection of garbage bags. The shrine is reduced to wood scraps.

We tie the loose parts together and throw it all onto the back of the truck.

Then we split up to leave. Two of them get into the truck, and I head towards my van.

I find Sokhem right next to it, smoking a cigarette. He is turned away as I load my tools in the back. When I slam shut the doors, he finally speaks.

"Did he go down easy?"

I look up, and Sokhem is watching my face carefully. I tell him, "I didn't take that assignment."

His eyes fall to my left arm, still bandaged from the cut where I drew blood last night. I can feel his suspicion. There's no easy way for me to explain it to him.

Sokhem is younger than me and a little older than Kiku, but not by much, I realize. The other guys always seem to instinctively look to him for guidance. If he keeps his head on straight, he might do well for himself. He can survive this life, provided he knows when to get out.

He looks away again and puts the cigarette back between his lips. "Must have been an outsider then. Can't be nobody from this neighborhood."

I reach under my coat, and his eyes follow my hand as I pull out the money pouch from Kiku's apartment. I hold it out to him. Warily, he takes it.

Sokhem unzips the pouch, looks inside, then zips it up again. He looks up and gives me a hard stare.

"If you hear anything about that…" I leave the rest open.

"Why go after the gun?" he says. "You know who really pulled it."

He's right. I do know.

For years, Wei Fang's been looking for someone to do one specific job that he refuses to do himself. And for years, those of us employed by him have continually turned it down. He must have, once again, gone outside the community to hire someone.

To me, Wei Fang is just an employer. My loyalty to him has always been conditional. He doesn't have anything on me to keep me here. My son's crimes are a matter of public record, and the time when it would have affected my work or social life has passed.

I don't have to spare Wei Fang.

I don't have to spare anyone.

I could spend all day slitting throats.

I just know it isn't going to fix anything.

You could turn the whole world into a killing field, but you'd still have to live in it.

There's a man I left buried in the old country. He used to fight for something. He used to lead an army. He used to believe in creating a better world. And in the end he had to bury everyone, his favored daughter and all his sons. He saved the last grave for himself. He knows it's still out there, waiting for him. He knows he'll make it back home someday, if only just to die.

Now, in this new country, in this afterlife, there is no purpose that he has found that will sustain him.

If you want to fix something, it's going to take more than a gun or a knife. Tanks can't build nation states.

Unfortunately, I've never been good at anything else.

Forgive me, Kiku.

My household fell apart years ago. I don't know how much of it was my fault. It doesn't matter. I have to accept responsibility for the part I played in its dissolution.

For months, Keiko's ghost dog haunted our waking dreams. It followed us through the streets, staying just out of sight, watching from a close distance. We knew it was bound by a blood oath, that it would not rest until its reason for existence was achieved.

An became increasingly paranoid. He wasn't sleeping. He claimed he couldn't sleep. His doctor suggested therapy.

I considered making a phone call. I considered turning in my own son. But I had no evidence. Only a father's suspicion.

Eventually, An was arrested after he strangled his counselor with a shoelace. She had been a youth volunteer. She survived, but lived on with the pain and trauma of it.

All of my suspicions were confirmed that day. He never confessed to anything else. But I didn't need to hear it.

His failure in life is also my own. I know. I know.

The parents of bad children can never look up and face the world with pride. We carry their crimes with us throughout our lives. The burden of it is like an anchor, binding you to a time and a place where bad things thrive. And no matter how many times you revisit your memories, you never find the answers that you need.

The house smells like food.

"What are you doing?"

Kiku doesn't even flinch at my tone. He's cooked the last of my rice. "I did some shopping. Your refrigerator was empty." His voice is still broken. His eyes are completely innocent.

This, I will never understand. His father has now twice tried to kill him. Who, with any common sense, goes out in public and lets their face be seen?

I take a breath. "Once those pain meds wear off, you're going to wish you'd stayed in bed."

"I made tofu. And vegetables. Do you want any?"

"Where did you find tofu?"

"The store on the corner. They make deliveries."

I know the place and the owners. The family has no connection to Wei Fang. He doesn't own that piece of property.

"Do yourself a favor and lay low for a while, alright?"

"Hm." A small nod. "So do you want this food or not?"

I really don't need a second wife. But then, it's been a while since I've had someone cook for me.

I set down the box from his apartment onto the table. "For you."

He looks at it but doesn't say anything.

After dinner, I clean up. And he takes the box with him into the bedroom.

I find him there later, curled up asleep next to it. The lid is off. Inside, there are some photographs. On top lies a snapshot of two children.

Fraternal twins are not identical. But they can still have a strong resemblance as siblings.

In the photo, it is clear that Kiku takes after his mother, and Rose takes after her father. Perhaps Wei Fang had chosen the wrong child to support. Had he not neglected her, would her severed foot have ended up floating in the canal?

Perhaps it would have been Kiku's instead.

Would that have changed anything?

In the shower, I come up with a plan. I'll have to send him to Mai. She runs a legal brothel on the mainland. He can hide out there. She'll do this one favor for me. There's no guarantee that she won't put him to work, but at least I know she's not a trafficker.

I pull clothes from the closet and dress quietly in the dark bedroom. I'll have to make that phone call tonight or in the morning.

"Do your tattoos have a meaning?"

I look behind me. He's still lying on his side, hugging himself under the sheets.

"They do."

"Are they for protection?"

I don't want to give away any trade secrets. But given that he is Keiko's son, he's most likely figured it out already.

"Yes."

"How long have you had them?"

"A long time."

"Who made them for you?"

"My grandmother."

He sits up. He pulls off his gloves and holds out his hands, palms turned up.

The only light is what filters in from the open bathroom door. I crouch at the bedside and take his hands into mine for a closer look.

His palms are marked with black ink. Characters written in the old language. I recognize Keiko's work immediately.

"My mother gave me this," he says. "She did it when my sister disappeared."

He would have been a child then. She had been that desperate to protect him that she was willing to subject him to pain.

His mother's power may be the only reason he's still alive.

I ask, "Who did your father send for you the other night?"

He gives me a startled look and pulls away. As if it were an indecent question.

"Why?"

"I'd like to know."

"What are you going to do?"

"Nothing. But you're here. In my house. I need to know if anyone might come around asking about you."

"Oh." He stays silent for a while. "If I tell you, you have to promise you won't try to find him."

"I'm not looking for any trouble, honey."

I can be good at lying when I have to.

"He was one of those lost souls who came by my mother's old shop every now and then. He left offerings at the shrine. We didn't talk much in the beginning. But he asked for a blessing once. So I gave him one. He told me that he'd done some bad things. I think he was looking for forgiveness.

"One night, we took a walk outside, by the water. He said he wanted to confess something to me."

Kiku stops here and doesn't finish the story.

"Did he tell you his name?"

He turns from me and falls back down against the pillows.

I keep pressing the point. "What did he confess?"

"I can't say."

"Did he hurt you?"

Kiku pulls the blanket up to his shoulder and doesn't answer.

I get up and turn to leave. I'll sleep in the couch in the main room. I'll try again tomorrow.

But, in a cracking voice muffled by the pillow, Kiku goes on.

"I sensed his loneliness the moment I met him. He told me about whales and how they communicate through song. They call out to each other under the water. When one whale hears the song of another, it answers back. But in order for them to hear each other, they must sing at the same frequency. If a whale were ever born different and sang at a different frequency, a frequency outside of the range of other whales, it would spend its whole life calling out and hearing nothing in response. It would go on believing that it was the only one of its kind. And no matter how much it called out, it'd never know another. And at the end of its life, the ocean would simply swallow it whole. And that sea of loneliness would be the only thing it had ever known."

I'm no marine biologist. Don't ask me if that story's real.

But I do know this.

I heard about a man who went to solitary confinement in prison. During that time, he would intentionally antagonize the guards so that they would go into his cell and beat him down. When he finally got let back into the main population, the other inmates asked him why he'd done it. He said that he'd been locked up by himself for so long that he just needed to feel something.

I run into Javier on the street. Alejandro is with him, making constant eye contact with nobody but the ground.

"Hey, you're Kiki's guy, right?"

"Sorry?"

"Kiku," Alejandro offers without looking up. His puffy jacket hides his narrow shoulders and normally stooped posture.

Javier glances at him. "What?"

"The name of grandma's aide. It's Kiku. I think that's how you say it."

"Right. So," Javier turns back to me, "you're his... like... uh, sorry, I don't want to be disrespectful."

I have to unclench my jaw in order to speak. "I'm not his anything. But I can deliver a message."

Javier has sharp brown eyes and well groomed facial hair. He stands with squared shoulders, half in front of his brother, as if to guard him. The bill of his cap is flat and pulled down low.

"Some guy," he says, "came around asking about him the other day."

"A guy…"

"Yeah. Just one. We said we don't know him. Made the guy leave."

Just one. That's not how Wei Fang normally does things.

"Okay." I shrug. "If I see the kid I'll let him know. I have no clue where he is."

Alejandro raises his head a little. "And let him know I finally got a gecko."

"A what?"

And like that, he pulls out a tiny lizard from his pocket.

"I named him Steven."

Javier is unfazed by his brother's antics. He just tucks his hands into his pockets and nods at me. "Alright then. Have a good one, boss."

I call Mai.

She sounds mildly annoyed.

"Tell me why I should help you."

"Not me. You'd be helping a kid."

"A kid? He's his mother's responsibility. Not mine."

"His mother already paid her dues. We owe her."

"…Keiko?"

"Her son."

"You're a real piece of work, Sam."

"But you understand."

"Knowing you, how could I not?"

I never faulted her for anything that happened. Though I did wonder if it was our combined genes that made our son what he was.

Of all the people in my life, at one point, she was the most reliable and self-sufficient. And with that, she's always had little use for me.

After the call with Mai, I remember the dream I had last night.

Again, I was at my father's koi pond. At the water's edge, two girls were playing. One was Bopha, the other was Rose. When they saw me, they came running towards me. They tugged at my sleeves with small hands. And they asked me when I was going to punish the bad man who had hurt them. I had promised to catch him years ago. Did I forget all about that?

I knew at that point that it wasn't a dream. I was being visited.

Keiko, from her nursing home bed, wanted to remind me that she hasn't forgotten about our shared past.

In the dream, a gate opened behind me, and from the dark, demons began to emerge. I grabbed the metal bars and slammed the gate shut and sealed it. When I turned around, the girls were gone. In their place, another small hand took mine. My son was a child again, begging me to protect him. I squeezed his hand and pulled him into a hug. Then I looked up and found the city in flames. In the sky, bombers flew low. And there came that shrill deadly whistle, a sound I knew, one that pierced through the smoke and sirens. When you heard it, all you could do was run because you knew what was coming but could never stop it.

In that fire was where I had found my first daughter, and in that fire was where I left her.

Her death, perhaps, was what made it impossible for me to properly care for my son.

If we ever meet again in the next life, I've already sworn to never leave her side.

"Are you coming with me?" he asks.

"No."

At this, Kiku looks away, silent.

"Mai will help you find work. She's got a place for you to stay. If things go well, you can still go to school. You like theater and stuff like that. There's plenty of that over there. Think about what you want out of this life. Forget about what happened here. Forget about your father. Work for the life you want for yourself. That's my advice."

"My mother is here."

"She's under the care of nurses and doctors. She'll be fine. You can still write to her."

"Someone has to look after the shop."

"I'll find someone to help you do that."

"It's not that easy."

"It can be. Tell me what I need to know about it."

"What about you?"

"Me?"

"Who will looking after you?"

"Me. I'm looking after me."

"I never told you this, but there are times when you seem even more lonely than him."

"Who? Your marine biologist?"

"You're both a lot alike."

"Why did you agree to meet him that night? Why put yourself in that position?"

"I won't turn away from someone who needs help."

"He went to you for help?"

"He has… demons. He wanted to get rid of them."

"Were you trying to perform a spiritual cleansing?"

His mother is powerful, and he must have inherited his abilities from her. But some things are too deeply rooted to be pulled out of a troubled soul.

Kiku ignores my question and wipes away tears with his sleeve.

"You're going to forget about me when I leave," he says. "Aren't you?"

"If you're that hung up about it, you can write me too."

"I won't speak harsh words to you if we're about to part ways."

A few hours later, I drive him to the ferry dock. The official transports have stopped for the day. But there is one last boat heading out. I know the owner. Arrangements were made.

The rain is only mist tonight. But I still hold the umbrella over both of us. He has everything he owns in one travel bag. Including his mother's box. There's an envelope of cash in there that he doesn't know about yet, the same amount that I had taken and given to Sokhem.

He stops at the boarding ramp. From here, the lights of the mainland are visible.

He looks out across the dark waters. "I never thought I would leave here on my own."

The ocean air is cold.

"You've never been away from home?" I ask.

"No."

"You'll be fine. It only seems scary at first."

But he shakes his head. I know he's reconsidering everything.

"I can't do this," he says.

"Listen…"

"I can't do it by myself." He's breaking.

"You can," I tell him. "You have to. I can't go with you."

"You're choosing to stay here, right? You want to? You don't want to leave?"

"That doesn't matter. What I want doesn't matter. It has to be this way."

"If things were different, would you change your mind? Would you come with me?"

"Yeah, sure."

"Really?"

"Probably."

"Okay."

"You better get going."

He turns, then stops. He looks at me. "Can I ask you something?"

"Make it quick."

He pulls off his gloves with his teeth. Then he reaches for me. His bare hands cup either side of my neck. His palms are warm.

He tilts forward until his forehead is against the center of my chest. He turns his face to the side, gloves still in his mouth, and I think he's listening to my heartbeat.

In another life, I would have held him. But my mind is already slipping to bad places.

Wei Fang isn't even the one I'm most concerned about.

By next morning, I may not be human anymore. When it comes to "work," that's how it has to be.

I let Kiku have his moment. Then I put my hands on his shoulders and step back. He lets his arms drop to his sides. Then he takes the gloves out of his mouth and slips them back on.

Before he can turn away, I grab one of his hands and slip the handle of the umbrella into his grip. He looks up at me without a word. His eyes are wet. I slide out of my coat and drape it over his shoulders. It's obviously too big for him. But he doesn't refuse.

Then he picks up the bag off the ground.

He bows. And, turning, begins to make his way up the ramp, under the umbrella, until he disappears into the ferry.

A hand signals from the window. My acquaintance. I signal back.

I watch the ferry leave. Then I walk back to the van.

The skin on my neck is warm. I don't fully notice the burn until I'm in the driver's seat, turning the ignition. It's now impossible to ignore.

I switch on the lights in the front cab and twist the rear view mirror towards me.

A mark is forming on my neck. Two of them. One on either side. Right over the carotid arteries and jugular veins.

Keiko's seal of protection. Handed over from her son to me. He just gave up his only form of defense. For me.

Why.

What the hell for.

I don't understand.

I make a fist and throw it into the ceiling of the van.

This isn't how I wanted things to go.

Life moves on like machinery.

Days pass.

Out on the street, one afternoon, I get a call from Sokhem on my cell.

He says, "Some guys are hanging around outside your house."

"I see."

"Just thought you should know."

"Thank you."

"Another thing." He pauses. "Kiku's mom. I know who sold her the bad synth. Years back."

"Go on."

"The guy who made the hand off didn't know it was bad. His boss gave it to him, said to sell it to her and only her. Said there was no cut this time; he got to keep all of the sale."

Like a confession. Kim would have been a teenager back then.

"His boss?" I say.

"Yeah. You get me?"

"Thanks."

There's another moment of silence. Then he says: "The universe has a way of making things right."

"Perhaps."

"See ya around, old man."

So I don't go home.

I eat a quick dinner at a takeout place. Then I go to Keiko's old shop.

I drop money into the donation box and take the stairs down toward the water.

I lay out my sleeping bag, plug my phone into the wall, and chamber a round into my gun.

I sleep.

Wake up to what sounds like a child's lullaby. There is the whisper of stirring water. Then it falls silent.

I sleep again.

In the early morning, before dawn, I get up to pray and clean myself up in the restroom. The ceiling lights don't work, so I light a candle. My cell rings while I'm shaving.

Boss has a job for me. Installing new fixtures inside of Kiku's old apartment. But first, he wants to go over the details in person.

This is not how we normally do things.

"Do you ever miss the old country?" he asks.

"Of course."

"There were these flowers that grew by the river where I used to live. I never knew what they were called. And I can never find them over here. I guess they don't grow out here."

On the other end, Wei Fang sounds no different than usual. I can picture him at the desk in the office of his house, the sleeves of a clean-collared shirt rolled up to his elbows, Keiko's work on his arms, covered up by another artist's ink. Cell phones don't work at his place, so he had a land line installed. The office window overlooks a massive garden. Like my father, he also raises koi. Like my grandfather, he also grows poppy.

His adult children live there from time to time when they're not traveling. They all work for him, except for the eldest son who currently resides at a psychiatric facility.

Over the years, we've quietly gathered information on each other. Just because we work together doesn't mean we trust each other. I am still a private contractor. I have the option of turning down any assignment I don't want.

His wife stays out of the family business. He tends to keep her away from his associates. I have seen her, only because I was asked to perform an exorcism on the property. I suspect that he only allowed me to get that close because he questioned the authenticity of my failed marriage.

They say that if you steal a man's wife, you'll get punched. But if you steal a man's money, you'll get shot.

Wei Fang is a business man. Family is just another extension of that. He raised his children to protect his assets because he knew they would be more loyal than his associates.

But his mistress and her children were loyal only to each other. Keiko fought Wei Fang for years over his lack of support for their daughter, and when that daughter disappeared, Keiko suspected him most of all.

Because he feared her wrath, he tried to end her before she could end him.

He had the skin that bore the lion tattoos cut off from his back. No exorcist he hired was able to destroy that patch of skin. When he tried to incinerate it, he suffered severe burns to the backside, in the spot where the tattoos once were. He had to be treated with skin grafts at the hospital. It was then that he sought my help.

I sealed the patch of skin in a box for him and told him not to open it.

I suppose I should not have done that. His fear of Keiko once kept his worst tendencies in check.

Kiku's mistake was interfering in his father's business. My mistake is giving a damn about the outcome of a situation that has nothing to do with me anymore.

"I trust you the most," he says, "to do this job."

We agree to a meet up spot. It is near the docks.

I have two hours to prepare.

Before I leave, I go back down to the shrine. I offer blood. I place my ancestors and my father's hopes and dreams into the empty box. I choose a God and hope it's the right one. I make a sign to the heavens and submit to whatever fate's decision will be for me.

And I extend a greeting to *her.* Not a request, not an apology, just a greeting. I only ask for a blessing for her son, as he walks alone now in a foreign country.

And then I climb up the stairs.

A shadow that isn't mine follows, one that walks on fours and breathes through gnashed teeth. It lurches as it walks, as if limping.

We don't know each other, but we've met before. This time, its ambitions toward vengeance aren't directed at me. I'll accept whatever ally I can.

The second I reach the top floor and open the door, I'm hit four times in the chest. I fall.

He has a silencer on that gun.

I land on my knees.

He fires another round into my face, under the left eye.

Everything goes fuzzy and black. Blood pools underneath me.

But it's not over.

From her hospital bed, elsewhere in the city, Keiko's eyes are wide open. We are connected now, and she knows everything.

He won't speak to me. He'll only watch me die. Which is what he's wanted to do for a long time.

In his last postcard, sent from corrections, he accused me of trying to interrogate him through the letters we exchanged. He claimed that the souls of the people I had killed during the war were coming after him in his dreams. That was why he never slept. He was tired of paying for my sins. He said he had no use for a father who never understood him.

A tattoo covers his skinny right forearm. It looks days old at most. It's one of Keiko's lions, the female.

Only Wei Fang could have given that to him. But the image is reversed, a mirrored imitation. The artist seems talented, but to bring that here, where the original was made, is to invite retaliation.

An, hollow eyed and sickly pale, is not the boy I remember. But he still looks a lot like his mother. Which makes it hard. Especially when he turns away from me and starts to walk away.

But the shadow of the demon dog has seeped into my wounds. Its hatred is potent. Smoke rises from the holes in my body.

It is then that I am able to pull back my blood. This, my grandmother taught me when I was young. The blood flows in reverse, off the ground, back to its source.

Under my skin, bones mend. It's painful. But I've endured it before.

I draw my gun.

I won't shoot him in the back. Not my son.

I stagger to my feet. And he turns around at the sound.

When he reaches for his weapon, I fire.

I aim for his lower legs. I hit him in the left shin.

He tries to take a step back and collapses.

I don't fire again. I deliberately avoided the kill shot. I just stumble my way towards him.

But the spilling of blood has awakened the lioness on his arm. I can feel her stirring. Then she shifts and reverses her position, assuming the posture of the original she was based on.

Keiko has taken over. Suddenly on An's face there is a look of primal fear.

His tattooed arm lifts up, weapon in hand. He raises his opposite hand and clamps it down onto his right arm. He struggles violently against his own body.

I realize that Keiko now has control of his right arm. And she's bringing the gun to his head.

An locks eyes with me, terrified.

I break into a run.

He lets go of his possessed arm and reaches for me with his left hand, screaming now.

The moment I reach him, the moment I grab his hand, is the moment the gun goes off.

The shot exits the opposite side of his skull, temple to temple, spraying his blood across the floor. And on me. His arms go limp.

And now.

Now.

What are we?

I am on my knees. Still holding his hand. The world is quiet.

The years of slow drowning are over. But there's nothing left anymore.

I'm swallowing air in a cold empty room.

The demon dog in my blood howls now, unrepentant, with sheer exuberance.

The image of the lioness inked on his arm scrambles itself, like an ink blot, becoming nothing recognizable, an abstract art piece.

Where has she gone?

And where has he gone?

I lay down my weapon. I reach over and stroke his forehead.

There are things I would have told you if you had hated me less.

I feel something settle down near me. Looking over, I see the dog. It is very real. Large with black fur, wolflike in form. An unidentifiable breed.

I take my gun and aim it at the animal. But it doesn't flinch or react.

A whisper comes. Unintelligible. I look around. No. It's coming from inside my head.

Keiko is pleased with this outcome.

I lower the gun.

I'm still holding my son's hand. It's still warm.

The dog whispers again, a childlike female voice, and offers a name I haven't heard in years.

Mah Yang...

I shake my head. No. Not that one.

What did your grandmother call you then?

I don't answer. Everyone knows there's power to a name.

"If the soldiers come, run away to the mountain."

Samnang...

"Don't wait for me, and don't come back. You won't find me here."

I shake my head again. And stroke my son's hand.

It hurts, she tells me. *But it'll be better tomorrow. And tomorrow. More and more better. And then you'll get stronger.*

I have nothing to say to that.

I'll call Amal in a bit. She'll help me take care of things. Then I have to call Mai. And my brother.

I'll pretend to be human for a little while longer.

There's a little girl in the water, the dog says. *We are friends. She taught me how to swim. Maybe she'll want to go home now.*

I remember my dream. The two girls playing. If their spirits are trapped here, it's time to send them off.

I lay my fingers over my son's eyes to close them. Whisper some things I wish I'd said to him years ago.

I pick him up. His weight isn't as heavy as I expect. Under his jacket, his shirt hangs loose. His body is bone thin. A habitual user's body.

I carry him down the steps.

The dog follows. Like a loyal friend. With a limp in its back right leg.

I'll stay, she says. *I'm going with you when you look for the other one. My time on earth isn't done yet.*

I shake my head. But I know she doesn't take orders from me.

I make a final prayer for my son.

If I see you in the next life, I want to be your father again. I'll do better next time.

Below us, the water is waiting.

It's cold, but I am colder.

Late Night at the Low Road Diner

Frances Rowat

The only way to tell that the woods lining the road are brown is because the sky above them is so black. The night is warm but not friendly. The diner is dwarfed by the sweep of the road, a tealight in a cheap tin lantern.

Marisse, like the little dark core of a candle flame, moves around the diner. This is the heart of the night, and the only things in the building except her are yellow light and empty tables and the smells of coffee and old grease. From the inside, the windows are printed with a long reflection of the empty room, backed with the ghost of the parking lot. Once in a long while something goes by outside. Usually it's a car chasing the fan of its headlights or a big truck garlanded in running lights.

Something comes by slower than most and she hears it pulling into the empty parking lot and around the diner, circling right to left, before it heaves into one of the spaces and the engine growls itself to sleep. It's parked under one of the blown lights and she can't see it clear, but she has an impression of some dark not-black colour, green or brown, on an old car. One of the big ones, a sedan made out of steel and hard angles.

She hears one of its doors slam and watches as two people come towards the diner, open the door and get into its light and warm air. One's a boy that probably thinks he isn't, mean mouth and thin clothes with cheap bravado printed on them. He's paying more attention than Marisse likes to who else is in the diner (nobody) and which ceiling corners are home to cameras.

The other one. Well.

It's pale enough that even next to the boy, Marisse thinks of it as the white one. It's quiet in more senses than one, hard to pick out even standing right there in the room, and if it had been putting on a proper face, she might not have noticed anything odd, certainly wouldn't have seen it for what it is.

Since it's not dressing itself up properly, Marisse guesses it's either very new or very weak, maybe both.

Still. Customers.

The two of them take one of the booths next to the window and she comes over with a carafe and a pair of mugs. "Coffee?"

"Sure," the shabby boy says. He glances at her for a second but doesn't really see her, looks across the table at his travelling companion. It looks like milky glass, almost translucent, but this close

Marisse notices its eyes. Traffic-light-green, like the last place you have to get through in the city before you can hit the open road.

"You know what you want?"

The boy starts speaking, couple of specials off the plastic menu standing neatly in its slot next to the salt and pepper, and she nods and gives back rote responses (white or rye? extra-crispy?), and he doesn't notice her watching him. His eyes are full of the pale thing across the booth from him, and some of the mean goes out of his mouth while he's gazing.

She's pretty sure the food will only make a difference to one of them, but she goes to cook it up. Glances through the serving hatch from the kitchen and sees the boy drinking his coffee, both hands wrapped around the cup, and the other one just gazing indifferently into space. After a moment the boy says something, leaning forward and speaking soft, and the pale one picks up its coffee and drains it at a go, never mind the steam coming off it, and puts it down and goes back to looking at nothing.

The boy looks like he's going to break something, but that's probably just his version of wanting to cry.

Marisse brings the food out on one arm, coffee in her free hand. She's not looking to start anything, but if the boy gets to be sudden trouble it won't be the first time she's cracked someone over the head with a carafe. Keeps her smile up, though.

"You been driving long?" she says, and maybe it's the smell of food or her just being the kind of person that kind of boy would never care to notice, but he answers while he's looking at the white one.

"Couple of weeks. Road trip." He frowns a little and drops his voice. "Babe, c'mon," he says to the white thing. "Please." It picks up its knife and touches it to the food on the plate.

This close, from the corner of her eye, Marisse can see it's wearing nicer clothes than the boy; a dark button-up shirt, maybe. Its hands are drowned-white, but clean, the nails pale as lilies; the boy has red-rimmed nails, a streak of dirt grimed into the knuckles of his littlest and ring finger on his right hand, a thin cluster of slowly healing scratches across the base of his thumb.

"Well, it's a good car to do it in, I guess," she says, topping up their coffee. "Lots of trunk space."

The boy looks up at her fast and ready to be angry, and sees her standing there wrapped in friendly-diner-waitress, and tries to cover his reaction with a laugh.

"It's rusted shut," he says. "It's an—it's an old car."

Way he looks at the white thing makes Marisse guess he'd jump if she asked if he was using the back seat, so she just nods.

"Well, good thing it still runs," she says. "You both got everything you need?"

The white thing seems to have forgotten its food in favour of gazing out the window and not moving.

"Yeah, we're good." The boy's voice is angry-going-to-cry, and Marisse takes the coffee and goes back behind the counter.

The flattop grill in back will be too hot to clean just yet. The coffee is down to the dregs and she pours it out. She's just measuring out new grounds and water when she hears the boy getting out of the booth and coming up to the counter.

Marisse thinks of the chewed-raw nails and the anxious shiver and decides she doesn't need to really worry yet. Not when he's drunk her coffee and probably eaten her food.

The sound of the gun's safety clicking off is not a surprise. She resists the urge to tell him *just a minute* and puts the carafe in the coffee machine, then turns around, wiping her hands on the dishrag hooked into her apron.

It does not look like the first time he's pointed a gun at someone. His hand is shaking a little, but his eyes are clear and looking at *her*, as much as he cares to, and that mean set is back on his mouth.

"If you give me all your bullets," she says, "I'll teach you how to keep your friend from starving."

Whatever he was expecting, it wasn't *that*. His mouth drops open a little and his eyes go wide. His grip on the gun loosens and its weight pulls it down enough that the well of the barrel, black as the night outside, dips away from her face. No denying that makes her feel better.

He takes half a step back. Marisse doesn't lean over the counter, but folds her hands on it.

"Fuck do you mean," he says finally, which as far as it goes is a sensible question. Doesn't feed her anything that she doesn't already know, and he probably wants to be very careful about that right now.

"Your friend," she says, pointing past the boy with her chin. "How long have you two been together?"

"Weeks," he says in a slightly strangled voice, then rallies. "Met him a couple of weeks ago. Like I said. We're on a road trip."

Him is good to know; Marisse doesn't want to argue with however the boy sees it. She nods. "And you buy the food and take care of him, but he's not eating?" The boy draws the gun back and points it a little more down, which is as good as a nod. "Or if you insist, food makes no difference. And sometimes you worry that he's thin enough to see through, that he's just going to fade right away?"

The boy doesn't say anything, but his mouth pulls down and breath heaves through his teeth like he's readying for a fight.

"You're not wrong," Marisse confirms. "Give me all your bullets, and I'll teach you how to feed him. Some way you can both live with."

The wanting is easy to see. The suspicion is as ground into this boy as the meanness. "How'm I supposed to know what you'll tell me actually *works?*"

"You'll see it for yourself. Right here." She looks past him at the white thing. "What do you have to lose?"

"My bullets," he says, sounding like his throat's dry, and lets out a confused little chuckle. Marisse feels bad for him a minute, but she'd still prefer to see that gun unloaded.

"Well," she says, "what good will they do you if you can't take care of him?"

It's a calculated guess, with the softening of his mouth and the worry over the white thing eating and the anxious *babe*. A couple of weeks isn't long but Marisse doubts a boy like this has much to look back on or forwards to, and once you look at the thing its green green eyes would be easy to find striking, even if you hadn't been travelling with it.

He does something ratchet-sounding to the gun. Its magazine clunks free, and then a single bullet falls out and skitters on the counter next to it. She sweeps them both towards her and puts them under the cash register, then turns back to the boy.

"Alright," she says. She takes out her order pad and marks what he's already ordered PAID across the bottom; better not to clutter up the lesson with outstanding debts. "What money do you have?"

"Hey, you *got* the bullets—"

"This is for your friend." Marisse doesn't look towards it direct, but the corner of her eye and the hairs on her arm catch movement; the white thing is on its feet, standing by the booth. "It will hurt a little. It will not do you any harm. Take out your money." She taps the counter.

He glances back at the white thing and then shoves one hand into the tight pocket of his jeans, pulls out a crumple of faded green and sets it between them. Marisse stirs it a little, so no one bill is completely hidden by the others, and leaves her finger on the pile.

"You see this?" she says. He leans forward a little, looking down and frowning, and Marisse punches him with her other hand. Her knuckles split the thin softness of his lip as it's jammed between her fist and his teeth, and blood spatters thinly across the money. He barks in pain and staggers back a step, and she sweeps up the bills.

"*You fucking—*"

"You had better keep listening to me, for his sake." She doesn't raise her voice, but she points past him and that gets his attention. He looks back at the white thing, which is watching her with the patience of a cat waiting for a mistake.

But it's watching, and he swallows back the cursing so he can listen, one hand across his mouth. He bleeds easily, and that has probably never made his life easier, but she guesses he'll be glad of it now.

"Look," she says, holding the bills up but not out. They're flecked with a dirty red haze, studded with a few fat drops. "This is what it takes. Money that blood was shed for and shed on. This is how you feed your friend."

"He doesn't eat *money*." The voice is slightly strangled, a little thin and a little high. His eyes are bright, in a way he would not want noticed.

"No," Marisse says. "Here. I give you this," she rubs the bills between her fingers, and they make a soft dead-leaf sound, "and then you use this to buy him food. Or shelter—gas for the car, a room for the night. Clothes, if he needs them."

Any material thing that would sustain the living, food or shelter or clothing, will do the same for the dead if it's properly paid for.

The boy's staring at her. She puts the bills down and after a moment he jerks forward and sweeps them up, fingers pressing into their awkward folds.

"Now," she says calmly. "Get him food with that—paying up front works fastest—and it'll help him."

He touches one hand to his mouth and glances at the white thing. It's standing behind him, nearly at his shoulder. It's shorter than he is; she hadn't expected that.

He looks back at her, tries for a cocky smile and drops it when it pulls at the split in his lip. "What's the best I can get him with this?" he says, holding a ten out to her. There's a thin line of red across Hamilton's face, like a long papercut.

"I'll whip something up." She takes the ten and tucks it into her own pocket, goes back to the kitchen. When she comes out with a plate, the white thing's sitting neatly at the counter, and the boy's hovering behind it like a nervous parent watching his kid ride a bike down the road for the first time.

Marisse wonders how they met, but doesn't guess either of them will answer if she asks. She sets the plate down in front of it, and it picks up the cutlery without prompting and starts poking gently at the eggs with a fork. The boy's holding his breath, and Marisse pretends not to notice him letting it out when it scoops up a forkful of eggs.

The three of them stay there in silence for a moment, except for the hum of the lights and the *tink* of steel tines on the thick plate.

"Just pay for things with money that I bled on?" the boy says carefully after a minute.

Marisse shakes her head. "Money," she says precisely, "that had blood shed on it in someone's getting of it."

"But I can't just get it and *then* bleed on it." He frowns when she shakes her head again. "What if I'd grabbed it before you got to it?"

"Long as you'd bled on it, that'd be fine. Fighting to get to keep it is still getting it."

He makes a thoughtful noise, touching his mouth again. "You gave it to me," he says slowly. "And it still worked. Could I buy the ten back from you and use it again?"

"If I was selling it."

He frowns but looks at the white thing eating and decides not to pick an argument. Marisse can see it a little better now, the shape of its face coming through. It looks like a young man, drowning-pale, but like a young man instead of something in a midnight closet trying to pretend to be one. It doesn't have a particularly pleasant expression, but she's not seeing the meanness of the boy's mouth anywhere on its features.

She does not forget that dead things are no less dead because they weren't killed out of meanness.

The coffee's done brewing, and she pours each of them a cup. The boy pokes at his, turning the handle in a slow counterclockwise drag, like the car pulling in to the parking lot. "Do I need—if I get us a room, do I need to pay for all of it with bloody money?"

"Wouldn't hurt if you did, but no. Could be just one of the bills. Long as *some* blood's part of paying; otherwise, it's not real to him, you see?"

He nods slowly. The white thing is shaking pepper over the last of the eggs.

"What if I got—like, a credit card? With blood on it?"

Marisse shrugs. "Maybe. It's not traded, but it lets you buy things. Blood rubs off plastic pretty quick, though."

His mouth narrows. "You said you knew how to feed him."

"I *do* know how to feed him," she says, calm. "Look at him. Doesn't mean I'll swear to how trying something different works out."

His shoulders fall a little, and he looks back at the white thing. Its face has grown clear enough to look mildly irritated, but it leans towards him a little, and the warm boy puts one hand lightly across the back of its shoulder. It's finished its food and is holding its own coffee cup, now, gingerly because of the heat, and Marisse can see the steam moving in its breath.

"Real to him. Does this mean we can get drunk?" the boy says, like he's looking for something to make a joke of.

"That will work, yes."

He smiles a little, thinly, and that mean streak is clearer in his mouth. "And if I'd made you open the cash register, and then I'd shot you while you were next to it..."

Marisse just looks at him, and reaches easily for the carafe. He's standing a little behind the white thing, but not too far. She has dealt with more frightening things than this tattered boy, working nights along the road.

"Rain," the white thing says, "she's done us a favour."

He looks down at it again and slides his arm a little further around its shoulders. "How you feeling?"

"Better." Its voice is soft and dry; it sounds not unlike the crumpling of the bills in the boy's pockets when he pulled them out. Marisse thinks it's quite young. If what it said about the favour is true, it probably doesn't understand itself quite yet either.

She thinks of the (purportedly rusted-shut) trunk of the car, waiting in the parking lot under the black of the sky.

"You okay with her knowing about us?" the boy says quietly, and he's still watching Marisse, but he's standing close enough behind the white thing with his arm far enough around it that Marisse would call it a hug. Not out loud, but still.

"What would I tell anyone about you?" she said. "Two men—" a stretch, that, but she guesses at least one of them would balk at being called *boy*—"on a road trip came in and paid for their food and left. Driving the car they came in, whose colour and license plate I did not see."

"One of them had a gun," the boy says.

Marisse sniffs dismissively. "With no bullets. A paperweight."

She could tell more, of course. There are police who drive this road at night, sometimes, and they understand the kind of things you can see in the dark. They know to keep their windows rolled up; if one drives home alone, they know to fill the front passenger seat with a folded jacket or a lunchbox so that they will never glance to the right and see

164

that where there should be an empty seat there is something that has moved into the space and is now grinning at them.

She could say there is a boy driving down the road, and maybe he travels with a pale thing beside him that is not afraid of police, or maybe there is a corpse in dark clothes slowly shrivelling in the trunk of his car, or both. She could say that he has a mean streak and an anxious devotion and those two are a bad pairing for anyone he decides he needs to cross.

The boy is looking carefully at her, but he only knows that if she decided to say something she'd have a reason to be afraid, and she isn't afraid. She guesses he knows the trick of putting things out of his mind, but he doesn't recognize it when someone else uses it.

And then, of course, the white thing's gentle remonstration—*she's done us a favour*—weighs with him.

"Okay," he says softly and then looks down at it again. "Okay, babe. Let me know when you're done and we'll get out of here, alright?"

It nods and drinks its coffee, slowly enough to be tasting it, then straightens up and gets off the stool. "Thank you," it says politely, and Marisse nods and murmurs a *you're welcome* that includes them both, but she swallows back the *come again* that's near reflex after so many years.

The door wheezes and slams, and they are gone.

She sweeps the bullet and magazine out from under the cash register and puts them in her hip pocket. Those and the ten-dollar bill she keeps separate from the accounting of tips at the end of her shift.

She drops the bullets down a storm drain in the paling grey light of dawn.

The ten-dollar bill, she keeps against future concerns.

Immaterial

Dan Grace

Eryn drops.

As she pulls the mask from her face the stink of the lock-up hits her. There's never been a time when, coming back from a payday, she hasn't felt her stomach turn at this smell.

The nausea passes and she's left with the image. Even from a distance she recognised the face. Dark brown eyes framed by those long black braids. But then the complete lack of recognition. Her back as she turned into the crowd. Her own inability to follow, to check.

The sound of a dozen or so others, the gasps, the faint murmur of voices, leak through the thin ply partitions. With an outstretched hand she unhooks the ties from the wall, loosening the knot of ropes that hold her suspended. The landing is awkward, her ankle turns. Slowly she pulls herself up, turns on the tap and hoses herself and the floor down.

A face she hasn't seen for three years now. Her sister's face. A face she assumed had vanished from her life. Moira.

Her belongings are still there, folded tight in a thick plastic bag. She pulls on underwear, overalls, boots. Limps out of the booth and glances up at the clock.

Late for work again.

He is a successful businessman. She forgets his name. She has no idea what his business is either, only that it is located in the Immaterial, and that means she has a job here.

He hangs from the ceiling encased in wires and tubes feeding stuff in and out of his body. His rig is a little more sophisticated than the one she so recently vacated, though it does the same thing. No open drain and hose here.

Today, to save time, she just vacuums everything, floors, surfaces, body. It fucks up the filters, but it's worth it if she's running late, filters are cheap compared to losing a client. It only really works for those that are in all the time, like him, the ones where she can come back later in the schedule and do things properly. People like him are always there, never here. What they know of this world, her world, is filtered through the haze of the Immaterial.

It's rote; she doesn't have to think about it. Instead she checks the lists in her head, the ways and means she has of getting through the next seven days until payday.

Home is a bunk in a dorm in a house in a street in a city that is slowly dissolving. Dissolving under a lack of funds, a lack of care, a lack of anything approaching a functioning public sphere.

Home is a word that she's pretty sure means something other than this.

The mess is quiet at this time of night. She pokes tofu chunks around her plate. Christy is eating fish again. Lifting soft white flakes to her delicate mouth as she reads.

"Where do you get that stuff?"

Christy looks up from her book, chews and swallows.

"Fishing. Out at the old reservoir, down the Rivelin Valley." She takes a sip of water. "Why? You wanna come sometime?"

Eryn thinks about it. The wet, the cold. Bright scales pulled from the murk.

"Maybe."

She hasn't known Christy long, a few weeks maybe, and you have to be careful. All kinds of stories about trusting strangers. She can hear Moira, advising, teasing. Ever present in the back of her mind. She can't always make out the words but the voice is always there, pulling her through each day, reminding her of what can happen if you get too close.

"Lend you the gear if that's what you're worried about."

Then again she hasn't known anyone long.

"I mean, yeah. That'd be good."

Christy grins and Eryn tries to suppress the smile she can feel behind her lips.

"Week after next I'll be heading up. Can even stay the night, I know some folk in the camp near there. If you fancy it?"

The smile pushes its way free.

"Yeah, I'd like that. That'd be cool."

It's an early start the next day. Back to businessman's place to clean up what she missed. Then on to half a dozen other places; small or large, wealthy or not so wealthy, but all on the spectrum of privilege, of a way up to the Immaterial.

Her mind is pulling in two directions and it's tearing a hole inside her.

Moira. Her face.

Christy. Her smile.

She has to go back up. To try and find her again. If it was her. No, it was. She is sure of that.

She finishes a job and pulls out her phone to check her balance. Digits slowly ticking down as debits are pulled for all of life's essentials. The answer's always there, in the numbers. And the answers always the same. She can't afford a trip before payday, before she has to go up and meet her employer and accept the transfer. A trip up is a trip up and it costs what it costs, no matter the reason.

She puts her phone away, picks up her bag and sets off for the next in a never-ending line of jobs.

◉

She pulls her boots off and massages her feet. Overalls and underwear follow and she rapidly hoists herself up, slipping the mask over her face.

It's a little different every time. Some say it's like an elevator, others a ladder, others a soft wind beneath them lifting them towards the light. Today it's none of these. It's like a bullet from a gun. She is up in the plaza, in the blazing white light quicker than a single beat of her heart.

Disorientated, she stumbles across the open space, tries to pin down the reason she is here. She gets pitying looks from those with their numbers flashing on their wrists, visitors like her. Those with the bright ourobouros, the residents of this place, ignore her entirely.

Payday. Numbers. She shakes her head and moves towards the queue outside the agency building. The representation of the agency building. Its interior, no doubt, not adhering the logic of its exterior. She's never been beyond the wide desk at the head of the queue.

Moira had explained all this to her before they came up, together, for their first payday. They'd clung tight to each other as they'd crossed the plaza. The eerie beauty of its residents hit like a brick. Moira had leaned in close.

"Projections," she'd whispered.

Computer simulations of beauty, uncanny in their grace and poise. That had been the fashion then, things had moved on since. Now imperfection was all the rage, a simulated realism. A simulacrum of the life the inhabitants of the Immaterial no longer had to live.

Moira had been so excited, always rambling on about the beauty and potential of the Immaterial, how the rising tide could lift us all. The clearer it became that this wouldn't be the case, that the new economy was just the old economy with a different face, the more Moira withdrew from her and from life in general.

Until one day she was just gone.

Eryn stares at the back of the head of the woman in front of her. Gone. Not a word. Not that they talked much by then anyway. She could have been gone a month, two maybe, before Eryn had noticed.

She shuffles to the front of the queue, receives her pay.

She drops.

"They realised their dream of a frictionless economic sphere, a digital informational nirvana of free production and consumption."

Christy shrugs.

"Of course the lack of friction just means they can't feel anything."

Eryn reaches around the edge of the fire, plucks the joint from Christy's hand and takes a lungful.

"That must be nice. To not feel anything, don't you think?"

Christy wrinkles up her nose.

"No way. You've got to have it all haven't you? The giddying highs and the terrifying lows, it's all part of the package. I mean, what's the point otherwise? And worse still they try to emulate it. They've shed the material world and its troubles and then they try to buy it back with projections, images of the real bought from the desperate and stupid."

Eryn nods. She thinks about saying something, but she isn't sure what it is she wants to say. A thought clots at the back of her head. She can feel it trying to push through into the foreground of her consciousness. Her mind wanders. They sit in silence.

The camp is up above Ladybower Reservoir. There are people here with no phones, with no jobs, at least in the real sense of the word. There are people here who have never been up. They laugh and they argue and they live and they don't concern themselves with what goes on in the Immaterial.

She imagines herself living here.

Christy breaks the silence.

"So what do you make of it then?"

She isn't clear about how it works, how they make decisions or get anything done. What do they eat? Lots of fish she guesses.

"I like it. I really do. I've never seen anything like it."

She surprises herself with how much she means this.

"Well, that's great. They don't plan on it being like this forever, but for now it works. I'm thinking about moving out here myself. You should come too."

Christy looks at her with bloodshot eyes, shrugs. Eryn studies the back of her hands.

"I'd like that, but I have some stuff I need to do."
Christy cocks her head, narrows her eyes and smiles.
"Stuff?"
Eryn sighs and leans her head back to look up at the stars.
"It's hard to explain."
Christy edges around the fire and pushes herself up against Eryn.
"No rush. Tell me when you're ready."

The tents are a bricolage of ingenuity. It's clear, as she gets deeper into the camp, that some of the people here know what they are doing. PV panels sit atop the more solid constructions, windmills too. Her mind is still floating free, like a balloon, only lightly tethered to her body. After they'd kissed she needed to walk, to put some space between them.

Too many new things at once. Moira's voice that.

A bell tent catches her eye. The outside is adorned with small flags, scraps of coloured material. The sides are up so she can see figures moving about inside. The thick scent of incense drifts out from its cool interior.

"Come in."

The voice comes from inside the tent. Eryn peers into the half-light. She can make out one larger figure and several smaller ones. Children she assumes. She feels like sitting down. Her head is starting to throb.

"Thanks."

She allows her eyes to adjust to the change of light. A woman, maybe ten years older than her, emerges from the darkness, a smile on her lips. Half a dozen children, none of them older than eight or nine by Eryn's estimate, sit around on cushions and a bench. A couple seem interested in her, others go on playing or eating. One of them shuffles along the bench a little. The woman gestures.

"Sit here."

Eryn goes to sit but a small voice pipes up from the opposite side of the tent.

"No, sit here."

She watches a small girl shuffle over on her cushion to make space. The woman rolls her eyes.

"Children, let our guest choose."

Eryn realises this means her. She shambles forward.

"I'll sit here thanks."

She slumps down next to the first child. A boy, maybe six or so.

"Ha!"

The boy wriggles against her side and grins up at her and then across at the girl on the cushion. Eryn notices that he's pretty dirty. Not in a neglectful sense, she'd seen far worse around the city, more in a child-in-the-woods sense. Mud, leaves, twigs, undiscernible bits and pieces. She smiles back at him.

"Soup?"

The woman hands her a steaming bowl. She gulps it down without thinking.

"Thanks, that was lovely."

The woman laughs.

"I'm Jessie, and I'm glad you liked it. You looked hungry."

Eryn grins and feels her cheeks flush red. She can hear Moira, laughing, telling her what a fool she must look like, wandering into a stranger's tent and eating their food with barely a word. But they'd invited her, hadn't they? She shook her head, tried to clear the fog.

"I'm Eryn, thanks, I don't have anything to give in return though."

"Oh, don't be daft, I'd made too much anyway. This lot are so picky sometimes."

Jessie gestures at the surrounding children. They ignore her. Eryn stretches and yawns. She feels awkward, like she's interrupting their mealtime.

"Well, ok, I should probably leave you to it."

Jessie eyes her.

"You're new here, right?"

Eryn smiles and looks down at the ground.

"That obvious is it?"

"You just seem a little tense, love. Like you've still got some of the city in you."

The boy next to her shuffles away.

"Eww, the city! I wondered what the smell was."

Jessie rolls her eyes again.

"Jack, that's not nice, is it?"

The boy pouts and glances up at Eryn.

"True though. The city smells funny."

Eryn laughs.

"He has a point."

Jack slides from the bench and points at Eryn.

"Hey, if you're new I bet you haven't been to the middle have you?"

Eryn blinks.

"The middle of what?"

He laughs, turns to the others.

"She hasn't been to the middle!"

The children weave around them as they walk the paths. Jessie points out the various tents of useful services, important people, interesting design and ill-repute. She seems to know everybody they pass, has a word for each of them. Moira's voice is clear in her head as Eryn passes through; hippies, the lot of them, never trust a hippy. She decides it's time to ignore her sister.

After a short walk they emerge into an open space, the middle of the camp Eryn assumes. It's larger than she would have expected. Planted throughout the clearing are young trees.

"Apples mainly."

Jessie's voice makes her jump.

"Some hazel and walnut. Pear too. A couple of quince and damson. A full orchard one day, hopefully."

Eryn nods, watches the children run off amongst the trees.

"That would be good I guess."

Jessie smiles at her.

"When we first arrived we decided we need to do something beyond just what was necessary. Make a mark in some way, even if this wasn't going to be permanent. Just something solid, something real, you know? We get a little more fruit each year."

There's a rumble of thunder in the distance and Jessie calls to the children. She turns to Eryn once more.

"Come and visit any time, you hear? When you're more settled."

With a final smile she's gone leaving Eryn stood amongst the trees. She wonders if she should have told them that she's just passing through, not here permanently. Back to the city soon, work to do. The thunder sounds again, closer this time and people start to head for cover.

Eryn stands and waits to feel the rain against her face.

"I'm going back you know. To the camp. To stay."

They're curled up in Eryn's bunk, thin curtain pulled across for a semblance of privacy. She can smell Christy's sweat below the spiky odour of cleaning products. She had forgotten how much smell matters, how it can set the heart racing or calm it in an instant.

It's been an intense few weeks. A tangled blur of work and limbs and paydays.

Christy rolls away from her.

"I'd like you to come too."

Eryn says nothing.

"I know. I know. You want to see your sister, but, Eryn, I've been thinking."

Eryn feels her muscles tense. She knows what's coming.

"You know it's probably not her, don't you? I'm sorry Eryn, but think about it. She's sold her projection, that's all. She's as good as gone. Her image, her voice, her mannerisms, all for the money to get out of here."

"Shut up. You don't know. It could be her."

She pushes Christy away. The spell is broken though. If you avoid saying a thing then it can never be real. Once it's said, you can't unsay it.

"Hey! Listen. There's a way to know. Without hanging around and hoping you might bump into her again. I can't stop you if you want to go. I wouldn't want to. I've heard there are places, beyond the plaza, where they know about this kind of thing. I'm guessing it will cost, I mean, what doesn't? But I also know that if I'm leaving I won't need these."

She holds her phone up so Eryn can see the flickering digits.

"I want you to have them."

Eryn shakes her head.

"I can't."

Christy smiles and pulls her close.

"Yes, you can."

The spaces beyond the plaza are an unknown. Each time she and Moira came up they'd talk of exploring, but each time, once they'd collected their pay, they knew that they didn't have the numbers for it. And so down they went.

This time she ignores the queue, it isn't payday after all, makes straight for the far side, the place she'd seen Moira move towards. Weeks ago now. Guilt breaks the surface in her chest.

The options are overwhelming. There are at least a couple of dozen exits from this side of the plaza, roads cut through solid cubes of rock or rising to twist around filigreed, impossible structures reaching up through the cloud layer.

The simplest, least daunting of the exits is an enclosed walkway. It's not unlike images she has seen of shopping malls, glass everywhere and behind the glass things she can see no particular use for but desires all the same. Her reflection, a simple projection devoid of any personality or deeper meaning, designed only to convey that someone is there, matches her step for step as she moves further and further from the plaza. She becomes increasingly aware of how out of place she looks.

From a distance she spots the sign she is looking for and makes for the doorway.

The room is cool and clean, sparsely furnished with few customers in it. Around the wall are projections. Naked human forms of all ethnicities, genders and body types. A man approaches her.

"I assume you are here on your employer's behalf?"

Eryn shakes her head.

"No, I'm looking for someone."

He sighs.

"We do rentals, my dear. But if you can't afford that," he glances meaningfully at her exposed wrist. "Then I will have to ask you to leave."

"No, actually, I can afford it. I can. I'm looking for someone specific and just for a short while. Do you have a catalogue?"

The man stares at her. Glances again at her wrist. He seems to be making a decision.

"Very well, here."

He gestures to one of the displays, shows her how to input parameters, move back and forth through options.

It doesn't take long, she knows precisely what she is looking for. Her voice leaps out of her when she finds it.

"This one, this one."

It takes a fraction of a second. No time to adjust. She never imagined when she saw her sister again it would be here. The cubicle seems to be made of pure white light, a microcosm of the pristine world of the Immaterial, and now she wonders about the sanity of this plan.

There's a full length mirror. She can't look at it. Not yet. Instead she looks at her wrist. Moira's wrist. She doesn't have long, but her strength is deserting her.

Now she knows. Her sister is gone. Like suicide but without the inconvenience of being dead, was how Christy had described it. Gone all the same.

But she was her sister and so.

She stares into the mirror. Moira stares back at her, dark brown eyes filled with recognition. She lets their hand trace the contours of Moira's face. She opens their mouth and Moira's voice tumbles out.

"I want to tell you that I miss you, that I wish you'd never left, wherever you've gone.

"I want to tell you about what it's like now, how it got so much worse, but how I think it's going to get better.

"I want to tell you about this person I've met, how they make me feel.

"I want to tell you not to give up, but it's too late for that, so instead I'll tell you I'll never give up. And that I'm not alone."

She glances down at her wrist, the numbers dropping away. Nearly zero.

Moira's eyes watch her from the mirror and she holds that image, lets it saturate her. And there it is, the familiar tug of the material.

She makes their hand wave goodbye to her sister.

Eryn drops.

Salt and Smoke

Storm Blakley

All the ghost stories seem to take place in conveniently creepy places like old manors at midnight, but not mine. It's in a family-owned corner convenience store, at about three in the afternoon, that I first see my true love.

I'm in for my usual restock of cheap whiskey and harsh cigarettes, and have already had too little to eat and entirely too much to drink. Don't judge me, you don't know my life. I don't even bother with a basket, barely succeeding in keeping the three brown bottles from spilling out of my arms. I look up, having prevented a small disaster, and there she is, short and curvy, just watching me with those stunning dark eyes, as knowing and unknowable as the sea at night.

She wears steel-toe boots and a dress with flowers of some sort on it, a large-brimmed straw hat with a wide ribbon hanging down back resting on her short dark hair. I can't tell you what colour any of it was, so don't ask. Ghosts don't have colour like the rest of the world; they belong to the in-between places, and whatever colour they might once have had leached out of them when they died. I don't mean to sound cold; it's just the way things are. Colour belongs to the living, not the dead. They exist in black and white and grey. Light and shadow, life and death, and the liminal spaces in between, that most people can't perceive.

But I can. I'm the only one I know who can, since Gram passed away five years back. I miss her, so much, every day. She was the only one who ever understood, and I count myself lucky to have had her to teach me all she could. She'd be disappointed in me now, I know. She saw helping ghosts as a responsibility, while I see it a lot more like a burden. I drink to try to keep the ghosts away, as well as the memories. It might not be so bad if she were around, but Gram understood death better than anyone, and it's highly unlikely she'd be stuck here, still. Her business was death, so no unfinished business there, as far as I can tell. It's not like she wouldn't come see me if she were still around, right? Right?

The afternoon sunlight shines right through the ghost, and she looks like gold, and it takes my breath away. She smiles, giving a shy little wave, and I almost drop my bottles when I instinctively try to wave back. This is met with a grin, but before I can react, it's my turn at the till.

I toss a handful of stained, crumpled bills on the counter, and ask Andray for a pack of jerky, as well. He slides a pack of Smoke 'em If

You Got 'em Assorted Jerky into the bag, beside my Hoarse Creek whiskey and Grove's Unfiltereds. Andray's a good man; he knows what I like.

"You need more to eat than that," he implores, as he picks up the bills and unfolds them, riffling through them quickly with long fingers and doing the math in his head. "You don't take care of yourself, my momma's gonna have a word."

I laugh, and tell him to keep the change, buy his mom flowers for me. They're good people, Andray and Mrs. M. They take good care of me, which is probably for the best, since I don't take care of myself much these days. Gram and Mrs. M would have gotten along like peanut butter and jelly, or something. Shut up, metaphors aren't my jam. Ghosts are, supposedly, but I hate it. Seems to me that we shouldn't hate the things we're best at, but life has a way of fucking with me. I feel like I've forgotten something, but it dances just past my grasp, as such things often do.

Outside, I start to make my way down to the docks, my ragged runners slapping the pavement in an unsteady rhythm, the peeling sole on the left flapping a counterpoint, and the ghost follows, noiselessly. When you don't really have feet, it's hard to make footsteps.

I chose the docks for a reason. Salt is a good barrier against spirits, supposedly, and my hope was that the salt air coming in off the bay would keep the ghosts further away. It's mostly worked, but the more stubborn ones get through. And they're all so damned stubborn. Not-stubborn people don't usually hang around after they've died. The noise of the boats coming and going, the susurrus of the sea rasping against the stones, can drown out the whispers of the dead, and that helps me sleep, which must be a good thing. Booze helps, but doesn't, at the same time. I used to dream, I think. I read somewhere that everyone does, that if we don't, our sanity starts to crack, but I don't, anymore, or at least, I don't remember them, and I can't remember the last time I ever felt rested.

My apartment sits over a warehouse, so I have a nice view of the bay, and the sunsets on the water can be spectacular. When I'm awake enough to see them, anyway. Not as often as I'd like, if I'm being honest. I used to love watching the sunsets. They're an in-between time, like ghosts exist in in-between places, and being drawn to them is part of my nature, I guess, as much as them being drawn to me.

I ignore the ragged armchair I'd hauled off the street a few years back, my only real piece of furniture, and sit on the floor by the window, out of the sun, thumping my bag down at my feet and reaching in to grab a bottle. The plastic cap cracks under my grip, and the top spins off easily, rolling across the floor and through her feet. I wince slightly, because that's incredibly rude, but she doesn't react. After a long drink, I rest the bottle in my lap and meet her eyes again.

"What's your name?"

"Alia." Her voice is louder, stronger than I expected. Ghosts fade with time, and it looks like she's been dead for quite a while. She looks thin, attenuated, like smoke pulling apart from itself as it escapes the fire. She sits down across from me, cross-legged in the shadows, and I can't help but wish she'd sit in the sunlight, so I could see her golden again.

"Hi, Alia. I'm Riley."

"Nice to meet you, Riley." It's awkward, but kind, and that's a nice change from the usual demands. You'd think that being dead would make people less likely to be assholes, but most of them, it just makes them worse. Especially when they find the one person in the entire fucking city, as far as I know, who can see them. Sometimes I think about moving to the woods, but that seems like such a pain in the ass, and there's no way I could ever afford it.

"You've been wandering a long time." I take another drink and light a smoke with the lighter I always carry in my pocket, though it's almost out of fuel; I knew I forgot to grab something at Mrs. M's.

There's something wonderful about a perfect sunbeam, angling through a shadowed room, and watching the smoke dance in it, eddies and spirals, grey in gold. She's watching it, too, with an indescribable longing in her eyes. Understandable; how long since she's been able to feel anything?

"Yes." She hesitates, twisting her fingers together in her lap.

"What are you looking for?" I ask, changing the subject. If she doesn't want to talk about her life or death, that's fine, and I'm not going to pry; ghosts deserve privacy as much as everyone else. Just because they're dead doesn't mean they aren't still people.

She came to me for a reason, though, so that's fair game to ask. Most ghosts stick around because they need something. Closure, usually, though sometimes it's an object, or someone they care about. Strong emotions tie people to places in life, so it stands to reason that that would last beyond death.

"It's silly," she laughs, looking away shyly.

"Can't be. If it were, you wouldn't still be here."

She's surprised at that, and a smile spreads across her face, chasing away the worry like the rising sun chases the morning fog off the bay. It's wonderful to see; most of the ghosts I meet are angry, though I expect a lot of that has to do with my own attitude and hostility. I shouldn't be, I know. Taking it out on them is wrong, but I didn't ask for this, and since Gram died, I've been so alone. I'm still in the wrong there, though, and I'm going to have to work on that.

Gram always told me to be gentle with the dead. They're lost, she reminded me, whenever I got frustrated. They're lost, and alone, and scared, a lot of the time. I can almost hear her voice, and feel the warmth of her smile, her hands, the joints swollen and painful, on my shoulder. Be gentle, she said. Be gentle, be truthful, be kind, and make them welcome in your home.

A gust of wind brings the salt air in through the window, stirring the ragged band flag I pretend is a curtain, and I'm ashamed, yet again, that I've let her down; this isn't a welcome place for the dead. There's no change in Alia's posture or expression, but for a moment she wavers, a reflection on water stirred by a breeze, and I'm terrified she'll vanish. Salt doesn't kill ghosts, just keeps them away, but she's been here so long, she's so faded, that for a moment it looks like she'll tear apart like old silk.

I offer to close the window, but she shakes her head, the ribbon on her hat sliding gracefully over her shoulders.

"I almost feel like I can taste it," she murmurs, and there's that longing again. How hard, how lonely must it be, to exist in a world that doesn't see you? To walk the ground of a place you called home, only to see everything change over the years, until nothing you knew remained, and to have to grieve your losses all alone?

"My dad ran a fishing boat, and he always told me the salt was in our blood." That smile again, only lightly touched with sorrow. "This is the first time I've been back to the sea in many, many years."

"That must have been hard, to be so close, but unable to come back home."

She nods, and smiles again, but she looks so tired, worn out like a favourite dress.

"I'm sorry I brought you here. Would you like to go somewhere else?" Awkward again, but I've never been good at talking to people. Gram charmed everyone, because who doesn't love a little old peach of a lady, but that's a skill I was never able to master.

She's shaking her head again.

"I don't think I have much time left, and if this is the end, I'd like to be able to be home again, or close to."

We sit in silence for a bit, her eyes on the sea out the window, drinking in the view of the sea as if trying to commit it to memory, while I do the same with every curve of her dark face. She doesn't, we both know. Have much time left, I mean. Days, maybe, at best.

"What happens?" she asks, turning back to meet my eyes. Direct, this time, no shyness, only fatigue. "When we go?"

I answer her truthfully, as she deserves, as Gram would have wanted.

"I don't know. Everyone has ideas, but I don't think anyone really knows. Most people, I think, just make up stories, because uncertainty and fear of the unknowable are scary as fuck.

"My Gram, she knew more than most. Your family came from the sea? Mine came from the dead. As far back as we can remember, women in our family carried the dead. That's what Gram called it: Carrying the Dead.

"Gram said that those we could help found their way home, but those we couldn't would fade like old cloth, the weight of their grief tearing them into smaller and smaller pieces until there's nothing left.

"Carrying the dead doesn't just mean that we carry them home. We carry their memory, as long as we can. Everything else might fade away, but the memory of the dead we carry until the end."

"Do you like music?" she asks suddenly, abruptly, her voice a melody all on its own.

That's a loaded question, and a sore spot, but fair's fair. If I'm going to ask her questions, she can, too, though I'm puzzled by the change in topic.

"I used to. I was in a band, once." My stomach growls, so I butt out my smoke and tear into the bag of jerky, careless of manners or propriety. I haven't eaten all day, so the smell is heavenly, even if it doesn't count as real food. To be honest, I haven't eaten much since Gram died. Everything tastes like ash. She'd be so sad to see me like this, I know, but when she went, so did all the light in my world, and I just don't know how to deal with it, let alone carry on.

Until today, when I saw a vision in black and grey and gold.

The sun has lowered while we've been talking, and the beam on the floor is almost touching her. Outside, the afternoon sun will be dancing on the waves, marking the sails in shadow and light. Ships and boats of all sizes will still be coming in and out, regular as the tides they use to work their trade. Maybe one of them belongs to her family, still on the salt despite the gulf of years between them.

"What did you play?"

"Bass."

"Can I listen?"

I stuff the last of the jerky in my mouth, as I get to my feet, leaving the packet crumpled carelessly on the floor. Gram never ate in front of the dead; she felt it was disrespectful to those who could no longer enjoy the comforts of the living. She'd have tea, and pour a cup for them, a small offering like we used to give to hearth gods, back in the day. I haven't done that since we shared a pot on our last day together, and I feel guilty, now. Alia deserves better, but I don't have any tea to offer. My stomach appreciates the sustenance, though, since it was already getting whiskey-sour, and the taste of salt and smoke lingers on my lips.

The speakers are dusty with disuse, and I have to use my sleeve to scrub out the docking port enough to clip my phone in. I'd wanted to delete the songs when the band broke up, but never did have the energy to get around to it. My own way of carrying that particular dead, I suppose. No one else had the recordings, so if I'd done so, there'd be nothing of it left.

It sounds tinny, coming out of the cheap speakers, but she closes her eyes for a moment, that brilliant smile spreading across her face again. "Atmosphere," Imani had called this one when she wrote it, and her guitar work was impeccable, rising and falling so as to reach the stars, my bass pulsing behind in a counterpoint as steady as the tide. Aditi had been a supernova on drums, always grinning, her impossibly solid rhythm the gravity that held the rest together. I wonder if she still plays.

I turn around, and Alia is behind me, one hand outstretched. She's in the sun again, and gods, she's beautiful. Here, away from the clutter of life, I can really see it. Glowing gold and black and grey shadows, the skirt swaying around her legs, and those eyes, like wells of night.

"Dance with me," she asks, a small smile on her lips. I don't know how, let alone how it'd be possible, but I don't hesitate.

I step forward, reaching out for her hand, and her arm goes around where my shoulders would be. There's no contact; there wouldn't be, since ghosts don't have mass, but somehow, our bodies move together as the music swirls around us, carried by the breeze off the bay, two strangers in tune with one another.

Imani's guitar sings higher, her voice meeting every note, singing of hope, of reaching our dreams. The bassline is a pounding heartbeat, matching mine, and I can almost feel the weight of the woman in my arms. Aditi's drums are inexorable as an avalanche, building towards a crescendo, and the suddenness with which the rhythm stops makes if feel like the floor has dropped out from beneath us, Imani's voice hanging in the silence, clear as crystal, a lifeline in the abyss of absence.

"Thank you," Alia whispers. "I always wanted to dance with a girl I liked."

She kisses me, and to my shock, I feel it. Salt and smoke on my lips. Salt to ward off spirits, and smoke as a gift for them to enjoy, Gram had told me, one of my first lessons as a child. How could I have forgotten?

Alia gasps, taking a step back as if burned, touching her fingers to her lips.

"Salt," she whispers in wonder, joyful tears in her eyes, and it's as if a weight has been lifted off her, as if she's come home after an indescribably long journey. Her body turns to mist, radiant gold in that perfect beam of sunlight. That sea breezes gusts through, sweeping her off her feet, her human form collapsing into a cloud, then carries her off through the window. I follow, silently, and lean my hands on the splintered sill to watch as she spreads out over the bay, headed towards the sea, going home.

There's a new hollow inside me, next to the one that came when Gram left, but somehow, the two together make the pain less. Strange, how we deal with grief, with loss. Sometimes, one loss creates a hole big enough to swallow the world, but a second can take some of the pain away, as if the first ached with loneliness, and the second keeps it company.

Entwined with that, though, ribbons of gold weaving through the darkness of loss, is a sense of purpose I haven't felt in a long time. Despite the losses she'd been through, Alia had always smiled, at least in the short time I'd known her, and there's a joy like nothing else in coming home. Somehow, watching her disperse over the sea, I've also found my way back home.

I will remember her, as I remember all the others, those from before, and those yet to come. I will carry their memory to the end, like my Gram taught me, and I will never forget a dance in the afternoon sunlight, and a kiss that tasted of salt and smoke.

Horangi

Thomas Ha

"*I wanted to be darker*," I said in Korean.

My grandfather let the unlit cigarette in his lips droop as he squinted at me. I remember him sitting on the cement steps outside of the Kalihi house, tucking the cigarette behind his ear while he looked me over.

My skin was raw from lying out in the sun all morning, my face already glowing like a tomato. I removed my sweaty shirt and shorts, and there were still pale patches of skin where my clothes had been and bright lines on my feet left from the straps of my slippers, little parts of my original coloring that I'd never quite erase.

My grandfather made me turn around, and he opened a bottle of aloe, filling the cradle of his palm with a big dollop before spreading the cool gel on my shoulders and back. His large, callused hands covered me in several sweeps, then he spread the last of the aloe with his thumbs across the crest of my cheeks and on my nose before letting me get dressed again.

I held up my skinny wrist next to his, a thin strip of pink next to his golden-brown forearm, to see whether I'd made any progress. I couldn't know it then, but darkening my skin wouldn't make much difference. My Korean cousins would go on calling me "the Haole" for most of my childhood, because I resembled my white father, and there wasn't anything I could do to change that.

"*You know*," my grandfather said, wiping his hands clean. "*In Korea, everyone wants pale skin like yours.*" He put his cigarette back in his lips and rested his elbows on the top step, staring out at the shadowy jungle at the end of the backyard that led into the valley. When I was older, he would tell me that it reminded him of the mountain forests in his hometown, of a time when people were few and far between, in their little villages, and beasts moved freely wherever they wished.

"*But we're not in Korea*," I sat next to him.

"*No... we're not.*" He rested his hand on top of my head, running his fingers through my light brown hair.

Those early years when we lived with my grandparents, long before my grandfather ever got sick, are more flashes than filmstrips when I look back on them now—fragments of sensations, like the smell of fresh, hot rice and the click of the cooker going off when it was ready. My grandfather's aftershave mixed with cigarettes in the bathroom.

Dewy grass in the mornings as low clouds passed through the valley, dropping light showers in the summer, or heavy rain in the winter.

But there were some days, like this one, that stood out in sharp relief from the rest.

I don't remember exactly when I noticed the black car sliding to a stop at the side of the Kalihi house, but I do remember the well-dressed young man who got out and stood for a second at the chain link fence. He looked at me, perplexed, as if he'd arrived at the wrong place, then relaxed when he saw my grandfather sitting in the yard. He turned back to the car and opened a door, helping an older gentleman up to the sidewalk.

Everything about the gentleman struck me as funny at first. He wore a dark, pressed suit, which was impractical and overly formal for Hawai'i. His chin was raised, like he was resting his head on an invisible bar and peering down at everything. His eyebrows, like his hair and beard, were a bright white, but just a little too wispy, like he'd forgotten to give them a trim. Before he even spoke, I knew he was one of the old beings, like my grandfather.

"*Horangi-sshi.*" The gentleman used my grandfather's other name, Tiger. "*Can we talk?*"

My grandfather leaned forward. The sleeveless undershirt he wore was dingy compared to our visitor's clothes, but he liked it because he could make a show of his bare arms, and he did so then, resting them purposefully on his knees.

"*Of course. How can I help, Mr. Yong?*"

The gentleman glanced momentarily at my pink face. "*It'd be better if we spoke alone.*"

"*It's fine. He can't understand,*" my grandfather said. He could see that I wanted to correct him, but he shook his head at me slightly. "Play," he said in English, waving his hand. I shuffled over to another part of the yard, kicking a soccer ball around as I stayed within earshot.

The older gentleman dismissed his driver, who walked further down the block, then he looked back at my grandfather when he seemed satisfied that they could talk.

"*Something's come up,*" the man said. "*It's Mr. Kim.*"

My grandfather laughed and removed the unlit cigarette from his lips, rolling it around with his fingers.

The old man cleared his throat. "*He has something that doesn't belong to him, and it's going to cause problems if he doesn't give it back. Problems for everyone.*"

"*I'm sorry to hear that,*" my grandfather responded politely, and he gave a smile that I'd often seen him give to the customers in his shoe repair shop, respectful, but with a little firmness to it. *"I'm not sure why you're telling me this. My family doesn't work for yours anymore, Mr. Yong."*

It only lasted a second, but I saw the gentleman's eyes harden and their color change to an icy blue. What little I knew of the old beings from Korea mostly came from folktales and songs, centuries-old stories about animals and monsters that were vague representations of what they were. But some of what I learned came from living with my grandfather, and I knew that his true appearance sometimes surfaced when he was overcome by emotion. A sharpened tooth here, fur forming there, little bits of his Tiger body bleeding through when he wasn't careful.

This visitor's expression, and the change in his eyes, were similar, like he'd lost control. But he quickly buried whatever it was that he was feeling, and his eyes returned to a neutral black.

"Of course," the man replied. *"But we all need things from time to time."* The gentleman's gaze passed over the Kalihi house and lingered on the weathered parts of the fascia, and the areas where the stucco was warped and cracked. *"If you do happen to see him and... set things straight,"* he gestured vaguely, *"I'm sure I could help you with something."*

My grandfather tucked the cigarette behind his ear. He ran his hand over the smooth skin of his head, an old habit, he said, from when he used to have hair. *"Well, I'm honored you'd come here, if just to tell me that."* He was quiet for a bit longer, indicating that he had nothing else to discuss. *"Thank you for the visit."*

The gentleman pursed his lips, restraining himself from going further. He nodded slightly as a farewell, then turned around as his driver opened the car door for him and got back inside.

The black car pulled away quietly, then disappeared down the street.

My grandfather looked over at me after they were well out of sight.

I kicked the soccer ball to him, and he stopped it with his foot before standing up, looking around, and scratching at his throat. I could tell that he was turning things over in his head. I had a dozen questions, but I knew it was better not to rush him. He'd tell me what he wanted to, when he wanted to, and I just had to wait.

"What'd you think of him?" he asked, kicking the ball back to me.

"He doesn't seem very nice," I answered. *"And I didn't like the way he looked at our house."*

"I didn't like it either."

"You don't want to help him, do you?"

"Not really."

"*But you didn't tell him no.*" I kicked the ball.

He stopped it. "*You don't ever say 'no' to people like that. But you don't say 'yes' either. It's tricky, but you got to leave it open, you know?*"

I didn't, but I nodded anyway.

We continued to kick the ball back and forth until my grandmother called us from inside the house, just as it was beginning to get too dark to keep playing. My grandfather picked me up and put me on one shoulder, like I was a light basket, holding me securely with one arm as he walked through the narrow hallways of the Kalihi house, his footsteps booming on the wooden floors with every stride. I always liked it when he did that, because I could see everything he could from up there.

The next day, after my parents went to work and my grandmother went to meet with her church group, I found my grandfather in the driveway, stooped over his car and pushing rubbish off the seats and onto the floor—a sure sign that he was planning a trip into town. Without a word, I hopped into the passenger seat and buckled up, waiting patiently until he eventually got behind the wheel, adjusted his mirrors, and started the car.

He pulled off our street and onto the highway, and I kept my eyes on the windows, watching the deep green blur of the forests and mountains as we passed the edge of Kalihi Valley.

There were only a few places we'd go to on trips like these. The main one was Ke'eaumoku, a street not too far from the heart of downtown, sometimes jokingly called "Korea-moku" by people because of the stores and restaurants clustered together in one small strip. As an adult, I realized some parts of it were a bit darker and stranger than I remembered, but back then, it was an exciting place to visit, if only because my grandfather was the one taking me there.

He pulled into a familiar parking lot, and I immediately sat up and leaned on the dashboard. "*Are we stopping at...* "

"*Yeah,*" he turned off the engine.

I was already out of the car, slamming the door closed and heading into a small storefront that set off a chime as I went in.

"*Usuhohsaey*—Oh." The woman at the counter stopped her greeting and lowered her glasses. "Your face. You got burned real bad this time."

Tokki Ajumma, also known to me as Aunt Rabbit, clucked her tongue and wiped her hands on her apron. She squeezed my red cheeks. "Sunscreen, boy. Sunscreen. Skin cancer is serious."

"I'm fine," I replied, staring at the different bins of food she had set out for the day in the glass display. *Tokki Ajumma's* store sold *banchan* of all types—from spicy pickled cucumbers and Korean style macaroni salad to crispy seafood pancakes and little salty anchovies. If there was a side dish I could think of, her store had it. And every time we visited, I knew I was bound to leave disappointed, because my grandfather would only let us get two or three things.

As if on cue, my grandfather entered, telling me to back away from the display. "*Easy*," he said. "*We'll take some pajeon and oi kimchi, please.*"

"*Really, Beom?*" Aunt Rabbit replied, using one of his other names. "*That's it?*" Because she was an old being, like him, she carried herself differently than the other Korean *ajummas*; she could be elbow deep in spices and fermented cabbage and she would still have a regal authority about her. I assumed it was one of the few reasons she could get away with speaking to my grandfather like that.

"*That's it*," he replied sternly.

She proceeded to fill plastic containers with food as she talked with my grandfather, ordinary chit chat about how business was going and how their families were. When she bent to get a bag for our *banchan*, I saw the smallest flash of movement, the only sign that she had used her power to move objects around faster than any human could, and I noticed an extra container of spicy rice cakes that she snuck into our shopping bag as she gave me a small wink. I only learned, much later, that my grandfather could always see her do this, but at the time, I enjoyed thinking Aunt Rabbit and I shared some kind of secret.

"*I was wondering*," my grandfather said, as Aunt Rabbit finished wrapping our food. "*If you've heard from Mr. Kim lately. You know, our Mr. Kim.*"

Aunt Rabbit paused. "*It's funny you should mention it. He's been by next door a lot at the...*" She looked at me and chose her words carefully. "*Adult... bar. Can't tell if he's celebrating something or mourning with the way he's going.*"

I looked at my grandfather at the mention of Mr. Kim, wondering if it was the same one Mr. Yong was looking for, but he did not meet my eyes.

"*Is he there now?*"

She shook her head. "*Heard there was an incident a couple of days ago. Some disagreement with another customer, and Mr. Kim ended up breaking the other guy's arm.*" Aunt Rabbit tsked and tied off our shopping bag. "*It reminds me of how he was in the old days, getting into trouble, if he wasn't already starting it himself.*"

My grandfather went quiet, scratching his throat. After standing like that a little longer, he looked back at Aunt Rabbit and took out a few bills and put them on the counter. "*On second thought, let me get a couple bottles of soju.*"

Aunt Rabbit opened a cooler behind her and took two green bottles. She held them and gave him a funny look. "*You working with the Yongs again?*"

My grandfather snorted. "*Like I would.*"

She put the bottles in another bag and narrowed her eyes. "Your grandpa was a lot of things in the old days," she said to me in English. "Handsome, strong. But not very clever. And *not* a good liar."

"Thank you," he said flatly.

Aunt Rabbit handed me our bags. "You're just lucky I never let you get too full of yourself back then." She smiled slyly. "Your grandpa ever tell you about the time I set him on fire?"

My grandfather cleared his throat loudly. "*So funny, Tokki. Always. So funny,*" he said as he began ushering me out.

"What?" She put her glasses back on and waved her hand dismissively. "Just a joke! Okay okay. Bye bye then, Tiger—*I'll tell you next time,*" she whispered to me.

"*Anyoungheegyaesaeyo.*" I said in farewell, bowing on my way out.

We walked for a couple of minutes to the far side of the shopping complex, and I already had a sense where we were headed before we stopped in front of the bar. The building was covered in neon signs, and the entranceway was open but completely dark, like a cave.

A heavyset Korean man in a black t-shirt emerged and stood in front of the doorway.

"Is your boss in today?" my grandfather asked in English.

The man shook his head. "He doesn't want to see you, Tiger." His eyes drifted down to my face, and he furrowed his brow. "That's a serious burn, kid."

"*I'm okay,*" I replied in Korean, which I made a point to use in front of strangers like this.

"But he's there," my grandfather said. He began to walk forward, and the large man pressed a hand to my grandfather's chest to stop him. The large man didn't notice it, but I saw my grandfather's arm twitch.

His fingernails grew longer into claws, and the veins in his forearm became more pronounced.

My grandfather took a long, slow breath, like he did whenever this happened, and his arm gradually returned to normal.

"Listen," he started over. "I heard about Mr. Kim. Tell *Kkachi*, I only want to help. It's in his interest, after all."

The large man seemed conflicted at first, but after a little consideration, he withdrew into the shadowy hallway. When he returned, he was with someone else, a short, lean man with salt and pepper hair who marched up to us, almost pushing his long, hook-shaped nose in my grandfather's face.

"You were always thick-headed, Tiger, but this is a new level of stupid. What the hell do you want?"

My grandfather raised his hands and nodded his head toward me. This man, who I assumed was *Kkachi*, noticed me and his face softened for just a second before he turned back to my grandfather with a stern grimace.

"So what? You shouldn't be bringing kids here to begin with. Spit it out."

My grandfather cleared his throat. *"Rabbit told me about what Mr. Kim has been up to. I'm concerned, and I was thinking of checking in on him."*

The little man gritted his teeth. *"So why the hell are you bothering me?"*

"I'm sure you guys have to call him cabs when he's had a few too many. If you could just give me the address, it'd be a big help. Then I'll be out of your way. I promise."

Kkachi squinted. *"Are you working?"*

"No," my grandfather said adamantly. *"Why does everyone—no."*

Kkachi looked around and muttered curses under his breath, words in Korean I didn't know but had an unmistakable gist. He pulled out a pen and an old business card from his pocket, then made his employee turn his back and lean forward so he had a surface to write on. After he scribbled the address, he held up the card. *"Mr. Kim's a steady customer, so you better not be working him."*

"I'm not," my grandfather said, taking the card. *"I really appreciate this. I know it's been a while, but you seem like you're doing—"*

"Oh, eat shit." The little man turned around and was gone.

My grandfather nodded to the bar employee and steered me away by the shoulders. When we were back to our car on the other side of the parking lot, he let out a long sigh. *"That went as well as could be expected,"* he said.

We both got in the car and sat as the AC started to blow, cooling the stiflingly hot interior. *"That man. Kkachi,"* I said while we waited, unsure of the best way to put it. *"He was really mad at you, huh?"*

"It's complicated," my grandfather said with a faraway look. *"When you live as long as we do, relationships tend to change. Sometimes, you're close with people, maybe even the best of friends. Later, you do things, and then maybe you're not. Eh. I don't know."* He shrugged.

"I just don't understand how anyone couldn't be friends with you."

My grandfather looked at me funnily. He patted the top of my head and told me to buckle my seatbelt. It seemed like he didn't want to talk about it anymore, so I didn't say anything else.

We drove east and north from Ke'eaumoku to a place I recognized as Manoa Valley. My grandfather seemed to have a general sense of where we needed to go, taking us up narrow, curvy roads along one of the mountainsides.

As we got closer to the address where Mr. Kim lived, the streets were suddenly blanketed in a drifting fog. Our car was sprinkled with a sheen of not-quite-rain as we drove through curtains of gray, and the sun grew dimmer, blocked out by the heavier foliage of the rain forest.

We turned down a dirt road that was marked only by a crooked mailbox, and the car shuddered over rocks and potholes as we pulled up to a small, blue house with peeling paint, surrounded by towering banyan trees, like a wall of gnarled roots.

My grandfather turned off the engine and looked at me. *"Why don't you crack open a window. I shouldn't be long."*

"You're leaving me?" I looked out at the dark forest.

My grandfather squeezed my shoulder. *"You'll be okay. This is better. Mr. Kim is... He's a good guy. But, sometimes, out of control."* He took the shopping bags we got from Aunt Rabbit's and pinched my cheek. *"Won't be long."*

I watched him walk up to the house and open a creaking screen door. He knocked, and the door seemed to slide open on its own. My grandfather gave me a nod and went into the house.

A few minutes went by, my eyes fixed on the small house and my mouth as dry as my hands were moist, when I saw something in the forest that made me draw back from the windshield. Between the long trunks of the banyan trees, a large, grey figure slouched slowly toward the back of the home.

I gripped my seatbelt and shut my eyes; when I opened them, the thing was gone.

My first thought was to warn my grandfather, to run and find him, but I knew he'd be angry if I disobeyed him. After fighting with myself over it, I unlocked the car and sprinted toward the house.

"Grandpa! Grandpa! There's something—"

I ran through the front door into a living room, where my grandfather was seated on the floor at a low table.

"My grandson," he said to another man, seated across from him.

This man, who I assumed was Mr. Kim, seemed to be my grandfather's age, but with a tan face that was more heavily creased and flushed with a tinge of red. His eyes were bloodshot and watery, and when he smiled, I could see that he was missing a few teeth.

"There's... something?" he asked.

I looked at my grandfather, who was stone-faced. He gave the smallest shake of his head, indicating I should stop.

"I just... wanted to join, if that's okay." I pointed to the table where my grandfather had set out the *banchan* we had gotten from Aunt Rabbit's.

"Of course," Mr. Kim said. "No need to wait outside. Sit! Sit!"

I tried whispering to my grandfather, but he looked away from me and cleared his throat. He opened a bottle of *soju* and poured some in a paper cup for Mr. Kim, then handed the bottle to Mr. Kim to have a drink poured in turn, since no one was supposed to pour for themselves.

As I sat down at the table, I looked around the inside of the house. There was really only one room and a bathroom as far as I could see, a kitchenette in the corner, a television on the ground, and a small couch with a blanket and pillow, where I assumed Mr. Kim slept. The paint was as peeled in the room as it had been on the outside, and there was a heavy, salty odor in the air, like fish.

"*This is something,*" Mr. Kim said, looking down at the *banchan* spread on the table. "*Still, I feel like we could use a little something more. Don't you think? Is there anything else you want? Anything at all?*"

"*I'm fine,*" my grandfather said.

"*What about you, kid?*" he forced a smile and reached under the table, picking up a long, black cane. "*Craving anything? Come on. I know.*" Mr. Kim waved the cane over the table. There were suddenly several wrapped burgers piled together on a plate that hadn't been there before. He waved the cane the other way, and another plate of hot fries appeared among the other dishes, filling the house with a more pleasant smell.

There was only one Korean creature I knew of that could summon things like that, and if Mr. Kim was one of those, then things could turn very bad, very quickly.

I was beginning to understand why my grandfather told me to wait in the car.

"*I'm okay,*" I said quietly.

"*Suit yourself,*" Mr. Kim replied, waving the cane one more time and making the burgers and fries disappear. He looked back at my grandfather. "*My daughter is all about that junk food now. Real American, I guess.*"

"*How's she doing?*" my grandfather asked, swallowing the *soju* in his cup.

Mr. Kim took a pack of cigarettes out of his shirt pocket. He removed one and handed it to my grandfather, but he shook his head and declined. Mr. Kim seemed surprised and kept the cigarette for himself.

"*She's living with her mother now.*" Mr. Kim lit the cigarette and took a drag. "*Applying for college soon too. Hard to believe.*"

"*She takes after her mother more than you, then.*"

Mr. Kim laughed loudly, puffing smoke, and he shifted over like he was off-balance. He'd clearly been drinking for some time before we came with the *soju*. "*She's going to study business, she says. Can you imagine that?*"

My grandfather refilled Mr. Kim's cup. "*I hear college gets pretty expensive.*"

"*That's true. But we'll be okay.*" Mr. Kim smirked, like there was a joke only he was in on. "*Anyway,*" he inhaled slowly and blew smoke as he stared at my grandfather. "*Enough about me. What's going on with you? Not every day you get a visit from the Tiger, after all.*"

My grandfather sipped his drink. "*Well, to be honest. Mr. Yong came by my house yesterday.*"

Mr. Kim's hand holding his cup stopped before he brought it to his mouth.

"*He thinks—*" my grandfather locked eyes with Mr. Kim, "*—that you have something that belongs to him.*"

Mr. Kim's face darkened, and he put his cup back down. He tapped the ash from his cigarette into the cup. "*Not sure what you...*" He stopped when my grandfather held up a hand, making it clear he didn't care to hear it.

"*I know what you're thinking,*" my grandfather said. "*But I'm not working,*" he continued calmly. "*And I wouldn't have brought my grandson if that's what I was after.*"

Mr. Kim looked over at me.

"*I just thought I should tell you that they were coming and give you some advice.*" My grandfather finished his drink. "*The only way out of this is to return whatever it is you took, before it's too late. That's all.*"

Mr. Kim gripped his cane tightly and looked around the room. I could see the sweat forming at his cheeks along the creases near his eyes as he stubbed the cigarette out. "*Of course you'd say that,*" he muttered. "*But I don't see why—I mean, I don't know why...*" he trailed off. It was clear he knew that he could not maintain pretenses with my grandfather.

"*What if,*" Mr. Kim touched his chin. "*What if you tell Mr. Yong you looked into it, and you didn't find anything? He'd believe you. I know it.*"

Mr. Kim waved his cane over the table, and a large stack of bills bound by a rubber band appeared next to the *soju* bottle, more money than I had ever seen in one place in my entire life. "*Anything you want.*" He moved the cane a few more times, and gold and bronze coins clattered on the surface of the table.

My grandfather paused and looked down at the money. "I haven't seen you summon so many things since the old days," he noted in English. "You must have a lot of power in *that cane.*"

When he said those last words, my grandfather tapped my leg twice under the low table. He would always tap my leg like that whenever he wanted me to get things from around the house—his cigarettes, a beer from the kitchen—so I knew what he was telling me.

"This is impressive, but..." My grandfather picked up some of the coins from the table and shuffled them between his fingers, as if he were testing them. "I still can't do what you're asking."

"Why the hell not?" Mr. Kim raised his voice.

"Because the Yongs will know. They always do."

Mr. Kim grunted with frustration and scratched at his scalp, trying to think. After a few seconds of muttering, Mr. Kim struggled to get to his feet, then he walked over to a mini-fridge and pulled out a small paper bag.

He brought it to the table, and tilted the opening toward us, showing my grandfather and me what was inside—an oval ball about the size of a grapefruit and off-white in color.

"*Is that...* "

"Yes," Mr. Kim said in English. "*Gyeryong.*"

I didn't know what that meant, but I could tell my grandfather was so surprised that he could not speak.

"The Yongs sent me looking for it, and I thought it was a joke. All the gyeryong died so long ago in Korea, right? So how could there possibly be any of their eggs still out there?" Mr. Kim folded down the edges of the bag to open it more. *"For years, I kept an eye out, but never came close. Then a few months ago I met a group of mul gwishin that was moving goods back and forth from home to the U.S. The one that had this thought it was some kind of Silla dynasty pearl. He had no idea."*

My grandfather studied the white shape more closely.

While they were both focused on the egg, I reached under the table toward Mr. Kim's cane.

"I was going to hand it over," Mr. Kim scratched his scalp. *"But the moment I touched it, I knew there was something different about it,"* he said. *"I felt my old power returning. No more weak little tricks or watered down spells. See for yourself. Touch it. Go on."*

My grandfather stretched out his hand toward the bag, but then stopped.

"That's okay," he said.

Mr. Kim's eyes flared into a deep, red color, while the skin on his face faded into a scaly grey. His teeth grew sharper, covered in dripping spit, and his true form, the *dokkaebi*, was beginning to surface. It was just as terrifying as I imagined based on the folktales and storybooks I remembered, and I gripped my grandfather's leg as Mr. Kim continued to change.

"Why?" He growled at my grandfather. *"Why the Yongs? You and I could keep it, Tiger. Couldn't we?"*

It seemed like Mr. Kim was feeling the floor for his cane. He had tried negotiating with my grandfather, then bribing him, and since neither seemed to be working, he was going to try something more desperate, maybe even violent. Only he was now realizing that the cane was no longer by his side—that I had pulled it from under the table and put it behind my grandfather, far from his reach.

"Sorry," my grandfather said to him with complete calm. *"But I'm not interested."*

Before I understood what was happening, Mr. Kim kicked the low table in front of us in a panic. The food and drinks went flying to the other side of the room, and I instinctively ducked my head and scrambled a few feet away.

Mr. Kim was almost fully changed, appearing more like a hunched, demonic animal than the shrinking man he was seconds ago. He loomed above us, almost touching the ceiling, just like the tall grey shape I had seen outside, stalking the forest.

He clutched the paper bag under one arm, his sharp teeth bared as he looked wildly around for a way out. Then he charged suddenly for the front door, not realizing, I think, that I was in his path and likely to be trampled.

Mr. Kim came crashing to the ground before he got to me, knocked aside by my grandfather who leapt forward between us.

There was a roar so loud that it reverberated through the house. My grandfather stood in front of me, his back swollen to almost twice its usual size, and his arms covered in black lines that looked like tattoos, growing across his shoulders and neck and up to his face. My grandfather looked back at me, and his eyes were a bright, golden color. The nails on both his hands had lengthened into claws, and his mouth was filled with glistening, white fangs.

I had never seen my grandfather turn this far before.

"*Just let me leave!*" Mr. Kim, the *dokkaebi*, screeched, and I realized he was shaking at the sight of my grandfather. "*Stand back! If anything happens, everyone will know it was you, Tiger!*"

My grandfather held up his hands.

"*I'm not going to hurt you,*" he replied, his voice deep and calm. He took a long, slow breath, and his claws began to retract, sliding back into his fingers. "*That's not... who I am anymore,*" he said, a strange note of disappointment in his voice.

Mr. Kim gripped the paper bag in his arm tightly and moved around the side of the room toward the door.

"*But,*" my grandfather cautioned. "*If you go, I won't be able to help you. And when they come looking—and they will—they're not going to stop with just you. Think about what that means... for your family.*"

Mr. Kim stopped, and the scaly grey color on his body began to recede. His glowing red eyes darkened back to black. His shoulders sank, and his face turned to the way it was before, but more frightened than I'd ever seen any adult.

At the same time, the black lines on my grandfather's body thinned and retreated under his clothing, and his body relaxed and returned to its previous size.

Mr. Kim sat on the couch, looking down at the paper and the *gyeryong* egg inside it for a minute. "*In the old days, I was nothing and had nothing, until I willed myself into being. My form, my power. I gave myself that strength. And I became something that people feared and respected, you know?*"

Mr. Kim folded up the edges of the paper bag to close it. "*But everything's different now. I don't even know what I'm supposed to be here, in this place, if I'm not that. Just getting weaker and weaker until... what? I'm nothing again?"*

My grandfather took a breath. "I know," he said quietly, then sat on the ground in front of Mr. Kim. "Sometimes, part of me still misses what we had. What we were. Our place in things before." He went quiet, as if he felt embarrassed to say anything further.

"But," he continued and looked at Mr. Kim. "If you just wanted to be a *dokkaebi*, and I wanted to be *Horangi*, you and I would have stayed there. And you'd still be a monster, and I'd still be a servant, and nothing would change. But we all decided to leave to try something else, right?" He nodded his head toward me. "Because sometimes, for something better, you have to give up something good. I think you know that."

Mr. Kim did not answer. He seemed very tired all of a sudden, and he covered his eyes with his hand. It was very quiet until he held up the paper bag, waiting for my grandfather to take it from him.

"It will be okay. I'll make sure," my grandfather said, patting him on the shoulder and grabbing the paper bag from him, then looked back at me once he had it.

"Let's go."

Mr. Kim continued to cover his face and did not turn to look at us as we left.

Outside of the house, when we made it back to the car, my grandfather let out a long sigh and held up the paper bag. *"That didn't go how I thought it would, but—"*

I didn't know why, but I clutched his side and began to sob.

"Hey, hey. It's okay." He picked me up with one arm and held me while I cried into his undershirt. I remember being embarrassed that I couldn't control myself, and somehow, that just made me cry harder.

"I'll never let anything happen to you. You know that," he said. *"Everything's okay."*

It took a while, but he waited with me until I was done crying, then he quietly put me in my seat, buckled my seatbelt, and drove us back home.

I don't remember how many days passed before the black car came to us again, but I remember going out the back door to the yard one afternoon and seeing my grandfather at the fence, holding the paper bag with the *gyeryong* egg.

Mr. Yong was standing at the sidewalk again, black suit and all, and stopped speaking when he saw me.

"It's fine. He can hear this," my grandfather said, this time making it a point to speak English. "Before I give this back, I want to know what you're going to do with Mr. Kim."

Mr. Yong kept his eyes on me and spoke quietly. "I can't let people break their promises."

My grandfather rubbed the top of his head. "I've been thinking. About the way we used to do things, and how we do them now," he said. "What about something else? What if you rewarded him instead?"

Mr. Yong blinked.

"If this is a joke, Tiger, I don't understand it."

My grandfather took the unlit cigarette he had behind his ear and moved it around through his fingers. "If you punish Mr. Kim, people will know that a *dokkaebi* fooled you somehow. And you're going to look weak, very weak. It's *Mr. Kim* after all. But if you help him?" my grandfather continued. "Then it only looks like he did a job for you and was... a little late at most. And you could even come out looking better, if you do it the right way."

"And what is the *right* way?" There was a flicker of blue in Mr. Yong's eyes.

"I hear his daughter is going to college, and those aren't cheap. I mean, nothing to you, and not as valuable as this," my grandfather held up the egg. "But a scholarship from the Yongs would probably go a long way for that family. Besides," my grandfather squeezed the paper bag slightly so that it made a crinkling sound. "I don't care what you do with this, personally. But if others learn the *gyeryong* are still alive, and can give them power like the old days? They might get ideas of their own. Better to act like everything's normal so they don't wonder too much. Don't you think?"

Mr. Yong stared silently at my grandfather for a long time.

My grandfather, in turn, held up the paper bag.

Mr. Yong took it reluctantly and glanced around with a grimace, once again resting his eyes on our house. "And I assume you'll want something out of this too?"

My grandfather put the unlit cigarette to his lips again, and he looked at the house briefly, then at Mr. Yong, and he gave him the smile, the one he gave to customers in the shoe repair shop. "No," he replied. "As long as everyone gets along, I'm just fine."

Mr. Yong seemed suspicious, like he thought he was being made a fool of somehow. But it didn't matter much, in the end. He had what he wanted, and he clutched the paper bag closely to his chest.

"Goodbye, *Horangi-sshi*," he said as he walked back to his car.

"Goodbye, *Yong-sshi*."

We waited until they left, the black car turning the corner and disappearing from the street, and I thought about asking my grandfather more questions, but I think I understood.

My grandfather, meanwhile, looked up at the sun and shaded his eyes. He asked if I was going to play outside, and I told him that I was. So he walked over to the cement steps and pulled out a tube of sunscreen from his back pocket. He told me to stand in front of him as he squeezed the white gunk into his hand and then rubbed some of it on my arms, then my legs, and then across my forehead and cheeks.

"*You have to take care of yourself in the sun, not worry so much about how you look,*" he said.

"*I know,*" I replied.

He dabbed his fingers in sunscreen and tapped my chin and my nose. "*In Korea, during the old days, when I served the high families, I was... very tough on people, you understand? Mean and cruel, because that's what others saw in me, and I thought that was what I was supposed to be,*" he said softly. "*But then, I came here, and I realized that's not who I was. And it's taken a long time to undo those ways. A lot of us old beings, I think, are trying to undo those ways still.*"

He made me sit down at the bottom of the steps as he covered the back of my neck. "*This will probably make more sense when you're older, but you're never going to be what people think you are, no matter how hard you try.*" He closed the sunscreen and put it away. "*So you just have to be what you are, whatever that is, okay?*"

"*Okay,*" I said, though I didn't fully understand. He was right that it would take years before I knew what it meant, let alone believe it. And only then would I realize, long after he was gone, that the thing I actually wanted was to be more like him.

"Okay. Go play," my grandfather said, rubbing in the last bit of sunscreen letting me run off through the yard.

He leaned back and rested his elbows on the top step and clamped his unlit cigarette in his lips, staring out at the trees that led up to the mountains, remembering, perhaps, the forests near his hometown and what it was like when people were few and far between, in their little villages, and beasts moved freely wherever they wished. Or maybe he was thinking of what it was like before, when he had more power and a better sense of his place in things, I don't know.

But after a while, he lost interest in the mountains, I think, his eyes drifting down and focusing on his grandson kicking the soccer ball instead. He stretched comfortably under the warm sunlight of the sleepy afternoon, while I ran back and forth on the grass until, eventually, my grandmother called for us as it began to grow dark.

Then he picked me up and carried me carefully on his shoulder, into the house, through the narrow hallways and toward the kitchen, where we knew we'd find the smell of fresh, hot rice and the click of a cooker going off when it was ready, just in time for all of us to gather for dinner in that small Kalihi house.

Siv Delfin

Damien Krsteski

I clutch a bouquet of white roses. The earth beneath my feet is soft, I can feel my body pressing down into it with each step as I approach a row of stones with names etched into them.

Siv Delfin.
The nightclub in Bobinki Rid nestled in a baroque building once part of a tobacco tycoon's estate, now owned by a branch of the Bug-eyed, where the first sample was found. The police chemists called the drug a depressant, a memory-suppressant, fear inhibitor, mighty curious molecule, a self-replicating wondrous African import, foaming at their mouths at the thought of studying it further—but to Claire it was yet another criminal thread managing to weave itself in Vasilegrad's warp-weft, remaking her city, one strand at a time, from within.
Siv Delfin. The crime scene gave the drug its name.

She went to Magda, an old informant, to find out more.
"It's not like any other," Magda said, her welding goggles resting on her forehead. "You don't space out. Don't lose focus or shit. On my first try I thought I'd been ripped off." She picked her nose. "Almost went to beat up the seller."
Claire listened, taking shallow breaths; the smog made Zheleza's air viscous. She knew she'd be coughing up fluorescent phlegm the following morning. "What makes it different?"
Magda bared her teeth. "Everything." She shivered, soot falling off her skin. "It makes you euphoric. It makes you feel"—her eyes widened, and for a moment Claire wished she'd put her goggles back on—"*eternal.*"
The noon sun baked the earth in the foundry yard to a dull amber but Claire felt cold all over. "And?"
"And it's popular. People talk. Use it. Pay good money for a sniff."
"Where does it come from?"
"Hell if I know."
"Who's pushing the drug on this city?"
She pursed her lips, shook her head. "Shit, Agent." Calling Claire by her former title, from when she'd worked privately, when they'd been cooperating. Magda glanced left and right, "You really think I know names?"

"What do you know?"

"One thing." The klaxon sounded, ending break-time. Magda placed the goggles back over her eyes; the Chief Police Inspector saw her reflection duplicated, a face twinned in confusion.

"What's that?"

"They're dangerous."

Claire let the car drive her out of the city's industrial quarter, her eyes sliding away from the rear-view mirrors.

When a user consumes Siv Delfin they forget about death.

Not forgetting in a *joie-de-vivre, bad-things-pushed-to-the-back-of-your-mind* kind of way, but totally, radically, as if the very notion had been uprooted from their head. Becoming completely oblivious to the concept of fatality, a user believes all life goes on forever, nobody ever perishes, nothing disappears, they forget about the manner in which close ones, or famous people, have passed away, the user's confused by the simple question, *Where is your great-great-grandfather?*

Not here at the moment, the user would say, *want to leave a message?*

Those pushing the product were also consuming the product. Bad news for the city, trouble for the police.

"They're going after the Bug-eyed," Police Inspector Radan said, staring at the white board. "Hard." A map of the city flickered on it, several spots crossed out in red. The latest crime-scene, a bar in a northern quarter, owned by a locally-known Bug-eyed member, had been demolished, several patrons maimed. Civilians. One adolescent.

But how could the attackers care about innocents if they couldn't even fathom the harm they were causing?

Claire nodded. "From the periphery. Not in BE quarters. No attacks in Delchev, Kamentsi, Mayadin." Jabbing her finger at those parts of the city. Chewing on a modafinil gum, a leftover habit from the old days in that private agency. "Fighting for contested territory, maybe?"

Radan tapped the board and the map zoomed out. "The drug producers are newcomers, but they're amassing a crowd, gaining power fast." He looked at Claire. "They don't have any borders to protect. For them, everything is contested territory. They're taking over the city, Chief. Starting with the most powerful gang."

"Let's say that's true," Claire said. "Where does that put us?"

"Normally, I'd say let them duke it out. Druggies versus Bugs. Let them claw at each other's throats. But this isn't a normal force we're dealing with. They won't stop with the defeat of the Bug-eyed."

"Why wouldn't they? Who'd they go after?"

Radan's lip twitched. "It's in the way they do things. Their modus operandi. They frighten me with their ruthlessness. After the Bug-eyed, they'll be bigger, stronger, capable of going against the other force controlling the city. Us."

Claire smiled humorlessly. "Vasilegrad's PD might be a target. Then again, it might not. In any case they are starting to dominate the scene." She rubbed her forehead, letting her exhaustion show. "Question is, what are we to do about it?"

Radan looked at the board, at the map of their city, with sad eyes. "We strike first," he said. "Preemptively."

This is my ritual. I've been coming here for months, years, always these flowers, always to these exact two stones. One next to the other.

The police paid informants, people to keep their eyes peeled for any Siv Delfin related activities, from all parts of Vasilegrad. The usual shtick.

Claire approached Magda first but Magda didn't want anything to do with it, and the next time Claire tried to reach her she was gone. Moved out of town, her foundry co-workers said.

No information trickled down to the VGPD; one by one, the informants were disappearing without a trace, as if swallowed by the earth.

Police had been deployed to several locations across town, near places operated by Bug-eyed—a gang of boy-scouts compared to the new folks in town—waiting patiently for any possible attacks. Software Workers had assigned probability values to each potential target location, based on previous activities of the new gang and the current goings-on of their enemy, and Claire and Radan, along with a group of well-armed colleagues, were sitting in a masked armored vehicle a block to the east of the locale deemed most likely to be targeted that night. *Rabotna Sabota* pub, Vervoolitsa St. 185.

She chewed gum in silence.

At exactly an hour past midnight—

A dull thud, a stretched-out boom, like a crowd stomping the ground all at once, and the van shook. Coming from the direction of the pub, announcing the arrival of the drugged-out terrorists.

The van's engine started up and they were on their way. Claire looked into the faces of the policemen and women. Curt nods while they all checked their equipment, the magazines in the machine guns, the maces, the batons, the canisters and the straps of their gas masks. She didn't have to be here, in the thick of it, but she always was, she could never play the part of the office bureaucrat, and her colleagues liked her for it.

Like a flicker, an unexpected flash of light in one's eyes, she felt a massive sense of deja-vu, like *he* was with her right then and there, beside her in the van, thigh touching thigh, his automatic in hand. Just like back in the day. She took a deep breath, closed her eyes, and banished him with an exhalation.

They poured out of the van onto a street overrun by chaos. The pub's front, smashed and broken, glass shards glinting in the cobbles, black smoke wafting from the inside, and people, civilians, emerging confused and crazed out, escaping the flames, shirts and skin torn, bloodied arms and legs, some still holding on to their beer glasses.

The pub was two-storied, and people jumped out of broken windows, breaking legs or arms in the process, getting up, screaming for help while limping toward safety.

The bomb had gone off deep within the pub, the area around the explosion marked by blackened, melting furniture, and charred corpses. As the police were about the step inside to look for attackers, and as the paramedics rushed toward the victims, a crowd of fifteen or so came in from the adjacent sidestreet.

They looked like ordinary people, a representative sample of the city's populace scooped up while waiting for the tram and cajoled into joining a gang. Running toward the pub's patrons with axes, knives, even scissors, as if they'd picked up the first sharp object at hand and had come, *en masse*, to finish the job.

Claire aimed her Whisperer at their legs, shouting warnings. She shot an incoming woman, middle-aged, polka-dot dress and white-lace boots, in the knee.

The woman screamed, looked at Claire with eyes empty but reflective. Diamond eyes. "Why would you do that?" Frowning, not understanding why someone would want to hurt her, she fell down.

"Drop the weapon."

But before the woman could get a chance to obey, a man from the drugged-out throng stabbed her in the neck in passing; for the purpose of the gang, their wounded were as good as dead. Nobody gets caught alive.

Claire shot the man and he slumped to the ground.

These used to be normal people once, she thought in disbelief, and with a flick of her thumb set her Whisperer to fire non-lethal neuroparalytic pellets.

"Ready," Radan said and they fell into formation. They took several steps away from the pub's entrance, their eyes scanning the throng, trying to differentiate between civilians and armed gang-members.

"It's their eyes," Claire subvocalized, and her colleagues heard her in their heads. "Glassy eyes. Shine back at you." She shot one—a healthy-looking teenager, beanie and punk band sweater. He spasmed and fell down, rigid, the ice-pick still in his grip. Having identified the differential, her neural prostheses could now pick out the assailants from the throng, outlining them in silver for easier targeting. "Don't kill," she added as the battalion stepped toward the crowd. "And don't let them off themselves. We need them alive."

The initial confusion had passed and help had come as all police units pooled toward Vervoolitsa St. They'd subdued the attackers within ten minutes, had the place secured and fire put out within thirty.

Claire's eyes scanned the scene—white sheets covered the bodies the paramedics couldn't save or revive. Her chest hurt. Beneath every sheet she pictured him, pale and bloodless and with a projectile wound in the abdomen, the way he'd looked when she'd been taken to identify him, and she almost wanted to pull back the covers off the bodies' heads, for just a peek, to make sure he wasn't really there. What would she think of it all right now, what would she feel, if she'd been like them, like the junkies, out of sync with reality?

She walked over to Radan, lying on a stretcher, about to be put into an ambulance.

"You holdin' up?"

"I'll live," he managed, then gave her the thumbs-up. He'd been stabbed with a buttering knife in the side—his armor had stopped the blade, but the assailant had managed to break a rib or two by blunt force alone. Enough to make him lose balance, and get stabbed again by another attacker, this time below the armor, in the kidney. "See you in the office tomorrow."

She smiled, squeezed his cold hand as the paramedics were lifting him into the vehicle.

The quarter strobed in red and blue, the vehicles splashing police-light on surrounding buildings and faces peeking from behind windows at the bloodbath below.

What would they think? What would they feel?

Claire came home exhausted. She walked past the hallway where the pictures on the shelves were flipped down or turned backwards to face the drab and flaking walls, and strode toward the cold bedroom.

She slumped in bed and plunged into nightmares.

Mayor Lagetti declared a police-enforced curfew. Nobody allowed on the streets of Vasilegrad past 19:00, and police had orders to stop, frisk, and, if need be, arrest disobeying citizens.

The police car drove Claire to the hospital. On the way, she didn't see a single civilian. When things got scary people stayed home, huddled together, turned to their leaders for guidance, and, most important for her, became obsequious, respecting the law and those who enforce it.

Radan was snoring when she got into his room. She set the chocolate she'd brought on the night-stand, next to the *get well soon* card from the colleagues (big-bosomed girl in black lacquered boots), and the flowers from she did not know whom. The older man who shared a room with Radan wasn't there tonight, his bed empty and stinking of disinfectant. Claire assumed he'd died.

She sat on the side of Radan's bed, careful not to touch any of the transparent plastic tubes connecting her colleague's body to the machines. She stroked his pale arm, and like always, felt a smudge of guilt, as if any affection felt after them was a betrayal.

He stirred. "Hey, Chief."

"How are you feeling?" She stood up.

"Not too shabby."

"Didn't mean to wake you up." But she was glad to catch him conscious; they hadn't spoken since the night of the accident.

"That's all right." Wincing. "Can't sleep much with this tube up my penis anyhow."

"I brought you something." She smiled.

He glanced at the bedside table, then blinked stupidly at Claire. "Flowers?"

"No," she said. "Footage."

Color crept back into his face. He grinned, though the smile never reached his eyes. "You got them talking?"

"They talked all right." She crossed her arms. "But we did jack shit."

"How so?"

"Being on Siv Delfin for long stretches of time messes you up. Bilateral lesions in the amygdala, Swiss-cheese like, the doctors say it's like watching a neurodegenerative disease on fast-forward."

"Who would've thought, huh?" His laugh turned into a coughing fit.

"Quitting, cold turkey, messes you up even worse. For seventy-two hours we kept them without the drug. They looked shittier than you do. Crying and pissing blood, projectile vomiting, the works. But after the partying came the crash. They passed out. And that's when they started babbling."

He gave her an incredulous look. "In their *sleep*? Let me see."

Claire nodded, pointed a finger at him. He raised an eyebrow at her when nothing happened. "Shit," she said under her breath, and smiled. She'd forgotten his neural prostheses were offline, and would stay that way while he convalesces.

"There's a display stuck to my bed," he said, lifting his chin.

She yanked out the paper-thin display off the foot-board—medical information scrolling on it—and, pointing her finger at its receiver, transferred the data. Again she sat beside him, holding the display before his eyes.

Two, four, then eight gray screens appeared on it, a grid of surveillance cam footage from St. Kliment's hospital. Tossing and turning in their beds were the citizens turned junkies turned terrorists. A stream of sound came, all jumbled at first, but the more Claire let the video play, the easier it was to pick up a pattern, words, repeated like a mantra, spoken by all the addicts in their sleep. *To break to wave and break a wave to stab and litter and junk, junkies, piling junkies flowing junkies flowing piles of junkies piled up flowing drowning junkies trunks and junks and flowing the river carries the junkies and waves of metal and waves of water...*

She folded the display in half.

"You think—" Radan's face was ashen again.

"They're dreaming of the drug," Claire said, replacing the display on the foot-board. It stuck to the wood like adhesive paper. "And of the place where they can obtain more of it. They're telling us where to go, Radan."

A swarm of centipedes crawled toward Mala Prespa. They crawled with little hair-like feet on the river bed through mud and fish bones, then, as they neared the sandbanks and the river's bottom became an incline, through rust, and chaff, and iron filings, all pulsating like a submerged amber halo around the island in the stream's flow. Past these, springs and coils and broken gears and robot parts further up the incline, until the centipedes no longer crawled over sand or earth but over man-made debris.

Out of the water, and onto the shore of the island, covered entirely in trash, the centipedes exposed their carbon-nanotube bodies to the foul air and transmitted, back to the police, everything they saw.

There was no other place, Claire knew. This had to be it.

A formerly pristine sandbank on the western outskirt of town, dividing river Plovna in two along its length, Mala Prespa had gradually turned into a horrid junkyard, as the people and industries of the city chucked out their broken belongings into the river, hoping they'd be swept off to the sea. Little by little they had amassed on the sandy shores, machine carcasses and mechanical parts like beached whales, carried shamelessly out of sight of the citizens of Vasilegrad by makeshift rafts. A disgust, an ecological disaster, a hotly-debated political topic, Mala Prespa remained and only grew, rusting in the fetid winds.

In police vans positioned a kilometer and a half away from the river island, Claire and her colleagues watched the many streams of the centipedes, stitched together into one video, on overlays before their eyes. Claire knew Radan was watching the stream on his hand-held display back in the hospital, too.

From Mala Prespa's vantage point, the city was a mist of pollution, a mirage shimmering on the horizon.

A blood-colored carpet of rust as screws, nails, bolts and nuts made the centipedes go up, down, up, down, converging from all sides toward the center of the island.

"Look at it," said Nenad Kanić. "Like pillars. Like an arch."

Half-rusted and flaking girders stuck out of the ground like iron gates. Through them, and past a graveyard of android body parts, ersatz skin peeled and flecked, deeper into garbage island. Switching on the audio, the police could hear morning river winds blowing and whistling on metal as the whole place sang and chimed. But there was nobody.

"They have to be here," whispered Claire. "Have to be here somewhere."

The centipedes made a sweep of the island, finding only dead metal. The day passed, the police growing impatient in their vans, slurping sugary and caffeinated drinks.

When the sky darkened, something started to happen.

Among the oaks near the river banks dark figures appeared, the few centipedes that stayed on the island shores turning their eyestalks their way to provide more detail.

Claire saw people, dressed in business suits and baggy pants and short skirts and high heels, crowding both sides of the river.

"A new batch of junkies," somebody said.

It took a couple of minutes for them all to gather, around twenty or so, then, in one sudden motion, everybody jumped into the water. Claire gasped, thinking they'd all just dived to their deaths, but heads emerged quickly above the muddy waves.

"What the..."

The junkies swam, undeterred by Plovna's strong currents. Claire counted heads, and when they reached the shores of the island she could see that most of them had made it.

They scattered across the island. Their wet clothes glommed onto their bodies, the fabric which sagged flapped in the wind.

Claire felt a vicarious chill in her bones.

Everybody seemed to be doing something different, each had a task to finish and they knew exactly where to go and what to do.

A plump young man dug out two pots and a cauldron from underneath a heap of broken plastic pipes. He carried them, the pots inside the larger cauldron and the cauldron by the handles, to a spot shielded from wind by a thin rusted metallic sheet propped on a girder. A group of junkies on guard duty patrolled the shores of the island, squinting in the wind. A woman with lanky blonde hair was stacking up bottles, vials, flasks, which the others dutifully pulled out of their pockets and handed to her. The man beside her poured the contents of each container into one of the pots, stirred it, watched it with eager eyes, and nodded in satisfaction.

They all had a role, yet nobody was issuing orders.

It took Claire a moment to realize what was going on, and when she did, she bristled all over.

The junkies were cooking their drug.

They made the drug—pouring liquids into pots, a dash of white powder here, a dollop of a black goop there, stirring until thickened to a paste, then leaving it to dry out in polluted winds—and consumed it. One after another, dabbing their pocket knives, spoons, fingers into the pots and taking a sniff.

Soon they left the island and headed toward town to cause trouble but were picked up by the police instead.

There, I can see the row of marble, rising out of green turf, where their names are written.

Claire talked to Robin. She had been talking to him for the better part of an hour.

She did it rarely, under extreme circumstances, when she couldn't hold it in any longer, when the stress she was subjected to made her feel as if bursting at the seams.

She staggered around her apartment, padding on the parquet (disturbing her downstairs neighbors, in all probability), a bottle of white wine, her second that night, carried by the neck.

She took a swig.

"Fuckers are always slipping away. We catch ten, another hundred pop up." To the patient walls, the hallway, the attentive furniture in the living room, she said, "How the fuck do I deal with this, now? And keep every-friggin-thing together so I can think my way out of this clusterfuck? To be the goddamn Chief"—she counted on her fingers— "to lead the investigation, to take care of my people, to make sure I don't show any weakness." She looked at her hand stupidly, then put it down, took another sip of wine. "I'm always out there, on the field, next to my people. I'm not some fucking bureaucrat cooped up in her office. I *care*. I go on missions with them, I ride in the same van, I use my gun, and still it isn't enough... So what would *you* do in my place? Pray tell how *you* would approach this case."

The apartment responded with silence.

"That's right! You won't fucking say! Because it's you who has to be the hero"—she was pointing a finger at nothing in particular, eyes squinting—"*you, you, you*, who had to go and be brave, and heroic, and the good Agent and good man and everything good, good for the city and everybody except for—"

As she was about to say it she suddenly felt very self-conscious, and sober. Lights from a car from the street below burst in through the slatted blinds, striping the room in yellow and red, then vanished, and Claire's vitriol and bravado drained with the color. She set the bottle down on the living room table.

"I'm fucking pathetic."

She slumped on the sofa. Looked around the room as if seeing it for the first time, buried her face in her hands. "No, I'm beyond pathetic." Her tongue felt numb. "I'm parenthetic. Paralytic, paraplegic, parapluie pour la plooee." She laughed.

Within moments, she was snoring.

She woke early the next day to a splitting headache, and an anonymous message. It wasn't until she was in the shower that her mind registered the red envelope floating in a corner before her, and on first impulse she swatted it away as if at a pestering fly.

Once toweled off and dressed, she opened the letter.

Encrypted source, textual, marked urgent.

We seem to be stepping on each other's toes. So why don't we set aside our differences, and cooperate. We have an enemy in common. V. K.

"Vladimir Koronski."

The policemen and women in the room blinked at the file overlaid before their eyes, then turned to look, somewhat skeptically, at Claire.

"Reaching out," she continued. "They've been aware of the junkies' presence on Mala Prespa, having observed them for some time now. We drove the junkies away from their hiding spot, and now they've lost track of them. He's proposing we share information"—she made an effort not to look at the ground—"in order to avoid similar, erm, blunders."

The deafening silence was broken by a young policeman. "Are you seriously suggesting we work together with the leader of a gang? Has the Mayor okayed this?"

"The Mayor leaves those decisions to her Chief Inspector." A smile tugged at the corner of her mouth. "And while they haven't exactly been model citizens, the Bug-eyed do obey a strict code of conduct. They haven't been real trouble to us. Not to the extent certain tabloids are making them out to be." She drank from her bottle of water. Paced left and right. The pill had flushed out her hangover but she still felt the vinegary aftertaste of wine in the back of her throat. "So, yes, we cooperate, carefully and for this case alone. I believe that old saying applies to our situation."

"The enemy of my enemy is my friend?"

"Was going to say beggars can't be choosers, but that too, Aleksov."

Koronski insisted on a face-to-face meeting, at night, in a Kamentsi gymnasium, the following Thursday. Said he'd always done business that way. More intimate, he'd said, than playing a virtual hide-and-seek across scattered servers. Claire agreed.

Radan came to work the next day, lifting everybody's mood. He was gaunt, yellow-faced, his walk stilted—leg-braces instead of crutches, keeping him up and taking part of his weight off—but when he walked through that door, to Claire he looked firm as a rock, a pillar of strength.

"You look like shit," she told him.

"Likewise, Chief."

"Glad you're back."

She left him to his colleagues. He had a lot of catching up to do; she had avoided bothering him with the minutiae of the case, not wanting to unload her worries onto him while he was supposed to rest and recover.

At the end of the day he swung by her office.

"I may not agree with everything but I trust your instinct," he said. "I'm coming with."

She took a long look at him. That was exactly what she wanted to hear. "Do you feel capable—"

"You expect action?"

She shrugged. "No. I think he's being honest."

"Then, of course. I wanna be there. I wanna talk to this guy."

"You understand how I'm operating here, don't you?"

He made a zipping motion over his mouth. "No time to bother the higher-ups." He grinned. "By the time they give us green light half our department will be snorting SD."

The car—non-police, non-camouflaged, as requested by Koronski—drove them to the wrought-iron gate of the gymnasium's yard. Stepping onto the gravel pathway, Claire motioned to the accompanying policemen to wait in the car. No need for protection. If Koronski wanted them dead, they would be dead whether four, ten, twenty, or just two. They were in his lair, after all.

Claire and Radan slowly crossed the yard—an overgrown, patchy lawn, metallic benches scattered around with dented or missing backrests. Several Bug-eyed strolled casually, eyes glinting with their distinct green hue in the dark. The facade of the gymnasium was half-white, the other half a daub of gray with graffiti all over—it seemed a renovation effort had recently begun.

As they approached the large building entrance, the door swung open. A Bug-eyed, not older than sixteen by Claire's appraisal, bowed, gesturing with his right arm toward the marble hallway of the gymnasium.

They nodded at the boy and walked in. Cold, gleaming marble, spotted in a cowhide pattern, their shoes clacking, announcing their approach to Koronski or to whomever listened at its end. Portraits of people Claire didn't recognize hung on the walls on both sides; names written on scraps of paper were scotch-taped beneath the portraits, and she realized these were scientists, writers, poets—*Marie Curie, Wilhelm Roentgen, Ivan Pavlov, Petre M. Andreevski, Maxim Gorky, Ivo Andrić.*

The boy stopped before a wooden door, green paint scratched off and flaking. Koronski's office. He knocked three times. The portrait next to the door was that of a young-looking, mustachioed man. *Grigor Stavrev Parlichev*, the inscription read.

Claire cast a brief look at Radan, and he nodded, mouth twitching in what probably meant to be a reassuring smile.

Footsteps from behind the door, and a tense moment later Vladimir Koronski was beaming warmly at his two guests. Avuncular, long-faced, looking more like the educator he'd once been and less like the gang leader described in the police files. Salt-and-pepper hair, tied up in a ponytail. Round glasses; crooked, thin iron frame.

"Welcome," he said, and they entered the office. It smelled of old paper and dust, even though at first glance it seemed clean. A desk and a cupboard in a corner, both containing stacks of paper. Koronski gestured at two wooden chairs that looked like they'd been borrowed from one of the gymnasium's classrooms.

Claire sat, then Radan did, too.

"Good to see you here." Koronski sat down and leaned on his desk. His voice was gentle, his manner professorial. "We have a lot to discuss."

"We do," Claire said.

"But not the past," he said. "Better let bygones be bygones," he added in English. "I am inexplicably fond of that cliché phrase." Claire couldn't help noticing the way he looked at her, a brief flicker of his eyes, as if scanning her face, in a flash, a wink, for some clue. If he was expecting a reaction from the Chief, he got none. She pursed her lips, and nodded.

"Of course," she said, and saw his face relax ever so slightly. "In this case, we are allies."

Vladimir Koronski exhaled, and smiled feebly. "Allies in this case."

"So tell us what you know."

He looked at her and Radan in turn, then started speaking in a soft voice, barely above a whisper, and Claire could picture this gang leader teaching mathematics to the poor kids of the quarter. "The new drug has been injected into our beloved city months, perhaps a year, before it announced its presence in the pompous manner of the junkie hordes. I am afraid that even though we were aware of its existence for much longer than you"—he inclined his head at the two guests, *meaning no disrespect*—"we know very little of its origin. Hearsay. Rumors from dark corners of the city. Corners which we, the Bug-eyed, inhabit. Said to be Kenyan in origin, synthesized in a Nairobi lab, then shipped across the Mediterranean to Europe, via Greece's porous borders into the Balkan Federation and its capital. Out of the lab and onto the street, where it adapted, where, thanks to its chemical makeup, it was easy to make more-of: just add, stir and leave to dry out, as you well know."

Claire remembered the police chemists' reports on the drug—how it had been self-replicating: add a few necessary ingredients and a pinch of the original drug and you'd have a pot-full in no time. She said, "On the island."

"Mala Prespa. But they'd been cooking well before then. We were observing them before the island, when the junkies weren't as organized, when they were making the drug in homes, parks, football playgrounds. Scattered."

"Why didn't you stop them?" Radan said. "You could've saved yourself heaps of trouble. Us, too. Nipped it in the bud."

"You mean stop a group of five, ten junkies?" Koronski shook his head. "No, that would have been a pointless exercise. These people were a mere symptom."

"Of what?" Claire said.

"Of our new reality. Chaos. Actions without reason." He squinted, and crow's feet appeared around his eyes, making him look older, worn out. "So we remained on the sidelines, content to observe. My people kept me informed on the drug flowing into our city, into our quarters, luring normal people to wade in, then carrying them in its current, somewhere… and I worried, but failed to act. What could I have done? I watched as the junkies started coalescing into communities; being easy to recognize an addict, they'd orbit one another, help each other out, always ready to provide a bit of the drug in exchange for raw materials and to make more, and more, and more of it."

"Their leaders—"

"None. Nobody to teach them. Nobody to show them how. Just the substance. They learn, they adapt to the drug and we adapt to them. That is the whole story."

Vladimir Koronski's words hung in the air of his office for a moment before Radan said, "But they attacked you. Club Siv Delfin. We assumed they saw you as rivals, that they wanted to take over."

"They attacked us because we attacked first." He sighed. "When I wised up to the fact that this new drug might turn into a big problem— you see, you and I might be on opposite sides, but we love the same city, neither of us wishes to see it brought down, into the grips of an addictive plague—I decided to take action. We tried to stop the supply of chemicals, dry out their sources, I thought only then this growing population of users would see daylight and resume their normal, boring, drugless lives. But no. They grew meaner. They figured out who was trying to keep the drug away from them. They barged into Siv Delfin, and killed. And that's how it began."

"And how we were brought in."

"Indeed." He looked into Claire's eyes, a sharpness creeping into him. "You know, I found it truly amusing that they would commit murder just to forget death."

The Bug-eyed had kept a close eye on the junkies ever since. They'd seemed to grow more and more organized, paradoxically, the more they'd detached themselves from reality.

"We wanted to see what their end-game was, figure out a way to get there first, to defeat them. We thought their gatherings on Mala Prespa—a different batch of junkies converging there each day to cook the drug, and consume it—were the apex. A miniature society, on the outskirts of town. Now," he said, "we may never know." He cast a brief admonishing look at Claire and Radan. "But they are self-organizing into something. They are working toward a goal."

"The abolition of fear?" Claire offered.

"Perhaps." He touched the tips of his fingers. "Or the abolition of the rival society."

The ride back was silent, the two policemen upfront, hands folded on their laps while the car drove itself, Radan and Claire in the back seats, turned away from each other, watching the grimy city roll by.

From the glistening ring road Vasilegrad was a seething core, burning around a tarry river which drained it of light, a vein pumping out bad blood. An oval of gold, beneath an indigo sky.

Claire thought of Robin, running conversations in her head, from when they'd been Agents together in PalPoliz, the long-dismantled private police agency. He'd died, mere days before she'd found out she was pregnant, on a similar case, when a turbulent political climate and private interests run amok had led to a crime wave sweeping over the city, drowning many.

And now, the drug and the junkies, and her collusion with the Bug-eyed. It was too much, her head ached and she touched it against the cold window. The road trilled on her forehead.

Was it her turn now? Was it time for the city to swallow her, as it had him, and their daughter, and all those others caught in this swirl of modernity and... new reality, clash of societies, action without reason? She mulled over the thought, felt herself plunging into that strangely comforting daydream where she took herself to them, mouthing, *I'll be over in a moment, tell her Mommy's coming will you?*

The car swerved right, out of the ring road, into the fiery belly of the city.

My heartbeat pounds in my ears; echoed by the two headstones before me, it grows stronger, louder with each pulse, gripping my neck and reverberating between my body and the stones until the pressure turns into a wave of memory washing over me, and the grip and the tension release me and I'm sobbing.

They used to breathe, used to talk, to move and dance and cook omelet with olive oil and jog in the park by the yellow river and wail and love and speak first words and hug.

I bite my lip. Tears stream down my face.

It took them three weeks to realize they'd hit a wall—painstaking days of collecting information, whispers from around the city relayed to the keen ears of the Bug-eyed, fed into VGPD computers, seeking patterns in the chaos, juxtaposing hearsay with hard fact, extrapolating, prioritizing.

Claire spoke to Koronski, privately and out of the office, on an encrypted line.

"They adapted," he said. "After your Mala Prespa stint they learned not to congregate. Their best defense is randomness. That's why we see no apparent self-organization."

"You don't know that yet, our Workers are crunching numbers—"

"Oh, to hell with your software."

She blushed; luckily, the call was audio-only.

"My people on the ground say the junkies are lost," he continued. "Which means they're lost. They've blended into the city's populace and are hiding behind crowds. One step ahead of us, always. Too flexible. A brittle structure."

He sighed. Claire paced around her apartment, eyes sweeping the parquet.

"What we can be sure of," she said after a while, "is that they're cooking the drug someplace, they can't go without."

"True."

"I've talked to my chemists, you know. To see if there's a chance to pick up on the compound's chemical signature, and look for it in the river, in the ponds, in the sewage pipes of entire neighborhoods if need be, and trace them. They say it might be possible. So I got them working on it. Even in this godforsaken hour somebody's in a lab coat peering down a microscope trying to make this happen."

"Good to hear." He didn't sound convinced.

"I'll deploy people across the city in a few days, and we'll get them."

He gave off a humorless chuckle. "You don't understand. They're too scattered. Too flexible for us. We're rigid structures." Claire winced at this lumping in of the city's police force with the man's gang. "We're too rigid for them," he said.

Chemical test results trickled in, and she kept Koronski in the loop. His theory was proven as traces of the drug were found all over Vasilegrad's quarters, no part of the city holding a bigger concentration of the drug than any other—an equally distributed, omnipresent affair, untraceable to a single source. Adding insult to injury, the combined amount of the chemical discovered was larger by three magnitudes than what the police and the Bug-eyed had previously estimated.

The city was saturated with Siv Delfin. Siv Delfin was an indelible part, an invisible latticework superimposed over the city, a new quarter manifesting itself in the actions of drug users, existing solely in a vicious cycle of fear and forgetting.

New ideas were proposed: engineered airborne bacteria set loose in the city, gobbling up the drug and excreting harmless byproducts; a neuro-vaccine, dulling the brain receptors tickled by Siv Delfin, gradually administered to every citizen; a counter-drug, carefully deployed across the city, similar in taste and composition to Siv Delfin but deadly to its long-term users.

Claire woke up before her alarm. She wolfed down her breakfast without tasting it, then got dressed and shot out of her apartment. The smell of bitumen and meat hit her nose as she stepped out onto the busy street: the burek joint ensconced between her building and the tall Vasilegradska Banka office had just opened, a line of eager customers snaking out onto the sidewalk.

She tossed a few coins in the cardboard box of the homeless woman, "Morning, Velika."

"Good morning, Ms. Yuleva," the woman said. "May God preserve your health, and may you have a very productive day at work."

She headed toward the subway station on Hnatt Ave.

Palls of gas slithered out of manholes like genies uncoiling from lamps, dirty sighs of a city waking to life. Cars and buses sped by, weaving around trams and trolleys, their motion perfectly coordinated by the Workers steering them.

Claire's reflection followed her as she walked, sliding from one shop front to another, sepia, emerald green, or cobalt-blue, a human-shaped absence ghosting through the city's mirror-image. She thought of her first dates with Robin, as she always did on her way to work, transporting herself to before his death, before their daughter and the disease which had carried her away. Music from those days played in her ears, a masochistic splash of fuel to her morning melancholy fire. She liked to relive those moments in her mind because she felt cozy, huddled with her loved ones inside a warm inner sanctum, carrying them, carrying her tragedies wherever she went, outside world be damned. Her whole past played out before her, the dates, the falling in love, the holding hands and long talks over lunch, the cases and the hard work and the techno clubs afterward, the death which shook her to her core, her daughter's birth, and the short-lived respite from grief she'd provided, her first words, her disease, her departure, too. It was a test of sorts, to see how much she hurt, gauge her strength by inflicting sharp cuts on herself; and thus, inevitably, training to withstand, raising her threshold of pain by a notch day after day.

She crossed the street.

Out of a corner of her eye, a sparkle, a silver gleam from the busy crowd rushing toward the steps leading to the subway station, over a person's face, and it took Claire a moment to realize her prostheses had spotted the differential, the diamond eyes of a junkie. She threw herself aside just as the person lunged forward with a weapon, and the person lost balance for a moment, time enough for Claire to slip away from the crowd, and for the crowd to disperse in panic.

The attacker recovered their bearing, looked around, and their hoodie slid back and Claire saw it was a woman—their eyes met and she launched herself at Claire again with animal ferocity but Claire had her gun drawn and yelled at Magda to desist but she ran on and Claire shot Magda in the head.

"No," Claire gasped.

Life drained out of Magda's body in spasms as she slumped to the ground.

At the passers-by, "Stay back." Claire's prostheses flashed her ID to them. "Police," she said.

She'd shot her former informant in the left eye, a charred and bloodied hole, the diamond sheen gone, forever. She knelt beside the body. "You stupid junkie." She shook her head. Softly, "Why didn't you leave town when you had the chance?" The Workers embedded in her prostheses had already called for backup, little counters in a corner of her vision promising their arrival in approximately three minutes. She straightened up again, packed her gun away and looked around. Her own eyes flashed back at her from the ground—the weapon, the kitchen knife Magda had brandished lay just beside her, polished and unused. Claire rubbed her forehead. The adrenaline was subsiding, she was starting to feel sick. Too early in the day for murder. On the other side of the body another, different kind of glint caught her eye. She stepped over, bent down to look at the vial. It must've slipped out of Magda's pockets falling down.

She stared at the grimy vial, half-full with russet powder. Crouched over, she felt giddy, stomach twisting into knots as mind raced and she just realized that soft music still played from her prostheses and she thought about *him* and *her* and how good it would feel to forget where they truly were and to be free and unburdened even for a moment—

Timers counted down to zero. Sirens wobbled, VGPD vehicles parked on the sidewalk. Pedestrians turned to gape at the body, and hurried on with their busy day.

Claire went to talk to her colleagues. She cut the music off. In the pocket of her windbreaker, she clutched the Siv Delfin.

◉

Two Junior Sergeants whose names escaped her stepped out of the first car. They looked at Claire and Magda in turn, colors passing over their eyeballs as their prostheses processed the scene. The female Sergeant approached her.

"Everything all right here, Chief?"

Claire nodded. "Yes." She spread her arms, showing them her torso. "Unharmed."

The Sergeants from the second car were getting out now, gripping their guns, but Claire waved them off and they replaced the guns in their holsters. One of them told Claire, "We better take you to the station, Chief. Jana and Mirko will secure the scene while the coroner arrives."

"Is Inspector Radan already there? Was he notified?"

The two Sergeants glanced at their younger colleagues, and the Junior Sergeants stepped slightly aside, busied themselves with scanning the body and the scene from every angle.

"We better take you to the station," repeated her colleague. "Now." His face had closed up, blank, unreadable.

"What's happened?" Claire said, a sense of dread coming over her.

"Let's get inside the vehi—"

"What the fuck's happened, Sergeant?"

He looked at his shoes. Sighed. "A coordinated attack, Chief." He looked up at her as if apologizing. "You weren't the only target this morning."

"No."

"I'm sorry."

"*No.*"

He placed a hand on her shoulder. "We better go."

Claire's legs buckled but she remained standing. The whole scene— the buildings, the gaping subway entrance, the body and the cars and the street and the passers-by—warped around her. She breathed out a syllable, "Who?"

The second Sergeant said in a strained voice, "Many, Chief. Too many."

◉

She couldn't bear to watch the murders; the videos extracted from the victims' prostheses were tucked in a shared folder someplace, but she didn't want to look for them.

Almost all assassination attempts had been successful. Hers, and Nenad Kanić's, the only exceptions. They'd killed Radan, in his building's elevator. He'd been too slow for the attacker, his body too weak to withstand another stabbing. They'd killed Tomi Aleksov, Viktor Petreski, Vasil Vasilev, Zlata Gelevska, Yordan Tsvetkov…

All butchered with knives, cleavers, scissors, strangled with garrotes. Half the city's senior police force eliminated, without a single shot fired at them.

"They won."

"Nobody's won."

"Today I got to bury half of my closest friends. They won."

"I'm sorry for your loss, but you can't give up on this. Give up on the city."

"Fuck this city."

"You don't mean that."

Silence. "I don't know. I think I do."

"We will break them."

"The Mayor's bringing other people in. This won't be a VGPD affair for much longer. I won't be able to cooperate with you anymore."

"Convince her."

"That would mean telling her we've been working together so far."

"So? Your career is pretty much over anyhow. With this tragedy, they'll push you to the sideline, retire you early."

"Maybe."

"That is what's going to happen and you know it."

Again, heavy silence. "And what if we just let them? Huh?"

"Let who?"

"What if we accept their existence and get on with our lives?"

"This is the grief talking."

"I'm serious. Why are we fighting them? What's so wrong with what they do to themselves? Everybody wants to forget the ultimate truth that everybody dies and that nothing holds any inherent meaning. We just go about it in different ways. We dive into fantasy worlds, we drink, we obsess over unsolvable cases, we go to comedy clubs, we do math. We invent a reason to wake up every morning."

"You're being pathetic."

"Am I?"

"Yes."

"Maybe you're the pathetic one—pretending to care about this city when all you do is desperately try to cling to power. Without the fear of death, how would your gang of green-eyed assholes hold people tight by their balls?"

"Nonsense."

"We're fighting to preserve our way of life, they're fighting to preserve theirs. They never would've started killing if you hadn't provoked them. You know what? Fuck you and your manipulating. I'm ending this war. Enough is enough is enough. We should let people choose—we're all adults, aren't we? Let them decide whether they want the drug or not. Let people choose which society they want to belong to."

"Look, I get that you're bereaved and heart-broken but—"

"Don't you dare."

Sighing, then, "Let's talk again in a few days. When your mind clears."

"We won't. I'm confessing to the Mayor and we're stopping this now. If you attack the users of the drug again you'll be considered responsible for any civilian deaths that ensue."

"Call me in a couple of days."

"So long."

Call disconnected.

◉

I gaze into the slabs of gray stone—sleek dolphins surfacing from an ocean of green, frozen in an eternal gasp for air—into the familiar names, and lay down the flowers. I don't know why I do this. Muscle memory, perhaps. But I do. I must.

The name of a father, next to his daughter, one he'd never gotten to meet.

I take a deep breath, and turn around.

I walk downslope, passing rows of stones, pods of dolphins, some bearing the names of my colleagues on their backs, and people shedding tears hunched over them, and I only think of them, especially my beautiful daughter, how good it would be to hear her laughter again, how long it's been since I've heard her laughter, and I hurry because I have to leave, have to go, because this place destroys me and it takes me days or weeks to remake myself after each visit.

But that is all right. That is what I do. What I have left.

I thought about taking it, the powder, and the sweet release it would offer, and maybe if I had taken it I might have heard both of them laughing again.

But I didn't. Because I don't want to see the world through diamond eyes, kaleidoscopic, made out of things which do not exist.

I owe them that.

The Bone Children and the Darkness

Lorraine Wilson

As the sun turned the last snow on the mountain-top carmine, the news came through the village that two boys were missing. Theos listened to Padma, the lines around her mouth shaping drama and sorrow as she talked, and then he ducked his head in the most cursory of bows before turning away to enter his house. Padma remained in the street, her disapproval matching perfectly the storm clouds piling against the southern sky, turning the sea sullen and hiding the far Africs.

Theos brushed his knuckles against the wood of his doorframe and left her disgust on the threshold where he could pick it up again later. The roof of the goat shelter needed tying down, and this would be a more bearable thing than listening to Padma's worn voice telling him worn things.

It had been two years since the last loss. Theos wrestled scavenged bricks into place beneath the wall and anchored rope around them once, twice, thrice; thoughts of vanished boys becoming one with the empty house behind him. A goat appeared at the corner of the building, its clever, mad gaze making him unreasoningly furious and Theos straightened up with the bones of his spine sounding years older than they ought be, as if all the days his father had been robbed of were added to his own soul. Allah, he thought to the goat and the mountain, where are the boundaries of guilt? How, Oh He Who Is Greatest, do I find the margins of my shame?

The goat did not answer, chewing steadily on the rope Theos had just tied, but the snow of the mountain slid from blood-red to black and shadows fled up the slopes, rendering olive grove and citrus, ruins and garrigue all unto ashes. Theos gazed upon Allah's answer; darkness and penance, he thought, and shivered.

Wind rattled the tiles of the house, the goat shook its head, and Theos could hear voices moving through the village. He knew where they would be going, what would be said, and his dearest wish was to stay here and be silent. But they would notice his absence despite the tarnish of dishonour, so Theos walked back through the darkening house, warmth already slipping from the tiles that had broken his father's skull. It would be raining by the time he returned but he did not take a coat, passing over the threshold and carrying that other burden with him into the crowd.

They came to the square at the heart of the village where torches formed an oasis against the night. The house here had once been large, although that was no measure of anything in a land scattered with buildings that had once been large and now were not. Many of them were nothing anymore, shallow soil making false carpets out of orchid and anemone, and the occasional twist of wire or unfathomable plastic. The ones with concrete had not lasted so well as the ones of stone, and these less well again than the tombs. This house was built of stone with a third of its roof made of wisteria and the branches of an orange tree.

"Effendi," one man called through the closed door.

The villagers waited, that coming storm pulling at the shawls of the women so that they seemed more restless than they were. Theos saw Agapé several paces away and might once have sidled closer despite her husband. Her hurt was broken glass in her eyes, but he could not separate out the memory of lying with her from the knowledge of his father falling. Illicit pleasure as his father bled; her flesh and his father's solitary death.

It was a relief when Nicanor bin Latif stepped from the house yet still Theos felt the muscles of his fingers tightening, felt others doing the same.

"Our boys," the tea-seller's wife said. "Our boys, Nicanor-effendi."

"Yet again, and once again," said the tractor-owner, whose tractor had not worked in living memory, but who cleaned it weekly with a cloth of rarest cotton.

Nicanor bin Latif nodded gravely, moving his smooth hands in a gesture of commiseration. "I have heard the news, friends, and I am saddened." Lypāme—I am saddened, and also, I am sorry; and Theos knew that Nicanor bin Latif had no honour.

"Where is she, Nicanor-effendi?" The tractor-owner said amid murmurs. "Where is your wife?"

Nicanor opened the door at his back and reached a hand into the shadows, pulling her into the light. The voices rose like drowsy bees or distant thunder and then died away. She was always so much smaller than Theos remembered, the thought of her a larger, more sharp-edged thing than her bird-thin body could ever contain. Her eyes were huge in the light of battened flames, oceans in a face delicate enough to belie the horror of her, the awe.

"Oracle," someone whispered. And then someone else, louder. "Oracle."

She tilted her head, her husband's grip so tight on her arm that even where Theos stood he could see the blood leaching from her flesh. Her free hand moved, floating in the air at the height of her ribs, and when she spoke it was to something there, within her palm.

"The place where the air fills with blood," she whispered. There was no other sound, even the wind waiting. "The allotted days are counted out. And bones. Knuckle bones are good for counting, and finger bones. Little bones are best. But not too small, oh no, if they are too small then they slip between your fingers and the old gods feast..."

Some-one began to wail, the ululation climbing alone and terrible until another joined it, and then another. Nicanor shook his wife, but she kept talking. "I saw them in the empty space with grey-red, rusty-red, old, old lines beneath their feet. I saw them laughing. I saw them stop."

Theos could barely hear her over the women so he pushed his way forward even as all the marks on his soul told him to stay in the shadows where the tarnish would not show. Everyone had other things to whisper of tonight.

"Where are they now?" Theos said before he knew he meant to.

She looked at him directly for the length of an inhaled breath, and when she smiled, he flinched. "Hello, son of kings," she said.

"Merciful Allah," he murmured, wishing himself away from this mad, bruised woman and her terrible eyes. "Where are they now, Oracle?" he asked again.

She looked at her husband, her eyes losing their focus so quickly that it made Theos' skin itch beneath his clothes. The sounds of mourning clamoured at his ears, and he saw the exact moment that she heard it too. "I... oh, they have gone too far, and I have lost them. I cannot see..." she looked back at her hand and her voice lilted again. "I cannot see in the dark. No, I can, I can, but only until the bone children eat my eyes. Then I will not—"

"Fool," Nicanor hissed at her, pulling again until she stumbled back against him.

"No!" she shrieked, so high and so sharp that the women fell silent and even her husband loosened his grip. "No," she said again, her face turning this way and that, eyes owl-like and desperate. "I will find them. I will go down and down and down and all the sunlight in my skin will make maps of the dark and I will find them by their laughter and their bones."

"Inshallah," said a woman's voice with all the finality of a decision that had been waiting to be made.

"She can find our boys," said a man. At the edge of Theos' vision, someone averted evil with their fingertips.

"You would send my wife down into the mines?" Nicanor said, but he pushed her forward.

"If she would go, Nicanor-effendi," Davos the Elder said quietly. "Inshallah, she would have a hope of finding our boys. More hope than any other."

"It is her fault they went." Thus, it began; the broken edges to the voice spoke worlds. "Her gabbling about the mines and what is down there, it makes them curious. She is Hades-tainted."

"It may break the curse of the place." Agapé's voice was harsh as a crow.

Nicanor nodded slowly, his head bowed. She had value to him, in pilgrims and fear. But Nicanor was a trader, and she also had a cost.

"I will go down and down and down," his wife repeated, her too-dark eyes drifting.

"She might die," Nicanor said, ignoring her. "It would be a great risk she took for you."

Theos turned away, pushing back through the crowd, disgust making his mouth sour. Nicanor disgusted him, the villagers disgusted him; he disgusted himself with his fear of her when she was so clearly broken.

Then she spoke, her voice pure enough to cut through the bargaining for her sacrifice. "The son of kings will go with me."

Theos stood still, his back to her, and again met Agapé's eyes three paces away from him. "No," she mouthed, moving towards him. "No, Theos." He looked down at the dirt and tried to imagine the mines beneath, remembering his father telling him of the thousand and one people lost in them hunting for riches or monsters or fame. He had said, a hand on Theos' shoulder, "Such things are not for us, Theos-jan. Only those who are already lost go searching in the dark." But the mountain had turned from blood to ashes in judgement.

Without looking at Agapé even as she reached covertly for his hand beneath the cover of her shawl, pressed it against her body, Theos turned back around.

"Theos—" Agapé whispered, but Theos shook away from her, and she fell silent. His father had begged him to stop seeing her. Theos had promised, and gone anyway.

"Son of kings," the Oracle sang. Her husband held her on the step of their house and frowned across the small distance at Theos.

"Who will go with the Oracle in search of your lost boys?" Nicanor bin Latif said caustically. "Is there anyone willing to volunteer, besides my wife?"

The wind raced in from the sea, rain whispering in the valley beyond them, coming closer.

"So many brave men," a woman's voice said. "I will go."

Movement, a sort of communal, systemic shame, and then Davos the Younger said. "I also, if the Oracle wills it."

"*I* will it," Nicanor said, shaking his wife's arm in emphasis. "Davos the Younger, and Pilar ibn Xanthos."

"And I," Theos said redundantly. The Oracle had spoken, as had the Allknowing. Here, then, was his penance.

"And Theos Athenas," Nicanor amended slowly.

By morning the clouds had passed on towards Athens, so the dawn fell against the entrance to the mines; a rock thrush sang from an oleander and wild tulips opened in the cracks of the old road. Theos waited, Davos and Pilar beside him. No-one else was there and yet the village below was busier than normal. People finding reasons to linger in the square, in their fields, with their faces towards the mountain.

"You have your knives?" Davos asked

"I do," Theos said, even though two of them were visible on his hips. "Did either of you go in, as children?"

Davos said "No" at the same moment that Pilar said "Yes." She and Theos shared a small smile. "You too?" she asked.

"Not far," Theos began just as Nicanor bin Latif and his wife came around the nearest bend, his hand still on her arm and her eyes on the sunrise. She was singing softly, a lullaby that Theos did not know he had forgotten until he heard it again. "But if the Oracle is still seeing rusted lines, then I know where to start."

"Kalimera sas," Nicanor said once he was beside them. "Although how can I bid you 'good morning'? Kalinihta, and kali tihi, instead." Goodnight and good luck. Beneath the light of an unblemished dawn, it was an offhand eulogy.

"Nicanor bin Latif," Theos said, his eyes sliding up again to where that bird was singing. There were white orchids beneath it and passing low above, two ravens conversing.

"Theos Athenas." The Oracle's husband lifted both his hands. "We shall be praying for you."

The Oracle half-turned so that the dawn sun gilded her face. Bowing, Theos touched fingers to forehead as Nicanor did the same, then he lifted a hand to the Oracle. Not to touch of course, but to usher

her into the darkness. Nicanor turned to Davos and Pilar, and held their gazes in a moment of strange, taut silence before bowing to them also.

"Down and down and down," the Oracle murmured. "To speak with the darkness and touch the bones and breathe the air filled with blood." They stepped over the line separating sunlight from the mountain and lit their oil-lamps.

"Merciful Allah," Pilar murmured, walking steadily. "He Who Is Greatest—"

"Not here," the Oracle interrupted, smiling childlike and unfurling one hand as if it held something precious. "He cannot see in here and it is crowded, so very crowded; chatter chatter chatter."

"She sounds happy to be here," Davos the Younger said to Theos, lifting his lamp with an uncomfortable twitch of his shoulders.

"She is," she said. "Yes, she is happy. Down here are all her nightmares, all gathered and waiting, and she will find them one and two and three, and they will feast and feast. It will be quiet in her dreams then. At last, she will sleep, and it will be finished."

Theos frowned down at the top of her head, the lamplight adding gold and red to the blacks of her hair. She saw her own death, and yet was fearless? It had never occurred to him that her madness might make her braver than them all.

"And the son of kings must come into the darkness," the Oracle added.

"Why does she call you that?" Pilar asked.

His father had always been kind to her, pitied her. Was it simply this? "I do not know," he said. "She sees someone other than me, perhaps."

"Does she?" the Oracle murmured to herself. "Does she?" and then, "Oh!" far more loudly two moments before the light from their lamps fell outwards. "The empty space," she said and ran forward with her hands stretched wide. Theos cursed and leaped forward to stop her, his fingers clutching at her clothes to avoid contact with her skin. Davos and Pilar both gasped, but she stopped at the first brush of his touch, her eyes drifting away and away.

"You saw them here, Oracle?" he asked, his voice echoing high above.

She did not speak or move. Then one hand lift to rub at her other arm and he released his hold on her tunic as if scalded, and when she turned wide eyes to him, he forced himself not to look away. "The red-rust lines at their feet and into darkness, small feet. Small bones. No good, the small bones…" she trailed off, and then said in the quietest of whispers. "I saw them here."

"The lines," he said after a moment, stepping back from her, his lungs expanding as he bowed. "The metal..." searching for the old word, rusted word for a rusted thing. "...rails. They are in the centre, I believe."

In one forbidden adventure, his boy-self had reached thus far, and then re-emerged haunted and defiant to face his father's fury and his terror. In perfectly parallel lines, black- and red-spotted with a dozen decays, the rails led them and this time he followed. *They* followed, into another tunnel which bore them down, and when the rails split, like some strange skeletal tree, they paused, all of them looking and trying not to look at the Oracle.

"Check the lamps," Theos said to Davos, and as Davos began to do so, Theos caught Pilar's eye. She lifted her chin and spoke loud enough to make all of them flinch. Then quieter, "Which way would you have us go, Oracle?" with a bow and her fingers hard against her forehead like one who had not made the gesture ten thousand times. The Oracle was brushing her hands against the peninsula of wall where the two tunnels parted, she did not turn to face them but pressed her cheek against the rock.

"Vucub-Came?" she whispered, so quietly that Theos took an involuntary step closer. On a long wavering note, "Ohhh yes. Seven Death and Wing, Packstrap and Bone Sceptre. They come to watch. They watch and their fingers are tap-tapping on all the bones they have eaten. A thousand and one. A thousand and one, and two, and three." She shuddered and pressed her face harder into the wall.

Theos stared at Davos and Pilar mutely. Davos was so pale that the soft light rendered him insubstantial, and Pilar looked half-enraged. This would not do, Theos thought. He took up his lamp again, crouching beyond their own footsteps to swing the light slowly over the dust and rust. First the right-hand tunnel, and then the left. He went slowly, and when he rose to his feet simply pointed right. The other two began to move, and Theos whispered, "Come, Oracle," then again, "Come" and on the third time, "Come... Aline," she stepped back from the wall and walked ahead of him. Their feet smudging the shoe-prints of children, and other footprints made by small feet unfleshed that Theos hoped no-one else had seen.

They could not measure how far they walked but the tunnel split twice more before they ate, and thrice more before they stopped to sleep. The dark was timeless, but their bodies were not and Theos was glad to stop moving, to sit with the mountain's vastness against his back and look at faces instead of the line where the light ceased. The Oracle trailed a finger in the dust between her leg and Theos' but Theos did not watch her, not wanting to know if she were outlining the imprint of heel bones and toe bones.

"Flesh and suns," she said, cutting over Pilar who was talking of nothing to hide from the silence, "Hmm," crooning, "new flesh and tiny suns have come into their house, and Bone Sceptre is smiling. Oh yes, we will deal out the flesh and deal out the bones, and the tiny suns that are so bright will die. The trapped one dreams of fields and snow and sunrise but in our house, there is no sun, only blood and bones and dancing."

"Allah, make her stop," Davos whispered. Pilar kicked her foot against his leg. They looked at one another and then quickly away, and Theos did not know what that meant.

"Where are the boys, Oracle?" he asked, because no-one else was going to.

She lifted her hand to study the dark smears on her fingertips. They looked like bruises. "Bones," she murmured, and then lifted her head so suddenly that Theos was trapped by her gaze before he could look away. There was the entirety of the universe in her eyes and a man could lose himself a thousand times over before he'd taken a single breath. "Packstrap wanted them, and Seven Death claimed them, and jackal-headed Anpu laughed with bloody teeth. Bloody Teeth had bloody teeth but was not laughing and the monster... the monster... oh, he is so trapped and so hungry. Little bones do not make the mountain open and even fresh blood is not like sunshine. It is sweet, oh yes, sweet; but it is not sunshine." She fell silent, then reached out swift as a bird to press her dusty fingers to Theos' face.

His heart faltered and raced and faltered again, the rasp of Pilar and Davos' breaths was like rockfalls but there were not enough muscles in his body to let him pull away. "Oh, son of kings," she said, and he would have sworn that all the galaxies in her eyes filled with the sea. "You will kill your son." He flinched and she tapped his cheek once, twice. "Thank you," she said, as if his flinch or this unfathomable foretold infanticide were a gift.

The Oracle curled into herself like a kitten and slept, and eventually Theos must have too because it was from sleep that Pilar shook him later. She placed a hand over his mouth and beckoned, Theos drew a knife and followed to where Davos waited several long paces away. The pack on his back brought Theos sharply awake.

"Is it morning?" he said.

"*Hush*," Davos said, lifting a hand and checking furtively behind Theos where the Oracle lay motionless as stone. "No, it is deep night, but we must go while she sleeps."

"Pardon?"

"Theos Athenas," Pilar said, pressing her hand around his forearm and looking up into his face with her brows lowered. "We must go. Nicanor bin Latif bid us do this. The Oracle belongs here, you have seen that this is so."

"The boys—"

"The boys are dead!" Pilar whispered harshly. "Or nearly so. We are hunting bones, and it will get us killed. We must go."

He still did not understand; he wondered whether this were a dream and if so, when his father would come to ask why Theos had broken his promise and left him alone to die. "Why leave the Oracle?"

Taking a long, hissing breath and dropping her hand from his arm to her hip, Pilar looked from Davos back to him, then spoke slowly, enunciating each word as if they tasted foul. "The Oracle is a curse on the village. It is her who tempts people into the mountain, and without her we will be safe from it. Her husband does not wish her back."

"She is a liability, and we must rid him of it?" He had an awful feeling that his father was not coming. He remembered Nicanor's farewells, the look shared with these two, that there had been neither look nor word for his wife.

"It is a kindness," Davos said quietly, rubbing a hand along his cheek and then hefting his pack's weight. "You know how it will go if we bring her out, if he does it himself. At least here it will be quick."

"Come, Theos Athenas, you know it is true. Let us leave her while she is sleeping."

Theos did not look over his shoulder at the Oracle because this moment was not about her. His father should not have died, and Allah had spoken his penance across this very mountain. Was this truly the price he must pay for a broken promise; for sordid pleasures stolen while the old man stumbled on steps he should not have been climbing? His father had always pitied the Oracle.

Theos closed his eyes then opened them again, moving back from the half-lit figures before him and bowing without raising his hands at all.

Davos simply shook his head, but Pilar said, "It will be your death."

It may be, yes. And the thought filled Theos with a sudden joy. "Perhaps," he said, not bothering to whisper now and the others twitched. "Yet if I die here, then I shall not kill my son as she foretold. And if I live here, then I live. I cannot lose," he said, smiling. It must have been a smile filled with madness and teeth, because they left him with no further words.

"Son of kings," the Oracle whispered when he knelt beside her, counting supplies quietly. "You did not leave me in the darkness."

Theos sighed. "No, Oracle, I did not leave you." What had she thought, he wondered, listening to a second betrayal? It seemed she was not quite mad enough to be spared understanding, and he found himself unsurprised.

"The bone children," she said, pushing herself up to sitting and brushing dust through her hair with both hands. "The ones still with marrow to remember. They are whispering."

The bone children. It was assuredly too late then. "What are they whispering?" he asked.

She tilted her head up to him and smiled calmly. "That he can see in the dark."

They ate, she barely, and then they walked. But the mountain had spoken down here, and fissures made rent twistings of the rust-red rails, until from some great paroxysm, the tunnel before them was obliterated by rockfalls. Theos rested his hand on the boulders blocking their way, and saw beside him a larger hand-print, black in the lamplight and each finger tipped with dots. He drew away and thought longingly of the thing called 'gun' that Nicanor bin Latif had on his wall. A useless ornament, but if it had not been then what comfort to have that, instead of blades?

"Which way did the boys go, Oracle?" he asked, turning away to look at her bent head. She was tracing something on the wall, her fingers making a faint *skritch-skritch* sound, like rats' claws or dead branches.

"We must go down and down," she said, watching her fingers. "To where the air fills with blood. That is where we must go."

They could follow the rails back to the village, Theos thought. But then what? For the Oracle, it was her husband, or the monster and the labyrinth; a poor choice and to leave her would make himself as bad as either. His lost honour was down here, in her small hands and the darkness. "What about the boys?" he asked one last time, gently because he did not envy her what she saw. "Aline, where are the boys?"

"Lost boys and broken men and bone children. They all go down to the place where he is counting his bones and dreaming of the sun.

Where the air fills with blood. Down and down and down." She flinched, shaking her head from side to side. "I do not want it," she said between clenched teeth and there were sobs in her voice suddenly. Theos stepped closer, one hand lifting. "Bloody Teeth licks his teeth. I do not want to drink this. Do not make me taste it. Please. Oh, please, I…"

Theos touched her, his fingers around her thin wrist, skin against skin and them both trembling. "Oracle," he said. "Aline." She sagged against the wall, her eyes mercifully closed, her flesh icy.

Even if it were not for penance, he could not leave her to this. To die alone, like this.

"We will go down," he said. "We will follow the children. I will fight the monster and you will have your peace. Is that what you want?"

"This way and that way and that way and this and down and down and down," she whispered.

Theos marked the way with white chalk, and they walked, taking the tunnels that lead downwards. Aline scratched her nails against the walls and sometimes he wanted to shout at her to stop, sometimes he wanted to beg her to sing again, like she had done in the dawn. But he could not fathom the horrors she saw and so he let her be. She spoke to things invisible to him, those strange names in her clear voice taking form at the edges of the light so that he began to think he could see them too, could hear them, when he knew that he could not.

Then they came to a crossroads where a vein of rose quartz ran a foot thick across the floor and up one wall, and Theos came to a halt, staring at it.

"We're going in circles," he said. It had been to himself, but Aline came away from the wall, brushing filthy fingers against her tunic and looking up into his face with a smile.

"We have been going that way and that way and this," she said. "No, no, no. The jackal-headed one is laughing."

"I'm sure he is," Theos said in disgust. "So is every other god, I would imagine." He heaved a breath metallic with frustration and the exhaustion of not giving in to fear. "We will sleep here, and I will decide what to do in the morning."

"Morning!" Aline laughed, the sound of it bouncing away down all four tunnels before coming back to them, murmurously. "Our tiny suns are no morning, son of kings." She spoke fondly and her face was beautiful in the lamplight. "They are waiting for their feast and my skin makes a map of the darkness," she added. "You will see." Then she staggered as if struck, her hands clawing at his arm and her voice brittle. "*Hush now*. Hush, he is done counting his bones and comes up and up and up. Wing and Packstrap can hear him, and *we must hush!*"

Theos did not sleep. He sat beside Aline with his two longest knives resting on his thighs and listened to the mountain. He listened until the silence was full of breath, echoes of laughter scraping against the nape of his neck like the tips of horns.

Once, when he rose to send light into the tunnels, one of them had fresh footprints pressed over their own. A man's bare feet, but larger and ending with scratches that passed through dust and into rock. The next time he rose, a second had these footprints. Hot air pressed against one cheek and Theos flung himself sideways, thrusting blade and light into the emptiness like a shout.

Aline moaned and when he turned there were tears on her dusty cheeks. He returned to her, wrapping his fingers gently around her wrist like he had done before. After a while the tears stopped and he sat with his thumb over her pulse, until she awoke.

He gave her food, his own hunger an irrelevance if he could not find a path. But scanning the tunnels again, tasting the air and feeling it move against his fingers, he still did not know which way to go. Scrubbing one hand across the back of his neck, his palm came away scarlet and wet. Allah, he thought, nausea in his stomach. Perhaps he did not need to find a path. Perhaps he need only wait here, and fight here, and die here. Allah.

Aline rose from drawing in the dust and showed Theos her finger. "I made a map of the darkness," she said. "You see?"

Theos looked at her delicate, filthy hand, at the outline of the monster by their feet, and shook his head. "I do not see, Aline. Lypāme."

"Oh, delam," she said, tilting her head and rendering him speechless, "I made a map so that we might reach the end." She reached out to tug at his wrist, and his entire body resonated at her touch. Pulling him to one of the corner walls, she pointed. He looked at her, and she pointed again, so he obeyed.

An arrow pointing down. Freshly scratched. *Skritch skritch skritch.* Theos went to another corner, an arrow pointing up; another beneath his own chalk, an arrow bending round upon itself. He pivoted slowly on one heel to face Aline across the vein of bright crystal, and she watched him steadily. "When I saw my father's body," he said, "I knew myself lost forever." It was not what he wanted to say, but those words did not exist.

Aline smiled. "And now you find me."

The words did exist, then. Now he found her.

They followed Aline's arrows, Theos waiting while she drew them. He heard who she spoke to as she drew and realised he would take this from her if he had been able. Instead, he checked the lamp and their water, and felt time weigh heavier with the lightening of his pack. Then he heard footsteps.

First one, then a dozen, hard-tapping rapid steps and Aline grabbed at his hand. "You must not look," she hissed, her head bent so that her hair made its own nightfall around her. "You must not look at the bone children, otherwise they can eat your eyes. Wing will scratch them out, Son of kings, and Seven Death will gather them, and the bone children will feast and feast and we will scrabble in the darkness with blood on our faces and they will follow our trail, Son of kings, *trip-trap trip-trap,* until they are thirsty, and—"

"Aline," Theos said desperately, "Aline, I will not look. It will be well, I will not look."

"—and Packstrap says they will save nothing for the monster but in the Duat and in the houses of Xibalba they are angry that Minos' monster steals their dues, and the monster is done counting days on bones, and he—"

Footsteps rattled around them; Theos touched two fingers to her chin and lifted her face to meet his. "Aline," he said again. "Look at me. Me, Aline. Only me."

"—and..." she fell silent, her eyes filled with tears and stars before she closed them, her bottom lip trembling like a child. "Delam," she said, as she had done earlier and something in Theos lurched. *My everything.* He fought a hopeless urge to tip his head down and rest his grimed forehead against hers. The footsteps circled once more, bone fingers clawing at his trousers sharp as blades, raising welts across his skin. He watched Aline, the shadows around her closed eyes and the flutter of breath in her throat. Bone fingers scratching, whispers of laughter, his skin against hers.

"The tiny suns always die," she whispered after a lifetime. They were alone again.

"Yes," Theos said, letting her go. "But not just yet."

They went down, the air growing ancient and the walls dense with handprints, with scour marks carving long wounds into the stone above the height of Theos' head. He knew the monster, it was as ancient and as brutal as their island, imprisoned for unimaginable centuries; besides, they had all seen Aline's paintings full of horns and darkness and blood. So he knew full and well what those great gouges were. The knives at his hips and in his boots felt like pins, like toys.

They went down, and the bone children followed them, and Aline whispered to unfamiliar gods who whispered back and ran their nails through the dried blood on Theos' neck. They went thrice down, and the lamp began to dim, their small circle of light retreating towards them, things breathing at their backs.

"Delam, " Aline whispered. Theos slipped his fingers through hers.

"Yes," he said. "I am here."

The light died.

And did not die.

Theos stopped walking. Aline pressing against his side, whispered, "They are calling for their feast. I wish they were quiet, but it will never be quiet in the dark. Never, never, never. I do not wish to hear. I do not wish to see."

But *Theos* could see.

Barely. But there were outlines to the tunnel ahead, and the truth made him wild. "Daylight," he gasped. Aline did not lift her head, so he turned to look down at her and cried aloud.

Blood was spilling from teeth marks on her arm, something was pulling her hair, a long cut was peeling open down the curve from ear to collarbone.

"*No!*" he shouted, a knife in one hand and Aline pulled behind him, but the darkness was full of scrabblings and whisperings and things were still biting at her, so he dropped the knife and bent, taking her featherlight body in his arms and running towards the faint grey edges that might be salvation.

He ran, and the light grew, his footsteps and his breathing loud, he ran until there was no-where left to run. The tunnel ended in a hollowed space, crystal and moss and dazzling light falling from holes far up the wall. Daylight and silence; silence behind because the voices and the footsteps had fled, and silence in his arms.

"Aline." He knelt, brushing blood from her skin and heady with relief at the shallowness of the wounds. But her eyes were closed, and she did not answer. "Aline," he repeated, taking her hand in his, willing his own tarnished strength into her. "Aline, please," he said, surrounded by shafts of sunlight and a thousand tiny bones. She said that they would take her, she had wanted it, even. Everyone had. Theos thought he might shatter. "Do not leave me alone, ātashé delam. Do not go with them. Please do not go with them."

To the shadows he shouted, "I will pay for her," and then to her again, as harsh as a raven, "Ghorbaṅat beram. Aline, I will be your sacrifice. It is right that this is so, I am soiled by death so let mine buy my honour, and your peace."

A darkness shifted along one wall. A vast shape, a sickle-shade, then the scrape of stone and the smell of old blood and musk. Theos laid Aline down amidst the light, brushing her hair from her forehead before he rose and bowed, fingers to forehead and to his heart. Then he turned towards the tunnel. "I am coming," he whispered to the nightmares waiting.

"Delam," Aline murmured, and he was beside her again between two heartbeats. Horns gouged at stone behind him, and the smell grew strong enough to fill his lungs. The monster moaned. "The air will fill with blood," she said, opening her eyes. "He remembers fields, he dreams of nights that ended. The son of kings must come into the darkness, and they will both wash their eyes in blood." She turned her face to Theos, and he helped her up so that they knelt facing one another.

"Son of kings," she whispered, "is the air filled with blood?"

Theos did not look away because there was hot air against his neck, one hand was on a knife-hilt and the light was moving, moving, meaning darkness would come even to this place soon. *Ah*, he thought, and shuddered, "Not yet," he said, "but soon." And then he added, "Say my name." Wanting to hear it in her voice just once.

She shook her head. "There are so many. Sons of kings and fathers falling and always guilt and monsters and death."

"Say my name, Aline," he repeated.

Blinking once, slow as a cat, she touched a fingertip to the centre of his chest. "This one, the one that is mine, is called Theos," she said, and all the bones of his ribs realigned themselves to encompass a different heart.

Then the light turned red.

All the shafts of sunlight falling across the cavern were carmine, refracting crimson, ruby, scarlet; the whole hollow space filled with blood.

The monster bellowed a challenge, dust and rocks falling around them, and Theos was on his feet, knives in both hands but Aline held him still, her grip impossibly strong.

"I wish they were quiet," she said, her voice trembling beneath the blow of another roar.

"They will be, once I have paid," Theos said. "You can find your way out—"

She shook her head, something scraped the floor behind Theos, and Aline's eyes were so wide that he could see the monster in them, night-black and massive. "It is not quiet in the dark. I thought it would be quiet and I could dream but my bones would not sleep and I would still hear and there would be blood on my teeth..." She was shaking as if she might come apart. "He remembers sunshine too. And he has been so lonely for so very long in the dark, but we are all condemned unless the son of kings sets us free."

We are all condemned, he thought.

He stared at her and stared at her. Night was coming and they had no other light but each other, and the monster who dreamed of the dawn was done with counting bones. Movement pierced the edge of his vision, sharp-tipped, but the red air slowed them all like water.

Unless the son of kings sets us free.

There might be a way, Theos realised. There was a way, but the cost... His blood faltered in his veins, and he could still choose penance if he just turned and raised his blades, then he would die and the bone children would claim their Oracle, and the world would continue to turn.

Or he could choose Aline.

Fleetingly, Pilar's face appeared, her hand pressing his against her stomach and there was something there that clawed at Theos' mind. But then he thought of Nicanor bin Latif and the voices in the square, Pilar's voice, and whatever that almost-thought had been, it was gone.

Theos' new heart beat loudly and one million suns revolved in Aline's eyes. She was worth them all. Without turning his head, Theos spoke above the monster's hunger, "We can lead you out," he said. Something sharp as needles scraped across his neck, down one shoulder, breath scalding his skin. "I am the son of kings, and I can set you free."

The air darkened to vermilion, burgundy, old blood, and Aline held Theos' gaze unblinking. Her fingers *skritched* a maze into the dust, laid two finger-bones inside it, a third.

The monster fell silent, that sharp thing unmoving just beneath Theos' shoulder blade, over his heart. "But this is the bargain," he waited, the sharp thing pressed harder, and with every breath, he bled.

"You guard us from the old gods and the bone children, and we will guide you and set you free."

She built houses from knuckle-bones, traced a sun and its rays. *Is this what you want?* His eyes asked hers. She rested her finger on the sun; broken nails black with dirt or blood.

Theos took a breath. "And when you are free," he said, "we two shall leave, and you may go to the village and feast."

In Praise of Interpretation (an afterword of sorts)

Fábio Fernandes

Are you satisfied, reader?

Did the stories you have just read quench your thirst for noir?

They should, because they are much more than that. Literature and cinema are the abode of clichés—in particular regarding genre. Science fiction is the realm of robots and spaceships, for example. But that, paradoxically, is only true for those who aren't quite familiar with it, as it's more than those gadgets.

Noir is another case of a genre that has become etched with fire into the hearts and minds of the average spectator. I use the word *spectator* because usually the first experience with noir is through cinema. After all, it all began there, when Nino Frank coined the term *film noir* in 1946 to describe movies like *The Maltese Falcon*, which favoured darker tones in the black-and-white palette, but were also darker thematically. Its roots, obviously, lie deeper—in literature, where the elusive falcon came from the pen of Dashiell Hammett. I could write a whole book about that golden age and everything that came after. In fact, dozens, probably hundreds of them have been written.

But you were looking for something else, right?

Because you are not the average reader. If you were, you wouldn't have come. Of all the anthologies, in all the genres, in all the world, did you have to come to this one?

Of course you had to come. Because, deep inside, you knew you would find something different here.

Difference in repetition. The old Deleuzian injunction still holds true. In these pages, you found find many interpretations of what noir is. Muslim noir, Korean noir, Latin American noir, to name a few. Exotic future drugs, alien monks, psychopaths with a twist. Also, locations vary. You were probably delighted to know that noir isn't bound to the United States. It can be set in Greece, Hawaii (ok, that's USA for you, but think broadly, think *colonization*), South East Asia, Brazil. There is also something to be said about our own prejudices when we finally realize that we are all human, so of course such things would happen outside the US—there is a whole world outside those borders, a world that doesn't care more about USian lives than they care about the rest of the world.

Another important thing: in many of the stories here you didn't find that special brand of nihilism that very much leant into the right-wing thought that predominated in the noir fiction of yore (and today, if I want to be honest about that, and I do). The concerns here are not (all) about terrorists and criminals. There is also some investigation of the horrors of colonization (of other nations on Earth, but also on other planets). And that makes this future noir all the more tasty—and relevant.

Are you satisfied, reader? I hope you are. Because these stories will remain with you for a long time.

Contributors

Djibril al-Ayad (editor) is the *nom de guerre* of a historian, futurist, writer, editor of *The Future Fire*, the magazine of social-political speculative fiction, and co-editor of seven anthologies. He studies myth, religion, magic and mysterious writing systems.

◉

M. Bennardo always enjoys his visits to Atlantic City, especially in the shoulder season, when only the most tenacious characters (and seagulls) haunt the boardwalk. Otherwise, he and his library of crime novels reside in Kent, Ohio. This is his third story for *The Future Fire*.

◉

Zoë Blade's stories have been published in *The Future Fire* and *Heiresses of Russ*, while her guide to avoiding Google's prying eyes was published in *2600: The Hacker Quarterly*. She's currently collaborating with artist Monosílabo on a comic book adaptation of *Inhuman*, in which a hitwoman discovers she's a replicant of her former self.

◉

Storm Blakley lives, works, and writes in the wild Yukon. When they learned, at a young age, that the markings on the pages told stories, there was no turning back. They spend most of their time with their partner and many animals, inventing new worlds and stories of their own.

◉

Saleha Chowdhury (artist) is a New York based digital illustrator who enjoys creating science fiction and fantasy illustrations serving as windows into new and unique worlds. She takes inspiration from astronomy, nature, video games, and animation. Her work has appeared in *Fireside Magazine* and *Lightspeed magazine*.

◉

M.L. Clark is a writer of speculative fiction and humanist essays: Canadian by birth, and now based in Colombia. Clark's science fiction has appeared in *Analog*, *Clarkesworld*, *F&SF*, *The Future Fire*, *GigaNotoSaurus*, and *Lightspeed*, along with four year's best anthologies. Humanist writings can be found at *OnlySky*.

Fábio Fernandes has written several books, among which the novels *Os Dias da Peste* and *Back in the USSR* (in Portuguese) and the collection *L'Imitatore* (in Italian). Co-edited the anthology *We See a Different Frontier* (UK), and the anthology *Solarpunk* (Italy). His collection *Love. An Archaeology* was published in 2021 by Luna Press.

Dan Grace lives in Sheffield, UK. His stories have appeared in a variety of magazines and anthologies including *Interzone, Big Echo, The Shadow Booth* and *We, Robots: Artificial Intelligence in 100 Stories*. His novella, *Winter*, is available from Unsung Stories: unsungstories.co.uk/winter.

Laura Gregory is a fantasy writer and graduate of Edinburgh Napier University's creative writing MA. Her feet returned to Canadian soil but her heart remains in Scotland. Working as a police records clerk, she fights crime by day and writes villains at night. Find her on Twitter at @lagregorla.

Thomas Ha is a former attorney turned stay-at-home father who enjoys writing speculative fiction during the rare moments when all of his kids are napping at the same time. Thomas grew up in Honolulu and, after a decade plus of living in the northeast, now resides in Los Angeles.

Damien Krsteski is a software engineer and science-fiction author. His stories have appeared in *Beneath Ceaseless Skies, GigaNotoSaurus, Metaphorosis, Mithila Review, The Future Fire*, and others. He lives in Berlin.

Lam Ning is a former gas station attendant who now works in the medical field. He came of age at the bottom of a mosh pit, and he does his best to write what he knows. His content tends to reflect immigrant and refugee experiences in urban America.

H. Pueyo (@hachepueyo) is an Argentine-Brazilian writer and translator. Her work has appeared before in venues like *F&SF*, *Clarkesworld*, *Strange Horizons*, and *The Year's Best Dark Fantasy & Horror*, and her collection *A Study in Ugliness* will be out later in 2022 by Lethe Press. Find her online at hachepueyo.com.

Frances Rowat lives in Ontario with her husband and a not-quite-startling number of cats. She has lived in England, Algeria, and Switzerland; currently, she's most often found behind a keyboard. Her work has appeared in such venues as *Fireside Magazine*, *Podcastle*, and *Cossmass Infinities*, and may be found online at aphotic-ink.com.

Benjanun Sriduangkaew has been nominated for the British Science Fiction Association Award and the Campbell New Writer Award. Her worlds are informed by Southeast Asia and post-colonial lenses. She is the author of the fantasy *Her Pitiless Command* trilogy and the space opera *Machine Mandate* series. She can be found at beekian.wordpress.com.

Valeria Vitale (editor) is an amateur writer, a passionate reader, and an enthusiastic editor in love with the darkest corners of literature: noir, gothic, horror and everything in between. She wanted to be a detective, but no one would hire her, so she became an academic researcher instead, working on historical maps and artificial intelligence. She secretly still hopes that one day she'll stumble on a case to solve.

Lorraine Wilson is a conservation scientist who now lives by the sea in Scotland writing speculative fiction influenced by folklore and the wilderness. Her debut novel, *This Is Our Undoing*, was released last year and a second, *The Way The Light Bends* is coming out in August 2022. She tweets at @raine_clouds.

Timothy Yeo is an aspiring author based in the claustrophobic island of Singapore. He normally writes short stories involving the supernatural, in an effort to explore the real-world monsters that lurk just out of sight.